Scoring
the
Player
Kit Grey

"Death will someday take me
    Hope I live a life worth taking
    Bored with you makes me right
    I wish we could be bored all of the time."

— ST. PAUL & THE BROKEN BONES

CONTENTS

CONTENT WARNING

Scoring the Player contains **heavy themes** that may be triggering or distressing to some readers. Your comfort and emotional well-being matter. Please review the following content notes to help you decide whether this story feels safe for you to read.

For an **exhaustive list** of potential triggers, please see the **Book Content Warnings** section (highly recommended) of Kit Grey's website (https://www.kitgrey.com/contentwarnings) or **scan the QR code below.**

Past alcoholism and substance abuse (parent)

Anxiety and panic episodes

Childhood trauma

Combat trauma (veteran character)

Complex PTSD (C-PTSD)

Confrontation with abusers

Depression and dissociation

Emotional shutdown in relationships

Endometriosis flares and related surgery of secondary character

Fear of abandonment

Harassment by sports commentators (coded and overt homophobia)

Implied/Referenced Sexual Activity Involving Unnamed/Unknown Characters

Missing family member

Nightmare that contains suicide (MC)

OCD-related behaviors

Profanity throughout

Queer identity in hostile or unsupportive environments

References of past suicidal ideation (secondary character)

References of past self harm (cutting) (secondary character)

Scene depicting near-drowning incident (MC)

Scenes depicting anger, frustration, and loss of temper (violence)

Self-control struggles under emotional stress

Self-isolation and emotional dysregulation

Sensory overload

Therapy and discussions of mental health recovery

Trauma-related flashbacks or panic attacks

DISCLAIMER

The views in this book in no way reflect the views and principles of the National Basketball Association (NBA), as it is a work of fiction. The author endeavored to portray aspects of the NBA schedule, rules, and regulations as accurately as possible. However, creative freedoms and liberties were taken for the plot purposes of this book. The teams, players, coaching staff, and agents, within this work and series, are completely made up and fabricated so as not to misrepresent the policies and values, curriculum, or facilities of real institutions.

While *Scoring the Player* can absolutely be read as a standalone, certain events referenced in the story occurred in Book 1, *Loving the Legend* (e.g., Arnaz's coming out article, existing friendships).
This book begins where *Loving the Legend* ends in a scene that is a major spoiler if you have not read *Loving the Legend* yet.
You may choose to start there for a fuller experience.

PLAYLIST

Scan the QR code below to listen to the full playlist on Spotify:

"This Bitter Earth / On the Nature of Daylight" by Clyde Otis and Max Richter, performed by Dinah Washington et al.

"Dark Stone" by Holy Fawn

"imagine" by Ariana Grande

"Self Control" by Frank Ocean

"Pockets of Light" by Lubomyr Melnyk

"Please Don't Fall In Love With Me" by Khalid

"Spring / The Promise" by Anna Yarbrough

"Out Of Your Way" by Snoh Aalegra

"Mother's Love" by The Vernon Spring

"Les Petits Gris" by Khruangbin

"Would You Mind" by Janet Jackson

"Lost Kisses" by Monster Rally

"It's Our Love" by Thee Sacred Souls

"II HANDS II HEAVEN" by Beyoncé

"Big Rings" by Drake, Future

"WIN" by Jay Rock

"I'm Ready" by Tevin Campbell

"Can We Talk" by Tevin Campbell

"All Night Parking (with Erroll Garner) Interlude" by Adele

"Ne Me Quitte Pas (Don't Leave Me)" by Orion Sun

"Regardless" by Naomi Sharon

"Pyramids" by Frank Ocean

"Wild Side (feat. Cardi B)" by Normani, Cardi B

"Focus" by H.E.R.

"Better" by Khalid

"guidance" by Jhené Aiko

"There Will Be No Crying" by Cleo Sol

"I Think It's Going to Rain Today" by Nina Simone

"when the party's over" by Billie Eilish

"Wyoming" by Elijah Fox

"dirty dancer" by Orion Sun

"Blessings - Extended Version" by Big Sean, Drake, Kanye West

"Swim Good" by Frank Ocean

"luther (with sza)" by Kendrick Lamar, SZA

"HYDRANT" by JIMMY EDGAR

"Lovers And Friends" by Lil Jon & The East Side Boyz, USHER, Ludacris

"Sunset Village" by The Vernon Spring

"Little Drummer Boy/Silent Night/Auld Lang Syne-Extended Version" by Jimi Hendrix

"Too Good At Goodbyes" by Sam Smith

"Lonely Love Song" by St. Paul & The Broken Bones

"Yes Indeed" by Lil Baby, Drake

"The Most" by Miley Cyrus

"EARFQUAKE" by Tyler The Creator

"NEW MAGIC WAND" by Tyler The Creator

"SLOW DANCING IN THE DARK" by Joji

"Simple Things" by Miguel

"Stand Still" by Sabrina Claudio

"Finally Mine" by Juliet Roberts

PROLOGUE: ARNAZ

FIVE SEASONS AGO

♫ **"Wild Woods"** ♫

What wounded souls monsters make.

Pop!

Pop!

Pop!

Welts from my rubber band thicken against my wrist.

"What's the matter? Coach won't let you play?"

I level my middle finger at *him*, Dallas' power forward. Salem. Jones.

"Cade," Coach warns.

I ignore him, so he redirects the warning. "Move along, Jones. Can we get through one game without you riling him up?"

Pop!

Pop!

"But it hurts to watch," he continues. "It's too sad. Why is he —yo, how are you sweating from sitting there?"

My finger levitates again, but our center steals his attention, cutting through their defense.

"Be right back," he tosses my way, as if he's earned a single fuck.

"Remember why you're sitting there," Coach reprimands, gaze tracking Jones, whose thick calves flex as he sprints away.

My jaw tightens, and I almost sail my finger Coach's way.

Our center continues a fast break up the middle lane, lobs the ball toward the backboard, and sets up to catch the rebound. The shot would be smooth, except Asshole Jones plucks it out of the air and then launches it downcourt to the opposing point guard, who hammers it in.

The crowd's roar vibrates under my feet as he races backward, arms outstretched, fingers curled, demanding more, and the sucker crowd answers, their bass drumming up my thighs.

Chin sinking into my jersey, my back slumps against the chair.

This score is an embarrassment.

Coach sticking me on the bench is an embarrassment.

Not to mention *this* fucker...There's something about him. Something that makes me want to smash my head into his face until I'm numb.

On the next possession, he dominates our power forward. Too damn slow to get around Jones, he passes the ball to Dickhead Andrews, our reserve shooting guard, who executes sloppy footwork with the confidence of an All-Star and fires a fucking air ball.

I groan.

How's Coach still punishing me for clocking him two weeks ago? *Look at him.* Dickhead had it coming.

Except now he has my starting spot.

"Coach." Jones returns. "Put him in the game. I'll pay you." He pats his chest and non-existent pockets, then shouts to the scorer's table, "Yo, Oldhead, let me borrow a twenty."

Coach ignores him and barks at our power forward to cover the wing.

"C'mon, Coach. He looks like cheese that's been out too long."

"What'ya call me?"

"Cade."

"Not *Cade*," I mock Coach. "*Jones*. All *Jones*."

"What's wrong with him?" Asshole asks. "His jumper broke?"

My jump shot? "Fuck you. Go find out why your point guard's aiming for a triple zero."

"Enough," Coach warns me.

"And you." I glare at him. "In case you missed it, that was Andrews's third air ball. You might want to, I don't know, give a damn about our twenty-point deficit and eight-game losing streak and put me in the game."

Coach stiffens, eyes shifting to icy slits.

The air stills like my bench mates and our assistant coaches —even the two randos at the end—are clenching their cheeks.

I shrug. *Where's the lie?*

"Mm-mm-mm." Asshole palms his chest. "Famous daddy ain't teach him manners."

"Fuck you say?" I fly out of my seat. "Say it again," I grit out, squaring up.

Black orbs swallow brown, except there at the edges, cutting like lightning, a bloodthirsty glint.

A serpent slithers awake in my belly, forked tongue tasting the air.

Oh, how we feast when we're mistaken for prey.

The bow of his top lip puckers.

A low-bellied hiss tempts me to sink my teeth in. Or latch on to his gold nose ring.

"Huh." His head tilts as his gaze trails down my body. "Thought we had a mouse in the house."

"Say. It. Again," I grit out, ignoring the weak jab. At six-foot-six, he only has two or three inches on me, max.

"Jones, knock it off," his coach yells from their side of the court.

"He ain't wrong," Asshole throws over my shoulder. "Andrews couldn't cop a bucket if you bought it for him."

"Nah." I close in. "*I* can say that shit. *You* can't."

"Just sayin'"—he steps back, raising his hands—"he ain't no sixth man."

I start to turn away...

"Forgive him, Coach," the fucker taunts. "Silver spoons scratch easily."

...but Christmas comes early this year.

He bobs to evade my first swing and the second. I fake a left hook, and my right crashes into his jaw. His head snaps quickly, then slowly, like it'll keep turning—until it skids to a stop.

A dark rumble, too skin-dancing to call a chuckle, crawls out of his lips.

My back uncoils, each vertebra a revolving bullet in a chamber.

Steep-sloped traps draw up and then sink down his back like steel being sheathed. The flex of his biceps pulls the cords beneath his skin. My heart rate drops to a slow thump as power surges between us. An ancient god of chaos curves time and locks us in a room, just me and him. Famished and unbound by the rules of civilized society, it only accepts offerings of blood in exchange for the sweet release you can't chase in a pill...or the tight heat of a man.

His eyes ignite, signaling he hears it too—the distant clank of a bell.

The sky opens, and he rushes me.

I thrust my elbow toward his jaw, but he ducks, throwing me off balance.

I'm yanked by my jersey.

Hard.

His head cocks up, then hammers into my face.

The floor arches its back, and a sweet crunch blares as the blinding burn of an ice pick twisted up my nose hits.

The chaos god accepts my offering. A rush of weightlessness lifts me from my body as iron and salt flood my mouth, and I'm freed of the knot jammed in the center of my chest.

The snap of a thousand rubber bands could never come close to the high of each metallic swallow.

"Get off," I slur as I'm ejected into a sea of moving lips from the wasted breaths of teammates and security guards pleading with me not to be me.

"Move!" I growl, pushing them away. I'd rip through this entire stadium for another taste.

Lasering the swarm of bodies and identical jerseys, I find *him.*

Forehead creased, eyes and lips turned down. *Is that regret I see?*

"Look at me!" My voice surges, meeting its mark.

The skittering under my skin increases as he steps back.

Don't you fucking dare...

More arms around me. More pointless stabs at getting me to stop.

"Get off of me!" I rip free and turn toward the bench.

If that ref blows his fucking whistle any harder, his head's gonna pop off.

My steps falter as my gaze clashes with crossed arms, rigid shoulders, and a sneer...

Coach, don't you see? Your disappointment is my pride.

They're telling me I'm ejected from the game.

Cool.

I lift my chin, and with a flash of my bloody grin—*Come and get me!*—I pivot mid-stride and crack through the guards on my six, except one grabs my arm, another grabs my jersey. Neither got the stamina to hold me. Charging my muscles, I barrel forward, dragging them, ducking and spinning off teammates.

Where is he?

I wrench my arm free, bolting away from Dipshit Guard One.

Zigzag.

Skrrrrt!

I lose Dipshit Guard Two.

Bingo.

He's staring right at me. Stoic, like his stillness is orchestrating the chaos.

You showed me your beast...time to play with mine.

I tense my muscles and blow toward the fucker like a battering ram, only he dodges left, sending me sailing through the air.

Shit.

My feet lift off the ground.

Holy shit.

Heart punching through my ribcage, wind smothering my face, I tuck in, curling my spine, and brace for a wipeout.

My back thuds against a floor of muscle.

"Hey, Blue."

"Fuck off"—my elbows crash against his ribs—"me."

Why's he always calling me Blue?

He winces, coughing up air. My elbow slices through the air again, the fire in my belly craving the crunch of bone, when a hand wraps around my leg and yanks me down Asshole's body. I kick hard, jamming my foot in the air until I'm freed of the guard. I flip to my knees, bear crawl up the fucker, and launch blow after blow, rage growing as each fist meets his elbowed shield. A movement of rushing bodies at the edge of my vision distracts me for a split second, and a sharp ache in my obliques buckles me over.

"Shh, that was just a tap," he soothes, rubbing the spot.

My hand wraps around his throat and squeezes, brightening the fucking glint in the fucker's eyes.

We're ripped apart.

He's barely contained, yet an army of guards circles me.

"Hey," he says hoarsely, rubbing his throat. "At least I got you off—"

My stomach bottoms out.

"—the bench. You're welcome."

"You got a death wish?" I growl, fighting to get free.

He smirks. "If you're doing the killing..."

"Stay the fuck away from me."

He turns toward the tunnel, palms clasped, offering amends to the crowd. And they eat it up, rooting for him and screaming, "Refs, you suck!"

He spins to face me. The distance between us not enough to hide the hollows of his dimples. "I wish I could, Blue, but I can't."

CHAPTER 1
ARNAZ
PRESENT DAY

♫ **"Do your worst"** ♫
Sometimes the arrowhead is a mercy.

The sun retches up a tormenting darkness that sits in the middle of my chest. I mistook it for the beginning of the end once. I grew impatient waiting, so I went in search of it. Turns out chasing death upsets some people. So now I take tiny lime-green-and-white pills, and one of the side effects is endurance. Handy, since last season, the league transferred me to the sunniest city of 'em all, Los Angeles, when I only want to live an East Coast October forever. If it weren't for my big homies, benzodiazepines and SSRIs, I'd never leave the house. They even managed to subdue the man who chased death to feel alive.

I'm no longer impetuous, but I did a thing.

I grew tired of hiding the fact that I love men, so I stopped hiding. And now everywhere I go, idiots ask me what it's like to fuck guys and play basketball. And I'm supposed to pretend it's not the most asinine question on the planet.

So many goddamn questions. Never mind the answers—they'll write whatever the hell they want. Apparently, I'm dating my best friend. Well, if that were true, it would make this shit awkward.

"Tyler, I want to spend the rest of my life with you."

Metal coats my tongue as I drag the beer from my lips. The cold press of the bottle burns my palm despite the rush of heat spreading up my neck.

How am I cold and hot at the same time?

Pushing back my chair, I inch closer to the bourbon less than ten...

nine...

eight feet away...

"I will strive every day to ensure that our family knows true joy, protection, and peace."

I study the object of everyone's attention—Sid King, my best friend—down on bended knee, proposing.

"Ours is an everlasting love forged through life's fires. Whatever storms may come to pass, we'll bear them together and come out stronger."

I search Ty's face for a sign that this isn't what he wants. He looks shocked. At least, I think that's shock. Hell, I could never crack him.

Draining the beer, I reach for the bourbon, and before the last of the pour can meet the bottom of the cup, it's falling down my throat.

"I am already yours, but would you do me the honor of marrying me?"

Pour, gulp, burn...again...again...

"No, no, no."

I search the faces of the other guests.

Oh no. He said no? That was a no, right?

My breath echoes in the air as Nicholas covers his mouth, and his eyes sink like that time in practice when I gut-checked him for elbowing me in the ribs. I scan one downcast face after another—until it meets one beaming with pride—Ms. King, Sid's mother. I trace her gaze back to Ty, who's lowering to his knees.

"No, because it's I who would be honored if you'd marry me."

Sid grins.

Holy fuck!

I blow out a breath and then add to the air of woots and whistles before tucking my head and weaving through the crowd.

I'll down the bottle if you push it back up, I warn my stomach as my back hits the bathroom door.

Snatching off my shades, the room spins slightly as the celebration gets louder.

Last game...twenty-eight points, eleven rebounds, ten assists...

I move toward the toilet.

...or was it ten rebounds and eleven assists?

Dragging in a resistant breath, I unzip my pants and then piss, ignoring the knock on the door.

There was the lob I threw to Nick, who posted up for a fade-away, and the one to Zeke for the dunk.

The doorknob rattles.

At least seven for Sid, who probably had as many for me.

I zip up and flush.

That's nine assists right there.

Turning on the hot water, I push the soap dispenser three times until my palm is full.

*Twenty seconds or...*I roll out my neck, ignoring the warning as I rub the soap between my palms and fingers and then rinse. I start to reach for a towel when my hands freeze midair.

Twenty seconds, or Anaïs won't survive surgery.

Grinding my teeth, I stab the soap dispenser again until my palms are full.

One Mississippi, two Mississippi...

I begin to rinse.

...three Mississippi, four Mississippi, five Mississippi, six Mississippi, seven Mississippi, eight Mississippi, nine Mississippi...

The knock, louder this time, rattles the door.

"Get lost." There are like a hundred bathrooms here. *Told Sid he should give out maps of their estate.*

Where was I? Eight Mississippi or nine?

For fuck's sake.

One Mississippi, two Mississippi, three Mississippi, four Mississippi, five Mississippi, six Mississippi, seven Mississippi, eight Mississippi, nine Mississippi, ten Mississippi, eleven Mississippi, twelve Mississippi, thirteen Mississippi, fourteen Mississippi, fifteen Mississippi—

I grunt and focus as the voices get louder outside the door.

...sixteen Mississippi, seventeen Mississippi, eighteen Mississippi, nineteen Mississippi, twenty Mississippi.

My lungs expand as I yank the towel free and dry my hands. Ripping open the door, I shrink back from the sun and throw on my shades.

"You didn't hear me knocking?" Nick asks.

"So?" I shrug as he slides by.

"Waddup?" Malik, Ty's teammate on the Knights, says as I reach for the bourbon.

Nodding, I tilt the mouth of the bottle toward his cup.

"Whoa, easy." He grins. "I tend to strip when I'm drunk."

Eyeing his cup, I shift the bottle to refill my own, stopping when I think the amount is even with his.

"That was epic," he says, facing the crowd. "Ty's my boy, but goddamn, right?"

The scent of grilled beef has my brain snitching to my stomach that it wants me to finish the plate I started.

Following Malik's gaze to Sid, who's chatting with our teammates, I quirk my eyebrow.

"I'm not even bi, but if I knew he was, I'd have given Ty a run for his money, y'know?" he rattles on.

Sid hugs his mother.

"N-nah." I clear my throat. "I don't see him that way."

He smirks.

Everyone believes headlines.

He starts to walk away, then pauses. "Yo, that Darius and Todd segment was bullshit. You belong here just like everyone else. Just ball and do you."

I wave it off. I caught a snippet of the show this morning. Fuck 'em.

"How's your pops? His Offensive Player of the Year speech had me dying. The funniest presenter all night."

Carter Cade, retired NFL tight end, and everyone's favorite dinner party icebreaker.

"A speech?"

He nods. "At the NFL Honors. He's good?"

I grunt.

Ty places a tender kiss on a seated Sid. They're so certain about each other. In the bleak span of mortality, what does forever even mean? Will it all have been worth it sixty years from now when one sleeps coldly in death?

Who will keep the other?

Ghosts do not warm.

"Because of you, I know that love is the greatest of mysteries..."

I crank up the music in my car until the bass is in the center of my brain.

"Whatever storms may come to pass, we'll bear them together..."

Maxing out the volume on my speakers until my teeth vibrate, I reach into the glove compartment and snag the psilocybin. Unscrewing the capsules, I pour back the dust. Soon, the slithering unrest beneath my skin will retreat.

"I am already yours..."

I chase it with another dose.

The faint echo of a car horn cuts through the music. Who could fault Los Angeles if she threw up her hands—or land—and evoked a 9.5 earthquake that careened half of the population and their cars into the Pacific Ocean? Cars digested to the depths, forming coral reefs. Bloated corpses burped up to the surface. Decades of congestion cured.

Solved.

My head swims through the reverberating bass.

Why does the sun have to constantly burn through the flesh here? I yank down my sun visor.

Everything about California is dramatic. Even the goddamn traffic.

I switch lanes and take the next exit.

My ringtone blares through the speakers.

"You're horrible at calling people back."

"My bad."

"How was it?" my sister, Anaïs, asks as I pull into a parking spot.

"Hold on." I reach in the back for my hoodie and then throw it on, popping the hood. *"You, whose beautiful soul is cast from love."*

"Wh-what? Is that one of your lyrics? It's beautiful."

"It's a line from Sid's proposal."

"Wait, what? He proposed?"

"Yep. Ty had a ring too."

"What do you mean he had a ring?"

"It turned into a surprise double proposal. There were tears, the snotty kind, and words like *everlasting* and *union*."

"Oof. You okay?"

I roll down the windows. "Yeah, he's my best friend. I'm happy for him."

"Bullshit. We hate sharing our best friends."

Yeah...She cried for a week after her best friend Isabelle got married.

"You still there?"

"Nah, I'm on my way home."

Home. The first morning I woke up there and squinted at its gleaming fixtures and blank, paper-white walls, I dry heaved, threatening to paint the marble. I canceled the unpackers and unboxed the essentials, which turned out to be less than a quarter of the boxes, and left the rest. Pulled up a hookup app and then got the fuck outta there.

When the guys came over for the first time, Sid took in the boxes and quirked an eyebrow. I arched one back. He said, *"It suits you,"* and I grinned and said, *"Fuck you,"* because I knew he knew why it suited me. I don't know where home is, but it sure as hell ain't LA.

"I've been thinking...maybe single life isn't best for yo—"

"Anaïs."

"Ever since your college coach, you've be—"

"Stop."

"I'm just saying, we love hard and we're loyal hoes. How freaking lucky are the bastards who'll love us back one day? They won't ever let go."

They won't be the ones letting go. "Mostly 'cause we're hoes."

"I checked your DMs. I'll never unsee that guy's sculpted face and horse dick for as long as I live. The hell was he going on about in the video?"

I shrug. "Like I speak Dutch." I track a group approaching less than twenty feet away and roll the tinted windows back up.

"I don't know how you're still single with dudes like that blowing up your DMs."

One of the guys pauses to video my whip.

The sun is starting to bleed across the sky, over-the-top watermelon and gold.

"Staying single is easy." I roll my window back down after they pass.

"You sure you good? Took your meds?"

"Yeah," I reply. "You take your meds?"

"Yep...I hear waves."

"At the beach."

"But the sun?"

My lips quirk at the note of worry in her voice. "It's almost down."

"Good. It's pouring here."

I'd kill for a rainy New York day.

"You heard me?"

"What?"

"I said Mom and Carter asked about you at brunch."

"Is it the third Sunday already?"

"Yeah."

"You okay? Was he—"

"Yep. I'm okay."

"Hold on." I check traffic. It's still shit, but it's starting to move. "Traffic is letting up." I start the car back up.

"Aight, I'll let you go. Call if you need me."

"Always."

I PULL up to my house and stare at the arched glass entry framed with white bougainvillea.

"I am already yours, but would you do me the honor of marrying me?"

I shift into reverse and back out.

REAL TALK SPORTS WITH DARIUS & TODD

"Darius, that's foul, man," Todd says, waving him off.

"I'm just saying what everyone at home is thinking. His performance is decent—"

"Decent?" Todd scoffs. "He's top five in the league offensively."

"But is that enough for the Royals to put up with other players' discomfort and the circus in the stands?"

"Sure, sure, but that's not Cade's fault."

"Come on, T," he says, throwing up his hands. "Be real. If Arnaz never came out, everyone would be focused on his game. I'm just saying, if I'm Ari Sealey—"

"Royals' GM."

"Yeah, if I'm the Royals' GM, I'm doing the math right now to determine if he's worth keeping. Tim Johnson is a free agent. He could take Cade's place."

"No offense to Art," Todd says, crossing his arms, "but he isn't close to Cade offensively or defensively."

"Is it fair that their security has to do the extra work of throwing out impassioned ticket holders for—"

"Impassioned," Todd cuts in with a laugh. "Some might call 'em homophobic."

Darius shrugs. "This is the free world. In case you forgot about the First Amendment? Isn't that what started this mess?"

"What'ya mean?"

"Cade's selfish article that no one asked him to publish."

"You're wildin', man."

"Nah, I'm keepin' it real. Let's ask our 3.7 million viewers."

"Man, let it g—"

"Put up a poll. Let our viewers weigh in." He signals to someone off camera. "Hashtag DariusNToddShow. Will Cade be dropped from the Royals this season? Yes or No? Sound off."

CHAPTER 2
SALEM

It's the second quarter when Coach puts me into the game. The crowd makes noise to commemorate my return. After five months of healing a stress fracture in my left foot, I'm ready to make the comeback of a lifetime. I've played for two other teams in my pro career, but ain't no crowd like the Brooklyn Lions'.

A lot has changed this season. For one, we have rookies who are pulling their weight. Then there's the bench that's proven to be deep enough to keep us in the running for playoffs when, like me, our star point guard and center succumbed to respective shin and shoulder injuries. Then finally, my favorite change this season—the league has an openly gay player! And I've had a thing for that player for as long as I can remember. Anyone in the league coming out as gay is exciting, but Arnaz Cade—or Blue, as I call him—coming out? It's the greatest discovery since electricity or Einstein uncovering that light is the fastest thing in the universe. Some might argue that my comparing Einstein's theory of relativity to learning my crush is gay is absurd. However, to me, the discovery is just as astonishing. I think my dude Einstein would feel me. He explained relativity as an hour talking to a pretty woman feeling shorter than a minute of having one's hand on a hot stove.

Unfortunately, Blue's rumored to be dating his LA Royals teammate, Sid King, but until it's been confirmed, I'm not giving up hope. Considering we play for teams on opposite sides of the country, I have to be creative when I make my move. Someone who has the balls to be the first openly gay player in the league deserves a bold play.

Jason, power forward for Minnesota, drives hard to the lane. *Cute!*

Before he can complete the dunk, I'm charging through the air. My shoulders eclipse the back of his head as I reach up to smack the ball away.

Not in my house!

Jason clasps his head and complains to the refs that I fouled him.

"Nah, bruh! That block was immaculate," I fire back.

I race up the court and catch a pass from our center.

I evade Minnesota's defense and attempt a fadeaway jump shot. It bounces off the rim, but Cillian, our shooting guard, rebounds and floats it in.

Damn, it feels good to be back!

Cillian kisses the horseshoe tat on the back of his hand, then winks at me. That's my homie. When everything went down with Blue and Sid, our team, like I imagine every team in the NBA, discussed it in the locker room. I hated the offensive jokes being made. I was tired of that shit. A new dawn had arrived. I could join Sid and Blue or stay quiet and let things remain the same. I remembered something my dad said about when one person chooses to evolve, however painfully, they inadvertently influence the people in their radius. I made a choice.

I stood up and faced my teammates.

"Yo! Chill. Some of y'all are talking recklessly. Watch that igno-

rant shit around me. I think it takes balls to do what Arnaz and Sid are doing. And for the record, I'm gay! Not that it's any of y'all's business."

Everyone went silent as expected. I stared into their faces, silently asking, "We got a problem?"

Cillian spoke up first. "My brother, Liam, is gay. He's the best."

All eyes turned to him. He stood up, reached inside his cubby, and pulled out his deodorant. He swiped some on and faced me like we were in the middle of a conversation.

"Uh—yeah? Is this the, uh, brother you introduced me to when we played Toronto last season?" I asked.

"Yeah, that's right, you met him. I forgot about that. His husband, Eli, couldn't make that game. Remember the picture of the Frenchie I showed you? That's their dog."

"The gray one?"

"Yeah, Loki. I love that dog, but he's a terror unless you give him treats. He has a weak stomach, so they buy him these crazy expensive small-batch treats with probiotics and a crap ton of healthy stuff. He goes wild for 'em. He begs by standing on his hind legs and spinning in circles. It's the only trick he knows."

I grinned. "Sounds like a character."

"Hey, if you're seeing anyone, you should bring them by for the next game night. Laila and I would love to meet them."

"I'm single, but thanks, man."

He nodded. "You ever need a wingman, I got you! I'm not saying I take all the credit, but Liam has me to thank for Eli. I'm the greatest wingman."

Over a dozen pairs of eyes ping-ponged between us. Cillian had to have felt it too, but he didn't seem to give a shit. It was so Cillian to have my back without saying he had my back. I shouldn't have doubted that he'd be someone I could trust to come out to.

Ezekiel, one of the guys taking jabs at Blue and Sid, hung back after most of the guys had cleared out.

"What's up?" I turned to face him.

"Hey, man, my bad with the jokes. If I knew you were, you know, I wouldn't have said anything."

"Gay. The word is gay. Your dick won't fall off if you say it. Whether you knew I was gay or not isn't the point. That shit's vile, man. It's hate speech. You never know who is or isn't gay around you. Every time you say shit like that, you're spreading hate and potentially hurting other people."

He rubbed his neck and winced.

"Anything else?"

He shook his head. "Just...my bad."

"You know, it's interesting how you insult in public but apologize in private. Next time, man up in front of everyone or save it."

I slung my bag over my shoulder and brushed past him.

I know so many dudes like him—constantly shitting on other people to assert their manhood. They're so committed to proving and performing their masculinity that they can't see how it's reduced their humanity. And if that's not fucked enough, they go and try to impose that crap on other people. To hell with that. I've spent too many years of my life feeling insecure about my manhood because of it. I have no interest in belittling and dominating other people to prove I'm strong, and I sure as hell won't be subjected to it from other people.

The opposing team's point guard gets jammed up by our small forward. He passes the ball to Dominic, their center, who drives three feet to lay it in. Dominic never sees me coming when I drop down from the wing, reach in, and block the shot. He attempts to retrieve it but ends up sprawled on his ass.

I gesture to the crowd that they aren't loud enough. They heed the call, screaming their lungs out. I stumble back, pretending to be blasted off my feet.

After the next three possessions, I force a turnover when their shooting guard squares up for a three-pointer. I run up behind him and tip the ball out of his hand before it's released.

Gimme that!

Our point guard, Onyx, takes possession and then sinks a three-pointer.

I end up playing a little over eighteen minutes before Coach benches me. She never keeps us in long during our first game back from an injury.

I'm tapped to join the post-game interview after I shower. Changing into matching pale blue corduroy pants and a long-sleeve, button-down shirt, I leave the top three buttons undone, partially revealing my chest tats.

"Salem, over here. Tom from CBS Sports."

I nod.

"Firstly, welcome back. It's official, Salem 'The Silencer' has returned!"

The room erupts into laughter, myself included. My defensive style has a way of silencing the opposing team's crowd, hence the nickname.

"You've been called the soul of the team, one of the toughest defenders the franchise has ever seen, and you can hold your own offensively. After five long months, how did it feel to be back on the court?"

"Thanks, Tom. It's been tough, but so many people behind the scenes helped me rehabilitate. I'm grateful to each of them. It felt amazing to be on the floor with my teammates again. It's good to be back."

"Salem, Erica from ESPN. You tallied five blocks, six points, a steal, two rebounds, and three assists to help the Lions clinch a W, 117–102. What do you think was the secret sauce behind today's win?"

"We got great stops and played to each of our strengths. Cillian made a huge splash in the fourth quarter, banking seventeen points, twelve assists, and four blocks. He's amazing. Ezekiel guarded the rim ferociously. Zyair was one assist away from a triple-double with eleven points, ten rebounds, and nine assists. I mean, I could go down the line. I'm proud of the guys."

"Salem, Sloan from NBA TV. You're coming back from an injury to play in a league with an openly gay basketball player. What do you think about Arnaz Cade and Sidney King's actions to promote inclusivity in the league for gay players?"

I grin and take a beat to formulate my response.

I think it's the best thing to happen to the league. Imagine if we could enjoy all the perks of our straight teammates, who often have their spouses and kids in the stands. Imagine if we could be out and not have that be the focus of our story as professional players.

Then there's Blue and his kaleidoscope eyes that resemble light-grazing ocean waves. Handsomeness wrapped in a golden-brown complexion, plum-colored lips, a perfect five o'clock shadow, and a sinful, though rare, smile. You take my seasoned interest in him and the fact that he's gay, and, well, damn—I have a lot of feelings about that.

"Sloan, I'm proud of the work they're doing, and I stand in solidarity. It shouldn't matter whether a player is gay or straight, but for some reason, it does, and that's a problem. I have no tolerance for homophobic speech or behavior."

As the words leave my mouth, it hits me—a way to shoot my shot with Blue!

Nah, it's too out there.

But, I mean, wasn't bold always the plan?

I rub my neck.

This could go one of two ways. One's great and gives me a shot with the literal man of my dreams, and the other...eek. Everyone will know I took a shot. It'd be mortifying. I once read about a government black site somewhere in the Arctic Ocean. Maybe I can hole up there for a decade until...*Okay, I sound scared again.*

Is the AC broken? I swipe the beads of sweat lacing my hairline.

Yeah, okay, I'm definitely scared.

Is it my scared or rational voice?

Does it matter?

It's Blue.

Blue!

Okay, okay...

Argh...here it goes...

I clear my throat, ignore the tap dancing in my chest, and lean into the mic. "But on a more personal note, I'd like to know if Arnaz is single 'cause I'd really like the opportunity to shoot my shot."

I flash Sloan a smile.

Like a blown fuse, the buzz in the room wipes out as my admission registers on the faces of the reporters. Then, a backup generator kicks in as a burst of frenetic energy careens reporters out of their seats, competing to ask the next question.

"I'll take two more questions!" I yell above the excitement. "How about you?" I point to a guy with the *Brooklyn Daily News*.

"Thanks, Salem. Are you coming out as gay right now?" He has to shout his question to be heard over the fray.

I plaster on my best shocked face. "I have to be gay to like him? Shoot!" I frown. "Nobody told me I had to be gay to like a guy."

Sloan's jaw drops.

"Can I just be gay for Arnaz?" I ask, looking into the camera.

I let the question sit unanswered. The energy in the room teeters close to combustion from the suspense. It's like I'm doing the equivalent of screaming "Fire!" in a crowded theater.

I stop fucking around and temper the tension.

"Yes, I'm gay. I have been since day one, and I've had it bad for Arnaz for a while now. Y'all got any advice for me?"

A reporter's eyes widen in shock.

Okay, to be fair, I didn't know I'd be coming out publicly today, but the way I see it, when it comes to your dream guy, you gotta put up or shut up.

"You could ask him out on a date!" someone shouts.

I follow the voice to its owner. "I could, Ciara, but I don't really know what he likes."

"How do we know you're being serious?" someone else yells out.

"Y'all don't believe me?"

Another hush falls over the room.

"Y'all journalists always need receipts."

I shake my head and fish out my phone from my pocket. I dial my dad on speakerphone. His call goes to his generic voice-mail. I hang up before his number is read out loud. I try my mom next, and she picks up on the second ring.

"Hi, dear. Is everything okay?"

"Hey, Mom, I'm good. Listen, I have you on speaker—"

I signal for the reporters to quiet down as laughter spreads throughout the room.

"That's good, baby. Your dad is driving me nuts. He's been in the kitchen for hours. He's on his third attempt at the double lemon cardamom cake you selected for this month's challenge."

I place the phone against my chest and whisper, "I can prove it—gimme one sec."

"Ma, I'm in a press conference. I'll call you later about that. Can you confirm for my friends here the name of the guy I've been crushing on hard since my second year in the league?"

"Of course, darling. It's Arnaz. You've been smitten since the first time you played against him. For what it's worth, I don't think he's with The Wonder Kid. If I were you, I'd go after him."

The room erupts into more laughter.

"I'm trying, Mom." I smile.

"Listen, please call your dad right back—wait, here he is."

"Wait, Mom, I really have to g—"

"Hey, son!" My dad's sonorous voice emits from my speaker-phone. "You picked a hell of a recipe this month. I don't know where I'm going wrong, but it tastes awful."

"Wait, Dad, I have to call—"

"It'll only take a minute. I added the lemon curd to two-thirds of the buttercream, then I—"

"Dad, I'll call you ba—Wait, did you say two-thirds? Isn't it one-third of the buttercream to two to three tablespoons of lemon curd, then you use the remaining two-thirds to mix in the cardamom extract?"

"That can't be right. Wait a minute. Let me put on my glasses."

I shake my head at the amused reporters as Dad mutters instructions.

"Holy cow! You're right. I don't know how I made such a mess of it. Thanks. Oh, and I agree with your mother. You're a handsome young man, and life is short. Stop pussyfooting around and go after Arnaz. I ain't raise no punk."

I burst out laughing, joining the reporters.

"Thanks, Dad. Call you later."

"You're a baker?" Ciara asks once I hang up.

"Amateur. My parents stayed with me after my surgery to help with things, and we binged *The Great Bake Off*. As you all now know, my dad and I started our own monthly challenge."

"Bake something for Arnaz."

My head tips to the side as I toss the idea around. "Huh." I think of the countless recipes I've bookmarked on my laptop at home. It'll give me the chance to flex my skills and make my interest in him clear at the same time. I'd have to figure out logistics since I live on the other side of the country, but I could use my parents, who live in Los Angeles. I could fly in during an off day—it'd be tight, but it's possible. Pretty quickly, the idea blooms into a thrilling plan of action.

"That's actually brilliant, Ciara."

I need more information, though. Best to go to the source. I peer into the camera.

"Hey, Blue, wassup? I have two questions for you. One, are

you single? And two, what's your favorite dessert?" I ask in my smoothest voice.

And with that, I jump up.

"Thanks, y'all. This was fun. Until next time."

I turn my head to Ciara. "I owe you one."

She mouths, *Good luck.*

I ignore pleas to answer one more question as I head toward the door.

Cillian is leaning against the wall, smiling. "Aight, lover boy. I peep you. Just one minor question. How the actual fuck am I supposed to follow that? They're going bananas. You gave 'em shock, howling laughter, and romance in under five minutes, not to mention a surprise cameo by your parents."

I chuckle as he stares at me in disbelief.

"My bad. I owe you one. You think I got a shot, though?"

"I mean, that was crazy romantic. I'd say so. Sid might kill you if they're dating, but I'm rootin' for you."

"You're a real one."

"And you do owe me. I want your millionaire's shortbread with extra ganache."

I pat his chest. "Say less. I got you, bro."

"Salem 'The Silencer', my ass," he grumbles as he heads toward the microphone. Somehow, the reporters are louder than before.

I grin as I watch him settle in to take the first question from Kevin. Knowing him, he's about to feast on their hunger for a soundbite.

"Cillian, what's your reaction to learning Salem is gay?"

"Pfft, old news." He dismisses the question with a wave, tilting back in his chair.

I burst out laughing.

"Oh, my bad, did you all only just find out?" he asks, wide-eyed. "Awkward," he whispers, staring at the table. "I wouldn't take it personally. I knew because we're, like, besties, but not many people know." He seems to consider that. "Well, technically, our coach knows, his family and friends, our entire team, my girlfriend, our cat Edgar..."

He offers a wry smile, meeting the gaze of the reporters.

"But, hey, none of it means anything. Surely, it was important for him to tell all of you. Because, of course, you would respect his right to privacy and not insist on asking every person on his team and across the league for their opinion on his sexuality. I'm sure you only asked me as a one-off because you know he's my brother from another mother. Given he's one of the greatest defenders in the league, and we're all here to discuss basketball, whaddya say we focus on that?"

It took less than two minutes for the challenger, Jo "Bull" Murphy, to knock out heavyweight Sal Corsetti. Cillian may have him beat tonight. It's like a giant ice bucket's been released over the room, dousing the collective fever. Silence permeates as the reporters exchange slightly dazed and embarrassed looks.

Cillian finds my beaming face and winks.

Extra ganache, caramel, and buttery shortbread, I decide as I head to the locker room.

Operation Bake-a-Cake-That'll-Win-the-Guy-of-My-Dreams begins now.

CHAPTER 3
ARNAZ

♫ "Winter" ♫

Spare me the shiftiness of autumn, where even the trees can't
decide what color to be.

"Would someone turn that off?" I grumble as a warm body tucks in closer to my chest.

My elbow hits soft flesh as I turn, shooting my eyes open to two heads sandwiching me in. I scan their matching wedding bands, and fragments of last night start to piece together.

"Loud," the one with the bun groans in his sleep.

Ack. That's my alarm. Disentangling myself, I climb over the one with the fade.

The room spins once I'm vertical, and I end up stumbling toward my phone.

Damn, what did I take?

Condom wrappers, poppers, and little empty baggies litter the floor. I had to have taken something to have stayed the night.

"Shit," I hiss as my foot lands on the underside of a beer bottle cap. Snatching up my phone, I kill the alarm.

"Stahp...spinnin'," I groan, pressing my forehead to my palm.

The demented ringtone blares again. "What?"

"Where the hell have you been?"

"Anaïs?" I pull back the phone to check the caller ID.

"Where are you?"

I rub my eyes. "Hooked up...wherever."

"You don't know where you are?"

My stomach gurgles. *Seriously, what the hell did I take?*

"Arnaz!"

"What?" I whisper-yell.

"Where are you?" The concern in her voice overpowers my annoyance.

"Hold on." I trudge to the window and separate the curtains.

"Never mind, I'm checking the app."

Recognizing a favorite hand roll sushi spot across the street that I quit dining in once I realized it's a go-to spot for insufferable first-daters, I grunt, "Downtown."

"Are you okay?"

I sniff my pits. *Yeesh.* "You still tracking me on your phone like a stalker?"

"One of us needs to know where you are. How dare you not call me as soon as you saw the video."

"Wh-what video?"

"Salem Jones."

The fuck he want?

Whatever I took thrashes inside my stomach and tries to kick its way back up. "Lemme hit you back."

I climb into my shorts. Patting the pockets, relieved to feel my car keys and wallet, I throw on my tee. I scan the room for my watch and spot it on the nightstand along with my shades.

Creeping over to swipe them up, I freeze for a second when one of the guys shifts, eating up the space I occupied, and burrows against his husband.

My shades slip to the floor as I reach for them. After neither of them stirs, I pick them up, set them on the nightstand, then pick them back up again. I start to turn when my legs lock in place.

Two more times or you'll lose tomorrow's game...

My fingers grip the sides of my shorts, forming a tight fist.

I step back and flinch as a cold wall presses against my back. I take another step back, and the cold spreads all over until I feel enclosed in an ice cage.

Staring up at the ceiling, I will myself to keep going. Just this once, not to give in. I take another step back, and the blunt voice cuts in again.

Two more times or you'll be the reason for a ten-game losing streak...

This is stupid.

Everyone will blame you because of your article.

My fingers curl around the lens until the bridge warps from the pressure.

The low zzzz between my jaw and ears fades, and the cage bars recede as I step forward and place them down in the same spot.

Coward.

I repeat it again, snatch them up, then race toward the door.

My phone buzzes as I leave the building.

138 text messages.

My stomach clenches.

Thirty-two missed calls.

The fuck?

I click on the first text at the top with a link to a video. One glance at the headline and I'm bent over the railing, emptying my stomach into a bush.

I NOD TO JO, a security guard, on the way into the arena.

"Well, what is it?" he asks.

"Huh?"

"Your favorite dessert?"

I shrug, clenching my stomach.

"I want an invite to the wedding."

I keep it moving.

"You the man, bro," Wes, always speaking on top of tens of thousands of people, whether it's game time or not, hollers at me as I enter the locker room.

"For fuck's sake." I pick up the card attached to the gift basket in front of my locker.

"Tell him I get the cologne this time," Johan demands, towering over the entire team at seven-foot-four.

"Nah, bruh, you got that old tequila last time," Ussef fires back.

"It's *aged*," Johan corrects, "And that's only 'cause Jamie, the asshole, skipped my turn and stole the Hermés watch."

Ever since my coming out article was published, this crap started rolling in from every dude who's read it and wants to bone.

"One to ten. Pick," I say, plucking a protein bar from Sid's stash.

"Five," Johan replies.

Ussef crosses his arms. "Eight."

I nod to Johan.

"Yeah, boi!" He fists the air.

"Bullshit," Ussef complains.

"It's always five, bruh," Johan replies, returning a middle finger.

"Yo," Sid starts as he walks in, "you got dudes propositioning you on national TV now?" He stares at my chair. "And more gift baskets?"

"That one's mine," Johan says, swiping it up.

"Enough, Shane." I glare at our PR cameraman.

He lowers the camera. "Sorry."

I still don't get why these gift baskets are interesting for the *Royals All-Access* series, but Shane swears viewers eat this shit up.

"Bruh." Sid scrunches his nose. "You need—"

"A shower. Yeah, yeah. I'm going." I polish off the protein bar.

"What Salem did was dope." He drops his bag. "I can connect you with my jeweler if y'all skipping dating to go straight to the altar."

"Drop it," I grunt.

"Salem's my homie, but he's on my shit list," Nick calls from across the room. "Cam's dropping hella hints for me to propose on national TV."

"What's up?" Sid asks me, ignoring Nick.

"I got messed-up last night."

"Because of Salem?" Sid's gaze darts past me. "Ay, let's give him some space. Johan, you stop recording too."

"We don't all got a half a billion followers," he whines. "Let me have this."

Three seconds of Sid staring at him, and he's killing the feed.

"What happened to you?" Sid asks, turning back to me.

I shrug. "Hooked up with a couple and took something, I think."

"You think?" He raises an eyebrow.

"I wasn't going to wake them and ask."

I got two rules. Don't stay the night if I can get home in one piece, and if I have to stay the night, be out by first light.

"So this isn't about Salem?"

"He's not the first dude who's wanted to bone me," I grumble.

"I think ol' boy wants more than that."

I snatch up a towel.

Like I give an ounce of a fuck about what he wants.

CHAPTER 4
SALEM
LAST SEASON

"Why would I let you near him when you both just got ejected 'cause he tried to pummel you?" the security guard asks.

I grin. "Yeah...he's a pistol isn't he?"

"A 'pistol,'" the guard scoffs. "You two are strange."

"I just need five minutes."

"No. It's a liability."

"Isn't he alone in there?" I slide him the hundred-dollar bill I brought to sweeten the deal. "The minute it goes left, I'll leave. Promise."

He stares at the bill and sighs before pocketing it. Scanning the halls, he nods toward the doors. "I'll have a nurse on standby."

I rush past him and pull open the locker-room door.

Back turned to me, Blue's bent forward, buck naked, shoving his foot in his briefs.

The sudden urge to eat a cherry off that taut peach has me swallowing hard.

Leaning back on the door, I whistle.

Most people would show a hint of surprise, but not him. He's too on guard to ever be surprised.

Head turning to the side, he stops chewing the gum in his mouth, only for a second, before his fist tightens around the waistband of his briefs, and he pulls them up.

It takes everything in me to keep my eyes trained on his face. If he caught me looking down, he'd know, and...yeah...not ready for that.

"Do I need to get a restraining order?" he asks.

"What's with the shades?" Except when he's on the court, I've never seen him without them.

He pauses before reaching for his jeans. "Just kick rocks, man."

"No one's around. You can stop pretending you hate me."

"Who said I give a fuck about you?" He wrestles the jeans on, pulling up the zipper, but not bothering to button them.

"Take 'em off. Let me see your eyes."

"No." He folds into a chair and bends over, tugging on his socks.

"Why? It's just us."

His jaw comes down hard, the sharp sound of gum being masticated filling the silence.

It's either a rubber band or gum being assaulted by him every time I see him.

"You know they surge to life when you hit a beyond-the-arc, step-back three or when you son dudes bigger than you on the court?" I ask.

His tatted hands fidget with his laces.

"But when I catch you watching me...that's my favor—"

He flies across the room and snarls in my face, "Stop talking."

"Or what?" I taunt.

His hand wraps around my neck. It's clammy.

I nudge my neck forward into his grasp, choking myself.

My gaze drops down to his hardened nipples.

He catches me looking and shoves me back. "Fuck you," he

sneers, his minty breath ghosting my lips. My body seizes for a breath, trapping in the "When?" trying to spring off my tongue.

I reach up and remove his shades, and to my surprise, the little monster doesn't try to headbutt me.

There's a bang on the door.

"We're good," I call out.

"Time's up," the guard says.

I twist the lock. "Heard about the trade rumors."

He steps back, glaring at me. "So?"

"Good. Your coach is a jackass. You're their best shot at making it to the finals, and he doesn't even have you starting."

"Yeah, well." He shrugs. "Some men fear glory."

I nod. *Or what it demands.* "Heard LA wants you. They're rebuilding their team."

He leans against the opposite wall and crosses his arms. The rhythm of his chewing betrays the calm he's trying to sell.

"Jones!" The banging gets louder. "Open the door!"

"You'll do well in LA." Philly doesn't deserve him. "Coach Derek was in our shoes just a few seasons ago. He's smart and hungry. And remembers what it takes to win. He'll know that the best way to handle all your fire is not to try to handle it." Some fires you fuel instead of trying to put out. "Maybe don't punch your teammate in the face, though."

"Says the asshole who elbowed me in the ribs less than an hour ago," he fires back.

My gaze travels down to the deep grooves emanating from his abs to his obliques. Every inch of him hammered into armor.

Like his chewing, the banging on the other side of the door intensifies.

"It was a peace offering." I turn my head and call out over my shoulder, "Yo, we're good. Chill."

"Open the goddamn door!" the guard demands.

"See? Right there." I nod to Blue's eyes when I turn back

and catch him watching me. "They're spilling with light. Puddles and puddles."

He straightens up.

"Watch me anytime."

The chewing stops.

"I like what it does to your face." I flip the lock and push back on the door. "Later, Kitten." I toss him his shades. "See you in LA."

CHAPTER 5
ARNAZ
PRESENT DAY

Remove the twenty thousand echoing voices, lights, and music, and the main court is my favorite spot in the arena. Dropping into a bleacher chair, I stare up at the jerseys of legends that came before me. Sid wants the Royals to be his home for the rest of his career. Me? I'm not sure. My teammates are my boys, and the current management is cool enough, but...I don't know. LA forever? I don't see it.

Still, I can't deny the questions that hang in the air whenever I'm here—Will my name be up there one day? And if not, will it be because of my game or because I decided to come out? I've only ever been good at a few things. Football, which I quit early out of spite. Singing, at least from what people tell me, though I haven't felt like singing for a while. I enjoy writing songs, and I guess it doesn't matter if I'm good at it, because the world will never hear them. Then there's playing the piano and guitar, which feel more natural than playing ball.

I've had to work hard at basketball every single day. Joining the Royals alongside Sid took my game to the next level, but it still takes work. More work than most would believe.

My phone buzzes.

I slide it out of my pocket and answer. "Hey, Cat."

"Oh, great! I caught you." The voice of Catharine, my agent, filters through. "How's my favorite client?"

"I know you say that to all of us."

She laughs. "Have I given you a reason not to trust?"

"Never."

"Exactly. This a good time?"

"Yeah." I climb to my feet. "Leaving practice."

"Coach Derek in a good mood?"

"Ha."

"That bad, huh?"

"We had to run penalty 17s and suicides because a rook showed up late."

"Ouch. I just had a client benched for a week for rocking a player who caused extra 17s every practice."

"I heard about that. Dallas?"

"Just 'cause you're my favorite doesn't mean I'll break client confidentiality."

I smirk. "Keepin' all of our secrets."

"Until the grave. So listen, I got you out of the CBS interview like you requested. As of today, your PR calendar is completely cleared. Well, actually, not quite. I confirmed the column for *Sports Illustrated*, but it's strictly about your game this season."

I dap Nick, who's also heading to his car. "They know no—"

"No Carter or coming out questions. Just ball."

"Cool. Thanks."

"You bet. So..." She clears her throat. "Salem's a client."

"Ah." I unlock my car, then open the door and throw my bag across to the passenger seat.

"One of my clients publicly expressing romantic feelings toward another of my clients is a new one for me. How can I support you?"

Romantic. I shake my head as I tuck in. *Is that what that was?*

"Yeah." I stare out the window. "1.8 million views."

"The video?"

I grunt.

"Hmm. I know that kind of attention is the last thing you want right now."

My head drops to the headrest, and I close my eyes. I need to eat soon, or I'm gonna pass out. Feels like I'm gonna pass out anyway.

She's quiet, which means she's racking her brain to figure out a way to fix this. We can't. It's out there now.

"Did you know he was gay?" I ask.

She sighs. "You know I can't answer that."

Yeah, I know. I'd have wanted her to answer the same way if someone asked that about me after I came out. She did know. Not at first, but eventually.

"How about this—I can add Salem and the press conference as off-limits in your media clause."

"Thanks."

"You know, if you are interested in him, Salem's a good guy."

I stab the temperature button to turn up the heat, then open the window.

"Honest to god, the kind of man you can take at his word. And he's charitable too—not just a throwing-money-at-the-problem type of guy. Like you, he dedicates his time."

I close the window and switch to the AC.

"You still there?" she asks.

"Yeah."

"You're quiet. Have I overstepped?"

I kill the AC, then put the car in drive. "Nah. Just tired."

"Okay. I emailed you the contract and details for next week. I'll send over the amended agreements with the updated media clause shortly."

"Thanks."

"Oh, hey, I didn't get your RSVP for my birthday shindig."

"I'm there."

"Wonderful. Call if you need me."

"Thanks, Cat."

"A-actually, wait—"

"Hmm?"

"I'm guessing you don't plan to respond to the viral post where a fan started asking about your favorite dessert?"

"Nope." I put the car back in Park. I don't even have a favorite dessert. If it's good, I'll eat it. "I don't need more shit showing up in the locker room."

"And you don't want me to pass it along to Salem in private?"

"Cat."

"Okay, okay. I had to ask."

"What?" I ask after she's silent for a few breaths.

"Nothing. I'm going. Call—"

"What, Cat?"

"Nothing, really. Well, except, I'm sitting here wondering, how?"

"How what?"

"With his press conference, charm, and objectively good looks, you're telling me you feel nothing?"

"No."

"No."

"Yeah. No. I don't find him attractive."

"Pfft. *Not attractive.* You want to come over here and man the phones? *The Rake, Vanity Fair, Essence, Out,* and *GQ* all want to know about his skin care routine, what he eats, and when they can meet his parents."

I hear her rummaging through papers.

"Calvin Klein wants his abs for their new campaign, Oprah

wants him for—I don't know what she wants him for, but her office called."

"Okay. I get it."

"Agh. I just have to ask again. What's with you two?"

"Meaning?"

"You can't be on the court together without it ending bloody or with more fouls than any other game. Why?"

"He's a dickhead."

"I've seen him simply look at you, and you go scorched earth."

"Not true. That was before. It's been chill this season."

"He was out for most of the season."

I shrug. "Ask him."

"I have. He said, *'That's just how Blue likes it.'*"

"How I like it?" I'm not the one who fucks with the other every game. "What part of my fist in his face screams 'I like it?'"

"What's the story behind the nickname?"

"Hell if I know."

She sighs. "Okay. You sure you don't want to come work here? You keep more under lock and key than I do."

"I seriously don't know. I've asked, and he never answers."

"Blue. Hmm. Maybe it's your broody nature. Or maybe you remind him of the color. Oh, crap. I'm late for my meeting. Let me run."

"Aight. Later."

"Hey, do what you want with this unsolicited advice, but maybe you should get to know the guy you hate. You might be surprised at what you find."

I'd rather eat through my arm than get to know Salem fucking Jones.

Mr. Anxious-For-No-Reason strikes again, and sleep drifts off without me. Picking up my laptop from the nightstand, I head to my favorite hookup site, but somehow, I'm staring at Salem taking a seat at his press conference.

2.3 million views.

The nausea from this morning returns.

Directing an I'm-friendly-for-now glance around the room, he settles into the chair.

The camera zooms in.

If autumn was a face...

Deep honey-brown eyes. Warm with an underhanded edge. Nothing like the unwanted inheritance of my murky, dark moss.

You can tell a lot about someone from their eyes. Like, how many words it'll take to get my point across. His tell me I'd use fewer words, and they may even read my silences.

God, I hate dimples. And plump top lips that curl up. And extra-as-fuck sharp cheekbones.

I roll my eyes as the reporters dick-ride his return.

A tat peeks out of the unbuttoned collar of the blue button-down hugging his chest and biceps. I make and then immediately delete a mental note to look for a full picture of it.

He thanks them.

So polite.

When his gift baskets start to pour in, he'll probably sit down at night and pen heartfelt thank-you notes.

A sheen of a winner's glow spreads over his brown skin and its undertones of gold—the same color of his small nose hoop. Stubble outlines a tapered V-shaped jawline. Like his crew cut, it's all so neat.

Yeah, the gift baskets will definitely be rolling in.

Fucker.

I hope he chokes on them.

A cover photo of him in a rust-colored sweater and dark

blue jeans standing in front of a stoop covered in snow has me hitting play on the pop-up video titled "Inside NBA Star Salem Jones's Sophisticated Brooklyn Brownstone."

"Welcome to Brooklyn! Come on in," he says, widening his glass front door. The video plays a montage of shots from the foyer, kitchen, dining room, wine cellar, and movie theater.

My mother would trade in her overpriced decorator if she saw this.

"This is Simba, my best friend," he says, bending down to pet a large, brown, shaggy-haired dog with a foggy gray eye. *"We rescued each other three years ago."*

Simba limps over to the camera and offers his toy.

"We'll play later." Salem pets him.

Simba's probably rented to capture the perfect thirst trap shot.

He climbs up and offers his forelimbs for a hug. Salem pulls him in, accepting a neck lick.

Okay, maybe they are best friends.

The camera pans the forest-green foyer as he talks about designing the place with intention, honing in on function, blah blah, textures, blah blah.

"My parents on their wedding day," he says before a large black and white portrait of a couple.

His dad's don't-fuck-with-me stature radiates from the photo.

His kind—or whatever—eyes and high cheekbones are from his mom.

Deduct ten points for unearned good looks.

He blah blahs about imported Congolese grass pendant lights that remind me of a sculpture Anaïs broke once. Mom was brutal about it. Listening when Anaïs yelled for me to get back in the room still litters the room of my regrets.

I fast-forward past the exposed brick in the living room, large float sofa, fancy art, blah blah.

I rewind. "*...reclaimed terracotta tile, a 1,200-pound carved-stone sink...*"

Damn. That smile.

So, the kitchen is his favorite place in the house.

I should've chipped those perfect teeth during our last rumble.

I fast forward, then pause on a room with a leather Eames-style chair.

The blue, almost-black walls are intensified by the glow from the metal and glass chandelier.

Simba stretches out across a midnight-blue rug in front of the fireplace as Salem crosses his arms and leans against the side post of the canopy bed with serial-killer crisp bedding in burnt gold.

I'm not fooled by the cream fur throw strewn across it. This dark sophistication can't belong to someone with vanilla fantasies.

And, damn, those pants are tight.

Heat skitters down my chest. I stare at the swell forming in my briefs.

Fuck, no.

I slam the laptop shut and blow out a breath.

Ain't enough meds in the world to make that make sense.

Scrubbing my face with my hands, I then reach for the half-burnt joint on the nightstand and light up. Plucking up my acoustic guitar, I return to the piece I've been struggling with for weeks. Leaving form and structure behind, the song'll find itself in the chaos.

The night air breezes in, mixing with the vapors.

Brooklyn's probably getting snow soon.

I'd kill for snow.

♫ ~~World Building~~ ♫
~~I've traveled millions of alien worlds alone.~~
~~Hoping that one day my ship will recognize its home.~~

♫ ~~Space Travel~~ ♫
~~I've traveled millions of alien worlds .~~
~~Growing familiar to everyone except myself.~~

♫ **Homesick** ♫
I'm scattered amongst unknowable worlds.
Hoping my ship will recognize its home.

REAL TALK SPORTS WITH DARIUS & TODD

"I spoke to a few top players who wanna remain anonymous, Todd, and I'm telling you, many of 'em aren't feeling Cade and Jones."

"Like who?"

Darius fidgets in his chair. "I just told you they wanna remain anonymous."

"That's lame. They should go on record if they have a problem," Todd says, stabbing the table with his finger.

"I think they are. They're talking to their management."

"About what?"

"It's a family sport. Parents don't want their kids exposed to that sorta thing." Darius shrugs. "Shake your head, but you know I'm right. This is the league that bears the legacy of Mo "Hammer" Bradley and Sniper Hedley, real men, who'd be turning over in their graves if they knew players like Cade and Jones were in the league."

Todd shakes his head. "The times have changed. This isn't your grandfather's league anymore. And some might say that's a good thing."

"Who?" Darius scoffs, twisting in his chair and scanning the room for effect. "The league's gotten soft. This is the beginning of the end. I won't be surprised if we start seeing viewership decline over the next few seasons." The camera zooms in on him. "Mark my words."

CHAPTER 6
SALEM

"**Y**ou're back from tennis early."

"I figured you'll need a hand with transportation," Dad offers.

"I appreciate it. I was starting to doubt my plan."

"Let's hear it," he says, standing next to me. His muscular frame that lives in my adolescent memories is now a softer, more lanky build, but the presence that garners the nickname The Chief among his friends is still alive and strong.

"Driving slowly with it in the front seat."

He chuckles, slinging his arm over my shoulder. "How about you drive, and I protect it with my life?"

"Deal."

"You deserve a date just for flying almost three thousand miles to bake and hand deliver your crush a cake on what I imagine is a much-needed rest day. That's old-school romance. And just when I thought you youngsters killed it with those impersonal apps. You've really outdone yourself."

I wish I could say the design came easily. Of course Blue didn't respond with an answer for his favorite dessert. That would be too easy. Nothing about him's easy. I asked Cat, but her lips were sealed, so I decided to wing it. After weeks of research and trial and error stretched around road games, my doubts backed me into a corner. Then I got a call.

"*Salut toi.*"

I grinned at Lucien's sing-song voice. "Hey you," I repeated back.

"*Tu me manques et je suis jaloux.*"

"Wait, say it again slower," I replied.

He did, and I was still lost.

"Tsk. Tsk. You've already forgotten the French I taught you?" he asked.

"I remember the important words."

"And what might those be?"

"Putain de merde, je veux plus, oh putain," I rattled off.

He chuckled. "The words you made me scream during sex are the important words? I said I miss you, and I'm jealous. You never made any grand gestures for me."

He saw my press conference. "Pretty hard to when I was in the closet."

"I'm jealous he gets to experience you out of the closet."

"He hasn't agreed to a date yet."

He scoffed. "Only an idiot would turn you down, and you're too good for idiots."

It hit me how much I missed my friend. We hooked up every now and then, but we never confused that with what we were—friends. "How are you settling in?" I asked.

"Eh, France will always be home, so it's easy to settle here. I plan to be back in Manhattan often. They're too proud to admit it, but my maman and papa need me here. They asked to meet you, by the way."

"Yeah?"

"They don't believe the beautiful, famous man on the screen is one of my best friends." He sighed. "They need me. Maison Laurent needs a strong hand. One of the pattern makers is a drunk, and I fear the head seamstress is sliding into senility."

"Isn't she like eighty-nine?"

"So?"

"Maybe it's time to order cake and champagne and throw her a retirement party?"

"You try retiring the tyrant. She threatens to go straight to the competition every time I broach the subject. They've been trying to poach her for years. I've resorted to having a chaise installed so she can nap when she needs to."

I laughed. "If I ever visit, I want to meet her."

"None of the men here are like you. Come before you get a boyfriend, fall in love, and forget about me."

"Only an idiot could forget you. I thought I wasn't an idiot."

My stomach dropped as I bit into the cake I'd been working on for the last twelve hours. "Hoh' on!" I ripped off a piece of paper towel and scraped my tongue.

"Ah bon? New recipe?"

"Ugh, and running"—I swished water around in my mouth, then spit it down the kitchen drain—"out of ideas fast."

"Oh non..."

And it felt like I was running out of time. It's not like I expected Blue to be waiting up at night for it. But still, it's felt like the kind of thing that loses its steam the more weeks pass by. "It's the fourth quarter, and I'm down like twenty points. Got any game-winning pep talks in the chamber?"

He hummed. "Start from the beginning."

We traced the steps that led to the taste that haunted my tongue before he offered, "When I design a garment, execution involves countless choices. Everything from the fabric, closures, and threads takes hours of consideration. They have to work on their own and in relationship to the other elements."

"So instead of focusing on the recipe, focus on the ingredients?"

"Oui. Deconstruct and assess each component. Don't be afraid to follow your inspiration, even if it goes against the grain."

"Hmm. Maybe I've been playing it safe," I admitted as I picked up the cake and dropped it into the garbage.

"La nuit porte conseil."

I slept on it like he instructed, and in the morning, I hit the ground running.

I STEP BACK as Dad snaps pictures.

"Your mother will kill us if we don't get one from every angle."

"Have you heard from her? How's her spa weekend going with Aunt V?"

"Spoke to her on the way home. They were headed to get facials. She sounded relaxed." He lets out a breath. "But I still received three text reminders to take pictures of the cake."

I chuckle. She sent me one too.

"How's your brother? I tried him this morning, but his phone's off."

"You sure it's off?" Wiping icing off my hands, I grab my phone from the counter and hit call on my brother's contact.

"So stubborn," I grouse as an automated voice confirms what Dad said. I hang up and dial the phone company, pin the phone to my ear, and retrieve my credit card from my wallet.

"He gets it naturally. At least he agreed to live with you. It only took years of convincing."

"We have an agreement, though. He's visiting his Marine friend in Minnesota."

"Hmm."

"I'm sure he's okay. I'll try him again tonight. Help me box this?"

He nods. "You know, if you and Arnaz start dating, I'll see my youngest more."

"I visit almost every other month. Gimme some credit."

"Alright." He pats my back. "Your old man is still holding out hope we can open a bakery here together."

"Think we're good enough?"

"Would you look at this masterpiece? With your tenacity, what can't you do?"

He gave me the same answer when I asked if he thought I was good enough to join the league. Then he hit the courts with me at the crack of dawn to practice, shuffled me to camps and tournaments. Tenacity aside, he and Mom are part of the reason I made it.

I rub my palms on my jeans.

"You're up," I whisper to the cake before I seal the box. "Help me score a first date with Blue."

CHAPTER 7
ARNAZ

♫ "No Trespassers" ♫
Sky-tall electric fences, overgrown thickets, guarded patrols.
Pray they keep you from the vacant rooms of my soul.

In a perfect world, each NBA team is a strong contender, which makes clinching a win challenging. In reality, there are games we go into knowing the win is in the bag for us because the team poses weak opposition. Such is the case with this season's Detroit roster. They hung their one shot at glory on their star point guard, who ruptured his Achilles tendon in the third game of the season. Coach benched our starting lineup after halftime. The score is 104-75 with less than three minutes on the game clock.

"Want to hit the weight room after?" I ask Sid.

"Can't," he replies, nibbling on his bottom lip. "Need to dip."

That's right. Ty gets home today after a stretch of road games.

"I can already see the hickey," I joke. They seem to cover more surface area these days.

He smirks. "No word from Salem yet?"

"Who?"

"I forgot that's dead." He rests his palm on my bouncing knee. "But why, again?"

"You know why. He's not my type."

He snickers. "All types are your type."

I fight a grin.

"You know, it took backbone to do what he did in front of the world. I think you—"

"Yurp!" We both fly out of our seats and yell props to Wes, who just swished a freak shot.

"At least the press has finally moved on." I crash back into my chair. "Well, most of them."

"Fuck Darius and Todd," he says, pulling my arm until my fingers drop from my teeth. "Let one of us run up on them in person. See if they question our manhood then."

Ten toes down, I know Sid has my back. He uses his considerable platform to fight homophobia, and checks anyone who gets out of line on the court. He's a real one. No doubt. But he and Ty aren't out to the public yet, and though they have every right to be offended, it's my name that's getting dragged.

Mine and Salem's.

"Yo! Special delivery for you," Nick calls over his shoulder as I enter the locker room.

"Give it to Ussef," I toss back as I cut through the circle.

"Uh," Ussef replies. "You might want to keep this one."

Heat flushes over my scalp as a tall, cream-colored box with a dark-red bow atop a server cart comes into view.

Johan hands me an envelope with my name on it, and I tuck it into the front of my shorts.

"Open it." I nod to him.

"Uh-uh." He backs away. "It looks fancy."

Christ.

I reach for the ribbon, then pause to blow on my hands before pulling and following the handwriting on the box along the edge that reads *open here.*

Gasps ping-pong around the room as the walls hinge down.

"What is it?" Nick asks.

"A 3D model of a building," Johan replies.

Sid cuts through the crowd. His eyes widen. "That's stunning."

"Yes, but what is it?" Nick asks.

"A cake," Sid and I answer in unison.

"What?" Wes scoffs. "It's too tall."

"Bruh." Jamie pats Sid's arm. "Tell me it's not like the fancy hotel you recommended in Miami near Ivy's."

"Yeah, the Art Deco one," Ussef agrees, stroking his goatee.

Nick tilts to take in the angles. "Shit's cold. This Salem?"

"What do you think the accordion folds represent?" asks Jerry, my favorite assistant coach, who I keep pleading with not to leave us in a few weeks for a head coach gig in Houston.

"'Accordion folds.'" Wes smiles. "That's good. I was thinking it's like poured stone." He points to the three middle layers. "But then check it, the bottom layer is the foundation, so like cooled stone, or maybe a light and dark marble 'cause it's so smooth."

"Nah." Johan shakes his head. "I think the top three are like sandstorms."

Nick snickers over his shoulder. "Yo, call MoMA, tell 'em to come get their critics."

I pull the envelope from my waistband and clamp down on the inside of my lip to stop the pounding in my chest.

Blue,

Do you remember the last time you clocked me? I headbutted you, and then you choked me.

Do you remember the first time?

I don't know how to explain what happened to me that day.

Or why a three-minute scuffle led to 1,895 days of unrelenting palm, neck, and chest sweats whenever I think of you.

You're probably wondering what's in the large box.

Well, it's you, or rather what I think of when I think of you. Five tiers for all 1,895 days.

The mixed gray concrete-inspired base, while a nod to your East Coast roots, reminds me of your strength in being the first out player in the league. Standing alone couldn't have been easy.

You inspired me to come out.

Thank you.

You ever met someone and sensed immediately that they have layers?

Layers that don't unfurl for just anyone?

Everyone with their labels wants to reduce us to one thing, but I know underneath that gorgeous package and I'll-feast-on-your-corpse swag lies someone very few of us will be lucky to know.

Back to the cake...

The dusty-peach textured tiers with alternating cream satin panels run counterpoint to each other. Shielded underneath is a Genoise sponge cake brushed with rose water.

Did you know rose helps with depression?

The filling is a vanilla and cardamom-infused crème pâtissière.

Why cardamom?

Well, it's known to enhance pleasure.

In case none of this is clear, I'll speak plainly.

I want you in all the ways I can have you.

You have walls, and that's okay.

Walls, too, are part of a home.

I'll stand outside on devotional guard, so you don't have to work so hard to protect them.

Put me out of my misery.

Go on a date with me?

Salem

P.S. It's dairy-free. Catharine wouldn't give me your number, but she shared that you're lactose intolerant. Full ingredients on the card in the envelope.

P.P.S. Why are you so beautiful? You turn a sidelines chair into a throne. You do know you minding your business on a bench is how this started?

"CADE, you want to weigh in here? Are we cutting the cake or not?" Coach asks, pulling me away from reading the phone number scrawled at the bottom.

"You good?" Sid nods to the letter.

My chest thumps so hard, they'll hear it if I open my mouth.

"Yo," Sid calls out. "Can we get a bottle of water over here?"

I stare at the rust-colored leaves and cream flowers emerging from the base of the cake.

How does he know I struggle with depression?

A bottle of water appears.

I tuck the letter back in my waistband and then down the water.

"Wes is gonna fall into it if we don't cut it soon," Nick says.

"We can't cut it. It's like slashing through an Amy Sherald painting," Johan protests.

Sid's head snaps back. "That's dark, bro."

"We aren't eating it?" Wes looks to me. "We have to."

"Agreed." Nick nods. "It's an immersive experience."

"Ah, I mentioned my depression in my coming out article," I mumble.

"He's talking to himself." Johan nudges Sid.

"Hey," Sid says. I look up, and he snaps a photo. "To show your kids one day."

"Fuck off." I step back and pull away from the crowd. "Do what you want with it."

"Ay." I nod to Shane. "Not this one."

He lowers his camera.

I snatch the weight gloves from my station and then head to the weight room.

I've always been fascinated by the origin of things. How one ripple alters the sea of change. Take the Fender Stratocaster sitting an arm's length away. A kid back in the sixties decided to break the rules by cranking up the volume of amps and manipulating the feedback from his guitar's proximity to create sounds and textures that unlocked new possibilities for guitarists all over the world.

Fearless experimentation, trusting in your own flavor, and starting from where you are. I thought about that a lot in the weeks leading up to my coming out. What ripples I'd create by honoring what I needed, even if it broke the rules. Maybe it explains why I've been sitting here for the last forty-two minutes, staring at the two large slices of cake haloed by a golden cake board.

He said I inspired it.

How?

I rub my lips between my thumb and index finger as I breathe in the spiced honey, rose, and vanilla scents.

Blowing out a breath, I slide my phone out of my pocket.

No energy to pretend, I'm headed to find him in my browser when an alert for unread texts pops up.

Sid sent the picture of me in front of the cake. A reddish color dusts my neck and cheeks.

Deleted.

I click on Nick's video.

Sid, scooping up a bite of the cake, laughs as someone lets out a loud moan off camera. The camera pans to Wes, who, hand over his heart, stares at the cake wide-eyed with a spoon hanging out of his mouth.

"I need two slices to go, Coach," Sid calls out.

I shake my head. Ty is probably smothered in cake, getting thunderfucked right now.

"Great job today," Coach addresses the room. *"I'd attempt a post-game speech, but you're all high on cake."* He wipes icing off his mouth with the back of his hand. *"If Jones is taking orders, I want in."*

"For your eighth wedding?" Ussef calls out, making the guys laugh.

"Smart ass." Coach tries not to grin. *"Cheers. Get your asses back here bright and early for practice. Wes and Johan, address the media tonight."*

Nick's face fills the frame, cream in the corner of his lips. "So, what's the verdict? Does my boy The Silencer get a date?"

Ussef starts chanting, "Date him! Date him! Date him!" kicking off a chorus with the other guys.

I exit the video.

Doofuses, all of 'em.

Pillowy layers filled with folds of cream were waiting at my station when I returned from the weight room. One slice has polished panels, the other striated, and both have flowers and branches that are even more vibrant under this light.

I curl and straighten my fingers, relishing the slight tremor coursing up my inner forearm from deadlifting 400 and benching 230 pounds until failure.

Ignoring the spasm in my stomach, I resume my nightly ritual, head dropping to the cushion as I hit play.

Quads coiled, Salem drops low, sweat-glistened forearms bracketing the shooter, whose face is a blur next to Salem's curled top lip and narrowed eyes. His thick calves and hamstrings pull tight as he stalks the player's movement. With just the broad plane of his chest, he angles in just a clip, throwing the shooter off balance.

I rub my sweaty palms against my thighs.

Denied an escape, the shooter stiffens, eyes darting left and right, feet shifting like the floor's on fire, before thrashing his elbow into Salem's chest.

I trail circles around my stomach.

Chest slumped, the shooter gets off a limp pass.

A hint of something subtle tickles my nose, and I press my eyes closed to fight the pull, even as my fingers extend and feather across the metal of the spoon.

Salem's neck muscles tighten as he zeros in on the new ball handler.

My tongue grazes my bottom lip as the spoon's metal stem presses into my palm.

No. I drop it and rub my palm across the couch cushion.

He pounces, his hamstrings and glutes powered up.

Massaging my erection through my boxer briefs, I bear down, contracting the muscles inside my pelvis.

One, two, three strides, and he closes in.

Pre-cum darkens the gray cotton.

Corded Achilles and calves spring-loaded.

I reach under my waistband and wrap my hand around the head of my erection.

His mouth parts slightly as he launches up.

Tightening my fingers, they glide back and forth, causing pre-cum to leak onto my stomach.

His gaze darkens, jaw tightens.

"Mmh," I pant as a toe-curling wave of heat crests up my spine.

His delts and lats draw back.

My free hand drags over the cushion for the lube.

His gold piercing catches the light as he flares his nostrils.

My fingers sink into the moist sponge cake, jerking my dick ramrod straight.

I swallow roughly and rub the cream into the pads of my fingers.

Releasing myself, I massage my knuckles against the knot forming in my sternum.

A low-frequency hum clouds my ears as I roll out my neck.

Like the controls have been hacked by an enemy combatant, the flat of my palm raises, my lips part, and my turncoat tongue slithers out until the tip collides with the cream.

Holy hell.

Plunging into the layers of cream and spongy cake again, I suck my fingers into my mouth.

I hate him.

I hate him so hard.

The pressure builds between my legs.

Goosebumps pebble my arm as I stare at the cake and then my dick.

No...definitely not.

Third time this week getting off to his videos. Whatever this is has gotten out of control.

He sets a screen that drops a guard on his ass. A dark grin dances across his face.

I claw the cake, squishing cream between my palm and fingers.

"Ngh." I gasp at the slick glide as my shaft is lathered in cream, warming with every roll of my wrist.

My toes curl as I rock my hips.

The first pulse sends a shock up my thighs.

My thumb spreads across my slit.

Mmm, damn.

The salty-sweet, pre-cum-laced cake dissolves against my tongue.

Ngh.

My eyes shutter, and like night after night, his sex-dungeon bedroom blinks to life.

My chest kisses fur, fists cling to the poster panels. His tongue, sunk deep, pulls out, and a blunt pressure pushes past my rim.

I choke out his name.

My breath chases a scream as he spreads me open...

Oh, god.

Moans echo through the room, a cold-hot shiver floods my blood, and my teeth crash into my lips. The hint of sweet has me bucking into my fist as the first strip of cum hits my chest. A fizzy roiling lights up my skin. Every wrist pump emits a low, humming plea from my chest until the last of my release drips down my palm.

Ugh.

Heart hammering in my throat, I stare down at the mess of cake and cum. My fingers trail up my abs, over my chest, until they're parting my lips.

I suck them clean.

I reach down for more.

Fuck. Me.

Fuck. Salem. Jones.

CHAPTER 8
SALEM

As soon as I settle into the back of my ride from JFK airport to home, I try my brother again.

"Before you say anything—" he starts.

"I thought we had an agreement. I don't press you if you remain reachable by phone."

"Sheesh," he grumbles, and I can picture his scowl. "It was off for one day. I was waiting for the cash to come in from that private security job."

One day. Not *weeks* of him falling off the face of the earth or his refusal to stay in one place when he got home from Iraq. Our only communications with him while he was deployed was when he called me or Mom and Dad. Every cell phone I bought him was disconnected within months. We let him be, ignoring the unease clouding us. Until the clouds burst, and a call came in last year. The terms of his hospital discharge included him providing a permanent address and an agreement to see a psychiatrist. Between Brooklyn and Pasadena, he chose to live with me. I would get him his own place, but there's no way he'd stay there, and I want to be close to make sure he takes his meds and makes it to his appointments.

"Use the credit card I gave you."

"I can pay my own way."

I can barely hear him over a scratching noise.

"I never said you couldn't," I reply. "Where are you, and who's sandpapering your phone?"

"I didn't survive combat overseas to come home and have my baby bro bust my balls."

"Yeah, yeah. Where are you?"

"I'm in Utah, out in the desert."

I pull the phone away from my ear as the scratching noise gets louder. "Yo, can you find somewhere quieter? And what happened to Minnesota?"

"Hold on." There's shuffling, then the sound of a zipper. "I spent a few days with my buddy in the hospital and then left."

"Your friend's sick?"

"Depends on who you ask." He sighs. "He tried to take his life."

That's three of his friends. Only this one made it.

That feeling of a latched roof lowering over my lungs hits.

My parents and I spent over a decade praying for his safe return home, and now my fears are of a different kind of horror.

"You, erm…" I pause to steady my voice. "You okay?"

"Yeah…I should go."

He's not okay.

"Wait. What's in Utah? Send me the address of where you're staying."

"This kid from the Marines was from here. Always talked about purple sunsets, red arches, and rocks. I'm camping, so no address."

"How you have enough dough to get to Utah but not keep your phone on?"

"Who said I didn't have enough to pay the bill?"

"You did. You said you were waiting for cash to come in."

"That doesn't mean I don't have enough."

My head hurts. "I set up auto-pay on my card for your phone."

"Hell, Salem."

"Cancel it, and I'll just set it up again. You have enough meds?"

"Yes, Dad."

"You can't disappear again, Denzel." It kills us every time. I know he doesn't mean to, but it does. I remind myself for the tenth time today that the latest cocktail of his meds works.

I hear the tone for an incoming call and lower the phone to peek at the screen.

"Send a pic of the red rocks, and call Mom and Dad," I say.

"Roger that."

"No disappearing, Denzel," I insist before clicking over to the other call. "Hello."

A throat clears. "H-hello? This is, uh, Arnaz."

Yes. "Hey, you."

"Your cake put—"

An ambulance speeds by, drowning out his voice. I turn up the volume on my phone to the highest level, but I still can't hear him.

"Sorry, Blue, one sec." As the sirens recede, loosely coiled air skitters in and out of my ear. "You were saying?"

"Your cake put my entire team and coaching staff in a trance."

"And you?"

Besides the sound of his breathing—nothing.

I push away from the seat cushion. "That bad?"

Maybe the rose water was too much?

Can I at least get points for presentation?

He blows out a breath. "Put it like this. If it were between winning a championship and eating your cake again, I might consider dying ring-less."

I shake my fist in the air. "Does that mean we have a date?" I ease back into the seat.

"I don't like you, and I don't date."

"Hold up." My head jerks back. "I think you might have the wrong number."

"Nope. I don't."

"Why don't you like me?"

He scoffs. "I lost my starting position for the rest of the season because of you. I was suspended for five games and ordered to see a therapist. And what'd you get?"

"A two-game suspension."

"Right. And that was fair how? You fuck with me every game."

"You can't still be mad about that. It was five years ago."

"Pfft."

"That can't amount to a lot of dislike. Like, 10 percent max."

"You think I like you 90 percent?"

"More like ninety-eight."

"Fuck off."

"And I don't *fuck* with you," I correct. "I attempt to talk to you, and you go ape."

"Whatever."

"Nah. What, you don't find me attractive?"

The squelch of tires dragging through the slush fills the silence.

"Five years is a long time not to like someone," I continue. "We should celebrate."

"Why's your voice so deep?"

I grin. "Blue, why don't you date?"

"I just don't."

"Cool. Have a meal with me."

"No."

"You like seafood? I make a plate-licking paella."

"Who's Blue?"

"I'll tell you over dinner."

A slow exhale is chased by a flat, "I can't."

"You got my letter?"

My fingers tap against my thigh as I wait for his response.

"I'm not who you want." He lets out an exasperated sigh. "I can't be."

"You're telling me what I want?"

"I'm telling you I don't have what you're looking for."

The thick conviction in his voice tells me he believes what he's saying, so it doesn't matter if I believe him.

"Okay."

"O-okay?"

"Mm," I reply. "If that's what you want. Okay."

"Can I at least pay you for it?"

"For what?"

"The cake."

Unbelievable. "It was a gift."

"You sure?"

"Good night, Blue."

After a few seconds of silence, my hand lowers, and I end the call.

Well.

Damn.

CHAPTER 9
ARNAZ

♫ "Futility" ♫

To my future lover,

I've felt shipwrecked on deserted shores.

You'll try your best to make a home for me.

Go gently when you discover you need more.

I'm so tired that I want to physically knock myself out. Every time I nod off, I jolt awake. It's after two a.m. when I give up. My exhaustion is the only explanation for why my resolve failed for the last week, and I'm covered in my own cum with Salem frozen on my screen.

My body thrums, recalling his last play that blocked a tip-in but sent him crashing headfirst to the floor, breaking the fall with his hands, lower body following in slow motion like a stripper about to hump the floor.

Fine. Maybe he just fell headfirst into a low plank, but the save was hot, especially at three-quarter speed.

If you're flailing, you might as well go balls to the wall. So I google him, picking up where I left off on page twelve. Scrolling, I pause on him at a fashion show for Lucien Laurent.

I'm bored ten seconds in, so I fast forward, searching for Salem in the crowd. With only forty-three seconds left in the video, I think I might have missed him and start to rewind when he emerges onto the stage wearing a silver metallic kerchief with a diamond-looking strip at the hem, no shirt, and a black—or is it blue?—tuxedo jacket and matching skinny trousers. Except when I zoom in, it isn't a two-piece—it's connected at the waist. It's like a tuxedo overall, with a silver belt that matches the kerchief. A massive round of applause comes from the audience as he strides down the runway, commanding awe.

The fashion designer, Lucien, who's a certified smokeshow, comes out next, and Salem turns to him. With an *objectively* sexy smile—the camera eating up the gleam of his nose ring— he joins the crowd in applauding the designer.

Lucien says thank you, shaking his clasped hands at the crowd. I shuffle to sit up when his gaze lands on Salem, and it both softens and heats up.

Hm...they're fucking.

Salem steps back to give him his moment, but Lucien takes his hand and gestures for the rest of the models to come forward and join in. They all take a bow before joining the crowd and showering Lucien with a final round of applause. As they turn and exit the stage, he turns to Salem and blushes as Salem mouths something to him. Lucien's long-legged with a lean frame. He's wearing pearls around his neck and has one of those trendy boy-band haircuts.

He's hot. *Ugh.* They're smokin' together.

I shut my laptop and rub the back of my neck.

A few seconds later, I flip it open again and type in my browser "Lucien Laurent and Salem Jones."

I skim the search results that are full of articles covering them individually. I switch to searching images, and after five pages, I'm convinced maybe I got them wrong, but then I see a photo of them together at an art gallery in New York.

Salem is in the frame talking to a random woman, and Lucien's in the background casting him a sideways glance.

They've been careful.

There's no dating history, or anything even linking him to someone, for Salem online. None that I could find, which I get, since he's only recently come out.

I shut the laptop again and jump out of bed.

I PARK IN THE ROYALS' arena lot, grab the paper bag sitting atop the passenger seat, and make my way to the side entrance.

Pulling out my phone, I scan emails as I walk. My thumb hovers over the one I've been waiting for. I'm always careful, staying up to date on my vaccines and PrEP, but since I can't remember what I took that night of the threesome, I need to be sure. My thumb lowers, and I scroll down and open the attachment with the results for my recent STI panel. I scroll through the pages and nod as the results reveal nothing out of the norm.

Pocketing my phone, I press my thumb against the biometrics scanner and wait for the quiet click before turning the metal knob.

"Sup, Gigi?" I nod to the security guard and hand her the bag.

"With extra guac and two sides of salsa macha?" she asks.

"You already know."

"Thank you! You and Sid take such good care of me." She sticks her nose in the bag and inhales. "Having trouble sleeping?"

"Something like that."

"You know, some people watch TV when they can't sleep."

"Yeah, but games are won in the gym."

I cringe, recalling the coach who taught me that.

"What are you working on tonight?"

I raise my left hand. "I need to improve my weak-hand finishing."

"You might cross over with Sid. He's usually here at the crack of dawn. I hope he brings the stuffed French toast that I like."

Ty's home this week. I doubt it. "Cool. You good?"

"Yep. Another day, another dollar."

I tap her desk and head toward the practice court.

Images of Salem and Lucien filter in, and my head falls forward...damn.

CHAPTER 10
SALEM

"You're quiet today." Cillian bumps my shoulder. "Everything all right?"

"Yep." I shove my foot into my sneaker and pull on the laces until they're strangling my foot. "Just getting locked in." I feel him staring. "What's up?"

He raises his hands. "I didn't say anything."

I grunt as I loosen the laces and re-tie them.

"Jones, what you got for us tonight?" Coach asks, hands on her hips.

I'm not feeling like I have the energy to be the pre-game hype man tonight, but still, I push to my feet. "Tonight's dub's for all the LGBTQIA kids out there. Who y'all reppin'?"

"Tara and Benny from Sunrise Pediatric Hospital," Cillian jumps in.

I nod and turn to Otis.

"Camden," he replies, tucking his phone away.

I nod to Nikola, who's mid-yawn.

"We're putting you to sleep?" Coach cuts in.

"Sombor," he rushes out, jumping to a stand.

"Onyx?" I turn to him.

"Inglewood," he replies, tucking his jersey into his shorts.

"My mama," Zyair throws out, stretching out his hamstrings.

Once the rest of the team has a turn, I reach my hand in for a huddle, and everyone—well, everyone except Rob—leans in. "Lions on three!"

WE LIGHT CHARLOTTE UP.

Well, for the first three quarters. They fought back in the fourth. We got a steal on the last possession. Onyx yeeted it to me. We needed at least two points to win. Though wide open, I didn't trust the shot, so I lobbed it to Cillian who, tangled up by their center and small forward, was already gesturing for me to shoot.

Sorry, partna.

He got free and launched the ball seconds shy of the game buzzer. A whistle was called. Juiced with too much backspin, the ball smacked the inside of the rim, and bounced out. Their crowd got hulked, then went zombie when the ref made good on the whistle. Their small forward shoved Nikola, which meant Nikola got to the free-throw line, where he copped us uno, dos buckets.

We won.

The crowd booed.

Coach ate us alive. *"Sloppy dubs don't win rings."*

And now I'm staring at the room of reporters, glued to my seat with dread.

"Did you bake a cake for Arnaz?" one of them asks.

"Next question." I cross my arms.

"Do you have a response to Darius and To—"

"I don't respond to critics," I grit out, cutting them off. "Next question."

Those fuckers.

My jaw tightens.

They're on the blatant end of the spectrum when it comes to homophobia, and they're not alone. After six-plus seasons in the league, you learn to hear the snake's rattle when fielding questions. An interviewer last week had Cat immediately expanding my interview restrictions clause after they asked inane questions like:

"Do you find it difficult being in the locker room?"

"Are you concerned that the latest media attention will distract your teammates from the game?"

"Was it harder for you to compete as an athlete?"

"Do you find it burdensome to represent all gay players in sports?"

"Do you regret coming out?"

And then there's this crap I started but can't finish. "Are you and Arnaz Cade dating?" a reporter asks.

"No." I straighten up in my chair. "Y'all got questions about basketball?"

Cillian's knee knocks against mine before he leans into the mic. "I'll take the rest of the questions."

"Good lookin'," I grunt, pushing to my feet.

I'm intercepted by Meghan, our assistant manager, on the way to the locker room. "What do you want me to do with this, boss?" She holds up a gift basket. It's like the seventh one this week.

"Send it back."

Just like the others.

I PICK up my dog sitter's fallen textbook, then tap gently on his shoulder until he stirs awake.

His eyes blink open. "You're back."

"How was he?" I ask, rubbing Simba's belly.

"Chill." He stretches his arms over his head, then stills as his eyes widen at the snow-covered window.

"Yeah, six to eight inches expected by morning," I inform him.

"Whoa. Mind if I stay the night and head home in the morning?"

"All good." Simba jumps up as I rise. "You know where everything is."

I head upstairs to change, Simba on my heels.

When I come back down, Josiah joins me in the kitchen as I finish heating up chili.

"I hope you don't mind," he says, burrowing into my hoodie I left on the couch.

I slide him over a bowl. "How's grad school?"

"Mmm." His bangs fall forward as he breathes in the chili's aroma. "You spoil me." He slides onto a stool.

I blow on my spoon as I lean against the counter. "Have you asked for accommodations?"

He shrugs. "Everyone has ADHD. I don't need special treatment. I didn't need it for undergrad."

I blow out steam as I swallow a spoonful of chili. "I have a teammate"—I take a sip of water—"who struggles with SPD. You know what that is?"

He nods. "Sensory Processing Disorder."

"Instead of handshakes or butt slaps, he prefers non-touch praise. Head nods, thumbs up, y'know that sorta thing?"

"Yeah," he mumbles as he chews.

"And when he's really amped, we hit a special two-step shuffle we made up together instead of a bear hug. He wears noise-canceling headphones before and after the game, and we know to give him space when his ears are covered. No one gives him shit when he skips nights out after a game."

"And you all are okay with it?"

"Yeah. He's our boy, and we want to make sure he's good.

And we need him to be able to do his job when it's game time. You get where I'm going?"

"Yep," he says, pausing to lick the spoon.

"Ain't no shame in getting the support you need. We all want you to graduate."

He sighs. "I knooow."

"Good." I smirk at Simba, who's circling the kitchen for fallen scraps.

"Okay, but all day I've been waiting to hear what happened with Arnaz."

I stiffen, lowering my bowl to the counter. "He, uh, doesn't date."

He drops his spoon into the bowl. "He turned you down?"

"Yep." I refill his bowl and slide it back over. "Thanked me for the cake. Even offered to pay for it."

"Noo."

"Yep."

"Eeek." His chin sinks into my hoodie. "I'm sorry."

Yeah, me too.

I rinse out the pot and load it into the dishwasher.

"What about you? How was your date with the artist?"

"Next." He blows out a breath. "Wanna see my date this weekend?"

I step closer as he holds up a picture of a cute guy in an oversized sweater.

"High school teacher."

"Handsome," I observe.

"Wait, look at this one." He scrolls to a picture of the guy sitting on a couch. "Look at his library collection!"

I grin. "Imagine your libraries together."

"Stahp! You know it's literally on my vision board to marry a guy with more books than me."

I do know that. Back when I was injured, Josiah stopped by with a bag of supplies and covered my floor in magazines, glue sticks, and poster boards. Next thing I knew, we were making vision boards. My brother came downstairs and grinned at the big fat "Marry Blue" text block glued to the center of mine.

So corny now that I think about it.

"I got it," he says when I reach for his bowl to wash it out.

"I'm gonna head up. Need anything?"

He shakes his head as he slides off the stool and bends down to hug Simba goodnight. "I'll finish reading a few chapters, then sleep."

Simba whines as he follows me up the steps.

Shoot. I forgot to reorder his dental treats.

"My bad, Sim." I start the fireplace, then kill the lights before crashing into bed. "I'll order them now."

He ignores me, curling up in his bed with his back toward me.

I place the order, then whistle and pat the bed.

He doesn't move at first, but then he drags himself over.

I turn and scratch behind his ears after he settles away from me on the far end of the bed. "You ever felt kicked in the heart and balls at the same time?"

He nudges me with his wet nose.

"Nah, everyone loves you."

He turns his head away.

"It's okay. You can be mad at me. I still love you."

I lean back and stare into the fire.

"I'm not who you want. I can't be."

I can't place exactly why, of everything Blue said, that's what's been on a loop in my mind. It's the way he said it. His voice sounded...like it was less about whether I believed it, but rather, his disbelief of it.

If someone were to ask me what it is about Blue that has me hooked, I wouldn't be able to give them a single answer. I crave planning and direction, and everything about him feels off map. There's this pull toward him. Every time we're in the same building, I have to get close, and the way he goes primal whenever I'm near only heightens my need to be close to him. I sometimes hold back on the court, doing just enough to protect our house. Blue is pure instinct. If he senses something he doesn't like, you see it immediately. He goes for blood. But it's different with us. Yeah, it gets bloody, but it's not from hate. Whatever I feel when I'm near him makes him afraid. I know there's a deeper reason we fire each other up. It's not friction for the sake of friction. That would be like looking at the thrash of waves and missing the ocean.

Still...

He said no, and even though it feels like someone has taken tweezers to the nerves in my gut, I have to respect that.

I have to fall back.

CHAPTER 11
SALEM

"Mom's been trying to reach you. Call her back. Still waiting for a pic of the red rocks. Love you." I hang up after leaving the voicemail for my brother.

"Denzel?" Cillian asks, stretching out his back.

"Yep." I take out my headphones and shelf them with my phone.

"He's all right?"

I roll on my compression tights. "Most likely."

"Ready for this?"

I raise my eyebrow. "And I wouldn't be because?"

He pauses. "I'd get it if you felt a way being on his turf. It wouldn't—"

I shrug. "It's a game like any other."

Silence the Royals' crowd and help Brooklyn clutch a dub.

Business as usual.

Arnaz

Those. Calves. And thighs.

I wanna shove my head between them and strangle myself until my vision goes dark.

He's ignoring me.

Good.

I don't need him in my face, saying some slick shit to try to get me off my game. I asked for this. And there's nothing worse than getting what you ask for and then crying over it.

It's not like I like his voice that much to regret his silence.

I don't.

The hell does it need to be so deep for anyway? Imagine it dripped in exhaustion at night, slipping lower, darker, kissing the ear of the person next to him, who means to sleep and now has to deal with a woody from some irksome line like "Good night, Blue."

Imagine.

Nah.

Stay over there. Please.

I emerged from the tunnel during warm-ups, and there he was. Standing sideways from the net, he swung his arm over his head in a smooth arc, swishing a left-handed hook shot. Tossed another one, he turned, dribbled...and caught me staring.

With a tip of his head so slight I questioned if it was even there, he took off to the hoop for a floater.

And the coldness wasn't just warm-up vibes.

He's defending everyone but me.

Nick drives to the paint with a clear path to the rim. Their power forward, Zyair, jumps up to contest the shot, but he's no match for Nick's speed. The crowd makes noise as Nick sets up for a layup. Then Salem curves in, the run-up so swift each step barely sweeps the floor before he surges through the air and denies the shot with a force that sends a line of reporters ducking. Landing in a squat, he straightens tall and then glares at Nick over his shoulder as he walks away.

I groan.

I will *not* be cashing out on that at the spank bank later tonight.

Definitely not.

I need to kick my nightly internet stalking habit.

But damn, the algorithm is tight.

It feeds me the compilation of him humiliating guys on the court. *Ngh.* I never last until the end.

And the one where he's being interviewed wearing slacks. Snug-fitting slacks.

Great, pop a semi in front of tens of thousands of people.

And it keeps recycling goodies. Like the tour of his house with him lit up in the kitchen—for fuck's sake, that smile.

Ugh, the hell am I grinning for?

"I got ball," I yell when Cillian takes possession, and I move in to defend him.

"You got shit," Cillian fires back, dribbling forward.

We're down seven points, 45–52, with a little under five minutes left until halftime, but I'm not worried.

Squatting low, I keep one hand up to block any pass attempts, my other hand reaching in, tracking the ball. He hesitates, and if I were a rook, I'd jump or push in, especially the way his eyes keep darting to the rim like he's about to charge. But the ball tells another story, and if I wait just one more...

He hesitates mid-crossover, and I lunge forward and swipe the ball.

Cookies!

Winging it behind my back to Sid, he makes a fast break. No one's catching him.

I nod to Cillian. "Tell Papa what you learned in school today."

He claps back, but I mouth, *I can't hear you* as the crowd

roars. Racing backward, my heel thuds against something, causing me to stumble, but a palm to my spine keeps me from falling.

"My bad." I turn and face Salem.

"No problem," he mutters before racing away.

Brrr.

Wide open on the next possession, Cillian feeds him the ball on the perimeter. He stares at me as I charge toward him, then he changes pace to a slow dribble, the kind that says *this play is mine, the defender can't contain me.* He pushes forward as I close in and releases a jumper that sinks through the net.

He's expressionless as he backs away, and it gets under my skin more than when he's in my face.

"Hey—" I call out just as our coach calls a time-out.

I can't tell if he heard me. He keeps walking and doesn't turn around.

"I'm eating for five right now," Sid says as he catches up to me. "Good D, but we need you to cook."

"Night's young, dahlin'. Don't trip."

"You wanna talk about it?"

"No." I keep walking before he gets in my head and has me spilling my guts, or worse, doing halftime meditation.

"He's got it bad for you, bro. It's not too late to change your mind."

"Who said that's what I wanted?" I glare at him. "Not everyone gets to live a damn fairytale."

Men like Salem don't end up with men like me. They end up with warm and fuzzy-looking dudes like Lucien. Dudes who sleep soundly at night.

How do you even sleep next to someone like that— someone who's so clearly won the genetic lottery? How do you wake up and not feel immediately depressed that the most beautiful thing you'll see that day is lying across from you, and everything will be downhill from there?

"Aww." Sid slings his arm around my neck. "You want him to be your prince?"

"Fall outta tree."

"You'd both rock the fuck outta tiaras, princess."

I push him off me, stifling a grin.

When the game resumes, I step up.

Grabbing possession, I cut up Ezekiel, then Nikola, forcing Salem to leave Nick to defend me.

Yeah, yeah, forcing him to engage with me is an asshole move. I never said I wasn't an asshole, though.

He's at my back as I pivot left, shimmy right, then left again, testing his speed.

He's quick, staying low. I fake another pivot, then spin fast, jump back, and get off the ball.

It tears through the air, bouncing off the rim before it sinks in.

"Mm," I hum. "That's in there deep."

His eyes narrow as he races away.

Onyx lowers his shoulder to attack the rim. I swipe the ball before takeoff and then charge up court. Opting to skip the easy layup, I toss the ball over my shoulder, and Sid slams it in.

The crowd's roar is short-lived as Salem feeds the ball to Cillian, who banks a half-court three.

"How's your back?" Ezekiel goads Sid, who tries to free me up to drive to the rim. "Shit's gotta hurt, carrying your bench."

Backing away, Sid raises an eyebrow at me. "Have fun."

"Word?" I hit a fake crossover, then pull back. The idiot bites, and I make him dance. "Tryna set me on fire to get warm?" I release the ball. It spins around the rim, then crashes through the net. "I'm too cold-blooded, dawg. Go home."

The buzzer goes off, signaling the end of the second quarter.

We're up by eight points, so I know what's coming next. The

Lions have one of the sharpest coaches in the league, and she's no doubt gonna assign their most ferocious player to guard me.

Perfect.

Salem

I know what Blue's doing, but I don't know why.

Third-quarter clock begins, and we double-team him. Johan sets a screen that traps Zyair, leaving me one-on-one with Blue. He holds me at bay with his elbow, keeping the ball out of reach. When his head tilts forward, fixing me with a rare unguarded stare, I look away, curbing the roil in my chest. Leaning in to force him toward the corner, he pushes back, holding his ground. I bear the spread of heat everywhere as he turns, looking for a pass, and his breath ghosts my neck.

I ignore the way his lips, those dark, sexy lips...

No.

I widen my arms to box him in. The shot clock winds down, leaving him no choice. He passes the ball. I don't need to look to know it's in Sid's hands.

That no-look dime he made to him earlier after stripping Cillian was bonkers. Somehow, we've all gotten used to the way they read each other.

He frowns as I back away. His energy is all over the place tonight. I keep catching him staring.

One second his gaze is filled with heat, the next fear, and the next it's unreadable. Not its usual song of wrath and unrest, or wild woods, dark and dense with lethal life. Tonight, the trees are parting, offering a barely lit path inside.

Christ. I can't guard him.

But I have to.

When he's on fire, the other guys struggle to contain him.

It's why he's one of my favorite players to guard—he's so dynamic. I wait for our face-offs all season.

Not tonight.

When it's their possession again, I fall back and let Cillian and Onyx cover him. His off-ball movement is unpredictable. If he isn't standing still to lull the defense, he's taking off in straight cuts or making tight curls, trying to shake whoever's on his tail, to get an open look. He just lost Cillian by reversing direction. Sid checks him the ball, and he tosses it right back with Onyx on his heels, then he reverses. I take off as he catches the ball and then cuts down the middle, and it's three of us surrounding him as he lifts off.

He threads the ball through my arms without drawing contact and scoops it in. I try to head off a collision with Onyx, rotating my torso midair as I come down, and a sharp pain shoots up my leg as the outer edge of my foot hits the ground, causing my ankle to roll.

"Shit," I grunt as I hobble around, afraid to put weight on it.

The crowd's already losing their shit, but they go bonkers as Blue, whose back is to me, points to the ground, signaling it's his house.

"Hey, you good?" Ezekiel jogs over to me as Coach calls a time-out.

"I don't know." I string my arm around his neck as my other teammates surround me. "Help me to the—"

"What happened?" Blue asks, pushing through my teammates.

I quirk my eyebrow. "Landed wrong."

"Don't put weight on it until the trainers check it out," he says.

"Duh," Cillian cuts in.

Blue glares at him, then turns to me. "It's not your left foot. That's good."

He knows which foot I injured?

"You want to go in the back with him too?" Cillian teases as the trainers take over.

He ignores him, grilling my hurt foot, as I turn and limp toward the tunnel.

Huh.

AFTER THE TRAINER asks whether I heard a pop—I didn't—rule out swelling and bruising, and guide me through testing the full range of motion of my foot, I am allowed to return to the game. She gives me a warning that one wrong move and I'm out. Only Coach isn't taking any chances and benches me for the remainder of the game.

As soon as my back hits the seat, I find Blue on the court, watching me. His eyebrows crease as he stares down at my foot before turning his focus back to the game.

He and Sid are unstoppable, banking forty points in the fourth, twenty-eight of them from Blue.

"Waddup, homie?" Nick, my teammate from my Dallas seasons, pulls me in for a hug after the game.

"Good game."

"Your foot's good?"

"Yeah," I reply. "It was nothing."

"Y'all flying out tonight?" he asks.

"Nah, in the morning."

A hand clasps my shoulder, and I turn and dap Johan.

"Come thru tonight," Nick continues. "I'll order some grub. Invite your boys."

"Aight, bet."

"Jones."

I turn and dap Sid. "What's good?"

"We missed you at the Olympics. How's the foot?"

"Eh, still kickin'. Congrats on winning gold. Nick just invited us thru. You free?"

"Yep. I'll stop by."

We track a camera crew moving in to interview him. "Man, that cake..."

I grin. "Yeah?"

"Best I've ever had. You need investors for your bakery, I'm in."

I chuckle. "Good lookin'."

My smile falters as I spot Blue in the corner, expression tense like he'd rather go another four quarters than deal with the mic in his face.

"Hey," Sid says, gaze pinging between us. "Some of us need to take the long way home to get clear in here." He pats his chest. "He's one of 'em."

My eyebrows lift, but before I can respond that I'm a patient man, he's circled by a camera crew.

I quit staring once Blue's head turns in my direction, then I retreat into the tunnel.

CHAPTER 12
ARNAZ

Spoils from life's war, dare drink from my cup.
Sustenance for the night, poisonous by sunup.

"Pizzas and wings are here," Cam, Nick's girlfriend, announces, Nick trailing behind her with a half dozen boxes piled high in his arms. Sid walks over and takes the bags from Cam. "The salmon's in that one," she tells him.

He eats clean all season. Claims he's less restrictive in the offseason, but I haven't seen it.

The doorbell rings.

Swigging the last of my beer, I rub my palms against my stomach.

I hear Cillian's voice first and then a husky laugh.

"You need help?" I ask Cam.

"I'm all done here." She looks up with a soft smile. "Help yourself. Vegan cheese on those three." She gestures to the pies.

"Thanks." I throw my bottle into the recycling bin and grab a plate.

The pie with pepperoni and sausage has three slices left, the one with mushrooms and peppers has five, and the plain cheese has four.

I start to reach for the one with pepperoni when my fingers curl in.

Fix it. Make it even, or his plane will go down on the way home.

Clenching the plate, I grab a slice of pepperoni and raise it to my lips, but my tongue recoils, as if the pizza's singed flesh.

Dropping the slice back onto my plate, I grab two slices of the mushroom and one cheese, then stare at the four slices.

I rearrange the three remaining in each box so they're side by side, and my stomach relaxes.

The noise in the room kicks up as more of the Lions pour in.

There's one voice I hear above all the others, throttling my chest with a category-four hurricane.

"Hey, can I grab a slice?"

I pass Johan my plate. "Here." I turn, and the hurricane kicks up to a category five. In a merlot-colored linen shirt with the top buttons undone and the short sleeves rolled up, Salem perches on one end of the couch as he talks to Sid and Cillian.

The slight bulge in his black slim-fit pants has my grip tightening on the beer bottle.

How is he still single?

Johan snickers.

"What's funny?"

He takes a large bite of a slice and walks away.

I look down at my black sweat suit and stifle a groan. All my internet stalking has revealed an undeniable fact—Salem's tailors never miss.

Cillian nods as he approaches, then he loads his plate with wings, veggies, and dip.

I nod back.

"That hurt?" He gestures to my knuckle tattoo.

I shrug. "The good kinda pain."

"This thing that's happening…" He glances over at Salem. "You know the scent of almonds?"

"What?"

"Almonds. You know the scent?"

I tilt my head in a half nod.

"Hurt him"—he steps closer—"and it'll be the last thing you smell."

"What does that mean?"

"Fuck around and find out," he throws over his shoulder as he starts to walk away.

I shake my head. "There's nothing happening."

"Yeah, okay," he replies.

I squint at his back as a warm sound coats my skin—Salem's laughter.

Telling myself it's no big deal, I pull out my phone, find Salem in my contacts and start a text.

Me

Cillian just threatened me with almond cologne or something. TF? How's your foot?

My hand hovers over send.

"Yo, who got next?" Wes calls out, holding up the game controller.

What am I doing? I backspace on my text.

When I look up, Salem's on his feet, moving toward the kitchen.

"Me," I answer, racing over and swapping spots with Wes on the couch.

"Thanks for coming," Cam says as I'm on my fourth round of the game. My head cranks left, and I catch Salem's wave goodbye. I hold my breath, as if all the fresh air is about to seep out the door.

"Bro?" Johan says. "You killed us." He stabs the buttons on his controller. "One more rou—?"

"I'm out." I toss my controller and jump up.

I say bye to Cam, then throw up my middle finger at Nick a split second before he fires one at me.

I rip open the front door and freeze as Cillian's and Salem's heads twist my way.

Ignoring Cillian's remember-our-talk smirk, I lock eyes with Salem before headlights have us glancing toward the black car slowing to a stop at the curb. He turns back to me.

My mouth opens, but no words come out.

"Ready?" he says to Cillian before turning and heading toward the car.

"Say something," Cillian hisses in a whisper.

Shit.

My feet start moving and don't stop until I'm sliding into the car next to him.

He raises an eyebrow.

The driver asks if we're ready as Cillian calls out, "I'll order another one."

"Y-yes," I croak to the driver.

Salem studies me before looking away.

We don't speak.

The entire ride.

He stares out the window, stoic like a sculpted god with ridged cheekbones and a sexy, plump top lip. Vampire memory from our fight all those years ago has my jaw clenching with hunger to sink its teeth in.

What's wrong with me?

I rip my gaze away and rub my palms on my pants.

I catch my reflection in the glass. I look terrified. I start fidgeting, but no matter how much I try, I can't get my spine straight enough.

Why am I here?

I should open the door and make a run—or roll—for it.

Just keep on rolling right into the ocean like two-ply toilet paper.

Ain't like I didn't cop fresh material for another episode of "Late Night with Salem."

"Thank you," he says to the driver when we pull up to the hotel. The car's barely at a stop before he's out and the door's closing.

The driver eyes me in the rearview mirror when I don't move.

I start to reach for my wallet. "Can you take me bac—"

My door opens, and I stare up into piercing eyes.

I move.

He nods thanks to the doorman as the doors are opened for him, then he leads us toward the elevators. I start to follow the couple waiting in front of us when the elevator arrives, but he extends his arm across my chest, holding me in place.

A second elevator arrives—this one empty—and I follow as he moves toward it.

I'm backed against the wall as soon as both my feet cross the threshold.

"You know what you're doing?" he asks.

"What?" I rasp.

"Why are you here?" The scent of mint and vanilla fills my nostrils.

Unhurried and unscathed by my chaos, he waits.

"I don't know."

"No." He reaches out and stops the door from closing. "I don't buy it. You don't strike me as someone who does things without knowing why."

His lips are *so close*. He catches me staring at them and pulls back. The elevator door beeps, signaling it needs to close, but he ignores it.

"Tell me why you're here," he insists.

"I don't date, but—"

"Cool." He nods toward the open elevator door. "Good night."

"Can I finish?" My nails dig into my palm. "Dinner and movies...they're not me. But..."

"So, you're here to fuck?" He asks it like he's asking if I'm in town for a concert.

My face burns as he waits for an answer.

I glare at him, then move toward the door, but he blocks me.

"It's a fair question."

"How?"

"I asked you out on a date, and you said no."

"I don't date."

"You said you don't like me."

"I don't."

He reads something in my face that quirks the corners of his lips.

"What?" I ask, fighting the urge to cross my arms.

"You've been mad at me for five years..."

"I hate you."

"Mm." He leans in. "How much?"

I should walk away, but I'm locked in place by his scent.

His lips are close *again*.

I swallow roughly.

That bottom one...

He wets it, and my fists curl in.

"Show me how much, Blu—"

He grunts as my teeth sink into his bottom lip, and my fingers dig into his back. My jaw tightens as I clamp down, and his moan makes my hands squeeze his waist to keep myself upright.

Fuck, that sound.

His tongue swipes across my teeth, making my eyes roll closed.

"Oh!" a woman shrieks. "W-we'll take the next one."

I release him as she scurries away.

He punches the elevator button, steps back, and leans against the opposite wall. Rubbing his thumb across his bruised lip, his eyes darken as they snake over my body.

"Come here," I rasp.

He winks at me but doesn't move.

When the elevator stops, we're both off it before the doors fully open. I couldn't tell you what color the hallway walls are, the carpet, or the number for his room, but I could draw in painstaking detail the stretch of fabric across his traps, the deep groove along his spine, and the way his muscular ass shifts in his pants.

Flicking on a low light, he then places his key card, wallet, and phone down on the nightstand.

"I'm on PrEP," he says, voice scratchy. "Up to date on my vaccines. Tested and cleared after my last partner." He turns to me.

I tense, thinking about him and Lucien. "S-same," I reply.

He nods. "Come." He lowers to the bed and leans back. "Get what you came for."

One night, I remind myself. *And like every man before him, he'll be out of my system.*

One night.

Even if he's worlds sexier than any man I've ever been with.

I push off the door and cross the room until I'm kneeling between his legs and unbuckling his belt.

I pause as he slides off my shades and track where he sets them down. He lifts his foot to help me remove his pants, and once I drag them down, I wrap my palm around his right heel.

"W-what"—I clear my throat—"did the trainers say?"

Removing his sock, I inspect his ankle.

"They said I'm good," he answers.

I put gentle pressure on the side of his foot, curling it right and left while searching his face for any sign of discomfort.

His eyes darken as he blinks slowly.

"Stop looking at me like that."

"Like what?" His voice comes out so low, I feel it trickling down my spine.

I lower his foot and then trace my fingers along the inner curve of his thigh. He tenses, tugging the skin along the band of muscle.

So thick. Mm.

I string my arms around his thighs and nuzzle my face between them, pulling them close to bracket the sides of my face. As if sensing what I need, he tenses and presses his thighs together, drawing out a low moan from the warm, velvet pressure. He lets up when I begin to move and rub the sides of my face along the skin there. Turning my head, I peel his briefs to the side and lick the patch of skin in the crease of his groin. He sucks in a breath as I suckle the skin.

He continues swelling underneath his briefs as my teeth graze over his balls before continuing up his shaft. Despite swallowing, I leave a wet trail soaking the cotton. Head arched sideways, my mouth slots over him, and I moan from the feel of him lengthening under my tongue.

When my tongue reaches his head, it encounters something hard, and I trace over one, two, three...fuck...four metal heads.

He winks.

No, no, no.

He shifts up as I drag down his briefs.

I groan.

Life is cruel. Some fucker who subscribes to forever will wake up to his face and hum around this gorgeous uncut dick for the rest of his life.

My tongue circles his piercing, and another prickle of heat trickles down my lower back as he moans.

I lick the skin between his magic cross, submerging into the white noise rushing in my ears.

Locking on to his dark eyes, I suck his head into my mouth.

Even now, his demeanor is calm and contained, like he gets his dick sucked on demand whenever he calls for it.

Of course he does.

He shudders as my fingers dig into his thighs, and his head hits the back of my throat. I pull up, suckling him, then I lower again, humming from him filling my mouth and throat.

"Come here." He cups the back of my neck.

I open for him, moaning at the pulse of electricity shooting down my spine as his mouth latches on to mine like he's been kissing me all his life.

My arms tighten around his neck as our tongues move in rhythm.

Swaying, anchoring, claiming.

Claiming?

I rip my lips away. His eyes blink open, and their fierce need has our lips slotting back together.

I rub his erection, and the pull to feel him fill my mouth again has me circling his cock and pumping with long strokes. He grunts against my lips before sucking the bottom one raw. I thumb the pre-cum pooling at his slit, then suck it into my mouth.

He releases my lip to bite his own, and I sink down and lick the underside of his cock to his balls. He falls to his back as I suckle on one before licking across and working the next one into my mouth. I pump him slowly, relishing the shift of him in my mouth on every tug.

My new obsession gleams, and I lick back up his shaft, taking him into my mouth again until the metal hits the back of my throat.

I groan.

Every night...every time I watch him humiliate someone on the court, I'll think of this fat, jeweled dick waiting to be worshipped.

"Fuck," he rasps, peeling off my beanie and carding his hand through my curls.

I'll think of crawling under his sheets as he sleeps and waking him with my tongue, sliding my lips around him until he's filling my throat, his back arching, like it's doing right now.

I gurgle, eyes watering.

When it's wet with fresh sweat after the gym...

I bury my nose in the soft hair lining his base and inhale.

"Blue," he rasps, fisting the sheets.

When he returns from a road game, back against the door, as my knees kiss the worn spot on the floor...

My thumb presses into his taint as my mouth massages under his head.

He grunts, stiffening, eyelids flattened to narrow slits.

When he's trying not to be late for practice...

"Ungh. C-coming...fuuck."

My hand drops to my dick as the first rope of cum coats the roof of my mouth.

The muscles in his thighs swell as I drink him down.

His chest heaves as my lips tighten around him, and my hand flies from my dick to massage his balls.

I swallow every fucking drop, and he shudders, his back falling to the mattress.

He twitches in my mouth, and my eyes roll closed as I lick his slit until the last bead of his release is blessing my tongue. Then he slides from between my lips.

The curve of his dick, the wet metal points pulsing against his skin...My tongue is reaching for one more taste when I'm pulled up his body.

One second, I'm drowning in his eyes, and the next, I'm on my back, being undressed.

Salem

Damn.

I should be brain dead with how hard I just nutted.

He's even more stunning this close as he makes these soft, feathery sounds and sucks on my tongue.

I love him in jeans and a tee, but him in all-black sweats and a beanie with a single gold chain? Lethal.

Speaking of lethal—his head game.

Best I've ever had.

Mhm.

I'd be lying if I said that him sliding into the car didn't flood my thoughts with questions like—*Did he change his mind about us? Is this really happening? What's changed for him? Was I right about us? Does he feel it too?*

As soon as he got out of the car, I wanted to throw him over my shoulder, skip the elevator, and fly up all seventeen floors, but I'm glad I stopped to think and ask questions to figure out where his mind's at.

I can feel there is more here—not just sex—but he seems afraid. Fear I can handle. I meant what I said about not rushing in to tear down his walls as long as I feel like there's a chance and there's something there between both of us.

He shudders as my fingers delve under his sweatshirt, the color in his eyes dissolving into dark-speckled orbs.

I nip the edge of his jaw as I pull on the hem, rolling it over his head, then pull down his sweatpants.

He reaches for me, and I intertwine our fingers and kiss each letter of "Disquiet" inked across his knuckles, then lean down and get the one on his upper arm of the boy leashed to a cloaked figure that's captioned with "What's death to the damned?" And the one on his lower arm that reads "Got?" with an image of a molecule I only recognize as serotonin because I looked it up years back.

I clasp his hands above his head and return to nipping the corner of his jaw. He moans, and I lean down. Before my lips touch his—that are almost the same plum color as his nipples—he's already opening for me.

Mmm.

Instead of slamming my mouth against his like I want, my tongue traces across his lips. I pull back as he tries to deepen the kiss and grin at his whimper, dotting each corner of his mouth with a kiss. I trail down to his Adam's apple, grazing my teeth across the swell. His head dips back, offering me the full sweep of his long neck.

Damn.

He's so good.

I ignore the offering and lick down the center of his chest. He wrestles with one of my hands and groans as he's over-powered.

I work his nipple between my lips and lap at the soft flesh, resisting the urge to pinch it between my teeth.

Turns out Blue isn't quiet at all.

The sounds he's making have me lengthening between my legs again. His leg raises, and his shin rubs against my erection.

"Be good," I croak.

His obedience makes me crawl back up to his face and feast on his tongue. The kiss is hard and rough, and with his hands restrained, he's powerless to do anything but open wide and take it.

Or so I thought.

He bites down hard on my lower lip. My hand wraps around his throat, trapping his moan.

I catch his hand just as it rises from the mattress. "Stay," I order as I travel down his body. He lifts his ass as I peel off his briefs.

"Damn," I rasp, taking in the curve of his cock that rises under my gaze.

I dip down and lick the pre-cum pooling on his stomach, eliciting a hiss as my tongue catches the tip of his dick.

I spread his legs, then pepper kisses down the inside of his thigh, sucking the taut skin into my mouth.

"Uh-uh," I warn him as his hand lifts again.

He glares at me, but his hand returns to the bed.

Beautiful.

His legs tremble as I take turns kissing and nibbling down the inside of his leg.

I feather kisses along his ankle bone as my hand wraps around his foot to remove his sock. My thumb barely begins massaging the arch when he lets out a soft moan.

Found a spot.

I deepen the massage. When I envelop his toes in the heat of my mouth, his eyes roll closed, and he clasps the sheet.

My free hand reaches in to massage his heavy balls.

"So close," he rasps.

I settle between his legs, my hand anchoring his hips in place as my tongue swipes up his taint.

"Ngh," he groans, jerking from the touch.

The tip of my tongue licks across his balls before rolling one into my mouth. His dick twitches up before slapping back against his stomach.

I reach up and massage his nipples. Thighs trembling, he gasps choppy breaths.

I work his other ball into my mouth.

"Please," he begs.

I grin as I take hold of the base of his dick.

Knew we'd get there.

As soon as my mouth wraps around the head, his hips jerk off the bed, trying to fuck my mouth. My tongue slowly circles his slit before lapping up his pre-cum. I release my grip on his base, rub two fingers over his slit, then feed him his pre-cum. The second I suck him again, deeper this time, rubbing his tip against the inside of my cheek and tongue, he convulses, moaning around my fingers.

I take his dick to the back of my throat as the first pump of cum shoots into my mouth. Licking his base, my throat fills with him. I drink until his legs go limp, and his hips crash onto the mattress.

I crawl up his body and replace my fingers, which he's absently suckling, with my tongue. Rolling us to our sides, relishing the feel of his high, muscular ass against my erection, we kiss, messily and unhurriedly.

Arnaz

Why do I taste so good on his tongue?

I shiver as he massages my nipple while his erection burrows between my ass cheeks.

I want to taste him again.

The hunger burns up from my belly.

I never cuddle after sex, but I'm too boneless in his arms to move.

He pulls back and dips lower, then licks a stripe across my neck before his teeth latch onto the skin.

He moans as I rut against him.

"Blue," he warns.

I reach back and press him closer to me.

"Christ," he moans, his forehead resting on the back of my neck as he thrusts over my rim.

He sucks on the skin at the base of my neck. The sting, his warm gasps, the heat from the friction, all have me reaching down to stroke myself.

His thrusts slow, losing rhythm. "How did this happen?"

My eyes shoot open as his fingers glide over the mangled skin on my back.

Static buzzes in my ears.

My throat narrows, locking in the lie I've spoken easily since childhood.

"Hey." His voice is gentle, but the soft touch of his finger singes my scar. "You okay?"

His breath snakes across my neck, and I rip out of his arms. Scrambling for the unmarred skin of my sweatshirt, I yank it over my head, shove my legs into my pants, then grab my kicks.

My head turns slightly, searching for my good-luck beanie.

I pat my pockets, and the alarm blaring between my ears kicks up. *Where are my shades?*

Fuck the beanie. I have good-luck socks that can replace it, but my shades—I need them.

"Blue, hold on." He starts to move, and I fly to the door and don't stop until the staircase door shuts behind me.

I'm a coward, just like Carter said.

CHAPTER 13
ARNAZ

♫ "Twilight" ♫

My soul is reflected in the looming darkness, strengthened by
the dying sun.

Sweat soaks my T-shirt.

Hell.

12:52 a.m.

Not even an hour of sleep.

Feeling like shit for running out on him, I've denied myself
my nightly ritual of watching Salem's videos until I fall asleep.

Blowing out a breath, I reach for my joint and lighter, then
pause, cursing early practice tomorrow.

I crawl out of bed.

Plan B.

Leaving my house, I pop in my earphones and scroll
through my watch to call the only person I know likely to be up
at this time.

"Hello," Anaïs answers.

"Waddup?"

"Watching *Exosphere.*"

"Cheater!" She was supposed to wait for me.

"How? I waited weeks for you to catch up. It's not my fault you're a whole season behind."

"Judas!"

"Nope."

"Delilah!"

She laughs. "Just lemme catch you up."

"Fine," I grunt, transitioning to a jog. "How you feeling about surgery?"

"Nervous." The *s* trails off into a sigh. "But also ready to get it over with."

"What can I do?"

"Besides flying home to binge movies with me while I'm recovering?"

"I'm there."

"Even though I'll be at Mom and Carter's?"

"It's not about them," I reply, jogging in place at a red light. "I'll be there."

"Thanks."

"Catch me up."

"So, the Martians land on Titan, but the Saturnians get tipped off by Earth, so they're ready for them."

"Hold up." I take off down the main road to the beach. "What happened to Kairis?"

"Whaddya mean?"

"The season ended with Skai and them fading from dehydration."

"Okay, yeah, so when they didn't respond to Noel's tightbeams, she boarded a ship from Mars and used the thruster thingy to space jump to their ship."

"She's a real one."

"But they couldn't save Kairis."

"Huh?"

"Yep, the ship's gone."

"Whoa." I slip off my kicks and trudge through the sand.

"And they lost someone from the main crew."

"Who?" I drop down to sit on the sand. "Not Moose!"

"God no. I'd have been bawlin'. Imagine if he survived the streets just to die from a drought."

I shake my head. "We'd all riot until they un-dead him."

An older man in red trunks passes me, beelining toward the shoreline.

Who the hell would swim in the ocean at this time of night?

"You heard me?"

"What?"

"Jenku died."

"Oh damn. Who's piloting the ship, then?"

"I just told you, they lost the ship."

The man dives into the water.

"My bad. What else happened?"

He braces for a rough wave. I look around to see if anyone else is seeing this, but besides a group a good distance away sitting around a bonfire, the beach is empty. His head disappears under the water. Crazy fucker.

"So, after the Martians took the L, they retreated, right? But the Saturnians didn't realize they activated stealth explosives before they left."

"That's the same stuff that wiped out Atlas Station?"

"Uh-huh."

"Damn."

"Yep. Remember the captain who went with her gut and stood down to prevent the battle with Mars?"

How long can someone hold their breath underwater?

I climb to my feet and move to the edge of the shoreline.

I bounce back. "Hell, that's cold."

"What's cold?"

I scan the area where the man disappeared. "How long can someone hold their breath underwater?"

"I dunno. Why?"

"This guy just..." I move forward, cursing under my breath as needles prick my feet as the icy water washes over them. I lean forward, searching.

Nothing.

This isn't my problem.

I step back and say, "Never mind. Continue."

I start to turn away when I hear Carter's voice, "*...fuckin' coward.*"

My feet plant in the wet sand.

I'm not a coward. If the man wants to kill himself, let him kill himself.

"*...fucking coward.*"

Both voices lock me in place until the echo of one drowns out the other.

My chest caves.

"Let me call you back."

FUCK, fuck, fuck, that's cold.

Imagine it's an ice bath.

I-it's j-just an i-ice bath.

I swim toward the spot where the guy went under.

Shit. I'm thrown backwards.

Goddamn current's pissed off tonight.

Wh-what was that?

A slimy hand rubbed up my leg.

I'm knocked sideways as my head whips side to side.

The clacking of my jaw's so loud it's a shark's beacon.

I dip below the surface, but it's like staring at a black curtain.

Where is he?

This is a horrible plan.

Okay, that's definitely a fin! Whatthehellisthat?!

My eyes pinch closed as I touch my leg to see if it's still there.

I'm dead.

Wait, no, I'm webbed in seaweed.

Where the hell is this dude?

How're my lungs on fire if I'm freezing?

Am I hypothermic? Or is it hyper?

Who c-cares? Time to go.

I try to turn when waves as hard as sandbags pummel me beneath the surface.

I kick my way back up, retching up saltwater.

Darkness in every direction with bullets of silver.

Where the hell's the shore?

Waves hit the back of my head—brick after brick—knocking me back under.

I'm being ripped in different directions by my legs, arms, and head.

I crunch in, tucking my knees, and fight until I break the surface.

I duck too late. The wave lands a sharp blow to my face. Then another.

I hear it again. "*...fucking coward.*"

A growling "Damn kid" echoes down the hall. The stomping gets louder before the door bangs open.

"How many times I gotta tell ya t' clean up 'fore ya sleep?!" Dad slurs.

He sways on his feet, the stench of piss hits my nose, and I wince at the wet patch on his pants.

"I'll clean it up," I tell him, knowing I already cleaned up before bed. But there's no point fighting with him.

"Now!" His sneering disgust coats every breath as I pass him on the way to the hall.

I grab the broom and start sweeping the living room again. He drags in behind me. I angle sideways, not to face him, but not to have my back turned either.

"Yer soft." He reaches for the vodka bottle. "Got no teeth." He tilts it toward the cup, and most of it splashes against the fireplace mantel.

He hates using the damn screen. Fire isn't fire unless it rages out in the open.

And if I go over there and try to put it in place, it'll give him ammo to keep me up all night to prove a point. The same point he always tries to make—that he'll always be more of a man than I will.

Like that time he took me hunting, and I froze when he put the rifle in my hand and told me to shoot. Seizing my hand, his fingers locked around the stock, wrenched the barrel into position, and pressed down hard on my trigger finger. An ear-splitting crack tore through the air. Then he dragged me to the carcass, handed me a knife, stood back, and told me to get to work. I barely cut through the elk's sternum before I keeled over, puking.

Hours passed, full of rambling insults and threats like he'd rather I die in the field than let me leave a coward. He started yelling when I asked what the point of dressing the elk was if the meat was already rotten.

I never understood why they call gutting an animal "dressing" and not something more accurate like "mutilation." I still smelled the stench of sun-rot and death.

"...fucking coward."

My head snaps to the side at the shatter of glass. Dad hikes up his pants and bends forward, swaying, his face close to the flames.

"Fuck," he spits as a shard of glass nicks his thumb. "Look what yer did."

I drop the broom and disappear into the kitchen for a towel. It happens so fast when I return. He's unfolding to a stand, then rocking sideways, leaning arm-first toward the fire. I race over and grab his arm, my foot slicing open in the process, and I lose my footing. My back lands on the glass with Dad on top of me.

"G'off me. I'm f-fine," he yells.

Maybe it is the sharp burn spreading over my back or the stench, but I snap and slam my fist into the glass.

His laughter disappears when he sees the threat in my eyes, and he sticks his face out, begging for me to act on my rage.

If I start, I won't stop.

"Thas... wha' I thought...coward."

My muscles are on fire. Every punch a fresh puncture to my lungs. I seize up.

THERE ARE WORSE ENDS.

No more suns.
   Or pills or headlines.

THE END of having it all except a hospitable place in my own mind.

WARBLED SOUNDS.
    It hurts.
    The mallet-blow waves hurt.

A MAN WITH RED TRUNKS.

Darkness returns.

A door, tattered clothes, the stench.

I vomit.

Why can't I hear the man?

Please...the burning.

"Son, stay awake."

"Son, stay awake."

CHAPTER 14
ARNAZ

♫ "3:33 a.m." ♫

Sinking, sinking, sinking.

I emerge from the darkness to a man in dripping red trunks, who looks like the one I tried to save, talking into a phone.

"...know if he was trying to drown. He's out co—"

My choking as I try to sit up steals his attention.

"He's awake." He pats my back. "You're awake. Breathe. The paramedics are on their way."

I start.

Paramedics?

I bolt to my feet, but my legs bend like rubber, and I retch up bile and water.

"Wait, they're on—"

"N-no...p-para...no."

"It's okay," he says. "I pulled you out, but you were in bad shape. You should have a doctor—"

"No." I stumble to my knees and crawl on all fours. Something sharp slices into my wrist, and the sting gives me enough of a rush to rip upright.

"Wait," he begs as I will back the cramping burn in my lungs and legs and stumble again.

I retch up more water, gasping from the burn in my chest. My vision blurs as hot tears scorch my face.

I lurch from the distant ring of a siren, fear licking at my feet, and I stagger toward the road.

"You alright, man?" Wes asks.

My grunt razors my throat, sending a pounding to my head, turning the corners of my vision blurry.

Each swallow—razor, pounding, blur.

Two bottles of Gatorade in the last hour, and I'm still so damn thirsty.

We're halfway through baseline sprints, and I still can't get power in my legs, so I'm trailing behind everyone in what's usually an easy jog.

I groan as Coach kicks up the intensity, ordering us to ping between the defensive and offensive ends of the court.

"What's the matter, old man?" a rook talks shit, flying past me.

I search for a comeback as the shower of sweat from my scalp has me drying my face against my soaked jersey.

The rook reverses course. "Dude, you look..."

The court spins as I gasp for air, and salt fills my mouth as each rapid blink submerges me into darkness.

The needle disappears under my skin. "Geez, Doc. An IV?"

"You fainted, and you're running a fever. You run into anyone with a virus or a cold?"

I shake my head.

"We'll run tests for the flu," she says, picking up her tablet.

"I don't have the flu."

She pauses and looks up at me. "How do you know?"

"I, uh..." I stare at the floor.

"Arnaz, everything we discuss here is confidential. Did something happen?"

I tried not being a coward. That's what happened.

"It doesn't feel like the flu is all I meant," I mutter.

"I am ordering you to skip the next two games to hydrate and rest."

"Not necessary," I argue.

"Non-negotiable. Have your meds changed?" she asks, staring at her iPad.

"No."

"Okay, sit tight. I'm going to order a few tests."

WHEN I GET HOME, I manage to put down a couple bites of the soup I had delivered and pass out.

DAD'S FIST *slammed into the table as he barked at me to never ever speak those words again. I stared at my food, hating myself for making him upset. I only mentioned that I wanted to marry Jimmy because he collected twice as many beetles as me. Mom and Anaïs would win Red Light, Green Light if they remembered to freeze like they are right now.*

Mom slammed down her fork, and I wished I hadn't drunk so much blue lemonade because I had to pee so badly. Squirming, I plugged my ears to block out the ringing. I always made them scream lately. Wish I could figure out how to stop doing that. I'm dragged under the table, and then arms are wrapped around me.

Anaïs.

He yelled that I was an a-bomb-a-nation, and I started crying, because if I were a bomb, what if I went off and my entire family exploded? The front door slammed just as Mom pushed back her chair. Anäis wiped my face and whispered that it was okay. She used to cry like me before the tiny lines began on the inside of her thigh. She wore Band-Aids there now—not my favorite ones with the unicorns. I wanted to be strong like her and never cry. He said real men don't cry, but when he wasn't around, Mom said he's an idiot, and I should cry whenever the heck I wanted. Maybe I'd start drawing my own lines on my leg. I didn't want mine to bleed like hers because then I'd have to wear the dinosaur bandages because he yelled at me the last time I wore the unicorn ones. Said I should wear the green dinosaur ones because I was a boy, but I liked unicorns more than dinosaurs. Didn't he know they had magical powers and got their energy from the sun?

Anaïs crawled from under the table and reached for me, but I shook my head. Covered in sweat, I squeezed my thighs together really hard. I just needed the world to stop for a second so I could get it under control, but then the walls shook as Mom's bedroom door slammed, and I erupted.

I gasp awake. Chest pounding, I kick back the sheets and shuffle to sit up.

I rub my face, then stab my phone screen.

The hell?

I slept twelve hours.

I get up to piss, then settle back under the covers and binge *Exosphere.*

I don't remember dozing off or setting an alarm, but the ringing stirs me awake.

Not an alarm.

I shuffle to the door, already knowing who's there.

I grunt.

"Good to see you too," Sid says, trailing behind me with grocery bags.

I crash onto the couch and bury my head under my pillow.

"How are you feeling?"

"Doc's overreacting."

"Yeah, looks like it."

Peeking from under the pillow when he returns from the kitchen with a tray of shit, I shake my head. "Nah. I'mma be shitting green for a week."

"Good. Detox all that garbage you eat."

"I had soup yesterday," I fire back as he hands me a fresh bowl. This one is mostly vegetables. I push the spoon around.

Ugh.

It's *all* vegetables.

He hands me water and vitamins next. No point asking what they are. When he's hellbent on shit, it's easier to just go along with it.

"You're in pain?"

I shake my head.

"Uh-huh. Where does it hurt?"

For Christ's sake. "I'm fine."

"Your head?"

I glare at him. How does he do it? I swear. People think we

have some secret mind-reading connection, but it's all Sid and his weird-ass ability to read people.

"Where are the painkillers?"

"My nightstand."

I've downed the soup by the time he returns with my head meds and the painkillers the doc gave me.

"Eat. Drink."

I shoot back the pills with a cup of the yellow liquid.

"The hell?" My throat burns, then it mellows. "Tastes like pizza."

"Oregano oil."

"What's the red stuff?" I nod to the second cup.

"Coconut water, kale, beets, celery, orange, and aloe."

My face twists. *Who comes up with this shit?*

"Not leaving until it's down." He settles next to me and picks up my remote.

I slowly sip the goo as we watch the Arizona and San Francisco football game. *I'll dip a toe in acid before ever admitting it doesn't taste half bad.*

The sun's up when I wake up to piss, and he's gone.

The fridge's stocked with a bunch of healthy to-go meals and green shit, and the sink's cleared.

Before I die, I need to erect a park statue or bench in his honor.

I GET a Brooklyn Lions app notification that a game started a few minutes ago. I grab the remote and turn it on. It takes me half a breath to spot him amongst the light blue and gold jerseys. He's held back by Cillian while arguing with a ref. They run a replay. Salem gets caught in a screen before shaking loose, then chases the point guard to the rim, shadows him step for step, leans in at full extension, and slaps the ball off the backboard.

The ref calls a foul.

Wait, what? I sit up. *Shit call. That block was clean.*

Even Kevin, one of the OG commentators, seems to agree with me. The Lions' coach should challenge it.

The camera zooms in on Salem's narrowed eyes, creased forehead, and distant stare from the sidelines as the opposing point guard misses the second free throw shot.

I gnaw on my nails to kill the army of ants swarming my blood in the spot where those smirking lips kissed my neck.

I ran from him, and even though I'm not surprised, I'm embarrassed. For a few minutes that night, I felt *normal*.

Better than normal—it's like I was a different person who liked after-sex cuddles and pillow talk. Then he touched my scar, and reality came crashing in.

He runs another block against the same flopper and drills the ref with a glare. Ignoring my semi, I lie back on the couch and watch the game for a minute before I fade to sleep.

It's exactly how it was, except everything is different. Salem's hand covers both of mine, locking them in place above my head...

The metal and glass chandelier casts a dim glow over the room.

I'm writhing and moaning under the heat of his tongue as it trails down my abs.

"Please," I beg as my fingers tug the fur throw underneath me.

The bedroom door bangs open.

Carter.

"W-wait," I scream as the quiet click of the safety being removed rings louder than Carter's maniacal laugh.

Salem stills.

"No!"

CHAPTER 15
SALEM

I click on the link in Cillian's text.

A highlight reel from the Royals' social media account of Blue arriving at the locker room to find gift baskets starts playing. His reaction is the same every time—tense eyes, hunched shoulders, flared nostrils.

The montage ends with a hook for viewers to tune in to the latest episode of the *Royals All-Access.*

Was his reaction the same with my cake?

I click on his profile, though I doubt there's anything new. Eleven posts in total, and only two of him.

One is of him and his teammate Ussef, who's donning a cape, shirtless.

The caption reads: *Happy Birthday, my G.*

I slide to the next photo. He's sitting next to Sid in a navy three-piece suit. I zoom in and peep a rose pinned to his blazer's lapel. Damn, the camera loves him.

I scan the thirsty comments, then trade my phone for the remote and pull up the latest episode of the *Royals All-Access* and hit play.

"Johan, get in here, man," Sid says as Johan enters the locker

room, already suited up for the game. Grabbing his chair, he joins the guys forming a circle.

The scene cuts away to a solo feed of Johan talking to the camera. *"Sid leads us through a couple rounds of breath work before every game. I wasn't into it at first, but I can't deny that it locks us in."*

The screen switches back to the guys huddled in a circle. Blue's knee bounces up and down, and tense lines edge his closed eyes.

The next scene follows him dapping a security guard.

"C'mon, man." He glares at the camera, dipping his chin, continuing down the corridor into their locker room. Cutting to a large gift basket waiting at what looks like his station, the camera pings back to Blue, zooming in on his flared nostrils and clenched jaw.

"What do I think of the gift baskets?" Nick snickers. *"I mean, we love 'em. Yo."* He looks off camera. *"How many have there been?"* His eyes widen. *"You heard that?"* He shakes his head as "At least fifty" appears in the caption. *"We fight over them."* He leans in as a muffled voice sounds in the background. *"Say it again?"*

"How does Arnaz react to the gift baskets?" is captioned across the screen.

Nick grimaces. *"I meeeean..."* He rubs his neck. *"Don't y'all got footage?"*

Blue approaches the locker room in a dark denim button-down, jeans, shades, and a beanie. The same beanie sitting upstairs in my closet. I couldn't bring myself to leave it out in the open. Every time I look at it, a dull ache steals my breath, and I feel his thick curls between my fingers and see his dark eyes, far gone, as he kneels between my legs.

Why'd he run? Because I touched the rubbery patch of skin shaped like the jagged edge of a key? I'm not afraid of scars. He should see my brother's.

His steps come to a stop as he zeros in on the gift basket,

and his lips flatten in a tight line. He approaches, reaches around the basket like it'll detonate if he makes contact, hangs his jacket, and walks away.

In the next scene, he's sweaty, like he's returning from a workout. He scowls at the gift basket, this one bigger than the last, tosses his weight gloves into his locker, and walks away.

His eyes roll as he enters the locker room with Sid, who bursts out laughing and shakes his head.

Different gift baskets, same scene of disdain, for what feels like three minutes.

I sit up straight as I brace for his reaction to my cake.

He said the team liked it, and Sid confirmed as much, so I'm guessing his reaction can't be so bad.

I pick up my glass of water and down it.

Nick appears again. I reach for the remote and fast forward past their team practice, an interview with their coach, and keep going until I reach the credits.

Wait.

I rewind back and then fast forward again until I reach the credits.

Huh.

They didn't film it.

Why?

CHAPTER 16
ARNAZ

They abandon themselves to be like people who hate
themselves.

"Champagne?" a violet-haired server with rolled-up sleeves and neck and arm tats offers.

"Whiskey neat?" I ask.

"You got it." He brushes my hand while taking my empty glass.

Straightening my shirt sleeves, I scan the room and zero in on a man clad in a tux who has Salem's complexion and build. My shoes tear across the ballroom floor, only to slow before coming to a stop when I'm an arm's length away.

What would I even say?

It's been three weeks.

Not that long, I guess.

He didn't text or call either.

Though I'm the one who got off and then ran like a coward.

A man with salt-and-pepper hair steps into my path.

Looking past his shoulder, my stomach plunges as *not-him* turns in my direction.

I turn and sweep the rest of the crowd. A part of me, the cringe-fest side, was counting on him being here.

"Arnaz?"

I turn around.

"Rocco," the man says, like it's been said before, and I missed it.

I shake his hand.

"You smoke?" He offers me a cigar.

"No."

"You enjoy the ocean?"

The fuck?

"It would be my pleasure to have you aboard my yacht."

Ugh, a yacht guy.

A husky laugh has my head whipping around and tracking the voice to another *not-him*.

Damn.

I turn back.

"...your career with keen interest, and given your exceptional talent and the new opportunities available to you following your recent...*revelation*, I believe there are uncharted territories that I'd like to help you—"

"Rocco, I'll stab you in the eye with my heel if you try to poach my favorite client," Catharine warns as she floats over in a black ball gown with one of those mermaid-tail hems.

"But you steal my top point guard at my anniversary party, and I'm supposed to exercise decorum?" he claps back.

"Babe. He came running to me. I tried to get him to stay with you. What was I supposed to do?"

She grins as I dip down and plant a kiss on her cheek. "Happy Birthday, Cat. You look gorgeous."

"You too. Love the dark blue. Look"—she nods to my cravat and then points to her red diamond solitaire necklace—"we're matching." Leaning up, she loudly whispers, "Watch yourself around this one—he likes 'em young."

"Oh, fuck off," Rocco scoffs.

She blows him a kiss.

"Don't leave without spending time with me," she orders.

I nod.

The server returns with my whiskey neat just as Rocco hands me his card and says, "Call me."

"Thanks," I reply to the server, stuffing the card in my pocket. "Restroom?"

"Follow me," he says, leading the way.

Once we pass through the doors of the event room, he points toward a staircase leading to a lower level. "There's one through there. But you should check out the secret one that way." He gestures in the opposite direction toward a long corridor. "It's in an old ballroom with a sublime fresco that, I kid you not, looks like something stolen from the Vatican."

I look down the long hallway.

"Go all the way to the end, ignore the red ropes, and hang left. Past the double doors."

"Thanks."

"Hey," he says, stepping closer. "You're too hot for that oily cat with the fake tan." He slips a piece of paper into my palm, his rings clinking together.

I quirk an eyebrow as he saunters away.

I'll never be *that* smooth.

I end up making a wrong turn before reaching the cordoned-off ballroom. Weaving through the stacks of covered furniture, I pause and stare out at the dense trees drenched in rain. I think about my plan for when I retire—cop a cabin in a deep forest and live there until I die.

I'll be silent when I need to be silent, which is a lot of the time these days. When the voices in my head get loud, the one in my throat skips town, only coming back when things get quiet. And then there's the space problem. I need space when I get home. I need space when my brain craps out. I need space in the middle of the night when I can't sleep.

I need too much space for someone else to feel at home with me.

I polish off the whiskey, then find the bathroom.

After taking a piss and then washing and drying my hands, I slide my phone out of my pocket and pull up my texts with Salem.

I begin typing.

Me: *Hey...*

And the thing that's happened all week happens. A maelstrom of conflicting thoughts paralyzes me.

Why text now?

What's changed?

You know what he wants, and you know you're not cut out for it.

I rub my throat.

He touched my scar, and I couldn't catch air. Every inhale tightened a drawstring that bound my throat closed.

I dump my phone back in my pocket.

Nothing's changed.

I weave back through the stack of covered furniture and am a foot away from the doors when a throat clears.

"Fuck!" I gasp.

"Blue."

Rubbing the heel of my hand against my pounding chest, I step back. Salem's back is to me as he stares out the window.

Always the prey with him.

I open my mouth to speak, but when he turns around and looks me square in the eyes, I choke.

"You ran," he says.

Goddamn his tailor. He's smoking in a mustard-colored suit. The smooth swell of his chest peeks through his partially open, pale blue button-down. I can make out a portion of his tat—

black spider legs. I open my mouth again, and I'm reminded of part of the reason I'm choked up. I'm a coward.

"I-I…"

The doors burst open. "Did you find the fresco? Isn't it a marvel?"

Salem clears his throat, and the server jumps out of his skin.

"Holy balls!" He lets out a nervous chuckle. "I didn't see you there."

"I'm *not* here," Salem replies, making for the door.

"W-wait." I dart in front of him before throwing, "We're in the middle of something," over my shoulder to the server.

"Find me later?" the server asks.

"He's free now," Salem answers, sidestepping me.

"Stop." I match his steps. "Can we talk?"

"Why?" he demands as the doors thud closed, leaving us alone.

I hang my head and release a strangled breath.

"Enjoy your night, Arnaz."

Fuck.

The fading sound of his footsteps is like a cold hand in the small of my back.

I bolt for him, blood rushing in my ears until it's washed out by my panicked, "Wait!"

My foot kicks out, catching him mid-step, and the world tilts as my knee buckles, and we crash to the floor.

"Seriously?" His palms flatten next to his sides.

"Just wait. I shouldn't have left like that. I'm sorry." I squeeze my thighs around him, and he goes still before he drags in a breath and pushes up. Suddenly, I'm riding him like a horse.

A horse with no reins.

Oh shit.

He lurches back, twisting left, but instead of bucking me off, he uses the momentum to reach back and yank me to the floor.

As soon as I land with a thud, his arms bracket my head. His stare doesn't hold the anger of a glare, but it's steel-cold and sharp, like he's assessing...me, my bullshit, if I'm worth the effort.

"Why'd you run?" His voice is dark and low. "Your scar?"

His lips are so close that the tightness in my chest makes each breath a miracle.

I can't admit it.

I can't think.

His scent sends my pulse into a frenetic spin.

Drawstring...throat.

"Hey." His eyebrows crease. "What's wrong?"

"Please." I want to melt into the floor as soon as the word slips past my lips.

I don't beg.

"What?" he murmurs, lifting my chin.

God, those eyes. Beyond their warmth, ferocity, and intelligence, something terrifying stares back at me.

Not *something.* An offer.

It's a mystery, the easy recognition of what I've never known. I was raised under the exacting hand of cruelty, so it's no surprise that I recoil from it.

Devotion.

A suffocating promise with its risen chest, iron back, and pledge of quiet sacrifice.

"Those wheels are spinning too fast," he says.

And on loosely screwed axles.

What am I doing? "I need to g—"

"No." His lips lower to mine, a gentle brush before he pulls back. "Stop running from me."

I don't know how.

I mean to push him away, but my legs spread, and my mouth takes over, hungry for another taste. I fight with his belt, faintly aware that I'm being undone too.

"Wait," he breathes, pulling back. He stares down at me and drags his thumb across his lips.

I reach for him, but instead of covering me again, he lies next to me.

He doesn't react to my stare.

I blow out a breath and follow his gaze to the overhead fresco.

Meh.

Mythical men immortalized in stone and ivory are no match for his sun-dipped, sinewy expanse and sculpted proportions.

I flinch when his hand reaches into my pocket and fishes out Rocco's card and the server's phone number and then rips them up.

I grin. *He saw all that?*

"I blame your face." He groans. "Way too many comple-mentary features. Or the tats and the sexy lilt that screams 'I'm badder than death.'

I snort. "I wasn't planning to call either of them."

After a moment of silence, he asks, "What about me? Were you planning to call me?"

I return to staring at the ceiling. "I tried. A few times a day. I didn't know what to say."

"Why did you run?" He asks.

I suck in a breath and hold it as my thoughts race with different versions of the answer. I sigh out, "My scars...I don't like to be reminded of them."

I expect him to lean in for more information, but he doesn't.

We lie in silence until a rumble from his stomach breaks it.

"Hungry?" I ask.

"Guess so."

He starts to move.

"Wait." I take hold of his arm.

He pauses.

"I'll be back."

I get to my feet and dust off my suit.

"This room reminds me of the sheet forts my brother and I used to make," he says.

"Sheet forts?" I ask.

His eyes gleam. "Yeah, you know, when you take all the comforters and sheets and hang them from the walls and ceilings to make a fort?"

I squint. "That's a thing?"

He scoffs. "Yeah, it's a thing."

I shrug.

He frowns. "Hold on."

"What are you doing?" I ask when he climbs to his feet, takes off his blazer, and rolls up his sleeves.

"Come." He starts rearranging the furniture. "Help me move this."

I help him push a table back.

"We're gonna form a circle with this stuff," he says, pointing to the chairs stacked on top of each other.

"Why?"

"You'll see in a second."

After forming a small circle with the furniture, he dusts off a cover and lays it down on the floor, then layers another one on top. Then he takes two more and, after dusting them off, strings them across the top of the chairs to create a tarp.

He kicks off his shoes and crawls underneath. My head peeks in, and I watch him sit cross-legged, assessing the height. "Not bad. It's kinda perfect, actually, with the rain."

"This is a sheet fort?"

"A makeshift version. Take your shoes off. Come here."

"Your parents let you do this?" I ask.

"Yeah. Dad would handle mounting the sheets to the walls since he didn't want us to fall using the ladder. This one time, we had a water gun fight. I don't know how it started, but Mom was a better shot than all of us. Man, we drenched everything."

I tuck my knees in as I scoot next to him. "Sounds...fun."

"You do anything similar with your family?"

I stare at the ceiling of sheets. It's cozy, like the closet in my room that I used to chill in. I usually crank up my thoughts until they're buzzing behind my ears and drowning out the person sharing their warm and fuzzy childhood memories. Not this time. And I don't think the tightness starting to fade in my chest is from envy.

"Blue?"

"Huh?"

"You and your family do anything similar?"

"Water fights in the house?" I scoff. "And ruin my mom's expensive art? Nah."

"Hm. She was strict?"

His stomach growls again.

"Let's take care of that."

"I can come," he offers.

"Enjoy the fort." I crawl out. "I'll be right back."

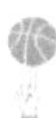

"It's me," I say a few minutes later when I enter and find him lying on his back with his arm under his head.

I hold out a platter of hors d'oeuvres.

His eyes widen. "Whoa."

"Under my arms," I say.

He folds up to catch the two bottles of water.

I spread out the mac and cheese balls, crab puffs, skewers... and a mushroom-looking thing.

"Sheesh. You raided the kitchen."

"Chef's sampler the caterer called it. These are the vegan

ones." I point to the mac and cheese balls separated from the other food.

There's a knock at the door.

I roll back to a stand and pluck my wallet out. "Be right back."

"Thanks, man," I say to the server, trading the cash for a tray of desserts and champagne.

"Seriously?" Salem asks when I return with the tray.

I shrug. "You were hungry."

As I lean down, he reaches over and kisses me in a way that I feel in my toes.

I groan. "You can't look like that, bake me a Wolf cake, annihilate men on the court, be packing a big, pierced dick, and kiss me like that."

He grins. "Why not?"

Salem

"Is it weird if I ask about Lucien?" he asks.

"Wh-what?" I cough, roughly swallowing a lump of food.

"You dated?"

"How did you—?"

"Google."

We were so careful, though.

"Why'd you break up?" he asks.

"Uh…" I take a sip of champagne and clear my throat. "He moved home to France." The way he's searching my face is unnecessary. I wouldn't lie. "We weren't *official,* official. Well, I mean, don't get me wrong, he's one of my closest friends…and there were benefits."

He sets down his plate. "Did he want more?"

"If he did, he never asked."

"What if he did?"

I snicker. "Is this how you are on dates?"

"Answer the question."

I almost ask "Or what?" to see that sexy, angry, feral side surface. Instead, I answer, "He didn't."

His eyes narrow like I'm full of it.

I draw in a long breath. "It wouldn't have been fair to him."

"And you always strive for fairness?"

"I try, yes. Don't you?"

He shrugs as he tucks his legs in. "I don't know if I believe in fairness. I believe in survival. Most days at least."

Am I supposed to know what that means? "I don't understand."

"I bear my demons and aim to harm no one, but if someone comes for me or mine, fairness should run the other way."

"Oh, yeah. Same." I ask the question I've been curious about for months. "What about you and Sid?"

He shakes his head. "Just friends. The kind that've never kissed."

"Cool." I swig the champagne.

"You allowed yourself to crush on a straight guy?" he asks.

So many questions.

"Uh…I guess? Though technically, I allowed myself to crush on a guy who I didn't know was gay."

"Wild." He bites into a skewer.

"What, like you've never crushed on a straight guy?"

"Not if I can help it. Most of 'em are assholes about that kind of thing."

"Word. Lucky me, you aren't straight."

"Not since my first breath."

Same.

"Is California home for you?" I ask.

Arnaz

"Fuck no," I reply. "I wouldn't even want to be buried there."

"It's like that?" His eyes widen. "Why?"

"The sun."

"Explain."

"Wish I could." I bite into the crab puff he offers. "You?"

"I love my home in Brooklyn. I hate being on the road."

"That's the best perk of the gig."

No boxes to unpack. It'll all be gone tomorrow.

"I can't feel at home unless there's a kitchen."

That makes me grin.

"What does your piercing feel like raw?" It's out of my mouth before I can stop it.

He coughs. "Wow." He takes a swig of water and drums on his chest. "You really"—he coughs and swigs another sip—"don't go on dates, do you?"

"Sorry." But dammit, I need to know. "I know your...ex told you."

He chokes out a laugh.

"What's so funny?" I ask.

"Your whole body just shuddered at the word *ex*."

Pfft. "I'm not the jealous type."

He pats my leg.

I'm not.

"Did he sleep over often in your sex-dungeon bedroom?"

He squints. "My what?"

"YouTube." I roll my eyes as a slow grin tugs apart his sexy lips.

"Answer me."

"Nah, we weren't exclusive, so we strapped. And yes, he stayed over often."

"Never?"

He arches an eyebrow.

"Raw?" I clarify.

He shakes his head. "Why are you grinning?"

"Pass me that strawberry tart," I reply, wishing the warm feeling in my chest would knock it the fuck off.

"What did you mean by a 'wolf cake?'" He pulls the strawberry tart back as I reach for it. "Am I supposed to know what that is?"

"It's a planet outside our solar system."

"Why is my cake from there?" He hands over the tart. "Did we give up trying to live on Mars?"

"Mars, bleh. Wolf has a red dwarf star that is cooler than our sun, literally."

"Ah, the sun again."

I bite into the vegan tart and moan at the salty and sweet strawberry glaze. "Twry thish one."

He leans in and takes a bite. His long lashes flutter as he groans.

"Right? Let's try the chocolate one."

He swipes a crumb off the side of my mouth and reaches for the mousse cup. "How's it been for you since coming out?"

I stiffen. "Let's see, what was today's headline?"

"'The Courage of Two, 79 Years Later?'" he asks at the same time I answer, "'Some Players Call for a Separate Locker Room for Gay Men.'"

"Wait, what?" he asks.

"Yep."

"That's bullshit." His voice has gone tense. "Let 'em try."

I attempt to tune it out, but some of it is hard to miss. "How's it been for you? Your teammates and management are cool?"

He shrugs. "There are definitely dickheads on my team, but they'd never say it to my face, you know?"

I'm not naive enough to think no one on the Royals would vote for something like that, but I can't see it. They had Sid's back first when he spoke out about homophobia in the league, and they've had my back since I came out.

"The response from your college coach was dope," he mentions.

My mouth goes dry. "Wh-who?"

"Your coach from college."

My fist tightens around the spoon. "What response?"

"Here." He dusts off his hands. "I can show you."

"N-no." I drop the spoon. "Don't."

Salem

My breath catches as the same glacial stare that sometimes clouds my brother's eyes pins me in place.

"You good?"

Like a taxidermy or wax figure, he sits rigid, posture bone straight.

"Blue?" I wave my hand in front of his face.

The motion flickers him back to life.

"Everything okay?" I ask.

"Yeah," he mumbles, averting his gaze down to the spoon he's gripping like a knife. He manages to partially lift his chin toward me before it falls back down. "I, uh, told Cat I'd spend time with her before I left. Should we…"

"Uh, sure."

He doesn't move, and I swear he looks just like my brother after a sound or word or some other untraceable button's been pressed.

It's so similar—I recognize it like my own face.

The vacant stare.

The eerie stillness.

Blue's haunted—but by the ghosts of what war?

Arnaz

"Hey, hold on. You sure you're okay?"

I freaked him out. I think I went quiet like I do sometimes.

"Yeah. I have a headache," I lie. "The champagne." Unlike mine, his face is too honest. He doesn't buy it. "Come on."

"You're still here! Get over here!" Cat calls, extending her hands to us when we reenter the party.

Drunk Cat is a rare Cat.

She's dancing barefoot with a small group. Most of the guests have cleared out.

"My two favorite clients," she sings.

"Hey, I thought I was your favorite," Salem replies.

"I knew you said that to all of us," I chide.

She looks around as if cameras are hidden somewhere, then leans in. "Just you two." She takes both of our hands and spins us around, and we duck to clear her arms.

"Where's Lys?" Salem asks, looking around for Cat's partner.

"They walked my aunt out," she says. With a wide grin, she twirls us once more and adds, "I knew you two could work. Can't think of two people better suited for each other."

Salem stiffens before he switches gears, twirling Cat around and then pulling her close. "Happy Birthday, Cat."

"You're leaving?"

He nods. "Early practice. Flying back tonight."

"Aww, okay. Thank you for coming."

He nods at her, then turns to me, glancing over my face as he buttons his jacket. "See you in Brooklyn?"

It takes a few seconds to remember our teams face off in a few weeks.

I nod.

He starts to walk away, then pauses. "Are you sure you're o—"

"I'm good."

"Okay. Safe flight home."

My shoulders slump as I watch him leave. I definitely freaked him out.

The closest to a date I've ever had, and I sent him running.

CHAPTER 17
ARNAZ

"Yo, we gotta fucking rebound," I drill into the guys.

"Play your positions and don't let up on the gas," Sid adds. "We got this."

Salem soars through the air as soon as the second quarter resumes.

We don't got this.

Eclipsing Nick's reach, he blocks his shot with a casual rage that leaves Nick stunned.

Fuck me.

If I freaked him out at Catharine's party, he isn't showing it. At all.

But how?

The times I've gone "quiet" in front of people, they're awkward as hell afterward. I've been dreading this game, fully expecting another ice-out from him like last game, but as soon as we saw each other on the court, he blew a kiss at me, making the crowd laugh.

Still, I tested the waters last quarter by lifting a middle finger at him.

"It's like that?" he asked, moving in to guard me. "It's my fault your boys out here just for cardio?"

"You talk like you're winning." My voice was flat as I pulled the ball back like I was about to drive.

"Just sayin'." He boxed me in. "You sure y'all on the same team?"

"Nah, they with us," Cillian interjected as he swooped in, attempting a steal.

I was faster. Dipping low, I pivoted, spun off Cillian, and launched the ball to Sid, who caught it without looking and swished it.

He smirked and shook his head. "Hey, if I win, come to my sex dungeon tonight."

"You're not winning," I replied as I raced backward.

But not before he winked, catching the twitch in the corner of my lips.

So, yeah, he's acting normal.

Huh.

Salem

Haters will say that home-court advantage is the reason it's twelve minutes into the third quarter and we're only down three points. If you listened to the pundits, the Royals and their "super team"—*guhk!*—were supposed to add us to their four-game road sweep.

Fuck outta here.

Sleep on Brooklyn if you're stupid.

Cillian's banked twenty-four points so far, including a circus shot at the end of the second quarter.

The crowd's been losing their shit all night.

Charging up court, Cillian cuts to the wing and then launches the ball straight at the backboard. Slicing past Ussef's weak defense, I catch the rebound midair and hammer a sideways windmill dunk.

Let's go!

Yelling, "Ball," Sid fakes a crossover on their next possession as Ezekiel and Zyair double-team him. Zigzagging back and forth, Blue manages to free himself of Onyx's defense. Johan and Ussef create a door for Sid to get the ball off. Barely five seconds left on the shot clock, Sid launches it to Blue.

Or he tries, but then I fly in with a gravity-defying steal.

Aaahh-haaa!

I hear, "Fuck this," before I'm rushed.

Landing on my back with a soft thud, my face is mushed with Blue's arm.

Adorable.

He scrambles up my body, trying to steal the ball, but I wing it to Onyx.

"Asshole," he grits in my face.

"You know this is what started this"—I gesture between us—"five years ago."

"Eat shit," he fires back.

I curl my arms behind my neck. "What are you doing tonight? Let me cook—"

His hand wraps around my throat.

"If I squeeze just right...," he mutters through clenched teeth. "Earthen eyes...bulge just so..."

I try to snicker. *Earthen eyes?*

"Cade," his coach yells. "Hump Jones on your own time. Get your ass on the bench. Marcus, you're up."

"H-he c-could...h-hump...me...n-now," I choke out.

Blue growls in my face and then releases me.

"The fuck you smiling for?" he fires at Sid as he storms toward the bench.

The ref must have gotten laid last night. That was an obvious flagrant two foul, but lucky for me he's still in the game.

CHAPTER 18
ARNAZ

♫ "Rot" ♫

Tomorrow you will reach for some dead thing.

Post-game interviews when you're on the losing end are really the high times of life. The media wants to know why you're a loser, and you have to keep your head up while confessing your and your team's shortcomings. Sid and I take turns grunting through one ear-stabbing question after another.

We're hauling our egos back to the locker room when Sid taps my arm and backs up.

Cillian and Salem take seats at the press table.

"How do you feel about tonight's game?" the same interviewer who just asked us in sports code why we're such losers, asks Cillian.

"Splendid. We just loved having them."

He turns to Salem, who nods and adds, "So respectful. You'd hardly know they were here."

The room echoes with laughter.

"In the third quarter, when Cade moved in to defend you—"

"Oh, that's what he was doing?" Salem quips, and the press erupts again.

Sid steps back. "Your boyfriend got jokes."

"He's not my boyfriend."

I'm just obsessed with the way his metal massaged the back of my throat.

I catch up to Sid and ask, "What were you talking to him about after the game?"

"Why?" He leans in and sniffs me, and I lurch back.

"Stop that."

"Smells like a crush."

"No." I sniff my shirt.

He smirks. "Ready to roll?"

WE REACH an elegant three-story brownstone with an iron-like gate, window railings, and polished brass numbers affixed to the glass and wood door.

"Pretty." I sweep my gaze over the tree-lined block.

"Fort Greene is one of my favorite neighborhoods," Sid says.

"Ty grew up around here, right?"

"Born and raised until his parents passed, then he moved to Jersey to live with his uncle." I expect him to ring the bell once we reach the top of the landing, but he pulls out a key and unlocks the door. "Besides my mom's house, this place is like a second home for us."

We remove our shoes.

"Mmm." I sniff the air. "Garlic."

He crinkles his nose. "And butter." He takes my bag and places it on the entry bench. "A-yo, we're here. Everyone decent?" he calls out as we make our way past a curved staircase with muted gold and black wallpaper and soft lighting.

"In here," a deep voice calls back.

My socks skate against the hardwood floor as we head down a hallway.

"In here" is a sprawling family room. I zero in on the Steinway on the far side of the room, adjacent to the dining room table, and my fingers tingle. "Sheesh." I whistle and spin. The high ceiling has embossed tiles in rustic gold, deep grays, and slate blue accenting the exposed beams.

Sid grins. "K, where you at?"

"In here."

I whip around, searching for the source of the voice, when there's a thump behind the laddered wall of built-in bookshelves with color-arranged books, artworks, and photos. A panel opens, and Kieran, Sid's cousin, whom I recognize from Sid and Ty's barbecue, emerges, balancing bottles of wine in his arms.

I jet over to help him.

"Thanks, hon!" he says as I lighten his load. "I'm glad you could join us."

"Thanks for having me."

"Feeling this 'fit," Sid says, taking the remaining bottles from Kieran. High cheekbones and chestnut eyes are family features, and Kieran's eyes are highlighted by black eyeliner and a dusting of gold shimmer. Both men have the sides of their heads shaved low, but where Sid has short coils, Kieran has golden-brown dreadlocks piled intricately high.

"This old thing"—Kieran twirls, voice almost as deep as Sid's—"is what some might call the result of having exquisite taste. On the bottom, the gentleman is wearing a pleated paper bag, ultra-high-rise waist, with a leather belt tied into a bow. The hem is hemmin'"—he points to his leg for emphasis, making Sid chuckle and me grin—"at a precise four inches below the knee. And up top, we have a mint-green, silk-tie crop shirt with a front concealed button placket and—"

"Hey, where'd you put the Cajun seasoning?" Tommy, their childhood best friend, enters from the kitchen, wearing an apron over his jeans and T-shirt that's stretched around his massive build.

"Bae-bee!" Kieran huffs. "I'm serving these lewks like a gracious host."

Sid and I laugh as Sid wraps his arms around his cousin, pulling him into a hug.

"My bad. You're gorgeous as always, babe." Tommy smiles. "What's good?" He nods to me. "Thanks for coming thru." Then he greets Sid. "Sup, bro?"

"Sup, T," Sid replies.

"Thanks for having me," I repeat.

"It's in the fridge," Kieran replies to Tommy, referring to the seasoning.

Tommy turns and disappears back into the kitchen.

"Dried seasonings don't go in the fridge, K," Sid teases.

Kieran sighs. "The man knows I'm hopeless in the kitchen, yet he still lets me unpack the groceries."

We're following him to the bar to transfer the bottles of wine when the doorbell rings.

"I got it," Sid calls out, heading toward the door.

"There's beer there." Kieran points to a silver beverage tub. "And lots of reds and whites. What can I get you?"

I flinch at the sound of laughter coming from the entryway —Salem's laughter.

"Whoa. Your face," Kieran says.

My heart pounds. "What'd your cousin do?"

"You didn't know he was invited?" Kieran touches my elbow, his brows furrowed.

I shake my head.

At the light thump of their footsteps, a surge of electricity makes me want to break for the window.

"You like him, yes?" He frowns. "Wait, no. I'm reading terror." His nose scrunches. "Aww, you really like him."

The hell?

Is the whole reading-people thing genetic?

"Your secret is safe with me," he whispers. "Shhh."

I school my expression to neutral as Salem saunters in, *not* looking wholly edible in a white button-down with a band collar and dark washed, slim-fit blue jeans. His socks are fancy, with a blue and orange chevron print.

Did he change after the press conference?

"He's scorching," Kieran whispers.

Where's the whiskey?

"This is my cuz, Kieran," Sid introduces him to Salem.

"Hi, Kieran," Salem replies, placing a grocery bag down to extend his hand. "Salem. Pleasure to meet you."

I *don't* forget how to talk or listen and catch only every other word of their exchange. My head *definitely* doesn't tilt in, sneaking a sniff of his fresh laundry and vanilla-mint scent. I *don't* stand frozen like a powered-down robot when he says, "Hey, you," in that *not-at-all* spine-tingling voice.

Tommy reemerges from the kitchen with a large tray piled with seafood and vegetables. He's introduced to Salem, pops back into the kitchen, then returns with two additional trays before passing around cloth bibs to protect our shirts.

"It looks delicious," Salem compliments him.

"Thanks, man," Tommy replies. "We make a seafood boil a few times a year."

"What are you both having?" Kieran asks, heading to the bar.

"That reminds me." Salem reaches into the grocery bag on the floor and pulls out a case of IPA and a bottle of wine.

"Chablis," Kieran says, smiling at the bottle. "Thank you!"

"You're welcome." Salem turns to me. "What are you having?"

His eyebrows crinkle when I don't respond.

And now everyone's staring.

"He likes IPAs," Sid jumps in, and when Salem turns away, he mouths, *4. 6. 8.*

I end up doing more of a 2-12-3 second inhale-hold-exhale technique.

Salem returns with our drinks, then digs back into the grocery bag. "Just in case," he says, placing a box of European-style vegan butter on the table.

"Are you lactose intolerant?" Tommy asks me.

I half nod. I think.

"Gotcha. I wondered why Sid asked us to skip dairy for one of the trays."

The four of us settle in, then Salem passes me the dairy-free tray after he whips me up a sauce with the vegan butter, lemon, and spices.

When Salem isn't looking, Sid mouths, *Marry him.*

I glare back. This is all his fault.

A HUGE MESS is made while we're cracking into lobster and crab and peeling prawns. I press the cold IPA bottle into my palm as Salem licks butter from the inside of his wrist before it catches his cuff.

I'm quiet, which isn't unusual—lately, I'm often out of sync with the mood of a group—but tonight's different.

I'd never admit to my quiet awe at watching Salem be a human.

He recognizes a painting hanging on the wall, which leads the conversation toward this year's Met Gala. He expresses curiosity about Tommy's chemistry professor gig, and we all learn that a drop in chlorophyll is the reason leaves change in autumn.

He turns to me often when he speaks, never letting me feel left out but never forcing me to contribute.

He's a human masterclass on being a people person.

Yeah, he's definitely more broken into his skin than I am mine.

He and Sid talk fashion, and then the charities they support. When I recognize the name of one that focuses on mental health services and shelter for unhoused LGBTQIA+ youth, I blurt out, "I support that one too."

He turns to me and quietly asks, "Yeah? Did Cat mention there's a seat becoming available on the board?"

She did. "Boards aren't really my thing."

He nods.

"Are you, uh, thinking of applying?" I don't even know if applying is the right word. I always imagine people in suits doing that kinda thing.

"I am." He wipes his mouth with a napkin. "If they could use me, and it works with my schedule." He stares down at my plate. "You liked the sauce?"

I follow his gaze to my plate filled with shells. "Mmhm. You're a baker *and* a cook?"

"I feed myself alright. You?"

I wince, making him laugh.

"That bad, huh?"

I shrug.

"I'll teach you," he says, brushing my knee, and I forget how to speak again.

LATER, when we take turns cleaning ourselves up after we eat and Salem heads to the bathroom, Kieran whispers, "He's dreamy."

"A keeper," Tommy echoes.

The ants are back, organizing an ant army invasion in my blood. "We aren't together," I mutter.

Kieran exchanges a glance with Tommy. "Why not?"

"Where's the remote?" Sid interrupts, crashing onto the large marigold-colored couch and kicking his feet up on the kidney-shaped footrest.

"Let me guess, you tryna catch highlights of the Knights at Madison Square Garden?" Kieran teases.

"So?" Sid smirks. "And leave Princess alone."

I glare at him. "You're a matchmaker now? You're dead to me."

"See." He catches the remote Tommy tosses him. "He loves too hard to love easily."

I take a swig of my beer, ignoring the squeeze in the middle of my chest.

Okay, he *was* dead to me for an hour. It's impossible to stay angry at him any longer than that.

We watch highlights of Ty banking mid-and long-range shots with the precision of a sharpshooter. The Knights shooting guard and power forward also do damage, collecting forty-two points between them.

"Speak of the angel," Kieran says as the front door shuts.

Our heads swing toward the hallway and a few seconds later, Ty walks in. He slides his key into the back pocket of his ripped skinny jeans, then daps Salem and me. "Wassup."

He moves to Kieran and Tommy, planting kisses on both of their cheeks.

Sid smiles, shuffles to a stand, and wraps him up in a hug. "Car ride over was smooth?" he asks before dipping down to kiss him.

"Yeah," Ty replies after he pulls away, returning an easy smile I've only ever seen reserved for Sid.

"It'll make sense in a moment," I mutter to a slack-jawed Salem.

Sid massages the back of Ty's neck, rubbing his thumb over his fading hickey.

"Guys. Salem..." I remind them.

"Oh," Sid says as they both turn toward us. "You wanna or should I?" he asks Ty.

Ty nods for him to shoot.

"You probably know from the media that we're best friends. We've actually been in a relationship and have recently become engaged," he tells Salem.

"We're out to close friends," Ty adds.

"It's only a matter of time before we come out to the public or our relationship gets leaked," Sid says.

I'm impressed that Salem's able to contain his shock enough to stammer, "Engaged? Wow." He huffs a laugh. "I mean, I knew you were close friends—everyone knows that. But engaged?" His gaze bounces between them. "Well, shoot, it isn't a hard sell," he jokes, making us laugh.

Sid was voted Sexiest Man Alive, for fuck's sake, and Ty's nickname is Pretty Boy. Only someone snorting too much Special K would look at them and not trade a year off their life for a top-ten spot on their threesome short list.

"Hey," Ty says to me. "I can tell from his face that he didn't know. Thank you for protecting us."

"Always," I reply.

TY EMERGES FROM THE BATHROOM, removing his beanie and moss-green sweatshirt, leaving a white tee underneath, and joins Sid, who's waiting for him at the dining table with the remaining half tray of food. He slides onto Sid's lap.

Sid congratulates him on the dub, and Ty boasts Sid's game stats.

I look over at Salem, who's just picked up the controller to start a game with Tommy.

He turns and catches me staring. His nose ring glints slightly as his lips spread in a warm smile. His gaze lingers on my face, the heat of it sending ants down my spine, before he turns back to the game.

"May I?" I ask Kieran, nodding to the Steinway.

"Have at it."

I finish my beer and then toss the bottle in the garbage before I pad over, adjust the bench, and take a seat. Opening the fallboard, I stare at the black-and-white keys as I crack my knuckles.

I begin with scales to loosen up my muscles.

"He's a pianist?" Ty asks.

"And guitarist," Sid replies as their voices fade, and I drift away.

CHAPTER 19
SALEM

The game controller, like my jaw, hangs limp as Blue transports us to a symphony hall. The thing I've only glimpsed before expands over the room as we're granted rare entry into the hidden scrolls of his psyche.

It's all there—melancholy, fatigue, heartbreak, terror, hope.

The invitation only deepens the itch of mystery that's hooked me from the beginning.

More questions than answers, which might be the case with us until the end.

The need for one particular answer burns above the rest.

What is the source of his pain?

It's the question I've been asking myself since I touched his scar, and the need to know only intensified after Catharine's party.

Because of my brother, I recognize a soul altered by grief.

But with Blue, there's something else. There are hollows.

Back erect, eyes closed, and a slight part of lips—his fingers are the only movement in the room.

I haven't yet explained his nickname to him. *Blue.*

My dad used to say, *"If you can't find peace, wait for the blue hour before dawn, and free your wrestled fears to fate."*

I'm not sure Blue has ever found that hour, but when I think of it, I think of him.

Pulling from beyond a veil, each press of his fingers to the keys draws us closer.

This song isn't for us.

Some songs are for ghosts. Locked away in rooms, preserved by its lack of exposure, and released for the haunted on their own time.

As it should be.

There's a kind of anachronistic thinking that's lethal to who we are.

Like the hate post I saw earlier about me and him. The drag of the past chains itself to our feet, making the present not present enough.

As the piece comes to an end, I want to wedge something through the door that's closing.

The chills running up my arm hint that I can let go. This song will play long after other memories from today fade.

Whistles and applause sound through the room, but I sit motionless.

He opens his eyes, and a lightness radiates from his timid smile.

"Is that one of yours?" Ty asks.

He clears his throat. "Yeah. A nocturne. Still workshopping the title. For now, it's 'Bitter Blood.'"

Or "Burial Solitude." It's like a graveyard hymn.

Kieran's face is a pristine mirror of our awe as he exclaims, "Wow!"

"Take a ticket," Sid teases. "He has a whole team first in line to buy the album."

Blue laughs and wrings his hands before beginning to play again. "The request line's open."

Tommy whistles.

"We love this song." Kieran swoons, blanketing his shoulders with Tommy's arms.

I force myself to move when the song ends. "Seriously?" My fingers mock-explode against my temple.

His smile deepens, coupled with the light in his eyes. *God help me.*

I point to my useless mouth.

He snorts. "We can't both forget how to speak."

I huff. "Those hands speak better than I ever could."

He stares down at the piano keys.

He's cute when he's being shy.

"An album?"

"Mm...maybe. I sing and play guitar too."

"Wow." I lean in. "I didn't think you could get any sexier."

He flushes, and I want to trail his lips with my thumb.

"Wanna see my sex dungeon?" I whisper.

His gaze darkens. "We're out," he says, jumping to his feet.

WE SAY our goodbyes and then pause at the door to put on our shoes and coats. As soon as Blue's tatted hands glide across the lapel of his leather jacket, I rush him, sealing my mouth to his.

He moans. Giving as good as he gets, he sucks on my tongue.

Wrapping my arm around his waist, I press against him, deepening the kiss.

I squeeze his hand between the press of our bodies, and he latches on to the zipper of my pants.

"What are you doing?" I rasp against his lips before moving down his neck and nipping his Adam's apple.

"One taste," he whispers.

"Blue—"

"Please."

I glance behind us, then move us to the wall shielded by the coat rack. He drops to his knees, unzips my jeans, then lifts me out of my briefs.

A sharp breath sends my teeth crashing into my bottom lip as he licks between the bars of my piercing, alternating latching on to the surrounding skin.

"Blue," I gasp.

He pauses to swallow, then licks the pre-cum pooling in my slit.

We both stiffen at the sound of footsteps. I start to pull back, but his fingers dig into the backs of my thighs, the only warning before I hit the back of his throat.

"Ngh." Streaks of white spread behind my eyelids.

His tongue massages the underside as he works me deeper down his throat. So fucking warm, the suction so tight it borders on painful.

"Fuck." My palm presses into the wall. "Someone's coming."

He pulls off, gasping for air, then sucks me down to my base. The pressure between my thighs builds as he rubs his nose in the hair at my root with a wet moan. His eyes shift to an inky charcoal color, lasering into me.

"Christ," I mutter around a ragged breath as his hands tighten on my ass, and he corkscrews me in and out of his throat. Each glide of his tongue sends a throbbing ache through my body. My fingers trace his sexy lips spread taut around my length, making him hum, shooting a vibration from my abdomen down to my toes.

Fuuuck. Grabbing his face, my hips snap, fucking his mouth.

The footsteps grow louder.

The pressure peaks, threatening the strength in my knees. Seconds of staring into his leaking, blissed-out eyes, and I'm biting my fist to stifle a chest-ripping grunt. His mouth tightens around me like a second skin as I tremor through my release.

After brushing a quick kiss to my slit, he stands, wipes his mouth, and weaves around me, leaving me with my dick out and panting.

"Hey, is there another bathroom on this side?" I hear him ask from farther down the hall.

My shoulders drop as both his and someone else's footsteps retreat. I tuck myself in and lean against the wall.

Gaht damn!

"GOOD, YOU'RE STILL HERE."

I jump at the sound of Sid's voice.

"My bad," he says. "I wanted to catch you while you're alone."

I look over his shoulder. "S-sure. What's up?"

"He'd probably chase me with a Smith & Wesson if he knew I was saying this to you." He leans against the wall. "But he's a good guy. I saw him struggling tonight, which means he's into you. He tends to give off the opposite of what he feels. Like, his fuck-you-and-die attitude could really mean *I don't hate you*."

I grin and nod for him to continue.

"If he seems disinterested or distant, it's probably not why you think. Be patient with him. He's a bit of a closed book, but I sense he hasn't had it easy."

"He hasn't told you what happened to him?" I ask.

Blue rounds the corner as Sid shakes his head.

"Thanks, man." I pull him into a dap.

"Bus leaves at ten sharp tomorrow," he says to Blue.

"Buzzz leevs at ten sharrrp," Blue mocks.

"So rude to his elders," Sid replies to me.

"I'm older than you." Blue scowls as he lifts his bag.

I open the door but pause when he turns and says to Sid, "Thanks."

Sid nods. "Have fun. Ten a.m. sharp."

"Say 'ten a.m.' again and see what time I show up," he fires back.

Sid meets my gaze, and we both laugh.

HE SIDE-EYES me as I lead him to my car. "What's so funny?"

"Hmm?"

"You and Sid just now. Laughing."

I slide my hands into my pockets and shrug. "I laughed?"

"Yes. Just now."

"No." I shake my head. "I don't think I did."

"You did. You have a habit of not knowing when you're laughing?" he asks, voice clipped.

"Normally, I don't. But you see, I haven't had my dick sucked that spectacularly since...well, never. Maybe uncontrollable laughter's a side effect."

The crease in his brow disappears as he rolls his lips. Whatever grin he's holding in fails to hide his dimples. "Cillian threatened to make me sniff almonds."

I huff out a laugh. *Of course he did.*

"What does it mean?"

"Cyanide."

"Ah." He stops walking. "That's your whip?"

"Nah, this is me." I point to the Prius next to it.

"Oh, my ba—"

I point my fob at my Maserati, and the matte-black butterfly doors expand. "Kidding."

"How?" His eyes bulge. "This is the MC20 Cielo Paradiso supercar with the Nettuno V6? The final collab with Sakamoto? They only made, like, a hundred. And they sold out in under three minutes."

"Yeah. You alright?"

"I don't know." He swallows. "I'm either having a heart attack or falling in love."

"It's love. Kairis has that effect."

He sucks in a breath. "You watch *Exosphere*?"

My middle finger curls to meet my thumb, and I turn my wrist to make a sideways E. "Animo Cursum Astra."

"Yooo!" he exclaims as I recite the show's slogan. "I've been trying to get Sid and the—One sec." His brows furrow as he reaches into his jeans, pulls out his phone, and stares at the lit-up screen. He accepts the call. "You good?" he asks into the phone.

I start to step back to give him space but hold when he says, "Hey, hey, what's wrong?"

My pulse kicks up as he blinks rapidly, and I step closer, resting my hand on his arm.

"I'm on my way." He shakes his head. "Nah. I'm coming. Meet you at home or the hospital? Okay. Be right there."

"What happened?" I ask as he hangs up.

"I need to get to Prospect Heights. Can you drop me?"

I'm already leading us to the car. "Who was that?"

"My sister, Anaïs."

"Is she sick?"

His nod is spacey.

"Is it serious?" I ask.

"Inflammatory disease. She's supposed to have surgery for it in a few weeks, but the monthly flare-ups are excruciating."

"Damn."

Once he locks his seat belt, I pull out quickly.

"We were gonna grab breakfast before I fly out tomorrow," he says, biting his nails as he stares out the passenger side window.

"I didn't realize your sister was in Brooklyn."

"My mom and Carter are in New Jersey, but she moved here a couple years ago."

He calls his dad by his first name? "Here. Plug in the full address."

"THANKS," he says, unbuckling his seat belt when we arrive. "Sorry we couldn't...you know."

"I really don't mind waiting downstairs and driving you both to the hospital," I offer again.

He pauses, hand on the door handle. "Maybe. It might be better for her than a random driver. Let me ask her."

"Go." I cut off the ignition. "I'll be here."

"Thanks.

He speaks to the doorman and then disappears past the glass doors.

CHAPTER 20
ARNAZ

"**T**hanks, Aaron."

"You bet. Call downstairs if you or Ms. Cade need anything," the doorman replies as he lets me into the condo.

"Hey," I call out as I slip off my kicks and drop my bag.

I follow the only light, which is coming from her room. The place is silent except for the sound of my socks sweeping the floor.

I slow down in the doorway of her bedroom, transitioning to a tiptoe. I kneel and sweep the curls from her face. She's out cold. I rub my thumb over the wet circles on her pillow, tracking back to the dried tears streaking her face.

Ignoring the burn in my eyes, I gently cover her with her comforter.

Fifteen years of this shit.

Life's cruel.

I consider waking her, but it's always the same thing at the ER. We wait for hours only to be sent home with 800mg of ibuprofen. Which, if I had to guess—I lift the open prescription bottle on the nightstand—she already took. The only real solution is the surgery she has scheduled, and even that isn't a full cure. But it gives her the chance of a life with less pain, and that's more than enough reason for her to try.

A tail of soft fur brushes against my leg.

"Hello, Alfie." I pluck up the tawny, black, and white cat, kissing him on his fluffy head as he nestles into my arms.

I anchor him in one hand while I shrug off my coat to leave on her door handle, so she'll know I'm here if she wakes up.

Salem

"What's her name?" I ask, bending down to pet the black pit bull who wandered over to sniff my leg.

"Sodapop," the man replies.

"From *The Outsiders*?"

His face lights up. "You'd be surprised how many people our age don't get the reference."

"I'm not, actually," I reply, and he laughs.

"Awesome game," he says.

Sodapop licks my wrist as I scratch the crook of his neck. "Thanks." Simba's gonna stalk me later, demanding answers for Sodapop's scent on my skin.

"You were hot. I mean—"

I glance up at him.

"Like, you were on fire."

The sound of a throat clearing turns our heads.

"Hey." I glance past Blue, searching for his sister. "What did she say?"

"She's asleep."

Blue glares at the dude who looks like he wants to ask for his autograph.

"It was nice meeting you," the guy says to me instead.

I wink goodbye at Sodapop.

"Don't let me interrupt," Blue says stiffly.

"Should we wake her?" I ask.

"He kind of looks like Lucien, doesn't he? If Lucien was a bendy yoga instructor."

"What?"

"Your ex." He takes a step back.

Arms crossed, light scowl, tight eyes. *Well, well.*

I clasp his waist. Before he can protest, I dip my head and pull him into a kiss. When my tongue gently brushes against his teeth, he opens for me, softening in my arms.

I'll never get used to the little moans he makes.

"Blue—" My voice hitches as I catch my breath. "If I wanted Lucien, or his lookalikes, that's where I'd be." I brush another kiss against his lips. "I've waited years for you."

The only sign that my words hit their mark is the tremble of his hands against my back.

"Should we wake Anaïs to take her to the hospital?"

"I'm not sure. I think it's better for her to sleep. You can leave your car parked here for the night. The doorman will watch it."

"You want me to come up?"

He doesn't answer as he walks away.

Such a dick.

A sexy, wrathful, gorgeous dick.

"SHE JUST MOVED IN?" I ask, looking around at the bare walls and sparsely furnished living room.

"Nah," he replies, returning from checking on her. "Why?"

"She's okay?"

He nods. "Out cold."

I smile at the photo of her and Blue on her otherwise bare desk. She has a warmer brown complexion than Blue's—it's closer to mine—curly hair piled high in a messy bun, and they share the same sharp eyes down to the dark circles.

"Doesn't seem lived in," I answer, placing the photo down.

Blue shrugs. "She's not really sure if this is home for her."

"I thought you said she's lived here for years."

"She has. Come on." He leads us to the opposite side of the condo, to a guest room that's on the smaller side of medium, with a bed, TV, and chair. He takes my coat and then hangs it in the closet.

I ask for the bathroom, and he points me to the en suite.

He's flicking through channels on the TV when I return. "An addict," he mumbles. "What are half these apps?"

I sidle up next to him. "Can I have some?"

His brow furrows as I lift his fingers away from his teeth and open my mouth wide like fangs are about to emerge.

He snatches his hand back. "You're nuts." He rubs his hands across his thighs, stretching and curling his fingers, then they're back at his mouth a second later.

"Blue?"

"Hmm?"

"What happened to you a few weeks ago?"

"Wh-what?"

"You missed a few games. They said you were sick."

He stiffens, then resumes gnawing on his nails and staring at the TV's home screen.

After close to a minute of silence, when I know an answer isn't coming, I ask, "Can I help you relax?"

His fingers still against his mouth, and he nods.

"Think you can be quiet?" I ask, swiveling my feet to the floor and jumping up to lock the door.

"I-I'm always quiet." The catch in his voice betrays him.

He sucks in a breath as I clasp his legs and pull him down the bed toward me.

"I'd like to know you." I remove his socks. "And you need to release tension. So how about we play a game?"

"Mmh." He moans as my thumb presses into the heel of his foot.

"Is that a yes?"

His eyes glaze over before his head falls back between his shoulder blades. "Don't stop."

"Dems the rules. You answer my questions, and I keep going. You're allowed four skips."

He grunts his assent as I rub circles into his foot.

I start with an easy one. "Salty or sweet?"

"Sweet."

"Date night out or at home?"

"H-home."

"New movie or old favorite?"

"New."

His eyes flicker when I use both hands to work his heel. "Wait," he breathes. "I want your answers too."

"Sweet, home, old favorite. Would you rather time travel to the past or future?"

"Neither...or future."

His chest rises and falls slowly as my thumb glides up his arch, applying firm pressure.

"Why not the past?"

He swallows quickly. "Skip."

Hmm.

He nods for me to answer.

"Past. Kindness or intelligence?

"Kindness. You?"

"Both."

His teeth scrape against his lower lip as my fist rolls along his arch.

"Skinny dipping at night or sunbathing nude?"

"Night."

"Night, if it's with you," I answer, making a tiny grin appear on his lips.

"Would you rather have a teleportation machine or the ability to control minds?"

His head tilts slightly as he considers it. "Teleportation machine. I'll finish a game in LA and then teleport to my snowy cabin."

"You have a snowy cabin?"

"I will when I retire. You?"

"Mind control."

"Of course." He hums and lowers to his back as I knead the ball of his foot.

"Why 'of course?'"

"I don't know," he rasps. "Control seems like your thing."

"Maybe."

I think about my next question as heat builds under my palm where it kneads his flesh. "Would you rather be able to talk to animals or be fluent in every language?"

"Fluent in every language," he answers, voice slurry.

"Why?"

"How am I gonna retire in a forest for peace and quiet if animals are yapping at me all day?"

Snowy cabin. Forest. I make a mental note to learn more. "I'd love to talk to animals."

His glazed eyes open a little more.

We're quiet for a few minutes while I concentrate on his foot and think of more questions. "I got one. Would you rather undo your deepest regret or live your wildest dreams?"

His foot tenses in my hand. "Undo my deepest regret."

"Why?"

"Skip. You?"

I nod slowly. "Live my wildest dreams. Would you rather know the date of your death or the cause of your death?"

"Date."

"Really? *Cause* for me, maybe I can do something to change it."

He shrugs. "I don't care how, just tell me when."

The resignation in his voice makes me pause before I lift his foot to my lips and place a soft kiss on the ball. "Last questions. Ready?"

He nods, his fingers intertwined behind his head as his foot gets heavier in my hand.

I rotate his toes in a circular motion, pulling each one upward.

"Do you think about me at night?"

His eyes lower. "Yes."

"I think of you too. Does it make you come?"

"Yes," he replies, his voice deepening, before he nods for me to answer.

"Yeah, Blue."

His foot twitches.

"Have you ever been in love?"

"No." His eyes blink closed. "Yes."

So, he *has* dated. Did someone cause him to stop? I switch to his other foot as I take that in.

"Did he love you back?" I question.

"Skip."

"You only have one more skip. Why were you out sick?"

"Skip."

"Dangerous." I click my tongue. "No more skips."

He doesn't reply, but his fingers return to his teeth.

"When you think of me at night, are you on top or bottom?"

"Bottom," he murmurs as I softly stretch his foot outward.

I hide how much I love that answer.

But, fuck yeah.

"Favorite thing about a man?"

"About or on?" he asks.

"Either. Both."

"Scent after they work out. Piercings."

"Favorite feature of mine?"

"Mm," he moans, lower back lifting as I squeeze his heel with both hands, and my thumbs press down.

As if he knows it's mine, he doesn't touch his erection.

"Your face, voice, body...the way you read and move on the court."

There's no masking my megawatt smile. I thought I'd get one grunted answer.

"You haven't answered any of the last few questions," he reminds me.

"My bad. Your entire package is"—I raise my fingers to my lips and kiss them with a *Mwah!*—"but your eyes..."

"Yeah. The green," he says, with an air—no, a gust—of boredom, maybe even disdain, and pulls his foot back.

"The green is the least captivating part, no offense." I pick his foot back up. "For me, it's their shape and depth and the way you wield them. They seem old."

He squints. "My eyes seem old?"

"Yeah. Like those eerie, beautiful houses covered in vines and wildflowers that, like, despite wars, famines, name your atrocity, still manage to stand."

"My eyes are like an eerie house?" The rawness in his voice overpowers the tone of skepticism.

"Yeah. You know the kind of house I'm talking about. The paint is chipping, the windows are storm-beaten, and when you stare too long, you run cold, sensing there's something staring back. Not just staring but daring you to approach. And most won't. But for me, I have to."

"So my eyes are possessed?"

I ignore him and continue. "You press your face against the streaked window, and there's overturned furniture, the beginning of a staircase, and tells where the floor creaks from too much life, and you want to break in, but something there in the shadows stops you."

Looking deep into those haunting eyes, I quietly and without so many words, tell him my plan for pursuing him. "The way in isn't force...it's patience."

Arnaz

My stomach clenches.

Please don't let the burn spreading up my chest reach my eyes.

"Hey," he speaks softly.

"Next question," I rush out.

He kisses the sole of my foot. "Do you think you could fall in love again?"

"Skip."

"You're out of skips."

"Come here then." I reach for him.

He shifts forward, spreading my legs, then strips me out of my jeans and briefs.

I've been on edge since I choked him on the court, and I swear I felt that foot massage in my cock. "I'll probably blow as soon as you touch me."

"Mm." He kisses the crease at the top of my thigh, causing my legs to tremor, which turns into a full convulsion when his tongue fondles my balls. As soon as his lips wrap around the head of my cock, I shoot hard, fisting the sheets.

I GRAB my briefs and slide out of bed before we do something stupid like try to hold each other. I lean against the bathroom door and squeeze my eyes closed, fighting the feeling of the ground slipping out from under me.

"Gonna check on Anaïs," I tell him when I return. "Extra toothbrushes under the sink," I add as I slip on my jeans.

"Cool," he says, sliding past me into the bathroom.

Anaïs is still asleep when I check on her. After leaving a note on her nightstand, letting her know Salem and I are in the guest room and to grab me if she needs me, I fill two glasses of water.

I spoke to her yesterday, and she didn't mention she was in pain, but the sink tells a different story—she can't sleep without loading it. After I press start on the dishwasher, I pop an unopened bag of Vietnamese food into the fridge. I fill Alfie's bowls with wet food and fresh water.

She'll need something bland to eat in the morning. After scanning her fridge, I end up pulling out my phone and placing a delivery breakfast order from a local health spot.

Salem's already dozed off when I return. I slide down the wall until I'm sitting on the floor and watch him sleep. My thoughts drift back to that night, choking on ocean, drowning in endless black. He's asked about it twice, but I can't bring myself to talk about it.

I stare at him until I can't fight sleep anymore, and I kill the lights and slip under the covers on the far edge of the bed.

CHAPTER 21
SALEM

Blue wakes up in my arms. In the middle of the night, I found him, back turned toward me, on the other side of the bed, and I nestled closer to him.

"Mornin'." I kiss his neck.

He grunts and burrows deeper into his pillow.

According to my watch, I have under an hour to relieve my dog sitter.

My hand caresses his stomach, then trails up to massage his nipple.

A low moan rumbles from underneath the pillow.

He pushes back, rubbing up against my erection.

We both still at the muffle of voices seeping through the door.

His head darts up from under the pillow.

"Nooo." He snatches his phone from the nightstand. He groans, staring at the screen.

"What's the matter?"

"It's the third Sunday."

"Okay." My gaze follows his where it's locked on the door.

"I'm sorry. Fuck."

I rub his arm, finding it clammy.

"My parents are here. They meet Anaïs for family brunch every third Sunday."

"Oh, cool. I dig family."

"Not this one," he grumbles, climbing out of bed. "Let's brush our teeth and get dressed." His voice is deflated, like he's losing air.

"Hey, hey, hold up." I reach for him. "I get it if you don't want me to meet your family. I can just bounce."

"Nah, it isn't that."

A man's voice gets louder, pulling Blue's attention back to the door. When it doesn't sound like anyone is about to burst in, he says, "I don't really mess with them."

"Oh. Why?"

"It's a long story."

"Okay. What can I do?"

"When we get out there, let me take the lead?"

"Of course. I got you."

THREE HEADS TURN in our direction as we enter the living room. Two I recognize from television, and one from the picture on the desk.

"Arnaz?" His mother's face lights up. "I didn't know you were here."

"Hey, Mom," he says, stiffly accepting her kiss on his cheek.

Round-tipped nose, sharp cheekbones, a full bottom lip just like Blue's. Tall and curvy, her hair is cropped low in a tapered bob. She has a deep brown complexion similar to my mother's.

"Hi, Salem," she says, extending her hand to me. "I watched your press conference." Her gaze dances between me and Blue. "I'm Liz."

"Hi, Liz," I reply, shaking her hand.

I've met a lot of famous people, but it's...different coming face-to-face with the anchorwoman who delivered the news to you and your family for your entire childhood.

Blue kneels in front of Anaïs, who's lying across the couch with a pillow between her legs. Her eyes have a delicate crescent-moon curve. They're foggy as she whispers, "I'm so sorry. I forgot."

"Why are you sorry, darling?" their mother asks. "And why didn't you call us to come over last night if you were sick?"

"It's okay," he replies softly to his sister. "How are you?"

"Woozy from the painkillers."

"I have breakfast coming for you." He kisses her forehead. "You want cinnamon tea?"

She nods and tries to sit up, but Blue tells her to rest.

"You just declined my offer to make tea," Liz replies.

The sudden feel of two torches being waved in my direction shifts my gaze to the green lasers beamed at me.

"Sir." I nod to Blue's dad, who's everywhere on TV these days.

He flashes a bright-white smile. "Hi, son."

"His name is Salem," Blue says with a sharpness that locks us all in place. He nods for me to come closer to him. "Meet my sister and best friend."

I cross the room and crouch to Anaïs's level. "Hi. I'm sorry you aren't feeling well."

She grins, and it's warm but kind of fragile, like it's costing her something. "Hi, Salem."

I release her hand and notice the blood-red lips with fangs and a black tongue tatted on the inside of her arm.

"You and I will be best friends too," she says, with a certainty that makes me smile. "Don't leave without giving me your number."

Blue scoffs, and she rolls her eyes. "Don't look at him. He doesn't like to share his friends."

We both laugh.

Their dad clears his throat. "Hey, can I talk to you for a second?" he asks Blue.

All the light drains from his face. "I'll be right back with your tea."

"I'm talking to you." His dad flies out of his seat to block Blue's path.

Blue jerks back. "No. And don't touch me."

"Son, hold on," his dad insists.

"Carter, stop," Anaïs pleads.

"Don't call me that," he snaps. "I'm your father."

"Don't talk to her like that," Blue growls back.

"I am your father, and you will refer to me—"

"Yo, you want him to go?" Blue asks Anaïs.

"Excuse me!" Carter scoffs.

"No, it's okay," she replies, a tremble in her voice.

"Arnaz." He moves like he's going to grasp Blue's arm, but Blue evades his reach before squaring up in his face.

"What did I just say?" The grit in Blue's voice has me moving to his side.

His mother beats me there. "Whoa," she says, trying to butt in between them. "Let's all take a breath."

The media overhypes their resemblance. Besides their eye color, tatted skin, and height, everything about Carter and Blue is different. There are the obvious differences like Carter's white skin and jet-black hair, but where Carter is big and broad, Blue is chiseled and slim.

On second thought, he may have his mom's downturned eyes, but the powerful rage and razor-sharp glare emanating from him are an exact replica of his father's.

"Hey," I place my hand on his back. "How about you and I go make that tea?"

"This doesn't concern you," Carter snipes at me.

"Don't talk to him," Blue sneers. "Don't even fucking look at him."

"It actually does, sir. I care about him, and he's upset."

"You care about him?" Carter repeats, glaring daggers at me. "This is *my* family."

"There aren't any cameras here," Blue scoffs. "You can knock off the good father act."

"You're such a big man now, huh? Can disrespect me—"

"Carter, stop." Anaïs moves to stand. With effort, she manages to straighten her back. But her eyes...

Whoa!

I dart across the room and catch her just as her knees buckle.

"Anaïs?" Liz races over. "What's wrong, honey?"

"I'm fine." Her hands anchor to my arm as she stands upright.

"Let's get you food." Blue transfers her to his arms and walks her toward her bedroom.

"I'm fine, really. I just need to lie down."

Carter, face stricken, moves in to help but freezes when Blue glares at him.

"Isn't there some tax write-off gala you're both missing?" he directs to his mother. "Can you just take your husband and go?"

"Now, that's enough," Carter snaps.

"No, Carter. Stop," Liz says, wrapping her arms around herself. "It's the least we deserve." She crosses the room and picks up her bag.

"We love you." Her voice is thick with emotion. "We only want to fix what we've broken. I don't know how to do that if you two won't let us in."

Anaïs's eyes well, but Blue's face is neutral, like Liz hadn't spoken.

"We'll leave." She raises her hands and backs off. "Please make sure she eats. We brought food. It's in the kitchen."

Carter stands there, between his wife and where his children huddle together. He opens his mouth, but the words are caught.

"Just go, man," Blue says.

Carter's face tightens like he's going to hold his ground, but his chest caves and he walks out.

"Come on," Blue says, helping Anaïs to her room.

A FEW MINUTES later he finds me in the kitchen, making Anaïs a plate.

"Are you okay?" I ask.

"I should probably hang with her until I gotta catch my bus."

I nod, then repeat, "Are you okay?"

"Yeah." He rubs his neck.

My stomach feels heavy from ingesting what felt like a lifetime of pain in a span of minutes, so it's hard for me to buy the indifference in his voice.

I step toward him and wrap him up in a tight hug.

His arms hang limp, waves of coldness wafting from him, until his body softens in my arms, and his chest trembles against mine.

It's gone in an instant as he pulls away.

"I should get back to her," he says, staring at my chest.

I nod and hand him the plate.

"I'll call you," he replies, taking it.

There's something in his voice that worsens the feeling in my stomach.

CHAPTER 22
ARNAZ

♫ **"Rigor Mortis"** ♫
Begins: fervent, buoyant, ached with pining.
Ends: bloated, rigid, ravaged with dying.

I flip up the collar of my coat as the icy rain licks my cheeks and pelts the brim of my fitted cap. Turning down a side street, I avoid the upcoming Main Street tourist trap. It's the third city since Brooklyn. I'm sure it has a name, but the number is what comes to me.

Three down, four more to go.

Last stop: San Francisco.

A sports bar spilling out with shivering smokers has me crossing the street. Keeping on until I hit the riverbank, I take a sharp left and descend a staircase. I blow on my hands as the wind lashes my back, propelling me along. Except for a woman in a plastic poncho and her dog, I don't see another soul for a quarter of a mile. Two zigzag turns and the crossing of a foot-bridge, my head raises and scans the area—unless you search for it, you'd never find it.

Slowly blinking into sight is the incandescent caduceus, settled in the inky, gauzy facade of a weathered stone building.

When I'm back home, I'll wonder if I imagined it, and that wonder will scratch at me until I return.

Sometimes I stare out of my bedroom window at the small birds perched on the cable lines. Every day, they reappear in the same spot, almost at the same time, and I'm further convinced I'm trapped in a simulation, and the wooly static of my brain runs on an entirely different operating system.

Almost everything in my life since my first breath has felt like it's running on a program, and I'm the glitch.

Not this bar, dark and out of sight.

A man aged enough to be my grandfather flicks a glance up when I enter. Our eyes exchange a quiet acknowledgment. Except for a couple in the corner, the place is as empty as I remember it.

"Toddy," I request as I reach for my wallet, peel off cash, and slide it over. Ignoring it, he gets to work on the drink.

The wooden floors and low-slung furniture creak from bearing decades of the troubled seeking a reprieve from the ills out there.

Or the ills within.

Ever since Brooklyn, I've been losing time.

Memory lapses.

Memory traveling.

Once or twice, you show your antenna's broken, people give you the benefit, but a third time?

The locker room falls silent when you enter, averted glances, breaths retracting from the stench of the two-legged disappointment.

I settle into the corner booth, facing the wall, and warm my hands over the tealight candle.

Always the same playlist: Nina, Coltrane, Ray.

Ms. Simone is right. It did rain today. All week, if we're being metaphorical.

Starting with game one after Brooklyn.

"Watch your mouth. I've been busting your ass for years," I reminded the cocky, trash-talking power forward after spectacularly embarrassing him.

Talking shit all game, I waited until the fourth when we were in isolation.

Catching the ball, I hit a slow dribble. He got low in anticipation of my next move. I lunged forward, making him jump back—an overreaction, food for the serpent in my belly. I followed with a hesitation dribble that had him trembling in wait. Then I finished him, hitting a sharp crossover dribble from right to left. The fool lunged left as I escaped, pushing back, crossing the ball behind my back, then powered to the wing. I set up for a quick release, drawing him in. With too much speed, he sailed past as I sidestepped left and fired the shot.

Bang!

I raced downcourt, laughing my ass off with Sid, when a blur in the crowd had me screeching to a halt. The build of a retired NFL tight end, ink-black hair, neck tats, cold glare. I wasn't only frozen, I was sweating bullets, and on each rapid blink, corners of the arena chipped away until I was back in my high school gym...

Carter had looked like he'd had a few drinks. It had been hard to tell from the court, but his knees had appeared to be wobbling. I'd frozen as he'd walked toward me. Was he so drunk that he'd walk directly onto the court mid-game? Why was he there? He'd never come to a game before. I couldn't breathe. A whistle had blared in my ear, and I'd stumbled back, each step feeding power into my legs until I'd booked it.

Coach and my teammates had yelled for me.

I'd run.

I'd reached the school basement, wedged open the closet, and crashed into the dark, shutting the door behind me. I'd tripped over a bucket, stayed down, and folded myself into the corner. Weak tears had streamed down my face as I'd gasped for air.

The cringey part is that I'd later learned it wasn't even him that day in the gym. When I'd finally crawled home way after curfew, bracing for the worst, Anaïs had told me that he and our mom had left town that morning on a media trip.

AFTER ALL THESE YEARS, I saw his ghost today on the court and froze. Again.

I must have looked like I was about to piss my pants because when I finally snapped out of it, everyone was staring at me. Thousands of lashing eyes.

My drink appears in front of me. "Thanks."

The man returns with pretzels. "You're always so blue when you come here."

"Blue?"

He nods.

I shrug. "Didn't know you did that."

"What's that?" he asks, tossing a bar towel over his shoulder.

"Talk."

He laughs, deep and rich. "I try hard not to."

He walks away.

Words to live by.

I raise the mug, and my hand stills as my phone lights up.

That's Salem's third call this week.

Take the out, man.

I'm not an expert at dating, but I'm pretty sure a crash course intro to the most dysfunctional family is the red flag you need to run free.

I resist the urge to cradle my head in my hands.

Speaking of outs, Sid saved my ass this week.

And how did I repay him? By damn near barking at him to back off when he tried to check in with me. No one knows about the shit Anaïs and I went through growing up, and I mean to keep it that way. Or meant to. But now Salem's gotten a glimpse, and it's been messing me up all week. Forget the foot pressed against my chest since that day. I keep thinking about climbing back into the closet in high school and staying there until...

Just until.

Still. Sid saved my ass, and I bit his head off.

During our post-game conference in Philly, a reporter asked what I thought about a call in the third quarter. The foul was against me. I apparently shoved a player into the stands. I had no idea what she was talking about. It happened again in Indiana when a reporter asked about another scrap between me and their point guard. I leaned in and said, "Nah. That was last game."

Sid laughed, instantly relaxing the sideways glances around the room, and said, "That's Arnaz's way of saying, no comment."

Confused, I took the out.

We swept all three games, so I could give two fucks about reporters, but I should definitely buy Sid a car or something.

One of these days, he's gonna get tired of myself. *I'm* tired of me. It's not like I'm doing it on purpose.

But, fuck, it *looks* like I'm doing it on purpose.

In Philly, I missed a critical wide-open pass. The moment it happened, I could see myself standing there, melting like a snowman. I raised my chin and took it when Coach laid into me.

I respect him, and I deserved it.

I'm so tired. My brain's turning into a super host rivaling my mother's galas. Sending invites to the uninvited, rolling out porcelain china, importing flower arrangements from Ikebana Grand Masters, and serving a twelve-course tasting menu. Mr. Anxious-For-No-Fucking-Reason having a rough time sleeping? No worries. We'll wake Arnaz up at two o'clock in the morning to accompany you. Since he's up, we'll have him carry a spine-caving load of emptiness.

Still, the feeling that I'm being backed into the corner by some looming, invisible monster has haunted me since Brooklyn.

There's a lot about that day I can't look at directly.

Including how good it felt to wake up in Salem's arms.

CHAPTER 23
ARNAZ

♫ "Exhumation" ♫
They found the note I carried to my grave:
These gangly bones bore unspeakable pain.
And the heart broke the day it was made.

Morale is low as we touch down in San Francisco for tomorrow's game.

When we're wrapping up dinner in the ballroom reserved for our team, I man up. I know I'm not the only reason for our two-game losing streak, but my spacing out hasn't helped.

"Ay," I say, getting everyone's attention as I rise from my chair. "My fault, y'all. I know I've been off since Brooklyn. I've been tryin' hard to get it back, but it's been a struggle. I'll be better going forward. I just need rest—"

"Nah, what you need is a boys' night out," Nick interrupts.

"Aww, man, don't ruin the surprise," Wes whines.

"What surprise?" I look at Sid. He winks and nods for Nick to continue.

"We know something's going on with you. And we have your back."

"So, tuck it in. We roll out in an hour," Sid finishes.

MY LIPS ARC IN A GRIN. "This is where we're going?"

"Let's get you laid!" Wes crows, pushing me into the Castro Bar.

Hell yeah. After dinner, I went back to the room to shower and change. Feeling it could go either way tonight, I prepped just in case.

"Wait." I stand in place. "This is a queer bar. A safe space for queer people. Men might hit on you. If it'll make you uncomfortable, then you shouldn't go in."

"Why're you acting like this is our first time?" Johan replies. "We're all good."

My shoulders drop. He's right. The guys organized a celebratory night out for me after I came out. It took me a while to let my guard down and accept they were really cool with me. When I did, it was one of the most fun nights of my life.

"Cool. Let's go."

All heads turn our way when we enter. One guy smacks the arm of the guy next to him as his eyes bulge at the sight of Sid.

Yeah...he's about to get eaten alive.

"My bad, man. I've been an asshole lately," I yell to Sid over the music.

"Yeah. You have." He slings his arm around my neck and pats my chest. "You know you can tell me anything, right?"

I nod.

"Let's get you loose." He maneuvers us toward the bar.

CHAPTER 24
SALEM

"Dude, are you listening?"

"What?" I ask.

Zyair arches his eyebrow. "Since you've been back, we've been unstoppable."

"Uh. Thanks," I reply, palming the glass the bartender slides my way.

They're riding high after we clinched a dub against the Bay Area Hawks.

"What's up?" he asks.

"Nothing. Just tired."

And confused by Blue's distance. Again. I keep feeling like I'm missing something with him—like maybe patience isn't enough.

"Look at this shit," Cillian cuts in, sliding his phone between us and hitting play.

A video of Nick shaking his ass fills the screen.

"Yo!" Zyair cackles. "Yo boi's turnt."

"He sent you this?" I ask, watching Ussef, who's squatted low, riding the air like he's competing with the guy in a jockstrap gyrating on the platform behind him.

"He wants us to come through."

"This is live?"

"I mean, kinda. They're not too far from here."

"Card, please," I call to the bartender as I jump to my feet.

"We rollin'?" Cillian asks.

"Yeah."

"Y'all know the bus leaves for Sacramento in like two hours," Zy reminds us.

"Cover for us," Cillian tosses back as I sign the check and pocket my card. "If we're not there, let Coach know we'll take a separate car and meet up with y'all."

Arnaz

My skin prickles as the energy shifts to my right, probably Sid again getting more thirst than the naked dudes on the stage.

I'm not prepared for the way the goth-nerd in my lap switches up when the beat drops, but his slow grind is kicking up the need to get off tonight.

I dip to keep up as the dude bends in half, the top of his head almost touching the floor. Strong hands anchor to my waist, and the scent of vanilla-mint fills my nostrils. "Hey, Blue."

Fuuuck.

My head whips around.

"H-how?" My voice catches, and my heart is pounding hard.

"Thought we deserved a last dance." He nibbles on my ear, heating my blood. "Pardon us," he says over my shoulder to the guy now dancing by himself.

Last dance?

My eyes roll closed from the brush of his lips against my neck as the thrust of his hips sends mine rocking forward and back.

He's done with me.

I don't blame him, but still...

My hands squeeze the arms he's wrapped around my waist as my head turns and catches his lips.

Heat builds with each rotation of our hips, his fingers snaking under my shirt to ghost along my stomach.

My feet leave the floor as I suck on his tongue.

Last dance?

His eyes tear open at the loss of my lips when I pull back.

"Let's go," I rasp.

I search for Sid and signal to him that I'm out.

His gaze pings between Salem and me, then he grins.

Salem

I've barely crossed the threshold of the bar into the night air when I'm pressed against the wall, and Blue's gorgeous face closes in on me.

I open for him, and he feasts on my tongue.

Whistles from the group entering the bar don't break the spell or stop his hand from gliding over my erection.

How can he want me this badly but be so distant?

I want answers, but not here.

I break our kiss. "I'm getting us a car."

He stares at my lips, pupils blown.

I order an Uber, and after what feels like an inconceivably long four-minute wait, the car pulls up to the curb.

As soon as the car door closes, he's on me.

"I'm going to miss these lips," I rasp.

His hands wrap around my throat as his teeth scrape against my chin.

"Got lube and condoms?" I ask, praying we don't need to make a pit stop.

He nods, then his mouth latches onto my neck.

BEFORE THE HOTEL room door closes, he's on his knees tugging on my zipper and then pulling me out.

The vibration of his moans mixed with the laving of his tongue over my piercings... *Goddamn.*

"Hey, wait," I murmur as my head falls back when his lips slide down my dick. "Blue."

He stills, staring up at me.

My thumb sweeps across his lips.

God, couldn't you have made him less gorgeous?

I can't resist stroking myself and spreading my pre-cum across his wet lips before I bend down and our tongues tangle, trying to lick it off.

I push forward, forcing him onto his back, and unbuckle his pants.

"Where're the lube and condoms?" I ask.

There'll be time for answers later.

He motions to his bag on the chair next to the bed.

I spring to my feet and rifle through it until I find them.

He's peeling off his briefs when I return.

I quickly strip, then lean down, my face upside down from his, and latch our mouths together.

Head tilted back, he murmurs something like a plea as he spreads his legs.

I shift down and wrap my arms under his thighs.

I hiss when his mouth starts to suckle the head of my cock.

Licking up the pre-cum spilling across his belly, my tongue moves down his balls to his taint.

I groan, biting my lip as he takes me to the back of his throat. His dick presses into my skin as his back lifts when the tip of my tongue massages his rim.

"Ngh," he moans as I knead the globes of his ass, spreading his cheeks, salivating at the pucker of skin, darker than the rest of his body.

Chin massaging his taint, I spit on his hole and lick it across his rim.

The feel of his hot, wet mouth around my dick sends pleasure skittering up my spine and has my stomach clenching as the first wave of my orgasm pulses through me.

The intensity of his shudder as my tongue tickles his rim makes me pull back.

Mmm, even this lightly, he feels it deeply. *Amazing.*

Tilting my head sideways, I extend my tongue and slowly

start to sink in. I get just the tip in, and his sweaty fingers dig into the back of my calves.

I flick the tip back and forth, relishing his "Ngh, fuuuck" and breathy pants.

I see white as his throat massages my head while his tongue tortures the skin around my piercings, a delicious mix of pleasure and pain.

"Pull off," I husk as a second wave hits, and I stiffen, grunting against his rim.

He gurgles as I slide out of his throat.

I clamp down on my lip as he tongues my slit.

"Mmh," I grunt. "You're gonna make me come."

And fuck me, he chokes as I hit the back of his throat again.

My fists dig into the floor to stop myself from fucking his throat until it's filled with my cum.

Grabbing the lube, I squeeze some on my fingers, then caress his rim before sinking one inside. I slam my eyes shut as his moan sends a ripple of heat up my cock. After I allow him a few breaths to adjust, I gently flick my finger back and forth.

His dick leaks against my stomach as I add a second digit and curve up.

He hisses when I can't hold back from running my tongue across the stretch of skin spread open as I stretch him.

He slips his hand between us to fist his dick.

He warbles something that sounds like "Fuck me" around my cock.

I keep going, opening him with my tongue and fingers as his fist drums against my stomach while he jerks his cock.

Needing inside him before he blows, I spit on his hole and finger it inside him before grabbing a condom and ripping it open with my teeth. When I reach down to roll it on, he takes over with his mouth.

A third wave of pleasure hits, shooting from my scalp down to my toes. "Ngh...stop," I warn.

He listens this time, using his hands instead. I push up to my knees and slather the condom with lube.

A warm breath blows over my crease. "Can I taste you?" he asks.

I look at his flushed lips waiting at my entrance and nod.

I squeeze the base of my dick as he licks a warm, wet stripe across my rim.

Christ, that tongue.

My head falls back as he rubs his lips back and forth, the friction and the heat ripping a curse from my chest.

And those fucking sounds he's making...

"Baby," I rasp.

He stiffens and then his fingers dig into my thighs—the only warning before his tongue is pushing in, swirling around, stretching me.

My fist tightens around my base as the pressure builds between my thighs.

"Wait." I thrust my hips forward, separating from his tongue. I take a steadying breath before I turn around and cover him with my body. He falls onto his back as I slot between his legs.

His pupils are blown.

Teasing my head across his rim, I lean down and kiss his lips.

"Fuck me," he begs, writhing underneath me.

"No," I whisper as I start to push in, and his tatted fingers dig into the carpet. "I've waited too long to 'fuck' you."

His lips part with a gasp as I sink into the tightest grip of muscle I've ever felt in my life.

Holy fuck.

"You...okay?"

His head bobs as he huffs out a breath.

His thighs tremble as he bears down around me.

"Hold on." I slide my arm under his back, tilting his pelvis up, and push in until I fully seat myself inside him.

A sound between a wheeze and a gasp spills from his lips. My teeth graze his chin before sucking on his neck, and his body quakes. I glide my hips.

"Salem," he moans, ruining my name for anyone else.

It has to be a kind of delirium to want someone as badly as I want him. *All* of him.

I lean forward, whispering in his ear, "You run and still end up in my arms." I thrust my hips. "Why do you think—Mm, fuck, you're choking me. Why do you think that is? Hmm? Look at me."

I tilt my pelvis and snap my hips. His eyes shoot open, and I kiss him as he cries out.

What I'd give to hear him cry out my name every day for the rest of my life.

The thought aches.

I fight the next wave thrumming up the inside and back of my thighs, and the one after that, swimming in his curved lashes and glazed eyes that flash wide and then shutter closed with every drive and pull of my hips.

I thrust harder.

He continues to ruin my name for every future lover.

My jaw clenches at the thought.

In every future I imagine, I only see him.

"Over five years," I whisper against his lips, "I've dreamt of you."

I tunnel deeper, memorizing the velvet squeeze of him.

Of boring days with you, gasps, moans, and cries in the middle of the night, and again in the morning.

"Why do you run?" I ask as I pull out to the tip and then thunder back in.

"Fuck!" he chokes out as his fingers dig into my back.

"S'okay." I grunt. "You run and still end up on my dick."

"Ngh." He spasms around me.

"So run, Blue." I squeeze my hand around his thick cock and stroke.

His abs contract, thighs press against my obliques, and his chin tilts up as the first shot of his cum hits my stomach. He convulses under me, crying out against my lips.

When the next wave crests, I let go, shuddering inside him.

CHAPTER 25
ARNAZ

My breath pounds against my ribs as I sink through the floor.

"Are you okay?" His voice cracks as he pulls out and kisses the inside of my thigh.

I suck in a breath.

For the first time in weeks, I feel inside of my body.

He removes the condom and ties it before tossing it in the wastebasket.

I groan.

His gaze shoots to me. "It hurts?"

"No." I swallow.

I just imagined what that dick down would have felt like raw.

Terrifying.

I barely survived tonight.

Fuck my life. I know what Salem The Silencer feels like inside me.

If the nighttime internet stalking was bad before...

But it felt like he was letting go.

"Hey—" I start, but he cuts me off.

"Should I stop holding out for you?"

A hoarse "No" is trapped in my chest as I shoot to sit up.

He was *letting go.*

But that was the first time I let someone make love to me.

At least, I think that's what that was.

I always thought when it happened, it'd feel just like that—like getting off wasn't the goal.

"Is it just sex for you?" he asks. "Is that why you disappear after?"

What? "You were there. You saw what I saw."

His brows draw together. "There, where?"

"At my sister's. With my family."

"I'm not following." He shifts closer. "Why would what I saw make you disappear?"

"Why would it make you stay?" It's out before I can mask it with something less direct.

"You and your family are going through a rough patch. Why—"

"No." I shake my head. "It's not a rough patch. It's been that way my whole life."

"What?"

I look away, drawing in a deep breath. "Carter was always Carter, but he got worse when he got injured and was forced into retirement."

"Worse, how? Did he hit you?"

I stand, grabbing my tee and briefs, and put them on. "That would have been too direct for him." I cross the room and stare out the window. "Mind games, mood swings, and insults were his weapons of choice." I shrug. "He drank a lot and reminded me I was a piece of shit every chance he got."

"Christ. What about your mom?"

"What about her?"

"She couldn't stop him? Take you away from him?"

"She didn't. She was checked out. Threw herself into work.

They fought a lot. She worked hard to keep up appearances—at least to keep us together in the public eye."

"That's messed up."

"That's fame."

"That's bullshit." His voice gets closer. "I'm so sorry."

I lean my head against his shoulder.

"But I need to understand." He kisses my temple. "Why would you think I would want you to disappear on me?"

"It went from you asking me over to hook up, to us sleeping at my sister's, then being stuck in the middle of our bullshit. That's...a lot."

"So?"

I turn my head and glare at him. "So?"

"Who said I can't handle a lot?"

I pull out of his arms. "Why would you want to?"

"You know why. Have I not been clear?"

I step back.

There it is again...risen chest, iron back, pledge of quiet sacrifice.

"How do you do it? How do you walk this earth so sure the ground won't cave in?" I don't wait for an answer. "I'm cold. I'm gonna take a shower."

"Hold on."

I'm already walking away.

"I said, hold on." His arm wraps around my waist. "I will fuck you all night if it means breaking through so you can hear this. I want you. *All* of you. I will keep the ground from caving in for both of us if you let me."

"You can't."

"I will give my last breath trying."

"No. I don't want that."

"Baby."

My body trembles, knees threatening to collapse at *that* word coated in his earnest voice.

"If there's anything you fear, it's not the ground..." He rubs the goose bumps on my arms. "It's your walls you're afraid of losing."

He doesn't know that.

He can't.

"I'm a grown man," he says, releasing me. "I don't need you to make decisions for me. If you run, do it because *you* need to."

I hear the clank of his belt buckle, and I swear I feel the floor quake under my feet.

"Don't go," I whisper, turning around to face him.

He pauses with one arm through his shirt. "You sure?"

"You can shower first." I gesture to my bag. "Borrow something."

His shoulders lower. "It's okay. You go first. I need to text my GM that I'll meet the team in Sacramento in the morning."

I WANT to believe it's no big deal, telling him about my family, but after trying to scrub the feeling off, it still feels like someone's stolen my skin.

I reach into my bag for a sweatshirt to throw over my tee.

After he showers, he climbs into bed next to me, wearing my T-shirt and shorts.

"You know, pain is nothing to be ashamed of."

"What?" I ask.

"I have an older brother, and he has a lot of pain. He tries to keep it from us, like it's an infectious virus."

I didn't know he has a brother. And the level of internet stalking I've done should get me on a short list for the CIA.

"What happened to him?"

"He was in the Marines."

"Oh. Are you close?"

"Close in the only way he knows how to be. I'll never stop trying, though."

"Yeah, sounds like you."

CHAPTER 26
SALEM

"My brother and I have matching tats," I tell him, lifting my T-shirt and showing him the black spider.

"'Fate bends to courage.'" He reads the inscription. "Are those droplets of blood?"

"Yeah."

He smiles. "Is your brother's in the same spot?"

"Mmhmm. When he got back from his first tour, we had plans to visit his favorite restaurants, catch games, and take a road trip." I lower my shirt. "Looking back, I think we were trying to fit both the years he'd lost and the years still to be lost into the span of a few weeks. And the whole time, I could feel he wasn't into it, you know? It's like our life didn't fit him anymore, and he seemed as lost by that as I did."

"Mmh." He hums low, chewing on the inside of his lip. "What was he like?"

"Quiet and serious. He's like that even now, which is weird 'cause I'd always been the serious one. It flipped, where even stories he'd tell me about his squad mates that were supposed to be funny were delivered with a kind of dead tone."

"He was depressed?" He curls a leg in and turns toward me.

"Maybe. I mean, yes. Though maybe the beginning of it back then? There were so many changes, it's hard to isolate."

"Like what?"

I blow out a breath. "Names of people I'd never heard of and would probably never meet, his vocabulary, the way he wore his clothes, and walked. He ran on way less sleep, couldn't even sit with his back to a door, and he scanned every joint we were in." I shake my head. "That's why we got this." I pat my tattoo. "I needed something to stay the same between us."

"I get that. Every tat I get makes my skin feel more like mine."

"Yeah, exactly. I thought maybe our skin could keep some part of us the same since everything inside us had changed."

"*Us* or *him*?"

"Hm?"

"It sounds like he was the one doing the changing."

I nod. "It kinda changed me, too, though. My parents too—day after day, year after year, praying for his survival."

He rubs my forearm. "Is he still in the service?"

"No."

At least not physically.

"He lives with me when he's not, uh, traveling."

Another call this morning, another voicemail.

I've crossed over from annoyed into full unease. My parents too.

Where the hell is he?

I WAKE on my side with a pillow in front of my chest and check my watch for the time.

If I don't get in a car soon, I won't hear the end of it from my

GM and coach. I lift the pillow slightly and inhale with my nose buried in Blue's curls.

I lean back. As soon as I start to move, gently untangling the arm stretched above his head, he flinches awake.

"It's just me," I whisper.

Pillow lifted, he blows out a breath and then buries his face against my chest.

I grin and kiss his hair. "I gotta go."

"Un-unh," he grunts, returning the pillow over his head. "Finish what you started."

"Huh?"

"You took your shirt off in the night because you were hot."

"So?"

He grabs my palm and wraps it around his erection. "Finish what you started."

I grin and reach for a condom and lube. "You gonna show your face?"

"Sun."

Vampire.

"You're not too sore?"

Turning, he tugs on the waistband of his briefs, pulls it down, and kicks the material away. "Get to work, Jones."

He shivers as the backs of my fingers sweep the hollow of his spine down to the swell of his ass, to his sculpted thigh dusted with hair.

Yeah, I'm gonna be late.

Lifting his thigh, I drizzle some lube on my fingers and then massage his rim.

He sucks in a breath as my finger slowly presses in.

I'm leaking by the time he's open, and I'm sheathing myself with a condom.

"You ready?" I ask, lining up against his rim.

"Yeah," he murmurs.

I grunt as I push inch by inch through his tight ring of muscle, watching my dick disappear inside him and listening to his muffled moan under the pillow.

I throw the comforter over us, so we're cocooned in darkness, and lift his pillow slightly to reach his ear. My voice still scratchy from sleep, I whisper, "I wish this ass were mine."

He shivers as I pull out to the tip and glide back in.

"Wish I could sink into it every morning..." My hand threads through his death grip on the sheet. "Wake you up with my tongue..." I nip the back of his neck as he pants into the mattress. "It's so good, Blue." I snap my hips. "Fuck, I wanna go slow, but I gotta go to work—"

"No," he begs, hooking his arm behind me, clutching my ass and grinding on my dick.

"I know, baby." I kiss his cheek. "I wanna stay inside you all day."

I angle to reach deeper and soak up his deep grunts on every drive.

I nip his ear. "Mmm. I can't wait to come inside you for the first time."

"Ungh, fuck, 'm close," he rasps, even though neither of us has touched his dick.

"Fuck. You want to be bred? You want to wake up on my dick every morning?"

"Salem," he whimpers.

"Moaning in our bed while I fuck you until you pass back out?"

His body tenses.

"And I empty all of my cum into this tight"—I spit on my fingers and then massage his nipples—"hole that's all mine? You want that, don't you?"

"Fuuck." His teeth sink into the side of my palm, and he clenches down so hard on my dick my balls draw up and I erupt as he shudders through his release. My hand flies to his dick to finish him off as I rock inside him with shallow thrusts, chasing his full-body shivers and his quiet moans.

He groans when I eventually pull out and fall to my back to catch my breath, peeling back the comforter to breathe.

I grin when, after a few minutes of us both panting, he mumbles, "Well done," under the pillow.

He trembles when I part his cheeks and lean in to inspect his rim for any tears.

"I'll be back."

I disappear into the bathroom, lose the condom, and return with a warm cloth.

He flinches as I gently pass the washcloth over his rim. "What are you doing?" He lifts the pillow, cracking one eye open.

"What do you mean?"

He looks pointedly at the cloth.

It takes me a second to realize what he's asking. I did this for Lucien all the time. "Have your partners never done this for you?"

"No."

My head snaps back. "Who have you been fucking?"

His eyes narrow. "You actually want me to answer that?"

"No," I rush out. "Lie back down."

He looks at me, and then at the cloth again, to see if I'm serious.

"Blue, if I'm inside you, I'm taking care of you after. Lie down."

Despite the deep forehead crease, he draws in a breath and sinks back down to the mattress.

I resume gently passing the cloth over his rim. When he tenses, I rub his lower back until he relaxes and then inspect him one more time.

He yelps as I place a parting bite on that perfect ass.

"I need to shower really quick, then head out. Do you need anything first?"

He returns the pillow and comforter over his head. "Call out."

I laugh as I push back to my feet. "I'll miss you too."

REAL TALK SPORTS WITH DARIUS & TODD

"He clearly doesn't respect the Royals." Darius crosses his arms. "Or the press."

"It's not as if he's the only player who hates the press," Todd rebuts.

"I heard rumors that he's..." Darius thumbs his nose.

Todd's head tilts to the side. "What's that supposed to mean?"

"C'mon on, man, don't make me say it."

"You're gonna have to, 'cause your miming is worse than your vision."

"Nah." He zips his lips.

"Well, well. The great Darius Williams scared?"

"I'm smart. I tell the truth on here, and I'm wrapped up in bogus defamation charges for thirty-six months."

"Fantastic. Be sure to add litigaphobia to your dating profile," Todd says, then turns to someone off camera and yells, "You know what the hell that meant?"

His eyes widen as he turns back to Darius. "Snow, crank, or smack?"

Darius shrugs. "Three for three? There's only one R word to describe his future, and it isn't Royals."

"Rehab." Todd strokes his chin. "Christ."

CHAPTER 27
ARNAZ

My palm's sweaty as it hovers over my phone.

Just do it.

I hit twenty-seven points tonight, helped clutch a dub, yet getting up the nerve to hit the call button has me sweating.

Who calls anyone anymore?

My finger plummets, taking my stomach along with it.

"Hey!" Salem answers on the second ring.

"Hey. You, uh, picked up."

"Of course I picked up."

"Bad time?"

"Nah. Never. Hold on one sec." He sounds like he's smiling. "How are you?" The music in the background fades.

"Yeah, I'm good. Is it cool that I called?"

"I mean, I've been waiting over five years for a call like this, so it's *cool* or whatever."

My mouth twists, wrestling the over-the-top bubble in my throat.

"How was your day? You, uh, had off, right?"

"Yep. It was chill. Took Simba to a dog park. Ran errands. Now I'm working on this month's bake-off challenge. Wanna see?"

"Uh"—I look down at my bare chest and light-gray sweats—"sure."

A FaceTime call comes in, and I hit accept. "Whoa. There's a bird sleeping on your cake?"

He chuckles. "The bird *is* the cake. Well, the nest and branch are also cake. It's all cake."

I scoff at the red beak and legs, jet-black neck, and indigo-blue feathers leading to a black-and-white striped tail. "I'm definitely staring at an exotic bird."

"A-ha. If you bought it, that bodes well for me. I need to crush Dad."

I laugh.

"It's inspired by the Formosan blue magpie. I don't know. I was about to dump it and restart. He beat me last month." He blows out a breath. "I need to bring it this month."

"If the challenge is to create a realistic-looking bird out of cake, I can't see anything topping this."

The camera flips around. "You know complimenting my baking isn't gonna help last time being our last time."

"That wasn't our last time," I tell him, then ask, "You dress like that when you bake?"

"Like what?"

I shake my head as my palm glides over my mouth. *Who bakes in silk PJs?* No, not PJs. I get catalogs with luxe loungewear shit like this.

I scoff. "You make no sense."

His eyebrows bunch, then lift. "I think in Blue speak that means 'you look hot. So hot, I think I'm gonna marry you.'"

"Blue speak?"

"Yeah. Sid gave me a primer. I'm competitive, though. I intend to be proficient in no time. No one will speak Blue better than me. Well, maybe your sister."

"You're not allowed to talk to Sid. Or my sister. And ignore her if she DMs you."

"Hater. You can't keep besties apart. She likes *Exosphere*?"

I grin. "Obsessed."

"Bam! Got my new watch buddy."

"You can't like my sister or Sid more than me." I know it sounds...whatever, but I blurt it out anyway.

He snickers.

Asshole.

He stops tweezing some shit on the cake and looks at the phone. "I could never like anyone the way I like you."

I try to minimize the self-view because the soft-boy face I'm making is bleh.

"What flavor's the cake?"

"Earl Grey sponge, lemon-coconut curd, and honey Swiss meringue buttercream."

"How are you single?" Apparently my filter has fucked off for the night.

He grins. "I got a date in a couple hours."

"Fuck you."

He bites his bottom lip. "Tilt the camera down—let me see what you're wearing."

I pick it up and angle it.

That shouldn't be visible from up here.

"Shut up." I groan, adjusting myself as soon as I see his dumb smile. "Cake makes me hard."

"Uh-huh." He picks up a can and mists the base of the cake with a muted gold dust. "And *I* make no sense? Seven seconds left to halftime, double-teamed by Boris and Allen, Nick wide open. What'd you do?"

"Launched that bitch."

"From the logo at mid court. Then turned your back and raced down court while it was still twenty feet from the rim."

I move to my couch and kick up my feet. "I knew it was clean."

"Tuff."

I nod at his look of awe. Mostly cause I've never known where to put genuine compliments.

I didn't think anything could top the sexiness of The Silencer until now. Lines of concentration, delicate touch carving grooves into the bird to create feathers.

Baker Salem. Nah, that doesn't sound right.

Baker Bae is hands down the hottest guy I've ever seen.

A FEW DAYS LATER, I muster the courage again and shoot him a text.

> Me
>
> Next Tuesday? You have a break.

I paste the link to the rental cabin and then hit send.

Stowing my phone on my shelf, I'm halfway to the weight room when I turn back for my gloves and see my phone lit up.

> Salem
>
> Hell yes

CHAPTER 28
SALEM

"Hey, if you're not gonna pick up, you could at least text me back so I know you're alive. Come on, Denzel—Shit." I turn sharply, almost missing the dirt road I've been looking for.

The windows of my car are ingested into a dense stretch of towering trees as I end the call. A few minutes later, GPS tells me I've arrived.

The "secluded mid-century cabin with private riverfront" listing description wasn't an exaggeration. Looks like nothing but forest and river for—I scan the listing—eight-and-a-half acres.

Pocketing my phone, I slip out of the rental and blow on my hands as I peer up at the two-story, A-frame cabin with a slightly menacing façade and large, inviting glass doors and rectangular windows.

Unlit string lights hang across the expansive deck.

If Blue were a cabin...

I unload the bags and follow the lockbox instructions to retrieve the key.

Placing my bags down inside the door, I peel off my shoes and search for the thermostat. A suspended, bright-red fireplace with a cone-shaped head and a tulip-style bottom steals my attention. Moving closer, I tilt my head for a full view of the interior. A wooden block hangs from a metal chain on the exterior with an inscription that reads: *Original 1970s fireplace. A little wood goes a long way. Enjoy!*

Stepping back, I snap a picture of it, then grab wood and kindling from the log rack to get a fire going.

I turn and sweep my gaze over the space. Bracketed between two camel-colored leather couches, I stare up at the bohemian wall hangings. I spot a projector up there, and I turn to see a retracted screen hanging from the ceiling directly across from it.

I pad over to the wall of windows to take in the dense forest and grin. Of course someone wild like Blue would choose a place like this to disappear.

I continue checking the place out, pausing to peel a vinyl out of its sleeve, dust off the record, slide it on the player, and lower the needle.

A distorted rustle leads to a crisp flow of piano emanating from the speakers.

Fighting the pull toward the kitchen, I'm headed upstairs to the open second level when my phone vibrates.

"Hey, Ma."

"Sorry I missed your call. Did you make it in alright?"

"Yes. Just now."

"Is Arnaz there?"

"Not yet."

"You feel safe?"

"Yep."

The bedroom's cozy with a king-sized bed in the center, two mid-century modern-looking nightstands, and a dark blue rug. Natural light fills the entire space.

I like all the light. Blue might hate it, though.

"Have you heard from Denzel?" I ask her.

"No, have you? We're both worried sick."

I'm getting there too.

I peek into the bathroom. A large whirlpool tub is situated in front of a window, providing a sick view of the treetops and sky.

"If we don't hear from him in the next few days, what should we do?"

"I'll hire someone to find him," I answer as I head back downstairs.

"Someone like whom?"

"A private investigator."

"What if he's back in the hospital, Salem?"

"We'll find him."

"What if he's worse off than before?" she frets.

"W-we'll find him." I wince as my voice shakes.

She won't miss it.

"I'm sorry, son. I don't want to ruin your night. Did you dress up?"

I grab the grocery bags from the front door and head to the kitchen. "Like how?"

"A dinner jacket. I suppose a tie's too much."

I snicker as I duck plants and stainless-steel pots hanging from an overhead rack and place the bags on the counter.

"We're at a cabin in the middle of nowhere." I open the vintage-style fridge to find it empty except for a few bottles of water.

"Okay. Well, let me leave you to it. Tell him we say hello."

I grin, imagining Blue meeting my mom. He'd probably hiss like a vampire in the sun as she went in for a hug.

"Love you."

After we hang up, I fill the fridge with lagers and open a bottle of red to breathe. Then I wash my hands and get to work on dinner.

Arnaz

An article on acoustics claims that when trees are thirsty, they let off silent screams. Vibrations flow from the trunk, the way our vocal cords vibrate for sound. I kneel and rub my fingers through the damp earth. This place definitely has a vibration. I fight the urge to toss my head back and howl just to hear my voice echo through the trees.

Movement on my right catches my eye.

A doe with ears perked watches me as she lazes with fawns by the river.

I wink at her.

The faint sound of music has my own ears perking. I grab my bags and make my way inside. The handle turns like his text said it would.

Soulful music, a peppery aroma, and an open flying saucer floating above a blazing fire in the middle of the room hit my senses all at once.

I drop my bags, climb out my kicks, and step deeper inside.

I whistle at the full view of the trees.

Who would ever move from here? We're too early for snow, but damn, it has to be stunning.

And then suddenly I feel him, more stoic than the ancient trunks before me. I breathe with the spastic thumping in my chest. Turning, he's there, leaning against the wall, basking in a honeyed glow from the setting sun, and watching me. For a second, neither of us moves, and a thrill feathers up my spine.

My coat hits the floor as he pushes off the wall, and we storm toward each other. As soon as our lips crush together, I breathe a sigh of relief.

Thank god he said yes to tonight.

I back him toward the couch.

"Hol' on," he breathes against my lips.

"Uh-uh," I grunt as our tongues compete, and he presses me closer to his body.

"Wait," he croaks, spinning us around so my back hits the couch before he straddles me.

I reach for his zipper. "I'm still keyed up from the game."

His tongue traces my collarbone.

I flip him to his back. "Means you gotta work me out."

His eyes widen at the surprise show of force. "Yeah?"

"Ye—" My breath is trapped as I'm snapped into a headlock. "F-ucker."

I grasp his forearm and tuck my chin to keep it from sinking in as he tightens his hold. I twist to the side and plant my feet before rocking sideways and crashing into his hips.

He barely budges, but it's enough momentum to push his elbow upward so I can duck until I'm free.

"Word?" I shuffle back.

"What, you got—"

I clasp his legs and yank hard. His back hits the rug with a thump. I drag his ass as he scrambles for an anchor, the rug easing the glide across the floor.

"You're dead," he threatens, a glint of amusement in his eyes.

I snort as he kicks, trying to break my hold. Crunching his obliques, he dips sideways and locks onto my wrists.

Shit!

With a rotation of his torso, he pulls my wrists across his body, and I'm yanked forward. Tucking my neck, expecting a guillotine choke, I'm caught off guard when his hips slide to the side, and my chest smacks the floor. I buck hard, but he's too fast. My wrists are pinned, and his knee hits the middle of my shoulder blades.

"Fuckface!" I snarl, tugging on my legs for strength.

I'm gripped by my collar like a fucking puppy and hauled to my feet, my cheek hitting the window.

"I swear to God, as soon—"

"Shh," he croons, cutting me off, then kissing my ear. Pinning one arm tight behind my back, his free arm reaches around and unbuckles my belt. "Thought you wanted to get worked out."

"Fuck you," I seethe as I'm stripped of my jeans and briefs.

"Plan to," he rasps, fondling my erection. He lifts his palm to my mouth. "Spit."

"No," I sneer, even though the husky command has me pushing back against his erection pressed into my back.

"Cool." He peppers a kiss along the back of my sweaty neck as he thumbs my slit. "You're wet enough."

"Wait."

He stops and raises his palm again, and I spit on it.

"Good boy."

The praise turns my knees weak, but I steel myself by trying to headbutt him, but he has me pinned so tightly, my head barely moves.

He fists my dick and strokes. I clench my jaw shut to stifle the moan, but the pleasure from the strain of my arm twisted behind my back breaks through, dragging a raw sound from deep in my throat.

His breath whispers against my ear. "Did you think about me during your game?"

"No." It comes out weak as I try to fuck his hand. "I hate you."

He abandons my dick to tug and massage my balls. "You've been saving all this for me?"

"You heard me," I pant. "I hate your face."

"Yeah? What else do you love?"

"Fuck your tailors."

He snickers.

"And the way your dick tastes."

"Aww, baby." His warm mouth nips my earlobe as he

releases my balls. The clank of his belt hitting the floor has me widening my legs. "You just told me you love me."

I push the limits of my range, turning my head until our lips slide back together. I moan in his mouth as his wet erection slots in between the globes of my ass and glides up and down.

I arch back, needing more. Needing him inside me.

"Hold on, I need to grab lube. If I let you go, you'll be good?"

"My pocket," I growl.

"Stay," he orders as he bends down and finds the packet of lube and a condom in my jeans.

I try to rip my arm free, but his hold tightens, as if he anticipated the disobedience.

"You just made it harder on yourself," he murmurs.

The warning sends liquid fire rushing through my blood.

The smell of latex and the wet drip of lube down my crease suspends my breath.

A sharp crack splits the air as his palm smacks my ass, pleasure and pain tangling, laughter spilling from me before I can stop it.

My back arches as the next slap lands, sending a deep thrum through every nerve and spreading a molten cocktail of heat that seeps deep into my muscles and bones.

"Ungh...again," I beg.

"No," he growls as his finger sinks into my hole and his teeth clamp down on my right shoulder until my eyes burn and flood.

"Fuuck," I moan as he slowly finger fucks me while licking his bite mark.

Needing his piercing on my tongue, I try to rip my arm free, and this time when his palm comes down, my eyes, nose, and dick leak as a roil of pleasure floods my body.

"Mmm, Blue." He sinks two more fingers into me and kisses my tear-stained cheek. "You're so perfect."

I shouldn't throw my head back to try to headbutt him, but I do it anyway, and I'm still barely able to lift my face from the glass. My spine tingles in anticipation of another slap, but then his fingers slide out of me, and the thick head of his erection rubs against my hole.

"Remember what you just asked for."

I break out in goose bumps at the dark warning in his voice.

He kicks my legs wider and tilts my hips slightly before a soft kiss lands in the center of my back—the only warning before my breath whooshes out from the stretch as he sinks inside me.

"You okay?" he croaks in a smoky voice once he's fully seated. I manage a nod, though I'm biting my lip so hard I taste blood.

"Wrong answer." He pulls back, then slams into me, hard.

"Salem!" scrapes from my throat as I dissolve into warm nothingness.

The slap of flesh rings in my ears as he bucks into me.

Eyes too wet to see, I wire them shut and hear my distant begging...grunting...cursing somewhere outside the silver static moving through me like helium.

If this is punishment, I'll be wicked forever.

I hear his dark chuckle, though I didn't speak.

He's so hard...and hot...and big. Every stroke...more static...

"Salem," I slur, part worship, part plea.

"Hm, baby?"

I open my mouth, but only a guttural sound comes out as he shifts and the curve of his dick reaches deeper.

"Come here."

His tongue tunnels into my mouth, his tight suck, tight palm, tight stretch from his cock...*Oh fuuuuck*. Lightning shoots down my spine.

"Imagine—hnn—someone walking by... seeing your fat

cock leaking all over my hands," he grits out, licking into my ear. "Hearing how fucking good you scream for me."

My full-body convulsion pulls a moan from him, makes his hips stutter, and when his fingers sweep down and scrape my balls, I blow with a brutal force.

"Let go." He kisses his bite mark while stroking my prostate. "I've got you."

I haven't felt my feet on the floor since he entered me.

I shiver in his hold as he rocks into me slowly. Setting my arm free, he wraps both of his arms around my chest.

His panting breath against my ear trembles as he stills, palm flattening over mine on the glass, holding me tight against his chest.

I kiss him sloppily through his release, each of his sighs and moans stealing my breath.

I'm expecting us both to land in a boneless heap on the floor, but he backs us slowly to the couch.

If he's surprised when I turn and straddle him, easing him back inside me, and suck on his neck, he doesn't show it.

His head falls back as I suckle his skin, and his finger circles my rim where I'm stretched around him.

When he slips out of me, he replaces his erection with his fingers.

"Whuh's that?" I slur as a pinging sound cuts through the crackle of the fire.

"Dinner."

"Smells good."

He raises my chin and brushes a kiss against my lips. "How do you feel?"

I snicker.

The right corner of his mouth curves up. "What's funny?"

"I'm literally plastered to you like skin, drunk off your dick."

He rubs a soothing circle across my lower back.

"You okay?" I ask, searching his eyes.

"Yeah, Blue." His voice scratches like coarse sand. "I'm living a dream."

"I BURNED THEM." I pluck the almonds off his plate.

His lips roll in.

"I told you I can't cook."

"They're not that bad." He takes them back. "And I'll teach you."

"I could never make this." I pile more of the cinnamon-y and peppery chicken tagine onto my plate. When I look up, he's watching me with a small grin.

"What?" I wipe my mouth.

"Nothing."

I shrug and return to my third helping. I usually hate when sweet mixes with savory, but I can't get enough of the glazed apricots.

After we cleaned up—more like he insisted on cleaning me up—and changed into sweats and tees, I followed him into the kitchen.

I had one job—to toast the almonds.

My head snaps up. "You knew they were burnt. Didn't you?"

He grins. "I mean, it was your third try."

I fling one at him, and it bounces off his chest onto the sheet we've spread across the floor.

His phone lights up next to me.

"Who's Josiah?

"My dog sitter."

"Oh. Simba okay?"

I pick up the phone and try to hand it to him, but he raises his fingers, sticky from biting off a piece of the glazed apricot. "8642." He tells me the code.

I unlock his phone, and my fingers clench tightly around it as I look down at the screen. "So, you're fucking."

His brow furrows. "What?"

I toss him his phone. "Why is he sending you a thirst-trap photo?"

He flips it over and stares at the photo. "That is not a thirst trap. He always sends a pic of Simba."

"Yeah, okay. That pic is 90 percent side piece and 10 percent Simba."

Salem

I shake my head. Though it *is* odd that Josiah is wearing my favorite hoodie again.

"He just finished pressing your draws to his nose while he jerked off in your bed."

I stifle a laugh. "Stop."

"He's trying to be Mr. Jones."

He's cute like this. "Well"—I shrug—"someone should be." I laugh, catching the spoon he wings at my head.

"I'm just saying." I set my phone down and lean forward until he's flat on his back and I'm hovering over him. "Has a nice ring, doesn't it?" I brush a kiss against his lips.

"I leave you downstairs for five minutes at Anaïs's, and a yoga instructor moves in." He glares. "What's wrong with you?"

I brush a kiss against the corner of his mouth. "If Josiah's my side piece, what does that make you?"

His face flushes as he digests his own words. I haven't pushed him about being exclusive, but I don't know...sometimes, he tells on himself. Other times, the fog in his eyes tells me to proceed with caution.

I'll wait.

I can wait.

Until the ache of not having him to myself becomes too much to manage.

He yawns as I pull back from kissing him.

"Tired?"

"Nope."

"Come here." I scoot back until I'm leaning against the couch and extend my arm.

He shifts up to join me, settling into the crook of my arm.

We finish eating while enjoying the crackle of the fire.

When he yawns a third time, I offer, "We can head up to bed."

"Nooo, not yet." The weight of his body against mine grows heavier, making me smirk. "I need to know things."

"About?"

"You."

I lean down and kiss the top of his head. "We have time."

He yawns again. "Let's play one of those board games, and I'll ask my questions."

"You sure?" I ask, running my fingers across the Q of his knuckle tat.

He nods.

CHAPTER 29
ARNAZ

See you're held in peace under midnight's keep.
Make haste. Gentle dreams await in sleep.

A light drizzle, or maybe dew, glistens on the trees, painting the treetops in streaks of silver when I wake up. For some reason, I never mind the sun if it's mixed with rain.

Climbing out of bed, I brush my teeth, wash my face, and then go in search of Salem.

I find him sitting on the steps of the front deck. The fawn stretched near his feet looks me over, pings back to Salem, then me again, probably wondering how a man who radiates the calming flow of the river found himself in the company of scorched earth. I take a seat next to him.

"Hey, you." He wraps me in his blanket cocoon. "I thought you'd sleep in."

I don't tell him that I slept peacefully until he took away his light snores. "Who's your visitor?"

"I think we're the visitors," he says, turning back to the fawn. "I don't know, but I kinda wanna buy the cabin so we can be together forever."

"What about Simba?" I rest my head on his shoulder as he rubs his fingers through the nape of curls.

"He'd make besties of 'em in no time."

"You found a dog friendlier than you?"

"Pfft. Simba has way more friends than me."

I grin.

"Even Cillian's cat, who tries to gouge the eyes out of every four-legged creature, sized Simba up, sulked away, then came back and slapshot a toy mouse at him." He extends his mug to me.

"What is it?"

"Chai, but I used oat milk for you."

I take a small taste first and then a larger sip. The ginger feels like drinking the sun.

"Have more," he offers when I return the mug.

"What did Simba do?"

"Huh? Oh, he hunched down to his belly and licked the toy. Edgar hissed and then disappeared for the rest of our visit. But, y'know, Edgar's like the Michael Corleone of cats."

I grin.

"So that's like an official sanction to enter with no smoke."

I want to meet Simba.

I sniff the air and follow the scent to Salem's neck.

"Want some?" He reaches into his pocket and pulls out a tiny vial.

He rubs the roller against my wrist and temples. I clasp his hand as he pulls it back. "Vetiver," I say out loud, reading the label.

"You like it?"

My eyes roll closed as I sniff my wrists. "It's kinda like wood in a new house."

"Yes, exactly," he says, twisting the cap back on.

"This is what you do in the morning?"

"Hm?" He sips from the mug.

"Rub on oils, make tea, and sit with Simba."

"Yeah...kind of."

"You're a real human."

His dimple deepens. "What are you? A mountain lion?"

"If I'm a mountain lion, then you can't be human."

"Nah." He smirks. "I'm whatever eats mountain lions."

Mmm. Hello, morning wood.

"Wanna go for a run?"

He hands me the mug to finish. "If I beat you, will you throw a tantrum like you did losing to me in Klask?"

"Fuck off!" I down the tea. "I won fair and square."

"You are a terrifyingly competitive sore loser."

"Whatever, I won."

"You did not."

"I will drown you in the river."

The fawn's head darts up.

"You're scaring the kids, honey."

"Say I won!"

He pulls my curls. "Do I need to discipline you again?"

A coil of heat stirs in my belly.

"Close your ears," he whispers to the fawn, whose head slumps back to the ground. He turns back to me. "If I win the race, you gotta give me something I want."

"Like?"

"Information."

I start to think it over, then stop thinking 'cause there's no way in hell he'll win. "Deal."

Salem

I tense as I stop drying myself. "Drowned?" I blink rapidly, wrapping the towel around my waist.

The need to know what happened to him when he called out sick weeks ago never let up. Especially after the first time I asked and he froze up. It was the first thing I thought of when I negotiated the terms of the race.

He rubs the back of his neck, staring at the floor.

"Did you tell anyone?"

He waves it off. "Wasn't a big—"

"No." I stop him. "You almost dying will never not be a big deal. You almost—"

The word catches in my throat.

"I'm fine," he says, putting his phone down on the nightstand, his towel still around his waist after showering first.

"Why didn't you tell me?"

"It wasn't a big—" He sees the warning in my glare. "I shouldn't have tried to be a hero."

"In no way was this your fault. You almost drowned. For Christ's sake, Blue."

He searches my face. "Why are you angry?"

"I'm not angry." I cross the room and kneel between his legs. "It's upsetting to hear, but I'm not angry. I just...damn."

"This is why I didn't tell anyone."

"That's not fair. Not to the people who love you, but mostly not to yourself."

"It is what it is."

"No, it's not. You deserve for people to show up for you. Was anyone there for you? Did you see a doctor?"

"Yeah. I dropped in practice a few hours later."

Of course he went to work like nothing happened.

"The doctor ordered me to sit out a couple games and rest. I slept it off, mostly."

"By yourself?"

"Sid stopped by with groceries."

"Thank God." I stand and lean forward, pushing him onto his back.

"Why do I feel like there's more you aren't telling me?"

He scoffs. "How do you know that?"

"Am I wrong?" I stare into his eyes. "Talk."

"It's nothing. It just, uh…brought up memories."

"What kind of memories?"

"Stuff with Carter. And weird dreams of him hurting people I…care about."

"Christ."

"Yeah, my psychiatrist doesn't think I need to adjust my meds, just recommended I bump up therapy."

"Have you?"

He looks away.

"Blue."

"I know. I wanted to see if it would stop on its own."

"And has it?"

"I start two sessions per week the week after next."

"Good. Really good. I'm proud of you."

He looks away again, but not before I catch the soft way my words land.

"I want to know what happens to you. A headache, a sore throat…"

"Why?"

"Because I care about you." I press my forehead against his as he wraps his legs around my waist, the backs of his heels pressing into my ass.

"Promise me." I separate his towel and wrap my palm around our cocks. The touch makes him shiver.

"Tell me you promise." I start stroking us, the heat from the shower still on our skin.

He moans.

My lips lower to his ear. "I don't want to lose you. Promise me, baby."

"Yes," he gasps.

"Immediately. Not weeks later. You call me as soon as you can." I pump us faster. "Yes?"

He nods, his mouth falling open on a choked gasp.

The idea of losing him to the ocean or fate terrifies me. I shut the thought out and get lost in his cries of pleasure.

AFTER, when we're tangled around each other, and he's caressing my scalp in soft strokes, he asks, "You think Simba would like me?"

"You?" I grin. "One hundred percent."

He rolls his eyes. "I would have believed you if you said, like, 55 percent."

"It's true," I say. "All his besties are feral."

He laughs. "What're your mom and dad like?"

I think about it. "They're chill. It never felt like being parents just happened to them."

"What do you mean?"

"It always felt like me and Denzel were intentional, like they had been waiting for us. I remember asking my mom if she regretted not having a daughter, and she said something like, '*Regret? I prayed for you and your brother.*'"

"Mm."

I turn my head and kiss his pec. "They were real, though. We had to be in by a certain time and check in often when we were out. They would shut stuff down the minute they thought our safety was compromised, or we were dropping the ball in school."

"Sounds like they cared."

I nod. "You ever think about being a parent?"

He blows out a breath. "I don't know. I can't really see it. But when I come out here to a place like this, I think a bunch of kids running around with me in the forest wouldn't be the worst."

I grin, imagining a bunch of curly-haired baby Blues barefoot in the mountains, living free in the way most of us forgot how to be.

"I could see that for you."

"Yeah?"

"Yep."

"What about you?" he asks.

"It could go either way. Though Sim is great with babies."

It's his turn to chuckle. "You have dad energy."

I snicker. "Uh...thanks?"

"I just mean, if they are yours, I don't doubt they'll question that you want them. You're too certain about things for them not to know."

"When I know, I know." And after a moment of quiet, I add, "And my parents will like you too."

I wait for him to stiffen or brush that off.

When neither happens, I grin.

CHAPTER 30
ARNAZ

♫ "Carry on" ♫
Stressed vines ripen fruit.
Dry spells strengthen roots.

"*Healing is a process.*"

My therapist's voice echoes in my ears as I scrub my hands over my face.

1:42 a.m.

I blow out a breath and will myself out of bed.

The air is crisp as I break into a jog. Instead of heading toward the ocean, I weave through the deserted streets.

Every time I think of the Tuesday three weeks away, my stomach stutters like a heartbeat.

Me. Him. The cabin. *Again.*

When he sent me the rental confirmation, I lit up brighter than Anaïs's neon-green skin that time we stole Carter's stash of LSD and cut school.

Seven miles later, I round the corner of my block and almost trip on a web of leashes.

"Sorry," an older man murmurs.

"All good." I get one foot free and lunge over the tightening knot, then manage to work my second leg free.

"You're always running," he says.

I hitch an eyebrow as I jog in place. "You talk to my therapist?"

His eyes brighten. "Therapy...beautiful."

I glance down our block. "I don't usually see anyone out around this time."

"Haven't had a good night of sleep in decades. I'm usually out reading on the deck when I see you pass by. Oh, quiet, Julie!" He huffs at the yappy, smaller of the two dogs. "It's my thirty-fifth wedding anniversary tomorrow, so figured I'd switch it up."

"Yeah? Happy Anniversary."

"Thanks." He reaches into his pocket and pulls out a folded handkerchief. His hand trembles slightly as he wipes a bead of sweat from his upper lip. "Soon, it'll be three years since she passed."

I stop bouncing on my toes. *Shit.* "I'm sorry."

"Chased her for years." His eyes crinkle at the corners. "Thirty-five years of being married to my crush."

He loosens the tension on the leash so the larger dog can sniff and then pee on the grass.

"My kids will be over to take me to lunch tomorrow," he continues.

He isn't alone. I roll my shoulders back, releasing some of the tension.

Thirty-five years. I don't know why, but I think of Salem. "How'd you know it was real?"

His head tilts forward slightly. "Say it again."

I clear my throat. "How did you know you loved her and she loved you?"

"Ah." He raises his head. "It's in here." He taps his chest.

"No." I shake my head. "I can't trust that."

I jump as both dogs growl and bark as a squirrel scurries by. He shushes them.

"I'll let you go," I say, taking a step back.

"Hold on, son." He closes the distance between us. "If he loves you, and I mean truly loves you, and you feel it in here"—he thumbs his chest—"then you can try like hell to fight it, but you'd be running from one of the greatest experiences of your life. If you want to run, maybe first know what or who it is you're running from."

He. He knows who I am.

"Uh...th-thank you," I mutter.

He nods. "I'll see you around."

"Yeah...see you."

With a slight hitch in his gait, I watch him disappear around the corner.

Anaïs's words from a few weeks ago bubble to the surface. *"Ever since college..."*

I think I've always known.

CHAPTER 31
SALEM

"He's one of the best private investigators in New York. He'll need to talk to you and your parents to get a full picture."

"Thanks, Cat." I kill the lights as I head upstairs. "You don't think this is over the top?"

"I don't, unfortunately."

My throat tightens. "Okay."

"He's the best, Salem. My team will continue to call hospitals, but so far…"

"Yeah." I clear my throat. "I appreciate it. I know this is a bit unorthodox."

"Not for me and my team. You know that. We want to help. I put all your upcoming press engagements on hold."

"Okay. Thanks. I'll look out for the call from the PI, and I'll prep my parents."

"Sounds good. Talk soon."

As soon as the line goes dead, I try the number I've called dozens of times over the last week, knowing I'll get Denzel's voicemail.

Where are you?

REAL TALK SPORTS WITH DARIUS & TODD

"Todd is sick with a cold, or at least that's the excuse he called out with. That means I'm flying solo tonight.

They call him The Silencer, but you all saw the head-scratching press conference that led Salem Jones to not only come out but also ask fellow gay player Arnaz Cade out on a date. Sources say that the press conference was just for publicity since Cade is secretly dating Sid King. Tonight, Jones played an abysmal game, fouling out.

Was coming out worth it?

Maybe he should have used his silencing powers on himself. In other news, Oklahoma fired head coach AJ Bell after a 12-18 start to the season. I say good riddance.

If only the league were as diligent with polarizing players."

CHAPTER 32
SALEM

Three weeks and no leads. The detective got ahold of Denzel's squad mate. Our only potential source of info, and he couldn't tell us anything. Apparently, he was so out of it, he didn't even remember Denzel being there. The hospital visitor logs confirmed Denzel visited over a few days.

No leads.

It always comes back to this.

No matter how hard I try...

What I achieve...

The choices I make...

How hard I hold on...

It always comes back to one unshakeable truth—very little in life is in my control.

Denzel knows what his disappearing did to us last time. There's no way he'd have willingly done it again.

Which could only mean he's gotten into a bad place somewhere.

Mom's frantic, calling me nonstop to make sure I'm okay. Dad's chest pains have returned, and he has to see a cardiologist next week.

"Where are you?" Blue shifts on his knees and frowns.

I look down at him. "S-sorry."

His thumb swipes across his wet bottom lip. "It's okay if you're not in the mood."

"I am. My bad."

My head falls back as his tongue returns to my slit.

He, well, *us*, is another area I can't control.

I want more, but the voice telling me not to push is strong. I think we're shifting. He's still taken by surprise for a few seconds whenever he calls, and I pick up. The night before my game in Denver, I was settling into my hotel room when my phone lit up. For the first time ever, he FaceTimed out of the blue.

"Hey, yo—"

A woman's shriek pierced through the phone, as a blur of dark hair flashed by the screen.

"S-Saahh—hehe! Salem—hff!—s-top—hihh— trying to get meee. Stahp!"

"Who's this?" I asked as out-of-control laughter blared over the line.

"G-hff!" Blue's voice cut in."G-gimme...the phone!"

A door slammed shut, and a smear of color flitted across the screen before a twisted neck and mop of curls appeared, revealing Blue's sister.

"It's you," I said.

"Bestie!" Her head swiveled to glance over her shoulder, and then she took off. "Wait—hehe—no, listen—guess what Arnie— ohmygod—hff!—s-top—when I asked—wait!—if you and him— Stahp!"

"Leave her alone, Blue!"

"She's toast!"

"Wait!" she shrieked as the sound of footsteps drew near. "Stah—Lemmetellhim!"

Hazy shapes and muffled laughter mixed in with Blue's "Lehh—it—nnngh!—g-go! Ow!"

There was an oof as the screen landed against a patch of gray.

I waited a few seconds, then called out, "Proof of life, please."

The phone scratched against the gray before Blue appeared, T-shirt ripped, curls in disarray.

"Um, clearly you won," I deadpanned.

"Oof!" He lurched forward as Anaïs's head appeared over his shoulder and her arms wrapped around his neck. "Get off of me."

She didn't budge as he tried to shake her off his back.

"I'm gonna DM you!" She winked into the camera.

"No!" he protested.

"Blue, let it happen."

"Aww, you have a nickname for him?" she cooed.

I grinned, and Blue blushed.

"Who let the two of you loose on Philadelphia?" I asked.

"I crash his road games a few times a year," she replied, bouncing over his shoulder as he walked them back to what I guessed was their room.

"Which I'm starting to regret," he said, offloading her with a soft thump. "I'll be back. Order food, demon."

"Salem, I'm DMing you now for us to grab dinner when I'm back," she called.

"It's a date," I replied as Blue rolled his eyes and shut the door. "Stop frowning. I'll always like you more than anyone else."

His blush returned.

"Hi."

"Hi." His eyes widened as they darted right, and then his fingers flew through his curls.

"I've already seen you." I snickered. "You're sexy messy."

He tugged on his bottom lip. "What are you doing?"

"Just got to my room. You wanna tell me what that was about?"

He joined the two rips of his collar and tried to pat them back together as he said, "It was nothing."

"About next week..."

He glared at me. "You're canceling?"

"Nah. Just three weeks feels like a year sometimes, doesn't it?"

Brows easing, a faint grin ghosted the corner of his lips. "Yeah. Like five years."

"Wow!" My jaw hung open. "Five years."

"Shut up."

"Nah, you can't take it back."

"Oh god."

"How do you even focus, missing me so much?"

"I'm hanging up."

I leaned back, scooting down until my neck hit the pillow. "I miss you times five years too."

He rolled his eyes but didn't try to hide the spread of a smile.

"I heard you're cooking for us this time," I continued.

"Fuck you."

I laughed. "Okay, let me let you get back to my new bestie."

"Wait! Tell me about your day."

And, damn, if the need in his voice didn't make me light up. Or the way he slid down the wall and listened as I told him about my boring day, and then he told me about his.

When we were finally going to hang up, the question of us being exclusive burned on my tongue, and I saw myself asking, and his soft, unguarded eyes darkening as his walls returned, and I choked.

Instead, I said, "I'll see you next week. Good night."

And then I'd laid there, swimming in thoughts like:

It's been going well, don't mess it up.

He told you he isn't the committed-relationship type. Instead of trying to force him, respect where he's at.

Is he seeing other men when we aren't together?

There's so much more I want to tell him—like about Denzel being missing.

Why haven't I told him about Denzel?

"Seriously!"

My eyes fly to Blue's glare. "Shit. I'm sorr—"

He jumps to his feet. "Bring the lube."

"What?"

He races toward the door buck naked.

The hell?

"Yo!" Yanking up my boxer briefs, I shuffle to my feet. A tight squeeze has my gaze dropping to my dick.

When did he roll on a condom?

I kick the bottle of lube across the floor. Swiping it up, I race after him.

I yank open the door, and a feral roar, jagged and raw, cracks the air.

My heart rages in my chest as he stands in the middle of the forest, heaving from unhinged laughter as icy rain pelts and pebbles his skin.

"Damn, that felt good!"

He throws his head back, fists balled, activating every taut muscle of his body, eyes closed, neck vein protruding, fat cock swinging between his thighs, and lets it rip.

His howl vibrates through the air, firing an electric charge in my chest, the weight of my control unraveling, pressing against my lungs, dragging higher and higher until a blue-black sound rattles my ribcage, tilts my face to the wrathful sky, and kicks free of my restraint.

He's right there with me, a blood-red, bone-chilling roar, lashing and slaughtering the wind.

The weeping sky answers to the dominion of our gut-hollowing purge.

Scraped from our blood, bones, and sweat—*media, headlines, slurs, humiliation for clicks, silent bystanders, missing brothers.*

Madness returned to the damp earth pulsing under my toes.

Blue beats his chest, and I don't have to touch them to know his tears are hot like mine.

Trembling as the window to my senses cracks open, and I surrender to the thrum in my blood, cleansing everything that is not us.

His gaze collides with mine.

As if he senses the fierce protection pulsing in my chest, his mouth slackens, and the lines of laughter vanish from his face.

Our chests rise and fall in rhythm as we meet each other with nothing between us.

I start toward him when he charges, tackling me to the ground.

Sharp razors cut through my pecs. "Fuck me like it's me you're inside of," he growls, ripping his teeth from my skin.

My vision wipes out until he's pinned under me, my hand wrapped around his throat, his legs creating a door across the mud.

I scrape my teeth across his neck.

His eyes mirror the dark sky, the only warning before his legs coil around my torso, and air whooshes from my lungs as my ribs press in.

Even now, as his dick stabs into my stomach, I must earn his submission.

I yank his curls, lifting his face, and then I clamp onto his lip until I taste iron, and he drops his knees.

Uncurling my hand from the lube, I squeeze some into my mouth, sink my chest into the mud, and lower my tongue.

His thighs cradle my head as he writhes against my mouth, and I lick and finger him open.

A growl rumbles from my chest, and I bite the inside of his thigh until he releases his erection.

I scrape the bottle of lube off the forest floor and watch him wet his lips as I sit up, pull out my sheathed cock, and douse it with the liquid.

"Look at me," I order when his eyes roll closed.

I throw his legs over my shoulder, folding him in half as I press my forehead to his, and cry out as I sink into his tight heat.

Warm velvet and molten silk envelop me like a second skin, molding around me and receiving me perfectly.

My fists burrow into the earth.

What power has given me the restraint to breach but not storm these walls I claim as my home?

My name is his chant—his eyes, stained glass windows into a soul I'll worship until my last breath.

Mine.

Yours.

Ragged moans echo as I tunnel deeper. Mud-covered fingers scrape at my back. I breathe against his mouth, ascend the ridge of cheekbone, and drink in the waters breaking through the mountains.

Cry. Let go, Blue.

Come home to me.

Wet, cold air spirals around us, thrashing the storm-drunk trees. I flow, submerge deeper, deeper still.

Hurtling wind and storm and slow-building rapture.

Look! We're the center of our own vortex, baby.

Sinking into the slick earth.

His lips wrap around my nipple.

My hips stutter.

His tongue laves my pit.

My thighs tremble.

Cries of mercy.

This is wholeness.

My teeth sink into his neck.

I shed restraint.

Tongue drinks iron.

Flesh pounds flesh.

Sob-soaked exaltation.

You arch and howl.
　　You cling to me.
　　You call for god.
　　You shudder.
　　You release.

I hold it all.
　　I'll.
　　Never.
　　Not.
　　Hold.
　　It.
　　All.

Unsheathed.
　　I give you what you ask for.
　　Cradled against your tongue.
　　Puffy eyes, bloodied lip, and bruised neck.
　　One, two, three glides.
　　I'm undone.
　　Chest caved in surrender.
　　Pulsing.
　　Coating.
　　Painting.
　　You in all of me.

Arnaz

"You'll sing for me one day?" Salem asks, resting against my chest as we settle into the bath water.

I wasn't feeling the glass walls surrounding the tub at first. But in the light, it's all treetops and sky. After dark, it's moon, and tonight, the gentle patter of rain.

He took the lead, kissing me, holding me, washing me, as we showered the mud off before climbing into the bath, and I clung to him.

One day, maybe at the end of my lifetime, I'll know how to describe what I felt out there in the rain.

Free, alive, and happy all sound feeble.

I thought he'd made love to me on the hotel floor in San Francisco, so what was that tonight?

My eyes burn as I kiss the top of his head. "Yeah, I'll sing for you."

Salem

"What's that?" I ask after returning with food.

He grins at the plates. "Breakfast at night?"

"It's too late to make the paella." I nod at the gift wrapped on his pillow. "This for me?"

"Yeah."

I hand him the plates of French toast and omelets, then pick up the box.

He arches an eyebrow when I sniff it before peeling back the paper.

"It's oil." His voice shakes. "You know, versus acrylic."

"Wow." I take in the painting. "Is this really how I looked?"

"Powerful?" He nods. "I grabbed a still shot from the exact moment you came out. You were so calm. You even smiled. I'll never forget it."

"I was scared shitless."

"Yeah?"

"Yeah." I huff out a breath. "A hundred percent."

"You know what happened the first time I watched it? I threw up. I don't think I ever felt that brave."

"How?" I lean in and brush a kiss against his forehead. "Your article—"

"It's not the same."

"How?" I ask again, shaking my head. "You kicked open the door for all of us."

"It took so much for me to get there."

"You still got there."

He shrugs.

Wild he can't see it. "You made the *Global Time* 100 list!"

"You like it?" he asks, biting his nails.

I stare at him. "Did anything I just said register?"

"Yeah, yeah," he garbles around a yawn.

"I'm sorry, is your greatness boring you?"

He snickers. "Wait, tell me if you like it."

"Am I really this hot?"

He rolls his eyes. "You know you are."

"Yeah." I lean down and kiss him. "But I like when you say it." I stare at the painting. It even captures the backs of the heads of the reporters. "Who's the artist?"

"One of Anaïs's friends."

I nod. "I love it. Thank you."

"I know how much courage it takes to come out. I wanted you to have something to remember the moment."

"I actually got you something too, but it's weak compared to this." I head over to my bag. "You can't open it until I tell you. It'll be better that way. Promise me."

"Okay." He nods. "But my promise expires in three days."

"So impatient." I laugh and put the gift bag directly into his bag. "In two nights, I'll call you."

"Is that an—?"

"Elk," Blue answers as it crosses the clearing just ahead of us.

He was watching me when I woke up this morning. We exchanged slow grins before I pulled him into my arms, and we watched the treetops sway through the window.

Instead of going for a run before heading out, we decided to explore the woods.

"It's huge." The elk lowers its head and chomps on twigs.

"We should stop until it sees us. I don't think we're supposed to approach."

We stop walking. "How do you know?"

He shrugs. "I just don't want it to be afraid."

A minute or so of our waiting for the elk to acknowledge us passes.

"Homie's gonna be here all day at this pace. He's not paying attention to us."

"She," he corrects me.

"How do you know?"

He raises and curls both sets of his middle and index fingers over his head. "No antlers."

"Oh," I reply, turning around. "Isn't it your dream to live in a place like this one day?"

"Yeah. Why?"

"No reason."

He faces me. "You don't think I can do it?"

I shake my head. "Never said that."

"Why, 'cause I can't cook?"

Where'd that come from?

"I'm serious." He glares at me. "You don't think I'm man enough to survive out here?"

"What are you talking about?" I step toward him. "Of course you're man enough. What's up?"

"I can learn how to cook," he says, pushing past me.

"It's all good. I'll buy the cabin next to yours. You can come over when you're hungry."

He turns. "And who will you be living with?"

"I don't know." I catch up to him, slinging my arm around his neck, ignoring the daggers in his gaze. "I'll probably shoot my shot with the hot city boy next door."

"You don't have a shot."

"Oh." I tilt my head back. "Word?"

He almost grins.

"Well, guess I'll just scrounge up a husband somewhere. Just walk on by if you see me giving it to him good against a tree or in the mud."

I rip my arm free as he tries to bite off a chunk. "Ay!"

I laugh, backing away as he grits his teeth and lunges for me.

"Don't be jealous of Mr. Jones!" I jump back as he swipes the air, then turn on my heels and book it.

"Run all you want," he calls out.

I kick up to full speed as I hear him gaining on me.

"You're already dead."

"Okay." I gasp for a breath as my laughter turns into a cackle. "But wait until after our wedding. Mr. Jones has been planning—"

Oof! I'm rammed from behind and taken down.

"Say it again," he snarls near my ear.

I'm wheezing with laughter as I'm bracketed by his thighs.

It doesn't take much to buck him off and flip over to my back. He quickly recovers and reclaims his position on top of me.

"Fuck Mr. Jones," he growls in my face.

I nibble on the bruise on his lower lip and clasp his hips, then grind up into him.

"Don't touch me," he sneers, crawling to a stand. I pull him back down and wrap him up in my arms.

I kiss the side of his face. "What?" I ask as he frowns. The beginnings of a mask appear. "Stop. Spit it out."

"It's nothing."

"Speak."

He breaks free of my hold but doesn't move from my lap. "It's just...we're on other sides of the country." He cards his hands through his curls as I rub his thighs.

"Blue, you could live on another continent...fuck, another planet, and I'd still want to be with you."

"But didn't you and Lucien stop dating because he moved to France?"

"Yeah?"

His eyebrows droop and then swoop up.

Ping.

"Is it starting to sink in that you're in a league of your own?" I ask.

"Wouldn't you get bored with me?"

"No. And honestly, with the kind of life we lead, I dream of boring days with you."

When he doesn't respond, I ask, "You heard me?"

He tenses in my lap. "What about days spent with someone diagnosed with CPTSD, generalized anxiety disorder, and persistent depressive disorder?"

I sensed some PTSD from him when he told me about his dad, though I'd have to look up what the C stands for. I knew about his depression from his coming-out article.

"I said what I said," I answer. "Though I pegged you as more avoidant than anxious."

Like my brother.

"The avoidance is from anxiety."

"Oh."

"I'm on meds."

I nod. "I'll do my own research, but will you tell me what it's like?"

His brows crease. "What what's like?"

"To be you." I lean up and kiss his cheek.

His shoulders relax a little. "What about you?"

"What about me?"

"Do you struggle with anything?"

I think about it. "Nothing I've been diagnosed with. Sometimes when I feel like things are spiraling out of control, I...uh... get bad anxiety, but it doesn't stay for long."

"Hmm. How aren't you always anxious? I never feel like things are in my control."

I think about my brother. "Yeah. I know what you mean."

Arnaz

"Is this what you see in my eyes?" I ask as we stare at the partially burned shack along the trail.

"What? No. This is in ruins," he replies.

We see me differently.

"Not all of it."

It's still standing at least.

"Why wouldn't they tear it down?" he asks, assessing the wreckage.

If the land were mine, I'd keep it too.

"It's sad," he says, wrapping his arms around my waist.

"Yeah?"

He'd never belong to a place like this.

Maybe I won't one day either.

CHAPTER 33
ARNAZ

♫ **"Before I Came to Know It"** ♫
At some point, I must have loved the world.

The thing that rarely happens happened—I overslept. I blame Salem—well, half blame—for our late-night video sex followed by hours spent doing absolutely nothing. He made us take one of those "What Animal Are You in the Wild" quizzes and got off when the results revealed that I would, in fact, be a mountain lion, like he guessed, and that he would be a wolf—specifically a red wolf—like he also guessed.

And then I made us look up which of us would win in a one-on-one fight and was hyped that it would be me. But then he kept reading and infuriatingly informed me that wolves travel in packs and mountain lions ride solo, and against a pack, I'd get eaten alive. So the fucker gloated and read some more, and none of it made me less infuriated until the mating section. He shook his head proudly and puffed out his chest as he read how red wolves are monogamous and mate for life, and…let's just say, one of us wanted to climb through the phone and sit on the other one's dick.

Instead, he was all, "Turn around and position the camera so I can see my hole. Yeah, just like that. Now, spread your legs…"

"Wait, position your camera so I can see you too," I panted.

He tilted the phone, then rolled his briefs down, and his cock had sprung up, his piercing glistening from his pre-cum.

His eyes darkened as I hummed at the sight while slowly sucking two fingers into my mouth.

"Remember the gift I gave you? Can you get it?"

I nodded and reached into the bottom shelf of my nightstand.

I pulled the black shoebox from the gift bag and lifted the cover.

Cackling, I said, "You bought me a dick."

He laughed. "Yeah. I did."

I rubbed my fingers over the thick, swirly vein along the side, then snatched my hand back. "Fuck, that feels real."

"Yeah…it's made of a kind of silicone to mimic human skin."

My mouth had watered. "It's the same color as your complexion."

"Yeah. I washed it for you too." Peeking out the side of the satin pillow it had been resting on were a card and a small bottle of warming lube.

"Goddamn," I scoffed, reading the dimensions on the card. "Length: eight and a half inches, circumference: six inches, diameter: two inches."

"That's my dick when I'm not with you."

"Fuck." A coil of heat spread between my legs.

"What's the shallow mixing bowl for?" I asked, picking it up out of the box.

"You stick the suction cup at the bottom of the dildo on it so that when you ride it, it doesn't move around."

"You thought of everything."

"Show me my hole again."

I uncapped the warming lube and squeezed some onto my fingers, then turned and slowly fed them into my hole, sucking in a breath from the stretch.

"Damn, you're so fucking sexy. I can't wait to tongue fuck you again," he crooned.

"Mm," I rasped, thinking of his long, warm tongue eating me out.

"That's it, baby. Add another finger now."

I obeyed, head dipping slightly from the added pressure.

"I'm gonna fuck my hole soon. But first, the rules." He tilted the phone up so I could see his face. "We're gonna play a game called start, stop, hold. When I say 'start,' I want you to curve up slightly and fuck yourself at the pace I set. Got it?"

"Yeah," I said with a grunt.

"When I say 'hold,' you stop but keep your fingers in. Okay? And when I say 'stop,' you pull out and let me see my sexy hole empty. Understand?"

"Yeah. I'm already leaking."

"You want to practice with your fingers first before using the toy?"

I shook my head.

"Yeah, we'll practice with your fingers first."

I glared at him. He tilted the phone down to show me what my glare did to him.

"Okay, I want you to finger fuck my hole slowly," he instructed. "Even slower," he said, and I slowed my pace.

"Slower."

"I am going slow," I grumbled.

"Reach under the satin pillow in the box," he said firmly.

"What?" I paused fucking myself, then reached for it with my left hand.

My ass tightened around my fingers as I lifted out a leather paddle.

"Fuck, Salem." I let out a groan.

"I know what you need, baby."

"I'm gonna come already, and we've barely even started."

"You'll come when I tell you to come. Now, rub the paddle across the right side of that sexy, plump ass cheek. And when I say 'lift,' you lift, and on 'punish,' you bring it down hard enough to make that fat dick happy. You can take your fingers out so you have something to lean on. But when my dick is in you, it stays in as I punish you. Got it?"

"Mmhmm," I murmured, getting into position.

"Yes or no?"

"Yes."

"Lift."

I lifted the paddle.

"Higher...higher...right there. When I say 'punish,' come down hard. If I don't think it's hard enough, we go again."

"Yes."

"Okay..."

Goose bumps broke out on my arms as I waited...and waited...

A string of pre-cum cooling against my shaft...

...and waited...

The handle of the leather paddle was moist in my hands. When I was about to glare at him, it rang out, dark and commanding.

"Punish!"

I came down hard, the sting burning as the slap echoed in the air.

"Mm. Good boy. Place the paddle down and rub soft circles along the spot until I say stop. Close your eyes and picture my lips parting and blowing soft air along the spot before I place gentle kisses."

I closed my eyes and imagined his full, sexy lips grazing the lingering burn, agitating and soothing the spot.

"Just like that. Now imagine my tongue gliding from those heavy balls to your rim. I woke up so hard this morning, thinking about how good you feel stretched around my tongue with your cheeks pillowed against my face."

I moaned.

"Start," he rasped, and it had taken me a few seconds to remember the rules. I groaned when my fingers sank back into my hole.

"Baby, start with my dick."

With a sigh of thanks, I'd squeezed lube on the heavy dildo and then reached around and pressed it to my rim.

"Slowly," he instructed.

I nodded as I tried to push the fat head in. By the third try, he said, "Sit on me."

I lowered the bowl to the mattress and used my headboard to lift and hover over it.

He sucked in a breath. "That looks...ngh."

"S'big," I hissed as the head popped in, and black stars lit up behind my lids.

"You can take me, baby. Just like that."

"Fuuuck." My thighs clenched together as I lifted slightly to catch my breath before lowering back down.

"Mm, you're so warm, hugging me so tight. Glide down my dick...that's it..."

I groaned from the pressure and burn.

"Start, baby. You'll feel better."

I gripped the headboard and slowly moved up, then sank back down in shallow thrusts, barely taking a third of the shaft.

I raised a hand to grab my dick but paused.

"Go ahead," he said, giving me permission.

After a few strokes, my head fell back as a spasm of heat

rolled down my back to my balls, and I rocked my hips, fucking myself deeper on every thrust.

Needing to see him, I opened my eyes and stared into the screen. His thick thighs were spread as he slowly pumped himself, his dark eyes half-lidded, bottom lip tugged between his teeth.

"You're so sexy," I breathed, then groaned loudly.

He winked. "You should see my view, baby. Hold."

I whimpered but obeyed.

"You're so perfect. I'll let you continue, but hands off that sexy dick."

I squeezed my nipple with my newly freed hand and continued riding *him*.

"How does it feel, Blue?"

"Mm." I panted a few breaths. "S'real."

"Like how I'd feel raw?"

I clamped my fist around the base of my cock. "Shhit."

He chuckled. "Faster."

I reached behind me to anchor my palm around the base of the dick and bucked faster.

"You know what I think about when I'm inside you?" he asked.

I shook my head.

"How is it so good? Making love to you. How badly I want to pump you full of my cum." His smoky voice sent a graze of heat down my spine.

"You want my cum?"

"Yesss," I moaned. "Fuck...yes."

"I want to give you my cum, baby, and then have you ride my face so I can eat it out of you and taste us together."

"Fuck, I'm com—ngh!" My body shuddered.

"Faster."

I cried out as I bent forward, lifting the dildo, and fucked myself hard.

"Hold."

I crashed forward onto the mattress in a heap on top of my cum with the gigantic dick sticking out of me.

I panted into my elbow, turning my face slightly to see him, beads of sweat running down my temples.

He was leaning back, watching me, cum covering his chest.

He blew me a kiss, and I surprised myself by blowing one back.

"You can pull me out when you're ready."

I winced as I pulled it out.

"Let me see."

I showed him my hole.

"Mm, damn, you took me deep. How do you feel?"

Yawning, I lay back onto the mattress and muttered, "Fucked."

"You did so well."

His pride bloomed inside me.

"You'll stay on?" I asked, rolling onto my back and swiping up the cum on my chest.

"Yeah. I'll be here."

We stared at each other, and an ache grew in my chest from wishing I were in his arms at that moment.

And he was there when I woke up this morning, light snores, handsome face, bare chest. I settled in to watch him and then looked at the time and bolted upright.

Unlike me, he could afford to stay up past three in the morning since he has today off.

I shoot Sid a text to tell him I'm running late, and he hits me back when I'm on the road.

Sid

Covered for you

Me

Good lookin'

I'm twelve minutes late when I slink onto the court, keeping to the back of the huddle as Coach addresses the team.

"...led teams to many NCAA Division I National Championships. While he's making his debut in the NBA, I have no doubt he'll be able to level-up each and every one of you. We'll miss Jerry, but after half a decade as an assistant coach, he's earned his spot as head coach, and we're proud of him. Let's give a warm welcome to your new assistant coach, Aiden Miller."

My head jolts up.

I push through Ussef and Wes.

"What the fuck?" I exclaim.

All heads swivel in my direction, except one staring at the floor.

"Problem, Cade?" Coach shoots me a puzzled look.

"What are you doing here?" I demand, staring at our new assistant coach, who's aged un-fucking-believably well.

"Hey! My office," Coach demands.

"Wait, hold up, Coach. Let me holla at him." Sid steps in, gaze gunned on our new *assistant coach*, who decides then to lift his head and look at me.

"We should tal—" Aiden starts.

"No!" Sid and I bark at the same time.

"Let's go," Sid says, nodding toward the door.

I don't stop walking until I reach the end of the hall, where I kneel and fold my head into my hands. My lungs burn like I'm back in the ocean.

"Tell me what's going on." Sid kneels next to me. "Who is he?"

Before I can answer, Sid's head darts up, and then he's on his feet.

"Sid, may I have a moment with Arnaz?"

I flinch at Aiden's voice. *Still so fucking polite.*

"Yo, walk the other way," Sid warns him. "He doesn't want to talk to you."

I screw my eyes shut and lean against the wall.

"Okay," Aiden says calmly. "You both should know that I was approached by the Royals for the position. It was the opportunity of a lifetime, and I couldn't pass it up. I don't mean to stir up any trouble for him."

I channel power that I don't feel and stand to face him.

It's fucking surreal staring into his dark, diamond-shaped eyes.

"I'm sorry if my joining has caused trouble. It's the last thing I wanted to happen."

"Why this team?" I question.

"Arnaz—"

I cut him off. "You know where we left things. What did you think would happen if you showed up?"

"A lot of time has passed. I thought it wouldn't matter as much."

"It doesn't!" I bark.

"Alright," Sid interjects, addressing Aiden. "You said your piece. Bounce."

"I'm out." I punch open the double doors. "Tell Coach I'm sick or something."

"Your team needs you," Aiden calls out. "You've worked too hard to let me mess with what you've built here. I'm no one."

I let out a scoff.

At one point, he was everything.

I drive around aimlessly for hours until Sid hits me up that he's home.

He's talking to his bodyguard, Jett, when I pull into his garage.

"You good with grilled salmon burgers?" Sid asks as I trail him into the kitchen.

"Yeah. Thanks."

He reaches into the fridge. "Make yourself a drink."

"Want one?" I head for his bar, pour a double of the eighteen-year Japanese whiskey, and throw it back, grunting from the burn.

"Nah, just water for—Actually, yeah. Can you grab a wine glass and the buns over there?"

"Yep. Where's the wine?"

"I have an open bottle of Albariño in the wine fridge outside."

I follow him out and unload the glass and buns next to the grill.

"You know," Sid tosses over his shoulder as I climb up his hill and stretch out on the grass, "the furniture is comfortable."

"I hate patio furniture."

He smirks, and I hear him mutter, "Who hates patio furniture?"

A few minutes later, I sit up when he brings over the grub. "Good lookin'."

He made a smiley face with BBQ sauce, remembered that I hate ketchup on anything but fries, and prefer sliced jalapeños over pickles on my sandwich.

"Good to see you smile," he says, lifting his burger for a bite.

"So, how much trouble am I in?" I ask.

"None. I talked to Coach."

I stare at him. "Seriously?"

He nods.

I make a mental note to definitely buy him a car.

"Wanna tell me why I was about to throw our new assistant coach out by his neck?"

"You knew he was joining?" Each team has its own dynamic, but there's no way the Royals would recruit someone for the coaching team without consulting their star player.

"Yeah. They shared their top picks with me a few weeks ago. He was leagues above the other candidates."

"And you didn't think to tell me?"

I wait for him to finish chewing, then he answers, "I didn't think there was anything to tell. You don't care about this stuff." He wipes his mouth. "And you never told me about him. You know you keep everything about your past close to the vest."

He's right on both counts. I still let out a grunt before taking another bite of my burger.

"So, what's the deal? Y'all used to date or something?"

My swallow sticks in my throat.

"You good?"

I polish off the whiskey.

"That bad?"

I shrug. "We got close. And I thought he... I made a pass, and he..." I blow out a breath.

"He what?"

"Turned me down."

"Oh," Sid says. A beat passes before he asks, "When you say *close*?"

"I don't know." I clasp my hands behind my neck and drop my head between my knees.

"What you mean you don't know?" His head tilts as he searches my face. "You weren't conscious?"

"No, nothing like that."

For years, I wondered how I got it so wrong.

"I was having a hard time freshman year. I think you've sensed enough to know home was trash for me. I always thought if I got out of their house, things would be better."

"And it wasn't?"

I huff a laugh. "No. It wasn't."

"Damn." He shakes his head. "I'm sorry."

"I actually missed Carter yelling and dragging me out of bed at night to remind me I'm a piece of shit. Can you imagine that?"

He tenses at my admission.

I can feel the questions buzzing around his head. I also know he's too patient to force it out of me.

And because I don't have it in me to talk about Carter *and* Aiden, I choose one. "Aiden saw me flailing." He saw *me*. Period. "Started coaching me one-on-one. Helped me strengthen my game. He really believed I had what it took to get drafted." No other coach invested as many hours in me as he did. "He invited me to hang with him in the coach's lounge," I continue.

"He doesn't look that much older than us."

"He isn't."

Sid nods.

"I always felt pulled toward him, and for a while I thought it was a one-way thing, but then there'd be moments when I caught him staring at me in a way that made me wonder..."

"Is he gay?"

I shrug. "I, uh, made a move one night." Even now, I can't tell whether I imagined him kissing me back, or pulling me into his body, or if it really happened. "Anyway, he stopped it and muttered some shit about not feeling the same. There was an inappropriate power dynamic or whatever."

"Damn. That must have hurt."

"Yeah..."

"What happened after?"

"He kept his distance, ended all interactions off the court, and I, uh...didn't take it well. I pretended like it didn't bother me, but I was spiraling. But the draft was around the corner, and I just kept my head down and got the fuck away from him."

He nods. "You lost a friend."

My only friend. Overnight, I was nothing to him. I had no one.

"Carter?"

I tense. "Yeah."

"Tell me."

I roll out my neck. "Pass me that?" I gesture toward the bottle of water he brought over with the food.

He hands it to me, and I unscrew the top and take a long swig.

"After he lost his NFL contract, he started drinking and made our lives hell. I think he always knew I was gay and hated me for it. But the alcohol and mood swings made him vicious."

"When'd he lose the contract again?"

"When I was young. Really young."

He hisses. "I knew there was a reason I can't stand him. He approached me at the ESPYS a few years back, before you and I met. Energy was off. Reminded me of my first boyfriend's dad." He pauses, meeting my gaze. "I'm so sorry."

The clear rage and sadness in his eyes have my ribs tightening, my mouth twisting, and my eyes cutting away.

My phone buzzes, and I lean back to dig it out of my pocket.

I stare at Salem's name, and a jittery warmth spreads over my body.

"You two are okay?"

I nod as I drop the phone between my knees. "I think... Fuck, I'm pretty sure I'm in love with him."

"Yeah?" He grins.

"Shut up."

"I knew it."

"How?" I question.

"How'd I know you'd fall for him?"

I nod.

"Besides him being objectively hot and looking like he'd bury a body for you at Kieran's house?"

I snort.

"You forgot how to breathe when he looked at you."

I groan. "Did everyone notice?"

"I mean, it was obvious to me."

"Yeah, but that's 'cause you speak Blue."

His eyebrows crinkle. "I do what?"

"I've been meaning to ask...How'd you know Ty was it for you?"

His gaze softens as he leans back on his elbows. "I don't think it was one thing. It felt like more than friendship with him from the jump. I was also craving something deeper. It had felt empty for a minute."

"Your bed?"

He grins. "Nah. I mean, yeah, I guess at some point that became true. Messing with people I didn't want to spend breakfast with got old. But mostly, it became clear that I couldn't imagine anyone else loving him or loving me, and it feeling so damn good...or right."

The rage I feel at Josiah, yoga guy, even Salem's ex...I don't think rage is what he means, but that's what I feel when I think about him with other men.

"How'd you know you could love him without hurting him?"

His head tilts to the side. "I didn't. We had a rough patch, and I hurt him by putting up a wall. He hurt me too. Honestly, I think that's part of it. It won't be good times all the time. I just try my best every day, and I see him trying too."

"It sounds like a gamble."

"It's a bond. And it's work. Anyone claiming it'll always be easy is lying. But I wouldn't trade what I have with him for all the world."

"T HREE HOURS of the same drills! For fuck's sake." I ripped off my shirt. It landed with a plop against the bleachers.

"Thought you wanted your name etched in the annals of NBA history," Aiden taunted, sweat plastering his black hair to his forehead. "It's this. Mastering the boring little things."

"The principles," I mocked, on cue.

I set up again and reached in, and his elbow blocked my reach. I tried every maneuver in the bank but came up short. I knew he was doing that thing where he scans every shift of my face to read me. I saw an opening and pushed in, hands swiping the air, as he switched up and got past me to the rim.

"You're reading what I want you to read instead of anticipating and watching the weak-side movement."

"Whatever, man."

"Get back here! We'll stay here all night if we have to!"

"It's already past ten," I fired back.

"You want to throw in the towel or you wanna get drafted?"

I stopped walking.

"Let's go again," he said.

And we did. Again and again. Defensive play after defensive play.

My phone died just shy of midnight, and that was hours ago.

My frustration grew every time he got to the rim. And he got to the rim eight out of ten tries.

He told me to channel it, and I tried, repurposing the fire and sweating out the shame.

After fighting and pushing and launching the ball across the fucking court, just to hang my head and drag myself after it, not twice or ten but seventeen times, it clicked. I felt the rotations, ignored the misdirections, and started to dictate the play, making him adjust to me.

My power as a defender grew with each successful steal until he was barely getting to the rim. And then he was never getting to the rim.

He stood, chest heaving, ball digging into his tapered waist, and smiled at me with so much pride I almost couldn't bear to look at him. But I did look at him, and it soaked in—the late nights, early mornings, speeches, exasperation-fueled arguments, excavating what he saw in me until no other voice spoke louder than what he fleshed out. Rushing from vapid conversations and stale class lectures to him, bent over his desk, bleary-eyed and serious. At the awareness of my presence, a curve of his lips, a glint of life in his eyes, like a greater obsession than game footage or complex court strategies stood before him. And every time, I would look over my shoulder, certain someone else was standing there, praying someone else wasn't standing there, to explain the surge of electricity that filled the space between us and the sudden relief that my lungs held air, that I wasn't slowly being vacuumed into an expanding emptiness.

Now, there he was, bright gaze slipping, and my tongue edged to the bow of my lips, wanting to taste him there. A sharp rise of his nostrils and squeeze of his jaw, which on the next brush of my tongue, he forgot how to use—mouth parting, then closing, then parting again.

Lines of fresh sweat streaked his temple.

"Arnaz—"

I was already closing the distance and slamming my lips against his.

He froze.

"It's okay," I whispered before kissing him again.

He moaned, mouth spreading in a gasp, and then his calloused hands were pressing into my waist, pulling me closer. My hand lowered and ghosted against his hardened dick, and he shuddered. The force of it shattered the moment.

I rip awake and blow out a breath. Turning to my side, I bury my head under the pillow and imagine I'm back at the cabin in Salem's arms as I drift back to sleep.

Teetering on the edge of a building, the wind blowing zigzags of wet salt from my eyes across my lips.

Crescent craters dug into my palm.

The steel-beamed titan and its blue-tinted glass towered over me, and I counted again. Down from fifty-two until I reached twenty-three, then I swept left to the corner office. I couldn't see inside from this distance, but I knew she was there. Giving her all to the only thing she'd known how to nurture. She'd hear the sirens, see the crowd form, and watch lines of yellow tape inconvenience evening plans that don't involve going home to her children.

A balloon of excitement lifted her heels, forehead pressed against glass, maybe it was her lucky day and the bastard with their innards plastered to the street—that poor misguided soul—would have a story that was sad, stirring, shocking because it was sweeps week, and those ratings needed to soar, baby.

And when her phone rang, she'd ignore it—how else would people learn to call her assistant? Even the school knew not to bother her on her cell. Even the children, who were old enough to feed themselves and thus old enough to figure out a flu or a fever.

After the road was cleared, and she'd changed out of her heels and freshened her lipstick, she'd hear her assistant gasp, and wonder if she'd done it, if the whispers were true. Her two-part investigative series on the neglect, abuse, and preventable deaths of those kids slain over there in Nebraska would finally win her a Peabody.

She threw her shoulders back and breathed in the rare air of victory when her office door opened and her haggard assistant entered, wide-eyed and shell-shocked, and delivered news that I, her back-stitched son, jumped from a seventy-story building, delivering the best sweeps week of her career.

Flipping around, I shifted until my heels hit air, whispered I'm sorry to Anaïs, spread my arms wide. And let go.

I lurch awake with a gasp, stomach clenched, fingers grasping at nothing.

Sid's living room crashes into focus.

"Fuck." I blow out a ragged breath and press on my throat to quell the burn.

I kick off the throw blanket and scramble to my feet.

A dim light illuminates the kitchen as I enter.

Ty looks up from a book.

"Hey." I slide onto the stool across from him.

"Chocolate mousse?" he offers. "Sid bought it."

"What's in it?" I lean sideways to fill my cup with water from the sink. "Butterfly pollen?"

His lips curl up in an almost grin. "Avocados."

"Of course."

"He also has beet yogurt in there."

I gurgle a groan as I gulp the water. What's next? Water alkalized from mermaid piss? He won't pass away like the rest of us. He'll just evaporate into frankincense-and-myrrh-scented air.

"I'll go with the avocados," I say.

He reaches into the fridge and then slides over a cup and a bottle of water.

"Bad dream?" I ask.

He shakes his head. "Still buzzing from the game. You?"

Sid and I caught some of the replay. Ty had made it rain, something like forty points in the second half alone.

"Weird dreams," I answer after swallowing a bite. "Old ghosts. Regrets."

"That should be your album name."

I grin as I scan the mousse cup's label. "Why is this so delicious?" None of the ingredients explain the creamy, salted, dark-chocolate flavor bomb.

"I know, right?" He recycles his cup and loads his spoon in the dishwasher. "Life's about learning to live with 'em, right?"

"What?" I ask as he retreats toward the door.

"Ghosts and regrets."

"Yeah, I think so."

"Night."

"Hey, that pump fake, fadeaway against Jimmy earlier... Fire."

He smiles. An actual, genuine smile. Dimples and all. Rare.

"I'll see you for mental health night?"

"Yep."

"Any of the guest room beds are comfier than the couch."

"Shh!" I cast a wary glance toward the living room. "She'll hear you."

His cat-like eyes crinkle at the corners. "There's more in the fridge."

I start to slide off the stool. "Don't tell Sid I like it."

I FEEL like I've slept five minutes when Sid shakes me awake.

"Go away," I groan.

"We have to be at the arena soon. You should head home and get changed."

"Nngh." I rub my eyes. "Go away."

"You hate it when you're late."

Ugh. *I hate it when he's right.*

My eyes blink open. "We roll together?"

"Nah. Ty got in late. I want to..." He grins. "Y'know."

"Horny fucka." I stretch my arms over my head. "Let the man sleep."

He smirks. "Who said he needs to be up?"

And now I'm up. "Hot!"

He laughs and backs toward the staircase. "Don't be late."

"Nah, you can't drop that visual and run. Can I watch?"

"And have my fiancé commit double homicide?"

"Mm." I swing my legs to sit upright. "I wouldn't share Salem either."

Sid chuckles as my eyes widen. "Yeah, you said that out loud."

I shrug. "He ain't a silencer in the sheets is all I'm sayin'.
"Word? Man, scoop him up and stop playing."
"Yo, can I take the Lambo?"
"Which one? Let me guess. The Revontón?"
"That's my baby," I croon.
"Bet. You know where the fob is."

CHAPTER 34
ARNAZ

Soak it in this brine of decay and deafness.

"You ready for this?" Sid asks as we head to the film room.

"No."

As soon as we turn the corner, Aiden's there, smack dab in front of the room.

"Ick." I stop walking. His I'm-smarter-than-you brows are brought down a peg by his good-boy eyes, only to confuse you again as you scroll down to the rugged five o'clock shadow a shade lighter than his black hair. "He looks better than he did back then."

"Yeah?"

"Mmhm."

Sid shrugs. "Salem's hotter."

I scoff. "Fuck off. Don't look at him."

He laughs. "I'm just saying, the last time a guy looked at me the way Salem looks at you, I ended up engaged."

"He's *so* hot." I groan. "You should see the thirst-trap videos his pet sitter sends him. And his ex is hot too."

"Who's his ex?"

"You two wanna get your asses in here?" Coach yells in our direction.

"Lucien Laurent," I reply as we haul it into the room.

"Oh, dayum. He *is* hot. He's been an annual sponsor of my criminal justice reform gala for years."

"Ugh."

"Aight. But did he go on national TV and tell the world he wants Lucien?" he throws back.

My grin vanishes as I pass by Aiden and take a seat in the far corner.

"LET'S GET INTO IT," Coach begins. "We know how Oklahoma plays. The key tomorrow night is to stop Miloš. We pull him out of his flow, everything else unravels. What does he feed off of the most?"

"Orchestrating the defense," Sid answers, and I nod in agreement. One of the best centers in the league, the more Miloš facilitates, the more power he generates.

Coach points to Sid. "Correct. What's our play?"

"Stay tight on cutters and shooters to limit pass opportunities," I reply.

"Correct. What else?"

"Protect the paint," Nick answers.

"That's right. His vision's 20/20 at reading the court. Stay on time with rotations, protect the rim, and make them go through us to get to the board."

"Yeah, but even if we don't give up passes," a rook chimes in, eyes pinging between us, "he's a sharpshooter."

"Good point," Sid says, making the youngin' puff up. "But

we're top three in the league defensively for a reason. Ussef, Johan, and I will body up and force him to take tougher shots."

"Make no mistake," Coach says, "tomorrow's game comes down to using the clock to our advantage and applying sustained pressure until the end. Aiden's gonna walk us through film from our last matchup and then we'll hit the court to work on adjustments."

The energy shifts as Aiden stands, his legs slightly bowed— and cut.

I can't fault the sideways glances coming my way, given yesterday's...reaction. It doesn't stop me from glaring at a rook and Jamie, nodding for them to move the fuck along.

It's not very hard to ignore someone you need to ignore because not ignoring them makes you feel smaller and smaller with each breath. It becomes hard, though, when that someone calls you out.

"...after the rebound, Arnaz trailed the play." His stylus draws an inverted triangle with me at the apex. "If you—" I shoot daggers at the screen as he turns to me. "If *he* sprinted and cut off the sideline instead, we'd force a half-court possession, thus preventing their point guard getting off a wide open three."

I grind my teeth at my obvious miss.

He's right.

Gross.

Everyone seems to be eating up the shit he's dishing.

"Your stance is too soft here," he calls out Johan. "Get bigger, hands higher, contest the shot. You don't let up on a player like this. Study the scouting report."

I roll my eyes when Johan's head nods up and down like a fucking bobblehead.

Traitors.

Still, no one can call me unprofessional or immature. I grit my teeth, but I listen.

Then we hit the court.

And…Eh. Professionalism is overrated.

"When he drives left, you need—"

"Nah." I stand up straight. "Go run drills with someone else."

"Arnaz, it's my job—"

"Yo, James!" I call over another assistant coach. "Can you cover us?"

Aiden exchanges a glance with James, who shakes his head and falls back.

"I'll fuck off once you listen to what I have to say," he says.

"I said no," I grit out. "I'm good to pay a fine. Back down, or I'm out."

He raises his hands and backs off. "It doesn't have to be like this."

"It is like this," I fire over my shoulder, giving him my back.

"Seriously?"

He's waiting for me in the parking lot after practice.

"Can you just hear me out, and then I'll fuck off?"

I keep walking, stabbing the unlock button on my—Sid's—fob.

"Why here?" I launch my bag onto the seat as soon as the butterfly doors expand and spin to face him.

"What?"

"Of all the teams. Why this one?"

"I told you. They came knocking."

"Nah. I don't buy it." I cross my arms. "You're telling me we're the only team that came knocking? All these years?"

He looks past me. "No. I'm not saying that."

I knew it. "Then why?"

"You're one of the best teams in the league."

"You never cared about coaching the best. You always preferred underdogs."

His hand swipes over his mouth, but not before I see the tiny smirk.

"Whatever you're feeling right now, it's not real. I don't know you. I don't want your coaching. You remember what you told me that day in the gym? Now it's your turn to stay away from me."

"How am I supposed to do that when I'm your assistant coach?"

I'm already walking away.

"We're on the same team now, Arnaz."

"Nah. Coach the other fourteen. I'm good."

"It's not that I didn't feel what you felt," he admits.

My footsteps falter.

I squeeze my eyes closed as he repeats the impossible.

"It doesn't make it right. I was your—"

I turn and lurch toward him. "You can't say that!"

I swallow down the taste of vodka.

"It's true."

"Don't..." My voice cracks as the years unravel. "You can't..."

"Okay," he whispers, eyes glassy. "Okay."

Ussef emerges from the arena, beelining straight toward us.

I can't fucking be here.

As soon as the doors lower, I rev the engine and take off.

CHAPTER 35
SALEM

Something's off with Blue. I can feel it. His texts over the last two weeks have been off. Every time I ask him a question about himself, he deflects by asking one back. I caught a few of his games on TV, and in each, he looked weary —dark circles around his eyes, sluggish energy, averaging fewer points per game. I keep feeling like I should do more, so he knows I'm here for him.

He's got to know. Right?

Damn, I miss him.

The private investigator still hasn't caught a lead on my brother, which makes no sense. I had this month's bake-off with my dad to keep me distracted, otherwise...*hff*.

"Psst, peep Easton." Cillian nudges my arm and nods to the new transfer, tatted from the neck down, raven hair, mean-mugging someone in the stands as Memphis' shooting guard heads to the free throw line for a foul Easton caused.

We woke up last week and found out that Easton was on a flight to don a Brooklyn jersey. The dynamic duo of Easton and Ray had officially separated. Best friends since childhood, they had the perfect contrast of power and finesse. Though lately their off-court tension has made headlines, and there were rumors of contract disputes.

Noise aside, we could use the defensive help.

He isn't much of a talker. I approached him during his first practice to welcome him to the team. He sized me up, and when I asked if he had questions, he grunted, threw on his headphones, and stared straight ahead like I wasn't there.

"Come on," Cillian whispers. "One more foul and I win a tres leches cake."

I still owe him his millionaire's shortbread, so that makes two bakes if I lose. I'm good for it, though.

I scan the crowd for the orange *Hey, Bestie!* banner I saw at the start of the game.

"Jones. Break time's over," Coach yells over her shoulder. "Get in there before Easton gets himself suspended."

I hop to my feet and lose the towel around my neck.

"Coach, keep him in. I'm close to making—" Cillian starts.

"Screw your bet," Coach cuts him off, making the entire bench snicker.

Easton ignores me as he skulks past toward the bench. I don't get his strategy. For half the damn year, all we've got is each other on the road. Why make it harder on himself?

"Yo! I got ball," I yell as I launch toward my mark, and the crowd gets loud for me.

"You wanna grab a drink?" Cillian asks.

"Can't." I shrug on my coat and unlock my phone. "I'm meeting up with Blue's"—I click on Josiah's text—"I mean Arnaz's…"

Josiah

Sorry boss. Think i caught the flu. Tried to walk
Sim b/4 i left but u kno how he is off schedule.

MY FINGERS START TYPING.

Me

No worries

Feel better

I'll head home now

"What's up?"

"Nothin'" I pocket my phone and dap him. "Josiah dipped early. He's sick."

IT DOESN'T TAKE LONG to find the orange banner as I leave the locker room.

"Is it weird that I had fun even though y'all lost?"

I laugh as I embrace Anaïs. "Nah, our arena's always lit. I like the fit."

She's reppin' my number seven blue-and-gold Lions jersey with ripped, black skinny jeans and all white Doc Martens. A leather jacket hangs from her hand.

"I don it with pride. There was an enemy in the stands in front of me, rooting for Memphis." Her dark-red lips part mischievously. "I almost poured my bottle of water over his head."

"Always violence with the Cade terrors."

Her tongue peeks out as she trembles with a low cackle.

"Ready, killa?" I lead the way out.

"Yeah, but only 'cause I'm hungry. Otherwise, I'd need you

to turn around and gimme a tour of the locker room, specifically the shower area."

I chuckle. "You know backstage access doesn't include showers."

"C'mon. You're supposed to be cooler than Arnie." She frowns. "He told you, didn't he? One time. One time I tried to peek Sid's dick, and now I'm banned for life."

I stop walking. "What?"

"Don't judge me. His nipples are pierced, and I was curious, y'know? I have a thing for dick pierci—whoa! Montenero GT!"

I'm smacked with déjà vu from Blue stopping in the middle of the street with the same expression.

"Nineteen hundred horsepower, slingshots from zero to, like, what is it, eighty miles per hour in under two seconds and zero to, like, 200 in twelve?"

I scoff. "Yeah. Eighty-five, damn. You and Blue share the same brain?"

She rolls her eyes. "I taught baby bro everything he knows about cars. Can I drive?"

I shrug and toss her the fob.

"Shut up! Don't tell Arnaz. He'll talk you out of it."

"Uh, why would he talk me out of it?" I call out nervously as she races away.

She pulls her glasses off her head and thumbs them on. "Get in, sweetcakes!"

Cillian sidles up next to me. "Who's the cutie?"

"Blue's—Arnaz's—sister."

He raises an eyebrow. "You already hanging with the fam? What happened to 'we're keeping it light?'"

I shrug.

We both jump as a screech of tortured metal music blasts from the car.

"Who is that?" I ask as Cillian whistles.

His face twists. "Death Spells, bruh!"

"Who?"

He's already gone, reaching into the passenger window and cranking it up.

"What the hell is this?" Zyair approaches, palming his ears.

"Death Spells," I repeat, grinning as Anaïs moves to her knees as Cillian swings open the door...and they bang their heads in unison, the motion trance-like.

Blue would hate this. I pull out my phone and hit record. My best friend on the Lions and his bestie—and now mine too —vibing.

When I'm about to hit send, I pause.

My shoulders sag as I slide my phone back into my pocket.

I thought we'd turned a corner and were past second-guessing after our time at the cabin.

With everything going down with Denzel, I just want to call him and talk.

It shouldn't be this hard, I think. Maybe my setup with Lucien spoiled me. When I called him, he came, and vice versa. And even though we hadn't been exclusive, we showed up for each other when it counted.

This feels different. Like sometimes the man I love is a ghost.

We've gone from talking every day to this.

What the hell happened?

"What's Blue's guitar music like?" I ask as I click my seat belt.

"Take a song with a post-rock, shoegaze influence, like the one we just heard, and then mix in soul."

I blink one eye closed. "Uh...I think I got it."

She nods as she takes off her glasses and uses the bottom of her jersey to wipe the lenses. "Okay, add soul, then spoon in Arnaz's melancholic moodiness, and mix that ish up." She slides her glasses back on. "His music would blow if it dropped. And"—she releases a heavy breath—"he'd hate it. I think he knows how good it is, and that's why he won't release it."

"I heard him play the piano once. It still gives me chills."

"Me too." She adjusts the mirrors. "Some of his stuff's so raw it makes me bawl. Where we headed?"

"I need to stop home and walk my dog quick fast. My sitter's sick."

"Thirsty Joshua?"

I snort. Blue told her about Josiah? I reach over and click Home on the navigation. "It's not like that."

"Uh-huh," she says, pulling out of my spot. "We're rarely wrong about that kinda thing."

"I'm not into Josiah. And I see the guys he dates. They don't look anything like me. And there's zero chemistry."

She side-eyes me, and it's magnified by her frames. "He wears your clothes?"

"That's new for him."

She frowns.

"It's cold out!" I say defensively.

"This is never off." She taps her chest over her heart. "We know what it's like not to be loved. When we feel it, we're fierce about protecting it. We can sense Josiahs a mile away. He's never getting off the Watch List."

"Watch List? Sounds like the CI—Ay-yo!"

My back hits the seat as she slams on the accelerator and guns it.

"Move it!" she yells at the cars on the road ahead of us as she swings across three lanes.

"U-uh, I think I see why Blue would've warned me."

"I'm not the one who—Not your turn, dickwad!" She cuts off a Benz, then switches lanes again like we're ducking the police. "I'm not the one who crashed my car a week after I got it for my eighteenth birthday."

"Was he okay?"

"No. He had a death wish."

The way she says it makes my stomach queasy.

"I once threw a jab about him having silver spoons," I admit with regret.

"Oof. And you lived?"

"He tried to take my head off," I tell her. "Right up here." I point to my townhouse up ahead on the right and open my garage through the app on my phone.

"Want to raid my kitchen while I walk Simba?" I ask as we get out of the car.

"Sure, but I wanna come on the walk first."

"Cool. Come on."

"I'VE MET MY SOULMATE," Anaïs croons as Simba begins his smooch show.

He ignored me and ran straight to her.

I unhook his leash from the peg.

His ears perk up when he hears the clank of metal, pauses for a second, then resumes rolling to his back and soaking up the belly rubs.

"I don't exist when we have guests over," I tell her.

"Like he remembers you exist when Arnaz is around," she coos to Sim.

I bend down and hook the leash through the metal ring of his collar. "Blue's never been here."

Her head pops up. "I thought...Really? Ohh. I messed that up the night when I was sick, didn't I?"

"It's all good." I stroke Sim's fur. "I'm sorry you were sick. How are you feeling now?"

"Surgery in a few weeks." She smiles nervously, offering her palm to Simba to slobber on.

"What's it gonna be like?"

"Doctors always downplay it, you know? You've heard of endometriosis?" I shake my head. "It's an inflammatory disease, and it's excruciating."

"Damn."

"They make a couple of small incisions around my abdomen and then go in with a camera to find and cut out any inflamed or scarred tissue around my organs."

"God. That sounds intense."

"I'll be under the whole time."

"How long's recovery?"

"Six to eight weeks if all goes as planned. It doesn't get rid of the disease—they haven't figured out a cure—but it's supposed to reduce the pain."

The three of us rise to stand. "Seriously, no cure?"

She shakes her head.

"Anything I can do?"

"Visit me during recovery?"

"For sure." Simba pulls me toward the door. "What's your favorite dessert?"

"Uh...Fraisier cake. Can I grab a snack real quick?"

"Sure," I say, and she follows me into the kitchen.

Scanning the fridge, she starts to reach for a yogurt and pauses. "Is that mac 'n' cheese?"

"Yeah. You okay with dairy? It has smoked Gouda and Gruyère."

"Mm." She pulls out the container and pops it open. "Is that truffle?"

I laugh when she licks her lips, making a slurping sound.

"There's also braised short ribs."

"Stop!"

"Top shelf, behind the sautéed green beans."

"Oh my god! How do you have all of this?" she exclaims.

"I like to cook."

I race over and help offload the pile of containers she's stacked under her chin.

"Why are we going out to eat?" she asks.

"I didn't think you'd want to stay in."

"I always want to stay in!" She peels back the lid on the ribs. "Ohmygod. Okay. New plan. You walk Sim, and I start heating this up. Come back and we throw down. Yes?"

"Yes, ma'am! The pots are—"

"I'll find 'em," she says, removing her coat.

"More wine?" she offers.

"Sure."

"You barely ate."

I look down at my half-full plate. "I ate plenty."

"No, *I* ate plenty." She points her chin at her empty second plate.

I rub the back of my neck. "I don't have much of an appetite these days."

"Why? What's wrong?"

"Did Blue tell you why he called out sick a few weeks back?" I question.

Her eyes narrow. "When he had a cold?"

Hmm. He really didn't tell anyone else he almost drowned. I can't tell her I'm worried something else like that happened to him. "Yeah. Um, just family stuff. My older bro is a Marine vet."

Sim comes over, looking for scraps, and she reaches down and scratches behind his ears. "Is he your only sibling?"

"Yep. He, uh..." I pause for a beat. "Struggles with PTSD and depression, among other things. Sometimes he disappears. The last time, it was bad. Luckily, the right people found him and got him to a hospital."

"That's scary. Where is he now?"

I expel a breath. "Hell if we know. We hired a detective to track him down."

She stops petting Sim, and the deep concern etched on her face feeds the gnawing in my stomach.

She leans forward, resting her palm on my arm. "Start from the beginning."

My mouth opens, but the words are choked.

"It's okay," she replies as my eyes well up. "Go slow." She grabs some tissues for me. "Tell me."

CHAPTER 36
ARNAZ

In me, an unceasing winter.
Heat bled out, blood blistered.

I hit rewind, then play.

He hangs his head as he walks toward the bench. The crowd is cheering him, but it's like he can't hear them.

I rewind the video again, then hit pause.

Clicking back over to the tab from his game two weeks ago, I drag it next to the one of last night's game.

I hit play on them both.

There!

I freeze both screens.

Shoulders hunched, bags under his eyes, he sinks into the chair, and unlike everyone on the bench whose head is turned toward the game, his stays facing straight ahead.

Shit.

I know what happens next, yet my throat still grows a lump when I hit rewind and watch it again.

I know this can't be about me.

So, who or what did this?

Ow. I pull my thumb away from my teeth and watch a line of blood form. I switch to my other thumb.

Who hurt him?

Climbing out of bed and grabbing my phone, I pace the room and call the only person I know who might have answers.

"Arnaz, what's wrong?"

"Cat, is he okay?"

"Who?"

"Salem. Who else?"

"Jones?" she asks, her voice more alert. I hear a thud. "Where are my glasses?"

Lys's voice filters through, asking, "What's going on?"

"I don't know. Something happened to Jones," she tells her. "Cade, are you there? What happened?"

"I don't know what happened. That's why I'm calling you."

"Why do you think something happened?"

"He looks sad. Something's off."

"Sad? What do you mean, sad? Where?"

"His last game. The third quarter. He's headed—"

"Wait, hold on. It's...two thirty-three in the morning, and you're calling me because Salem looks *sad*?"

I hear her whisper off the line, "Go back to sleep," as I pull the phone away from my ear and wince. *The hell?* The last time I looked, it was just after ten.

"Shit."

"Did you take something? Where are you?"

"No. I'm sob—"

"I can send Dr. Thomas over. You know she's trustworthy and discreet. Whatever is needed, we'll handle it privately."

It sounds like she's the one pacing now.

"I'm not high."

"Name the last three teams you played."

"Cat, I'm not high. I'm home. My bad for calling so late."

"Arnaz, wait. You know I can't disclose client information."

My pulse takes off. "What does that mean? Are you saying something's wrong without saying it?"

"No. It means that even if something was wrong, and I'm not saying there is, I wouldn't be able to tell you. Are you two having a fight?"

"Cat, if something was seriously wrong with him, I'd need to know."

"Okay, now I'm worried again. You sound really upset."

"Just please..." My ribs clench tight, squeezing the words into a watery whisper. "Tell me. Please."

"Hey." Her voice softens. "Sweetheart, what's wrong?"

I crash into my armchair and cradle the side of my head. "Nothing. I'm fine."

"But you're crying."

"I just need to know. Tell me. Please."

"I will call him, okay? If there is something wrong, I'll be there for him. But I am more concerned about you right now. If I leave now, I can get to you by the morni—"

"I'm fine. Tell Lys I'm sorry."

I hang up and drop the phone.

CHAPTER 37
ARNAZ

♫ "Demons" ♫
I envy the lonely, all that empty space.

"A rnaz?" My therapist frowns. "Can you tell me if you're experiencing thoughts of self-harm?"

Eight points, one assist, and no rebounds.

Why didn't I rebound?

I release a long yawn.

Thirty-two minutes past six, only eighteen minutes left.

Eight points. Pitiful.

I wince from the burn in my throat. "I keep tasting vodka."

"Thanks for letting me know. Let's address that in a moment. Can you tell me if you're experiencing thoughts of self-harm?"

"Just vodka."

"Thank you." She scrawls something down. "Okay, you said you taste it all the time?"

"Yeah."

"If I recall correctly"—she scans the screen of her tablet—"that was your father's drink of choice."

Four fouls. Three were my bad, but the fourth was definitely a bad call.

"Coach benched me for the second half yesterday."

She observes me in silence before replying, "He did? Can we hold that thought for one second?"

I nod.

"The vodka. Do you think it's related to your college coach joining your current team's coaching staff?"

I shrug, crossing my arms.

"That's okay. If there is a connection, it may not be obvious. We can go slowly. Coach benched you for the second half of the game. How did that make you feel?"

Every time I swallow, it burns.

"I keep chewing these tea tree toothpicks." I pull the one I'm gnawing on out of my mouth and hold it up to her. "Sthyyll vaahd-kuh," I say on a yawn.

"Hmm." She angles her head. "When did this start?"

He said he felt it too back in college. What the hell am I supposed to do with that?

"It makes me feel sick. I hate the taste."

"Arnaz, may I share an observation with you?"

Why does every hotel room have generic art? Ocean views, mountains, clouds...

"May I?" she asks.

Vodka burns worse than salt water.

"Sorry?"

"May I share an observation with you?"

I reach into my pocket to swap my toothpick for a fresh one. "Shoot."

"You know how we talked about the window of tolerance concept?"

"Yeah, you said I got a narrow window."

Her eyes crease at the corners. "We observed that your nervous system becomes overwhelmed by big emotions, and dissociation can kick in as a protective mechanism. What else do you remember?"

I clench the toothpick between my teeth.

Sid won't let me lose my starter position. I need to buy him a car. I think I know the one.

"It's okay if you don't remember. I can provide a refresher. When you're inside your window of tolerance, you feel present—"

"I *am* present. Every game. That's why I'll be tight if Coach doesn't start me."

She waits a beat, then continues, "Tell me more."

"'Cause I'm a starter. I've proven myself," I explain.

"Okay. I don't doubt that. What would it mean if you didn't start?"

"I just told you. I'll be tight."

"You'll be upset?"

"Yeah."

"Let me ask it differently. If you don't start, you'll be upset, but then what happens?"

I rub my sternum. All week, some dick with heavy boots has been flicking around a lighter in there.

"I'm gonna have a talk with him."

"Okay, and if you have a talk with your coach and he still benches you, then what?"

"I would…" I bounce my knee. "It's fucked-up."

"Mm. Because you earned your position as a starter?"

"Yes."

She nods and places her stylus down. "I hear you. I do." She leans back in her chair, looking out the window. "I don't know." Her chest rises, then falls as her fingers tap on the screen. "I'm sensing there's something deeper at work here. Are you open to us trying an exercise?"

Oh god.

I cross, then uncross my ankles.

Thirteen minutes...

The heavy-footed dickhead behind my sternum discovers a blowtorch. I grunt out an "Okay."

"Close your eyes."

I rub my palms on my thighs as everything goes dark.

"Great. Let's take a few deep breaths. Ready?"

"Mmhm."

"Okay, breathe in deeply for five seconds. Good. Now release the breath for seven seconds."

My lungs fill on three, so I'm stuck holding air until she tells me to let go.

"Again. Deep breath in for five."

I crack one eye open as I suck in air.

Twelve minutes.

"And release for seven."

"Last one. Deep breath in. And release. Great."

I was kinda on beat for that last one.

"I want you to imagine showing up to your game tomorrow night, and your coach announcing the starting lineup, and you're not listed."

My eyes shoot open.

"Don't worry, we're not going to call it into existence if we imagine it," she assures me.

Releasing a shaky breath, I close my eyes again.

"Tell me when you're there."

If Coach doesn't start me, I can already hear the pundits. *Welp, folks, it's written in the glitter. Arnaz Cade—new face of progress or failure? Is this the last dance for the first out player in the league?*

"Are you there?"

"There," I mumble.

"Fantastic. Can you tell me what comes up for you the second you're informed you aren't starting?"

Another obvi question? What's up with her today?

"I'm upset," I grit out.

"Okay. Can you describe where you feel it in your body?"

"I feel upset."

"Could you describe what sensations you feel and where?"

"Here." I flick my hand from my head down.

"Okay. You feel it in your head, neck, and chest? I got that right?"

I nod.

"What about your stomach?"

Vodka and bile.

"Yeah."

"Okay. Focus on just your throat. Keeping your eyes closed, can you tell me what sensations you feel?"

"Like?"

"Hot, cold, tight, sore?"

I swallow. "I told you, vodka."

"So, it burns?"

I nod.

"What else?"

I try to swallow. "Feels like someone's doing this." I wrap a hand around the front of my throat.

"Like someone's choking you?"

I nod.

"Can you see who's there choking you?"

My eyes shift, searching behind my eyelids.

I shake my head.

"Are you still standing before your coach?"

I flick her words out of the way to look around.

"No," I mumble.

"Can you describe where you are?"

I can't see shit, but I feel...something. I clear my throat. "It's dark."

"Okay. What else do you see?"

I rub the heel of my palm into my sternum as a room comes into shape. "Same room."

"The large room with a fireplace?"

I nod.

"Is the fireplace on?"

I nod again.

"Okay, and where are you?"

Where I always am. Sliding down the wall.

"In the corner."

"Standing or hunched down?"

"Hunched down."

"Okay. Does it feel okay to stand up?"

I sink lower until I'm on my butt with my knees bent in front of me.

"I'm good here."

"That's fine. Let's have you stay there, then. Do you feel like yourself? Younger? Older?"

I study my hands. "I feel like me."

"Okay. Anyone else there now?"

I shake my head.

"Can you tell me what you're feeling now?"

I hate that question.

I *hate* it.

"My throat was just starting to open."

"Do you know what's making it close?"

"I hate that question."

"It's closing because I asked what you're feeling?"

Her voice is never cold or rushed. Always even, with a warm lilt, even when I know she can tell she's annoying the shit outta me.

"Yeah. There's a door."

"Can you describe the door?"

The fuck? It's a door.

"The hallway is dark."

"The hallway that's in front of the door?"

"Yes."

"What or who do you think is behind the door?"

I feel...it...cowering, and my eyes prick with rage.

"I don't know."

I hate him. He's so fucking useless. Always hiding in there, stinking of fear.

"It's okay that you don't—"

I dip my chin inside the neckline of my shirt. "I hate him."

"Could you tell me who you see there? Is it the same six- or seven-year-old as last time?"

"He's so useless. Afraid all the time."

"How does it feel to hate him?"

I swipe my cheek against my shoulder.

The fuck am I crying for?

"He's just so scared..."

"Is he still really young? Like six or seven?"

I nod.

"Phew." She blows out a breath. "To be six or seven, scared and alone in that big house. That sounds really scary."

She takes a moment and then asks, "Do you think—and you can absolutely say no—do you think we can invite him to sit with us for a while?"

No! He's dirty, and he smells.

I shrug.

"Yes or no? It is completely up to you."

I don't open my eyes because her eyes are open, and she'll catch me checking the time. So, I don't know how long I sit here, but it feels like it's long enough for this session to be over.

Why isn't it over?

"Okay," I mumble.

"Are you sure?" she asks.

I sure as hell ain't gonna be scared like him. "Yeah."

"Okay, you can invite him in whenever you're ready."

I don't speak or look up as the door creaks open. Keeping my chin tucked, I stare between my legs.

She has this way of breathing that's contagious, like yawning. I breathe in deeply.

Then I hear it...the barely-there shuffle.

"Is he there?" she asks.

I nod as the fucker with the blowtorch discovers a ladder.

"What's he doing?"

I don't have to look to know. "He's hiding by the door."

"Think we can help him feel safe enough to come closer?"

My nostrils flare.

Why did he even come out if he's so afraid?

"Okay. How about we sit with him for a minute?"

Listening to the stilted breathing across the room, I nod.

My feet press into the floor as I push back against the wall.

"Alright. Maybe we can let him know, with or without looking at him, that he can leave whenever he's ready, and that it was really brave of him to come out and sit with us today. You think we can do that?"

I scrub away the tears that have dripped onto the knuckle tat on my left hand.

What she said. You can go now.

"Open your eyes when you're ready."

I minimize my reflection in the small square in the corner, wiping my eyes on the shoulder of my T-shirt.

She does the thing where she smiles at me with her eyes before they close, giving me permission to close my own eyes and take a second to breathe.

After, she asks, "Would you like to take a minute to get a sip of water, stretch, or just breathe a little longer before we talk about what came up?"

"I'm okay," I answer.

"Okay. How was that for you?"

"Peachy," I huff into a tissue as I blow my nose.

"Mm. That was really hard work. You know how we talked about how complex PTSD can lead to these fragmented selves or parts due to chronic trauma experienced during childhood or over long periods?"

I nod.

"And all of those selves of the psyche hold different, at times conflicting, memories, emotions, and behaviors?"

"Yeah," I reply. "You said part of the trauma work is to integrate those parts."

"Yes, that's correct." She pauses as I take a sip of water. "We just did some of that work today. I am so proud of the way you showed up.

"Our brains separate overwhelming experiences to keep us going. And these separate parts don't always speak to each other, which makes it hard to know what's in there and, in turn, how to regulate our emotions. The abuse you suffered when you were young points to a wounded child inside of you who is now getting the healing he needs and deserves. How did it feel to be in his presence?"

I rub my ear. "Gross."

"Gross. Hmm. You know, you felt angry that he was so afraid. I think what you were really tapping into is his helplessness. He was forced to hold so much pain and fear."

My knee bounces under the table as pressure bubbles up in my throat.

"And no adult showed up to help protect him. He is so brave for holding it all. It's not easy. The relational and developmental trauma that he—you—experienced was complex. You were punished for needing safety, connection, and love. Your pain is not dramatic. The work that you have been doing to process it all is really difficult work."

"Isn't there an easier way than this? Like a pill?" I ask.

"This is part of the work. Unfortunately, there isn't a magic solution out there. But work is being done to explore supportive avenues. For example, I just read about a nonprofit that's helping PTSD survivors access plants and other medicines, with the help of trained medical professionals, to revisit traumatic moments. It isn't FDA approved here in the United States, but there are clinical trials in places like Mexico and Peru that have had encouraging results. I offer that to say, with more resourcing, we'll continue to learn more ways to approach trauma work."

"Plant medicine?"

She nods. "We're seeing funding for private clinical trials to treat post-traumatic stress disorder, depression, and addiction, using psilocybin and MDMA. Again, it's just an example. It won't be for everyone, and it will be critical for this kind of work to be facilitated by trained professionals."

Wild.

"What do you think about us visiting him again in the future to help him feel safe and less alone? Of course we'll move slowly here."

I don't know. "Can I think about it?"

"Of course. I want to know what else comes up for you after leaving here. We'll do a check-in, but if you need additional support before then, you can call me."

"Thanks."

"You bet. Well, we started our session by discussing Aiden. Based on the exercise we just did, it is not surprising that feelings of rejection trigger core wounds. He reenters your life, pressing right up against them, triggering very painful feelings of shame, rejection, and unworthiness. What do you think?"

I scrub my hands over my face as the thought settles in. "So, you think it's really not about Aiden? It's about my parents?"

"I think it could be both. I don't deny that he hurt you. He was the first man you fell in love with, and when he turned you down and stepped back from your relationship, it was deeply painful. You found a connection with him, and when you went to explore that connection, you lost it. It may have triggered a core wound that love is not safe. I am also following the thread of rejection and shame that started before him, and yes, with your family."

He's six or seven years old...that's long before Aiden.

"Damn." I blow out a breath. "It always seems to come back there."

"It is no small thing that you experienced. During critical developmental years, you didn't have the safety or care that comes with an adult mirroring emotional regulation. I am a trained therapist, and as you know, a CPTSD survivor like you, and knowing what's happening in here"—she gestures to her head—"is just as much of a mystery at times. We can *shoulda, woulda, coulda* all day, but it takes healing, and nothing short of it, to understand what's happening in here. All we can do is practice grace and show up for our healing. And I probably sound like a broken record, but healing is a practice, not a goal."

"How do I face Aiden? It's like he dropped a bomb in my lap."

"Admitting that he had feelings for you?"

I nod.

"Hmm. I think that will take some time to process, which we will continue to do through our work together. We need to get you regulated first. That's the priority here. So, let's talk tools to support you as we move to close out."

I nod.

"Okay. You have a pad of paper and a pen?"

"Yeah." I reach for both.

"Let's come up with two to three things that feel really good for you with the goal of introducing calm into your nervous system every day. I want you to spend at least five minutes daily doing one of the activities that we list. We'll start with three, but you can add to the list. I just want to know what you've added when we meet, to ensure it's actually restorative. Okay?"

I nod.

"You're great at visualization exercises. So, let's add a few. I want you to think about someone who makes you feel really good when you're around them. And by good, I mean safe, seen, heard, like you can let your guard down, and if there's joy too, that's great."

Salem.

"I want you to think of a memory with that person or visualize them sitting next to you. If it feels safe for you two to touch, go for it, but if you don't want to be touched, just imagine them sitting with you. How does that sound?"

I think of the last morning at the cabin when we hugged goodbye. When he went to pull away, I held on longer, and he wrapped me up tighter. "Got it," I respond.

"What else feels good?"

"My music, playing ball, writing."

"Fantastic. One more?"

I gnaw on my lip. I haven't had much of an appetite all week or the energy to do much, so I rule out food or going out. Except... "I don't know if it counts, but Ty, you remember Sid's fiancé?"

She nods. "I remember Ty."

She remembers everything. Sid and Ty are famous, though. But she also remembered the unicorn bandage story I told her that one time.

"When my article came out, he heard from a couple of guys that they also struggle with stuff, so he's putting on a night for us to, like, drink beers or whatever."

"That sounds like an amazing way to be part of a community. Are you thinking of going?"

If she had asked an hour ago, I would have said I was planning to skip, but now I don't know. "Maybe."

"Remaining in connection with people we trust is hard when we're struggling, but it really is healing for us. Trust me. I can self-isolate like nobody's business, but my therapist reminds me that we were never meant to struggle alone. Healthy communities and societies lean on each other." She leans in slightly. "If you can, I encourage you to go."

"Okay."

"Alright, Arnaz. Again, fantastic work today. Really big work. Be gentle with yourself. Practice grace and compassion. Reach out if you need additional support. Okay?"

"Yep. Thanks, Zuri."

"You bet. Let's close out. Any thoughts or questions? And what's one takeaway from today?"

I lean back and stretch my arms over my head. "I can't taste vodka."

CHAPTER 38
ARNAZ

♫ "The Truth" ♫
Traveled ahead, long ago.
Waiting for my arrival.

I'm grabbing my towel and climbing out of the shower when my phone lights up on the sink.

"Hey, you good?" I answer.

"Hey, how's Milwaukee?" Anaïs asks.

"Haven't seen it. Went straight from practice back to my room. Hold on." I place the phone and switch to speaker. "Go ahead." I towel off and then pad over to my duffel and pull out briefs and a T-shirt.

"You saw Zuri?"

"Yeah."

"She helped?"

"Yeah." *I'm still hit with OCD flare-ups, but I don't feel lost anymore.* "Turns out it really isn't about Aiden. Tell you more when I see you."

"Okay. Have you spoken to Salem?"

I pause getting dressed. "Why?"

"Nothing. He's fine."

I blow out a breath and continue sliding my tee over my head. I owe him an explanation for being distant lately.

Fuck. I miss him.

"I wondered if you heard an update about his brother?"

"His brother?" I reach for my phone charger. "What about him?"

"If they found him."

I pick up the phone and kill the speaker. "What are you talking about?"

I KNOCK on the hotel door.

"Yo," Sid calls out.

"Got a sec?"

"Yeah, hold on." There's a shuffle. "You solo?"

"Yep."

I hear his footsteps approaching before the door opens.

"Hey," he says.

"Why'd you ask if I was solo?"

He turns the iPad screen pressed to his chest toward me, and a sleepy Ty appears on screen.

I nod. "My bad. I need to duck out, but I'll be back in the morning. Cover for me?"

He raises an eyebrow. "Going out? We're in Milwaukee, bro."

"The Lions beat Chicago a few hours ago," Ty says.

"Ah!" Sid replies with a smirk. "Have fun."

"Good lookin'."

CHAPTER 39
SALEM

"Want in?" Cillian extends the pool cue to me.

"I'm good."

"I want in," Onyx says. "Zeke?"

"Yeah," Ezekiel replies, sliding off the stool next to me. "I need a refill first." He polishes off his beer. "Want another round?"

"Sure," I reply.

"White wine, right?"

"Yeah, Pinot Grigio. Thanks."

"Can you grab me a glass too?" Cillian throws over his shoulder, but Ezekiel is already making his way to our private lounge bar.

My phone lights up on the counter next to me.

I glance at the screen, click accept, and I'm on my feet. "Hey —hello."

"Hey." Blue's voice comes through the line. "Hey, one sec." I turn to Cillian. "I'm out."

As I beeline for the door, Zeke shouts, "Yo, your wine."

"Give it to Cillian," I throw back.

"Hey, my bad. How are you?" I push the elevator button. "You've been kinda quiet."

"Uh, are you staying at the Regis or Four Seasons?" he asks.

"Regis. Why?"

"I'm, uh, in the lobby."

"W-what?"

"Yeah. I'm downstairs."

"Seriously?" I start to move toward the staircase when the elevator arrives. I hop on and stab the button for the first floor.

"Yeah. Is that okay?" he asks.

"You're here, like, in Chicago?" I repeat, not quite believing it. I stab the first-floor button again. "Hello?" I pull the phone away from my ear and see that the call dropped.

As soon as the door opens, I beeline for the lobby. I make it a few steps when I hear, "Hey."

I turn so fast that I flinch when I spot him standing in the corner.

"Hey!" I exclaim so loudly that he grins.

Removing his shades, he pushes off the wall. "I almost tried the Four Seasons first, but our team stayed here last time, so figured it was a better guess."

"You're really here." I pull him into a hug. "You flew from Milwaukee?"

"Took a car." He says, hugging me back. "Tell me about Denzel."

Huh? I step back. "You're here because of Denzel?"

The sound of voices drawing near makes us shuffle toward the elevator.

"Yes," he replies as the doors open and we get in. "Anaïs only told me a few hours ago." He removes his beanie. "Are you okay?"

He drove a car two hours to ask if I'm okay?

His shoulders draw up slightly, and I realize I'm staring and not speaking.

"Yeah. I mean no." I lean against the elevator wall. "I'm actually kinda freaked out."

He moves closer. "Why didn't you tell me?"

"I wanted to, but the door had just opened with you and me. I was holding out hope that he'd pop up and all our concerns were for nothing." We arrive at my floor, and I lead him toward my room. "It never felt like the right time."

I unlock the door and flick on the light.

"But the cabin..." he says, and I wince at the hurt in his voice.

"I know...I'm sorry." I turn and perch on the bed.

"We talked for hours."

I know.

"I knew you were off that last time at the cabin before we made love in the rain," he ruminates out loud as he tosses his coat on the armchair. "I don't want you to be sorry." He walks over and lifts my chin. "I want to know everything. Tell me."

Arnaz

The sun is breaking through the night by the time I'm out of questions, Salem's out of answers, and we're both out of ideas on how to find Denzel except for abandoning the season and searching for him ourselves.

I don't know what I'd do if Anaïs disappeared. It would be a reality I'm not sure I could face.

"Hey," he says, lying across from me. "You've been quiet lately."

I've been waiting for him to bring it up. I still don't know how to tell him about Aiden, and how he brought up stuff with Mom and Carter. I have to soon, though. Tonight, I just want to be here for him. "My bad for that. Things got off track for me for a minute. My therapist helped me work through it."

"Yeah?" he asks.

"Yeah." I lift my head from the pillow and lean forward to press a kiss against his lips. "You deserve an explanation. I'll tell you more soon."

"I missed you," he says.

"I missed you too." I press another kiss against his lips, then his cheekbone, and then his neck, my mouth latching on to the skin there.

"Blue," he moans.

I release him, already hating my next words. "I have an early shootaround." I kiss over my bite mark. "I have to go."

"No, fly back," he groans, tilting his head up and drawing me into a kiss.

The flight options were shit when I looked last night. If I leave now, I'll beat traffic.

"Salem," I moan as his hands explore my body.

"Stay," he begs at the same time I rasp, "Fuck...Lube?"

"Huh?" His fingers work my belt.

"Got lube?"

His hands freeze. "Shit." The back of his head slumps to the pillow. "No lube or condoms."

Damn.

I reach for his waistband. "This will be even quicker then."

After we 69 and clean up, I order my car and dress quickly. Or at least I'm trying to get dressed, when my chest is pressed against the door, and my chin is turned sideways for a kiss. I melt into the breathless rhythm of our tongues curling and stroking each other.

"Thank you for coming," he pants after pulling back.

I reach in for one more taste, chasing the taste of our cum.

"When can I see you again?"

"Soon," he answers. "Promise."

CHAPTER 40
ARNAZ

♫ "CPTSD" ♫

Surviving yesterdays.

There are more of us than I thought there would be as I pull in next to the cars filling Ty's driveway in Topanga Canyon. Ty lived here before he and Sid purchased their estate in Hidden Hills. It's kept for appearances for situations like this, where word got around about tonight and not everyone knows they're a couple, or that Sid's bi and Ty's gay.

Killing the ignition, I call Salem for the second time today. It goes straight to voicemail again.

"Hey. It's...um"—I clear my throat—"Blue. Call me."

We've talked every night since Milwaukee, except last night when we missed each other.

I hang up.

Damn, I miss him. It's been less than a week.

I didn't know it could feel this way—like my lungs don't have enough space to expand.

Sid rushes out, shutting the door behind him, as I step out of the car. "I saw it was you on the security camera."

"And you felt like escorting me inside?" I tease.

"Good, good. You're in a good mood tonight."

"What's going on?" I ask as he leans against the door.

"You know how I extended an invite tonight to everyone in the locker room?"

"Yeah..."

"Including the coaching staff..." He winces.

"Seriously?" I groan.

"My bad. He wasn't there when I told everyone, *but* Wes and Jamie brought him. I can kick him out."

We've already made practices tense by ignoring and avoiding each other. I rub my neck and stare at my car.

I'm not trying to bring that energy to Ty's event.

"Don't leave. I'll make him go," he says.

"Nah," I grumble. "It's whatever. Come on."

"You sure?"

"Yeah." I step forward, forcing him back until the door opens.

He hands me a plate as we make a pit stop at the food table.

"Thanks," I say absently, staring out at the view. Being this high up, it feels like I can reach out and touch the treetops and mountains.

It makes me think of the family of deer at our cabin.

I check my phone to make sure the ringer's on.

"Thanks for coming through," Ty says as I approach the patio, extending a dap.

"Thanks for having me."

"Wassup?" I say to Ty's Knights teammates, Idris, Tevin, and Malik, sitting around the circle, and nod to Wes and Jamie.

I slide into the empty seat next to Idris, avoiding the empty one near Aiden.

"Alright," Ty says, "I think we can get started. The idea of creating a chill space for those of us in the league who struggle with depression and stuff came to me during a phone call with my uncle. When I told him about a friend I'd met, he said something like he couldn't tell me how many times a conversation with a friend helped him or that friend off a ledge. He's a retired firefighter who's seen some messed-up stuff on the job. And then, Arnaz, when your article came out, and you talked about your depression, it helped me see that I'm not alone."

He pauses to acknowledge me, and I nod, feeling like an impostor. I came out because I couldn't stay in the closet anymore. This is different.

"I've also had similar conversations with some of you here," he continues. "We all know why we're here. Thank you for showing up. Before I open up the floor—"

The doorbell rings.

"I got it," Sid says, hopping up.

Ty lays the ground rules, asking us to assume best intent when someone is sharing their experience, give the speaker the floor, step out if we need to take a call, and keep what's discussed here private.

As footsteps approach, we all turn to find Ray, the other half of the Easton and Ray duo, trailing behind Sid.

"Still cool for me to join?" Ray asks, dapping Ty.

"You're right on time. Want to grab some food?" Ty replies.

"Good lookin', I just ate."

Locking eyes with me as he passes, he arches an eyebrow, then backsteps to sink into the seat next to me.

"Nice ink," he says, pointing to my arm tat.

It sounds like an invitation to pound town, but I learned from our face-offs on the court that's just his vibe. Dude has more swag than he knows what to do with. Or maybe he does. He's like Sid before Ty, always seen with a high-profile woman.

"None for you?" I ask.

"No, that was always East's—" His eyes, that look permanently outlined with kohl, glaze over. "N-no." He crosses his arms. "No tats."

"Cool." I tune Ty back in.

"... encouraged to share, but you don't have to. If you choose to speak, share only what feels safe and comfortable. If someone asks you a question that you don't feel comfortable answering, just say 'pass.' This is supposed to feel chill." He rubs his hands together. "Aight. I know that was a lot. Any questions?"

"Just a comment," Tevin pipes up. "I've known my boy Ty for a minute, and he's a hella private guy. It's not a small thing for him to open up his home and life to us. How about we give a quick shoutout to him for setting this up?"

We all make noise for Ty, who waves it off as he takes a seat.

"I'll go first," Malik jumps in. "What's up? My name is Malik, and the Knights are taking it all the way this season, suckas!"

I fire my middle finger at him, adding to the mix of laughter and boos as Sid balls up a napkin and wings it at him.

"For real, though. I'm curious." Tevin raises his hand. "With a show of hands, how many of us struggle with depression?"

Everyone raises a hand except Malik and Sid.

Even Ray.

And then I see Aiden's.

Hm.

"So, most of us. One more question." Tevin lowers his hand. "How many of us are in therapy?"

Everyone raises their hands.

"Like you, Arnaz," Tevin continues, "I've struggled with depression since way back. I'm talking as a teenager. I mean, everyone around me kinda seemed depressed in one way or another, but it took me leaving Chicago to realize it was me."

"Do you know if something caused it?" Wes asks.

"For a long time, I thought it was just me," Tevin answers,

straightening the leg of his jeans. "My dad passed during surgery when I was seven."

"Damn, man," Wes cuts in.

"Remembering him in the casket still messes me up. Mom was depressed after."

"That's brutal. I'm sorry," Sid says, and we all murmur in agreement.

"Growing up broke was definitely the villain in my life. It's why I sometimes sit around my house, bugged out when I look around and realize I've made it. It's still wild to me," Jamie says.

"That kinda touches on what I struggled with for years," Sid says. "Besides grief from losing my best friend and my dad splitting, for me, it was impostor syndrome. I experienced this sorta cognitive dissonance when I entered the league. On the one hand, I knew I worked my ass off to be here, and even when I started making strides, putting up points and breaking records, internally I still felt like I wasn't good enough, and it made me anxious all the damn time."

Ray, Wes, and Jamie nod their heads. I know this about him, and while I can't pretend to know what it's like to grow up poor, I know what it's like to feel like you don't belong in the room you're in. And I think I'm the only one here who knows what it's like to grow up in the shadow of a famous dad—one who hates you.

"It's like the external success didn't matter because internally I felt like a fraud," Sid finishes.

"There's impostor syndrome, and there's the struggle of finding your worth when your dreams don't come true," Aiden jumps in. "A failed physical exam in college closed the door on my career in the league and sent me playing overseas. I was shattered. Some of my favorite players played overseas at least once in their careers. I knew that, but I hated it. After a few seasons in Spain and then France, I decided to call it quits and came back home. I hit rock bottom."

"That's tough," Idris cuts in. "I don't know what I would've done if I hadn't made it."

"To say I felt like an utter fuckup would be putting it mildly. I got piss-poor drunk every night. Things came to a head one night when I grabbed my father's pistol and drove out to the woods with a pint of Henny. It was the single worst moment of my life."

I suck in a breath, but it's drowned out by the sounds of shock and disbelief.

He pauses. "By some guiding hand, I made it to morning. I'd been dodging calls to interview for an assistant coach position with an NCAA Division I team because I felt like even considering it would mean accepting the end of my basketball career. But then something snapped in place, and I realized that if I didn't find a new purpose for my life—and fast—I wouldn't survive the year. So, I begrudgingly took the interview and landed the job. I figured finding purpose in the work would come later.

"And then—" he smiles, huffing out a breath—"my first year as a coach, I met this really talented kid who possessed all the underpinnings to not only make it to the league but to soar. He had a lot of anxiety, something I also struggled with in college. Only five years his senior, I saw so much of myself in him. He was so hungry to be great, we'd stay behind after everyone left and run drills. Hours and hours, practice after practice."

My knee starts bouncing, and I can hear my teeth scraping against my nails.

"He was tenacious. He made me realize that if I couldn't live out my dreams, I could at least take everything I knew and had learned to help him and others like him pursue theirs. That became my purpose," he says.

"Did the kid make it to the league?" Tevin asks.

"Yeah, and he's phenomenal," he says, and goose bumps

break out against my skin when his gaze darts my way quickly, then away.

Sid glances at me, silently asking if I'm good.

My knee stops bouncing when someone asks the question I knew was coming.

"Who is he?" Malik asks.

"Pass," Aiden answers.

"I'm glad you're still here today," Ty says.

I think about him sitting in his car, drunk and armed with a loaded weapon. I think about what my life would have been like if he'd never entered it.

I push to my feet. "Bathroom," I murmur.

Ty nods as I step away.

I've been so focused on my own shit, I never considered his perspective or experience. I knew about him not making the league, but he never shared how it impacted him. He was—he *is*—so damn good at coaching, I just thought he was happy doing it.

"Arnaz. You in here?"

I stand and peel open the bedroom door.

Aiden's hand hovers in the air in front of the door across the hall.

"Hey." I nod, and he slides past me into the room.

I press my back against the door. "A gun?"

"Yeah," he says, barely above a whisper.

I screw my eyes closed as the weight of that hits.

I thought he had all the answers back then. Like he woke up every day knowing exactly where he was supposed to be.

"I never wanted to hurt you, but you have to understand I couldn't cross that line."

"Why?" I shuffle in place. "I was an adult, and it's what I wanted."

"It's not what you *needed*, and I don't mean that to sound patronizing." He raises his hands. "You were in so much pain when I met you, and you had your whole life ahead of you. I knew you'd be leaving within the year for the league."

I rest my hands over my head as the pain from back then breathes instead of the anger.

"You never doubted for a second that I'd make the draft. I swear, sometimes your confidence was literally the only thing that kept me from—" My voice cracks.

"Listen to what you just admitted. You needed a coach and an advocate more than you needed a boyfriend."

"You could have been all that."

"There was also the power dynamic between us. What if I crossed the line, and we got into a fight after? How would that affect your game? It was too risky. I didn't want anything to risk your chances of making it. Not even me and my feelings for you."

"We should have talked about it. You ghosted me. Fuck. For years, that shit twisted me up. You could have been honest instead of cutting me off."

Maybe then I would have been able to fully commit to the man I'm in love with without being scared shitless that he'll wake up one day and reject me too.

"I really didn't mean to hurt you. I'm sorry I disappeared. I just..." He sinks down to perch at the edge of the bed. "I didn't trust myself to be around you and not give in to what I felt."

"I thought I made it all up in my head."

He stares at his hands. "You didn't."

Silence hangs between us.

I wish he'd told me. For so long, I felt like I'd done something wrong. That I was delusional.

I blow out a breath. "I'm man enough to admit that my pain back then wasn't on you. And I'm not sure I would have made it to the league without your help."

"You would have."

Another thing we'll have to disagree on.

He stands up. "You don't owe me anything, and I'll respect your need for space. I meant what I said out there. You've become a phenomenal player, and I am so proud of you for coming out."

I feel years of tension seep from my shoulders. "Thank you."

He nods.

"For real." I step away from the door.

He meets my gaze. "You're welcome."

"Truce?" I offer.

He grins. "Yeah. You coming?"

I pull my phone out of my pocket. "I'll meet you out there."

I close the door and then try Salem again.

I get his voicemail. I wait a few minutes, then try him again with no luck.

Where are you?

THE CIRCLE IS BROKEN up when I return.

"We're about to hit up that new spot along Highway 1. You rollin'?" Wes asks.

"Uh." I turn to Sid. "You down?"

"Yeah. They're hanging back." He gestures to Ty and Ray across the patio.

"He's good?" I ask.

"I don't know," Sid answers. "Seems East's trade messed him up. Ty invited him after their game yesterday. He'll help sort him out."

"SHEESH," Wes yells over his shoulder as we squeeze our way into the dimly lit bar and lounge, following behind Sid, who's being escorted to a roped-off area where three tables are being joined together. "Should we get a couple of bottles?" he asks.

The guys pick their poison. My stomach turns at the mention of vodka.

I lower my fitted cap. "I'm gonna grab a beer from the bar," I call out before turning and cutting through the crowd.

I'm yelling my order to the bartender when a ripped dude takes over making my drink, flashing his bleach-white smile.

My head turns as Aiden squeezes into the sliver of space next to me.

"What?" I tilt my head down to hear him.

"Now that you're out, what's *that* like?" He lifts his chin toward the bartender.

"Like I still have blinders on 'cause I missed whatever you just saw."

He laughs. "I'll have what he's having," he calls out to the bartender, then turns back to me. "I'm all caught up on *Royals All-Access*. I've seen the gifts. Even with blinders, you can't miss the attention."

"It's different," I admit. "But not in the way I thought." I take a swig of my beer.

"Single life not for you?"

"Maybe not." The answer doesn't scare me as much as it should.

Never feeling what it's like to wake up in Salem's arms again? That's what's terrifying.

"What about you?" I ask. "Still single?"

"I date. I don't have men making moves for me on prime-time television, though."

I grin.

"Jones has balls of steel," he says with awe.

Yeah, he's the bravest of 'em all.

"Why didn't you tell me you were gay?" I ask.

"Bi," he corrects. "I don't know. Same reasons, I guess."

The sudden feeling that we're being watched has me looking around. "We should head back."

"WHERE'S SID?" I yell over the music after returning from taking a piss.

"He just dipped," Malik replies. "Aight, peace," I say, then weave through the crowd toward the door.

"Yo!" I catch Sid, who's climbing into his whip. "You're my ride."

"Get yo' ass in then," he throws back.

I nod to Jett as he opens the opposite back door for me.

"Play the good shit, Jett," Sid says, typing into his phone.

"Yes, sir," Jett replies as he buckles in.

A Christmas song comes on, making me snicker.

"Good man." Sid leans back and slowly strums his air guitar.

"Are we picking up Mr. Washington?" Jett asks.

"He's already on his way to the house." Sid nudges my shoulder. "You have to cover this on your album."

I shake my head. "I told you, only Jimi can play like Jimi."

"Yeah. Who else would think to mix 'Little Drummer Boy,' 'Silent Night,' and 'Auld Lang Syne'?"

"Only the greatest ever. On late-night TV, all soft-spoken in his silk kimono and fro..."

Sid snorts, and then we both crack up.

"...toying with the thread on his pants, avoiding the camera like he wasn't the rock god."

"Yeah, but he was smooth with it." Sid grins. "Witty."

Word. The kinda cool you could never buy.

I reach into my pocket, and my stomach sinks as I check my phone—still nothing.

"Hey, I think I need to cop a plane."

Sid looks at my phone and then smirks. "Yeah, I think you might."

"Who put you on to Jimi? You never told me. Lily?"

He nods as he rubs lip balm across his lips. "Yeah. Didn't appreciate it until I was older. You?" His face lights up as we pull into his driveway, and he catches Ty emerging from his Porsche.

He rolls down the window and catcalls him.

Ty grins.

"Good god. I'm the luckiest man alive," he says, a raw scratch to his voice as he reaches for the door handle. He turns and daps me. "Call Salem. You'll be the luckiest man alive, too."

"Trying." I reach up and climb through the sunroof.

"I can grab my whip in the morning?"

Ty nods. "We'll text you the code to the gate."

His eyes widen as Sid climbs out of the car and holds onto the door for support.

"Yeah...mezcal Negronis, a shot of tequila, and Jimi Hendrix Christmas album on repeat. Good luck," I say. "Ooh. Don't hurt 'em!" I call out as Sid starts slow grinding the air, making us burst out laughing. "Yoooo. Why ya boy trying to shake ass to Christmas music?"

Even Jett's smiling, and he looks like he'd rather eat glass than do that.

Ty backs away, laughing, as Sid slams the car door and guns it toward him and tosses him over his shoulder.

He turns, and his hand raises in a salute, but a shrill yelp flies out of his mouth from something Ty's doing to his back.

Slapping Ty's ass, he salutes me and Jett before hauling him inside.

"Home, sir?" Jett asks.

I fight the urge to tell him to take me to LAX, but there's not enough time to get to Brooklyn and back with tomorrow's home game.

"Yep, home," I answer.

At least I'll see him in LA next week for our face-off.

Next week's too far.

A FEW MINUTES LATER, my head pops up from my phone when Jett says, "Sir, wait here. There's a man standing in front of your house."

I lean forward as the headlights wash over my driveway.

Holy fuck!

I'm out of the car before it rolls to a stop.

CHAPTER 41
SALEM

His steps slow as he draws near, searching my eyes like I'm an apparition. For a breath, I wonder if I got it wrong. It's ballsy to show up out of the blue like this. But then again, he did it first in Chicago.

He sucks in a breath when I tell him, "Anaïs gave me your address."

The quiet wisdom that speaks to me about Blue whispers to be still as he reaches out and grazes my sternum. It aches to witness the tremble of disbelief that I wouldn't cross an ocean to be near him.

I needed to cross the ocean for him but also for me. My fears about Denzel...they're getting harder and harder to shake.

His chin lifts, and the second our eyes meet, he's there, falling into my arms.

I peel off his fitted cap and kiss his mop of curls as he holds tight like I might vanish. "I missed you, too, Blue."

I let out a deep breath as I'm grounded by the press of his weight against me. Each breath bridges miles and miles of distance.

The headlights from the car that dropped him off startle him as it reverses out of the driveway.

He lingers for a breath before stepping back.

"How long do I have you?" he asks.

I let out an incredulous breath. *Forever if you'd have me.* "Just tonight."

His shoulders curve in. "Come on." He reaches down and lifts my duffel. "Are you hungry?"

"I can eat."

"I'll order us something."

He unlocks the door with his phone app, and I follow him through the arched entryway.

We peel off our shoes and then continue through a dark foyer.

"Watch the steps," he says before flicking on a switch and lighting up a sunken living room. He stuffs his hands in his back pockets as he looks around. "Uh, there's a bathroom through there." He gestures to a door along the hall that we just passed. "I'm still decorating the place."

I bite the inside of my lip.

He's cute when he's shy.

A cute little liar.

I smirk. "Yeah?"

He looks around and squints. "Yeah, no."

I snicker. We both know this is as moved in as he'll ever be here.

"I like your couch. The olive color is nice."

He rocks forward a little as I sweep my gaze over the gaming system, milk crates, and coffee table.

The peek of a rug through a half-closed door steals my attention. "What's over there?"

"My music room."

"May I?"

"Yeah. Come on."

We step inside, and he clicks on a floor lamp that casts a red light. There's a grand piano in the middle of the room, a wall of guitars, and scattered papers strewn across the lid of the piano. I recognize the amps but not the black metal board with glass tubes protruding out of it that sits atop a console table.

"What's this?" I lean down and peer inside the glass.

"An amp."

"Huh."

"It's an updated version of an OG that's been around for decades. It has a buffered output, so you can use a powered subwoofer with a low input impedance. Basically, less resistance allows more electricity or sound to flow." He reaches for a half-burned joint in the ashtray on the piano. "Mind if I hit this?"

T-shirt hugging his biceps, he slides the joint between his lips and then hikes up his low-slung jeans.

The hunger hits quickly, and I rush him, wrenching the joint from his lips. I slam my mouth against his and push him against the wall.

He moans as I clasp the back of his neck and unleash the raw need that's been caged since the cabin.

And if I'm hungry, he's ravenous. His fingers dig into my back, pull on the loop of my jeans, grip my waist.

He shivers when his head arches back, and my teeth graze his Adam's apple.

He caresses my erection and shudders as my teeth sink into his throat.

"Mmh." I pull back, resting my forehead against his shoulder.

He cards his fingers through his curls and swallows roughly.

Opening my palm, I lift the joint back to his lips, reach back for the lighter, and ignite it. The tip disintegrates into the fire as he takes a pull.

"If you ever want to find yourself on my dick in under sixty seconds, talk amp and woofer shit," I croak out.

His gaze darkens.

I press my lips to his and suck in the smoke. He tries to latch onto my tongue, but I pull back, soaking up his groan. His tongue glides across the seam of my lips before he rests the paper against them for a pull. We lick, suck, and inhale from each other as we shotgun the rest.

"You like Ethiopian food?" he asks.

"I like everything," I reply as my head tips up. The edges of the room curve like a rotunda.

"Cool. Gotta piss. I'll order us grub on the way."

My socked toes press into the floor cushion.

There's a name for it. I stare down at the floor. Looks vintage. Cranberry. No, burgundy but brighter. *Muh-genn—tuhh, midnight blue, ivory. Ivory rectangle frame, ivory threads. Floor cushion.*

Rug.

I snicker. *Fuck. I feel good.*

What kinda ancient scrawl is this? I bend down and pick up one of the papers and grin at Blue's handwriting. Angling the paper under the dim light, the letters swim into hazy focus.

*S*ANGUINE

Brown skin, gold dust.
Nose ring, gold rust.
Parts protected, parts doomed.
Death will never claim parts of you.

*B*LOODLESS *S*KIN, *brittle bones.*
I dream him, him alone.
A slow drip, a slow bind.
Death'll never claim what's mine.

I READ the words again and again. They feel humid on my skin.

"I ordered Ethiopian and Sri Lankan and bourbon crème brûlée donuts, but I think I want dim sum." He leans against the doorframe. "How hungry are you?" He unpeels his gaze from his phone.

"Take a shower with me?" I ask.

"Mm." He spins and heads into the hallway, typing into his phone. "You eat pork?"

"Any chicken or fish?" I catch up to him, wrapping my arms around his waist.

"Chicken, fish, and beef," he mutters, pulling us along.

"Shrimp stuffed eggplant?"

"Hell yeah," he adds.

I think about mac and cheese, and my stomach grumbles. "How long?"

"Adding priority delivery. Should be quick."

I let go of him to swipe up my duffel.

"I'm gonna grab water. Meet you upstairs? It's the only room with a bed."

I nod as I head up. I pass two rooms with boxes before I reach the one at the end with a bed and nightstand.

I strip down before entering the en suite. There's a stack of fluffy towels and washcloths neatly folded in a cupboard. He isn't a total caveman.

The water in the large marble shower heats up quickly.

There's a spoon hanging out of his mouth and a pint of ice cream in his hand when he enters.

I grin. "Hit me."

"It's cashew-based." He scrapes the tip of the spoon against the top, then feeds it to me.

"Mmm." Mint chocolate.

He feeds us both a few more bites, then sets the ice cream on the counter and undresses.

His arms wrap around my back when he enters, and we stand that way for a while, letting the water wash over us.

Placing soft kisses along my back, his erection slots between the globes of my ass. "When can I have you?" he asks.

"You want to top?"

"So fucking badly."

"It's been a minute since—"

"Hey," he whispers in my ear as his hand wraps around my dick and strokes.

I suck in a breath as he nibbles on my ear. "Y'think I want to hear about other men who've been inside you?"

I breathe a quiet laugh.

He pumps soap onto a washcloth, then sinks it between my crease and cleans me. "I hate them."

I know, my feral vampire.

He wrenches the spray nozzle free, and a blast of liquid heat against my rim sends shivers up my spine. "Can I taste you?"

My hips roll forward, easing through his hand. "Yeah."

"Hold on." He releases my erection as he places the nozzle back.

I look over my shoulder as he steps out of the shower. I laugh. "Seriously?"

He laps up a bite of ice cream. "I'm sho hngree."

I pop my head out and open my mouth for him to feed me some.

"Hands on the wall," he instructs as he slides the carton back on the counter, then steps back in. "Spread your legs."

I glance over my shoulder as he lowers to his knees, and his mouth and nose slink past my crease.

My hips lurch forward. "Cold!"

The demon laughs as his hands dig into my waist, pulling

me back, and he continues licking up toward my rim. Forehead falling to rest against the shower wall, the dizzying heat of water rains down my back, and his icy tongue massages circles before pressing inside.

"Mmm." He moans low as his stubble drags across my rim.

I grunt as his fingers dig deep into the flesh of my backside.

"Baby," I moan when his tongue sinks back inside.

He stills, then his head lowers, and he crawls between my legs. By the time I realize what he's doing, his lips are wrapped around my dick.

His glazed eyes are raw with hunger and possession. He cards a hand through his curls, pushing them back. The dark letters scrawled along his knuckles...the suction, caress, stretch of his lips...*Fuck.*

I bite my fist as a blast of pins and needles vibrates through me from my fingertips to my toes.

I hear my dark moans as my whole body sinks into Blue's tight, soft mouth. He pulls me close—so close, the back of his head presses into the wall as his mouth moves slowly, grinding me down his throat. A burning spreads behind my eyes as his throat constricts, choking on my release, and sending a shiver up my dick. I pull out and spread the last drops of my cum across his lips.

"Come here," I pant, lifting him to his feet. He licks my release off the corner of his mouth, and my tongue chases it, his head dipping back in surrender as I claim him.

"You're so beautiful," I rasp.

"No," he whispers.

I raise his chin. "Blue, you're the most beautiful man I've ever seen."

I nibble on his bottom lip when he tries to pull away.

"Why are you still fighting this?"

He sinks his teeth into my shoulder as his arms curve under my arms.

"I can feel it right now. How much you want this," I say.

He clings to me as he latches on to my shoulder, but he doesn't answer. I kiss his curls. "It's okay."

I love you.

I know that scares you.

I reach past him for the other washcloth, then soap it up. He doesn't let go as I lower the cloth to his back and lather him up.

He startles at the sound of the doorbell.

He starts to step back.

"Will they leave it?" I ask.

"Ye—" He clears his throat. "Yeah."

"Turn around." With his back pressed against my chest, I continue cleaning him. I let him turn his head and suck on my tongue as I wash his shoulders, raise his arms to get to his pits, and scrub and rinse down his chest. When I get to his cock, I mix soap and warm water in my hand and massage him.

He shudders as my hand wraps around his length and slowly starts stroking.

"See? So beautiful," I whisper, gazing into his eyes as he comes undone.

Arnaz

He's on my couch.

He's on my couch, looking more at home than I've ever felt here. There are moments so blinding in their arrival that they'll take years to see. Finding him standing in front of my house earlier is one of them.

After our shower, we got dressed, then he helped me carry in the boxes and bags of grub waiting on the porch.

Now his eyes are half-closed as we watch a replay of tonight's game with Detroit sonnin' Cleveland.

Too full to move, I'm melted into the cushion as he gives me a lazy foot massage.

His eyebrows crinkle, and he says, "You're staring."

How are you here?

"The other night, I fell asleep at Sid and Ty's—"

He angles his head to fully face me.

His nose ring glimmers, gold against silken skin.

Arched cheekbones.

Dangerous.

"You fell asleep at Sid and Ty's."

"Y-yeah. And when Sid woke me up so I wouldn't be late, I asked if he wanted to roll together. He was like, nah, 'cause Ty got in late. And I was like, let ol' boy sleep, and he goes, '*Who said I need to wake him up?*'"

His mouth spreads into a lazy grin.

"Tell me that's not hot," I say.

"It's hot," he agrees.

"So, I'll wake up on your dick soon?"

He wets his bottom lip. "Sure."

If I wasn't full, I'd rehearse it right now. "Sid called you hot."

"That's nice."

"That's it? *Nice*?"

His eyes flicker. "Yeah. Hot is nice. I prefer *fine* or *beautiful*."

I roll my eyes. "You know you're fine."

He grins. "Fine just hits different. So, what now? He's on the Watch List?"

My jaw separates. "You're banned from talking to Anaïs."

"Nah. That's my homie. What did you say to Sid when he said I was hot?"

"I told him not to look at you."

"Why?"

"Why, what?"

"If he looked at me, then what?"

My jaw tics.

"I'd be waking him up on my dick in the morning inst—" he starts.

I fly out of my seat.

"What?" he whispers, his hands cupping my butt and settling me into his lap.

He tries to kiss me, but I clamp down on his lip.

He chuckles. "Always so violent."

"Fuck these dimples." I try to eat them, sticking my tongue and front teeth in. "Did the gift baskets start coming in?" I ask, pulling back.

Silence.

"Ugh," I groan.

"Blue—"

"You're too fine. I hate it."

"Blue—"

"They don't even know about your big, pierced dick."

"Blue—"

"Of course they know. You reek of big, pierced-dick energy."

"Blue—"

"Do you pen handwritten thank-you notes on the back of thirst-trap postcards of you and Simba?"

"Blue—"

"Wait until they find out how you bake, or cook, or look at night."

"*Blue!*" He practically shouts to get my attention.

"What?"

"I want to hold you. Can we go to bed?"

"What?"

"Can we go up? I want to undress you and hold you."

His eyes are shadowless. The clearest hue of sincerity.

Yet, I still hear the warning—the siren song.

If I surrender to this, us, and he changes his mind...

But, god, is it becoming easier to ignore.

"I meant to ask you in Milwaukee, your last home game against Portland..."

He nods.

"...seven minutes and thirteen seconds into the third quarter, you were headed back to the bench. And I don't know...You looked off. Kinda sad."

He blinks and rubs his stubble. "That's a really specific timestamp."

"Just answer the question."

"You didn't ask one."

"Was it because of Denzel?"

"Yeah, most likely."

"You'd tell me if something else was bothering you, right?"

He fixes his gaze on the floor.

Now, those are shadows.

He rubs soothing circles along my back. "Yeah. I'd tell you."

CHAPTER 42
SALEM

The ping of an alert stirs me awake. I must have turned at some point in the night because Blue's no longer in my arms. He's there, curled against my back. I shuffle forward to create space, turn, and slip my arm across his chest, then pull him closer.

I think it's morning, but his curtains are blacked out, so I can't tell. I reach behind me and pluck up my phone, and my fingers scrape over paper.

I angle my head, hoping to get a peek at more of his lyrics. Instead, I see the envelope I had delivered with the cake.

He kept it.

I would have too, but you never know with him.

I turn and kiss the side of his head before I click on my screen and catch the time. *7:47 a.m.* Damn. I have to head back sooner than I thought. I click on Cillian's text.

Cillian

You gud, bro?

Me

Yeah. Why?

I'm about to toss my phone back when three dots appear. Huh. It's early for him. Wait, no, he's three hours ahead.

Cillian

Cool. Know y'all aren't exclusive. Just checking.

Me

?

My stomach churns as three dots jump around.

Then a link pops up. My finger hovers over it.

I stare down at Blue, then back at the headline "Arnaz Cade's Secret Affair with Assistant Coach."

Bullshit.

A photo of Blue appears. He's in the same clothes as last night, and he's huddled close to a man I immediately recognize as his college coach, who spoke out in support of Blue when he came out. I scroll down and double back on Blue's *apparent* quotes.

"Still single?"

"Why didn't you tell me you were gay?"

Calling bullshit, I'm about to exit when voices blare from the screen. I scroll down, then back up again until I find the video.

He stirs as I fight through ads to try to hit pause. My hand hovers as the ads end, and Blue's there trading an easy grin with his coach, who blushes and shifts closer—*too close.*

"Said wake me with your dick," Blue groans. "Not your phone."

I lock my phone and rub my hand over my mouth. *He was with me last night*, I say to myself, despite the unease in my gut.

It just looks bad because they're standing so close.

Why *are* they standing so close?

"Lube. Condom," he mutters.

His eyes crack open when I don't respond.

"Hey." I try for calm, but my throat's too tight.

"What's wrong?" he asks.

I shuffle to sit up. "I'm sure it's nothing but, you, uhm..." I take a deep breath to steady my voice. "You and your coach from college. I saw him on the bench at one of your games. Have you two, uh, dated?"

He blinks rapidly. "Wh-what?"

For all that he tries to hide, his face conceals very little.

Huh. "You're seeing us both?"

"What? No." He sits up. "'Cause he joined my team?"

I unlock my phone and pass it to him.

He scrolls up to the headline, and his eyes narrow. "This isn't true." He thumbs through the article. "I'm not into him like that."

"Were you ever?"

He stills. "This isn't true."

"Answer the question."

He blows out a breath. I see the wheels spinning as he averts his gaze to the curtained window.

"We were close back in college. Nothing happened, though. I was messed up back then, and..." He crosses his arms over his chest. "I did try to make a move, but he..." He shakes his head. "Nothing happened."

"Okay—"

"Hold on. Let me finish. I got drafted a few weeks later, and I put it behind me. But then he showed up."

"To the Royals?"

He nods. "I didn't think I'd see him again, and there he was. It messed me up."

The low-scoring games, the tired eyes...It's all snapping into place.

The damn-near ghosting me.

The spasms in my gut intensify. "Because you're still in love with him?"

"No." He shakes his head. "I'm not."

"Then what about him returning messed you up?"

"The practice after he joined the team, he, uh, told me he felt the same for me back then."

A sharp chill spreads across my back. "Why would he tell you that all these years later?"

He shrugs. "I don't know, and I honestly don't care."

"Just like that?"

He squints. "What do you mean?"

"I'm missing something. You went from being 'messed up' to being plastered together yesterday. How?"

"Salem. I'm not lying to you. I don't want him."

"Answer the question."

"We were at Ty's house."

"Ty and Sid's?"

He shakes his head. "Just Ty's. I mean, Sid was there too. Ty invited some guys over to talk about mental health and stuff, and Aiden showed up. I didn't invite him."

"How did it lead to the bar?"

"He talked about what he was going through back then, and it led us to clear the air."

"There's clearing the air, then there are bodies pressed together," I point out.

"It wasn't like that. We were all at the bar—the whole group. It was crowded, and he slid into the spot next to me."

I look away from him and try to get my thoughts straight. I'm angry, and I don't know why. Lucien saw other people— people we'd run into sometimes—and it didn't bother me.

"Let me see if I got this straight. You fell in love with

him in college. He rejected you. You haven't spoken in years. He's back now. And not only is he back, but he told you he was in love with you too. And all of it messed you up. Is that the reason you fell off from us before Milwaukee?"

He doesn't answer.

"Wow."

"Hold on. It wasn't like that," he hurries to say.

"Yeah...I'm gonna go."

"Come on, Salem. I'm being honest with you."

A dark chuckle leaps from my chest. "Why? 'Cause of the article?"

"What?"

"Were you gonna tell me about any of this if the article didn't drop?"

"There isn't anything to tell!" he insists.

The hell there isn't.

I scoff. "The man you were in love with is back in your life, and he admits to you that he was in love with you too. And you work with him every day. How isn't that anything to tell?" I pull my jeans out of my duffel and stab my foot through a leg. "I get having unfinished business. But you straight-up put me on the back burner to deal with him? You didn't think you could tell me?"

"Hold on." He moves to stand in front of me. "I disappeared from everyone."

Cool. So, I'm *everyone.* "I have to go."

"Wait. Hold up."

I pause.

"I didn't understand it until my session with my therapist, but I dissociated or something."

Was I just a replacement for the one that got away? "This whole time, were you just dragging me along 'cause you've been holding out for him?"

"No. That's what I'm trying to explain. These last few weeks weren't about him at all."

Brick by brick, the dread I've felt the last few weeks crumbles, but instead of relief, I feel dislocated. I've been dreaming of a future with someone still in love with the past.

"Talk to me," he pleads.

"I..." I shrug. "It shouldn't be this hard."

"What. Us?"

"Yeah. Us."

"Bullshit."

My eyes narrow. "What?"

"What about this shouldn't be hard?"

"I don't know, Blue. Usually, when you love someone, it feels easier than this."

"Yeah, for you, maybe. I don't date." He jabs his thumb into his chest. "I. Never. Dated. Until you. When have I ever hinted that any of this is easy for me? I don't have a clue what I'm doing. I didn't come from a perfect family—"

"Perfect?" I huff and bend to grab my duffel. "Denzel missing is perfect?"

"I didn't mean it like that. Wait."

Arnaz

"Give me five minutes and I'm gone." He doubles back across the room and grabs his phone off the nightstand.

I *want* to be better at this. "Salem."

He ignores me, typing into his phone.

My back hunches like the ceiling's collapsing and the floor's drawing up.

"Salem," I say a little louder.

"My car is on the way. I need to clean up and then leave."

"At least let me take you to the airport," I offer.

"I'm good."

"Can we talk later?"

He shrugs. "I don't know."

"Salem—"

He's already gone.

I stalk across and snatch up my phone, hell-bent on chasing after him, when a call comes through from the Royals' GM.

For fuck's sake.

"Yeah," I answer, reaching for my jeans.

CHAPTER 43
ARNAZ

♫ **"When It's Time"** ♫
Hear the steel-hoofed drum of wild horses.
Jet entrails rumble the sky, roaring voices.

"Sir, Arnaz Cade." The GM's assistant announces my arrival.

"Cade, get in here," Ari replies, seated at the head of a polished conference table with Coach on his left and Aiden on his right. "Take a seat."

"No HR or union rep," I observe.

"It's not that kind of meeting. Take a seat, please," he insists, rolling up the sleeves of his white button-down.

"I'm good." I stand at the other end of the table. "What's this about?"

"Before you bust our balls, we know the articles are fabricated," Coach pipes in. "You're here because we need a plan to smooth this over as quickly as possible. Elizabeth is stuck in traffic, but she's on the call."

"Hey, Arnaz." The voice of the Royals' PR director filters through the speakerphone centered on the table.

"Liz."

"As you know, the Royals have a strict workplace conduct policy that discourages any relationships between staff—including coaches and players—that may cause a conflict of interest, disruption to the team, or pose potential legal issues," Ari says.

I cross my arms. "Why the policy reminder if you know the article's fabricated?"

"Yeah, Ari," Liz replies as he glares at the table, yanking his tie loose. "What the hell?"

His resting corporate asswipe face crumbles. "Fuck. I'm sorry." He holds up his hands. "I haven't had a good night's rest since baby number one. Baby number three has colic, and my GERD is fired up." He tightens, then loosens his fist. "So, I'm hanging on by a thread without my Americano. Please sit." He nods toward the chair. "We want to help."

I drag out a breath and then fold into the seat in front of me.

"Let's game plan, shall we?" Coach adds.

"Hold on." I nod to Aiden, who casts me a wary glance. "You good? Did I out you?"

"N-no," he replies. "I, uh, thought I made it harder for you."

"How?" I uncross my arms. "Everyone knows I'm gay."

"We know Aiden's bi," Coach chimes in. "Not that it's anyone's goddamn business."

"Something told me you might be seeing someone," Aiden answers.

Oh...yeah.

I lean my elbows against the table and scrub my hands over my face.

"What's happening?" Liz asks. "Why'd everyone go quiet?"

"Cade's lookin' like he could use damage control in his romantic life," Coach says.

"Oh no," Liz replies. "Can I help?"

I'm about to clarify that there is no *romantic* life, but I catch myself.

Denying who Salem is and what he means to me is part of the reason we got here.

I clear my throat. "I've been dating someone. I don't want to go into details," I admit.

"I knew it!" Coach exclaims.

I glare at him, but it only makes his shit-eating grin spread.

"Pay up." He turns to Ari. "Told you that press conference would score him a date."

"Just to be clear, we're talking about Salem Jones?" Liz asks.

I shake my head, then nod.

"Uh, did I drop? Can you all still hear me?" Liz asks.

"My bad, Liz. Yeah, it's Salem," I answer.

"Okay," Ari says with a smirk. "Maybe keep this under wraps for a few more days. I'm still due the next gift basket that comes in."

For fuck's sake.

"I'm happy for you," Aiden speaks up. "You deserve to be happy."

Happy, eh? I see Salem's hurt face from this morning every other time I blink.

"Okay. If Aiden's not getting fired"—I move to stand—"then I gotta go."

"Wait. We need a plan—" Coach insists.

"Sorry, Coach. I'll support whatever you all come up with, but I need to go."

I SEE missed calls from Cat. I shut my car door and hit her back.

"Hey," she answers. "Thanks for calling me back. The article—"

"It's bullshit, but Ari's handling it. Listen, Cat, I think I messed up with Salem. Me and the new assistant coach have history. It's not like the articles claim, though."

She sighs. "Oh, hon, I'm sorry."

"Yeah, me too. Check on him. Okay?"

"Of course. And I'll give Ari a call to discuss the team's stance and come up with a joint statement for you."

"Thanks."

"Obviously, I don't know the details, but Salem's reasonable. Maybe just give it time?"

I may not be good at the relationship thing, but I know time isn't how I fix this.

CHAPTER 44
SALEM

"Ay, force him to pass. Step up!" I yell to Ezekiel.

San Antonio's point guard sold the drive hard. Ezekiel sags forward, feeding right into the setup, and the guy drives straight for Zeke's chest. He sells the contact, catching two free throws.

"C'mon!" I shout.

Zeke shrugs. "Chill, man."

"I'll chill when you step up and stop giving the opps so much cushion."

"Man, whatever."

"Whatever?" I square up in his face. "You ain't a free agent yet, dawg, so stop acting like they signed you."

"Hold up." Cillian reaches in and separates us.

"Get him before he says some shit that gets him laid out," Zeke growls.

"Two tips," I start, not budging as Cillian tries to push me back. "You put the round thing in that hole with the net. Then you try to stop them from putting the round thing in the other hole with the net."

"Say it to my face," Zeke bites out.

"I just did!"

"Enough!" Cillian barks.

"Get off me." I push Cillian's arm away and move to my position on the block as the point guard sinks the first free throw.

"The hell you looking at?" I wing at Easton.

He appraises me with his dead, black eyes from the bench. His chest rises like he snickered, but his face doesn't move at all.

On our next possession, Cillian sinks his shot.

Our crowd yells "Defense!" as I yell "Weak side!" to get coverage for the left wing and wide-open point guard. "Rotate! Weak side!" I repeat as I box out the shooting guard, who's scanning for a pass.

Zyair and Onyx continue double-teaming their power forward despite dawg being the weakest shot.

Changing pace, their shooting guard tries to rip past me to the rim. I lunge to cut him off, and my face slams into a shoulder. Bouncing back, I fight to get around their center's screen when the guard snaps the ball to the open point guard, who gets off an easy three.

"Goddamn!" I glare at Zyair and Onyx. "You hear them yelling 'defense'? The fuck you think they talking to?"

They trade confused glances as Coach calls a time-out.

"Bro, you gotta chill," Cillian says, trying to calm me down.

"Talk to them," I snap at him.

"Seriously?"

"Yeah, I'm serious. If they ain't got hops, handles, or D, why are they here?"

Cillian shakes his head and falls back.

"Jones, a word?"

I sling my duffel over my shoulder and follow Coach into her office.

"Have a seat. You played hard tonight," she says, taking her seat behind the desk. "I like what I saw. Tough love is needed around here. Especially nights like tonight when the team's off. You, Cillian, and Easton played well and fought hard for our win."

"Thanks."

"It's been a while since you and I had one of our talks." She removes her glasses. "Everything okay inside the locker room and out?"

"Yep."

My dad's steely gaze prepared me for people like her, who are impossible to read.

"We've talked about how difficult it is to be different in a society that punishes nonconformity."

When I came out publicly, she pulled me aside after my press conference and told me she was proud of me and had my back. And she hasn't wavered.

"Yep," I reply.

"Good. You remember. The door's always open if you need to talk."

"I appreciate it. I'm good. Looking forward to Wednesday's game in LA." I pick up my bag.

She leans forward. "You'll bring the same heat against the Royals as you did tonight?"

My fist tightens around the strap. "I plan to rain hell down on them."

"That's the spirit."

CHAPTER 45
SALEM

"I don't understand. It's been weeks. How are you still coming up short?" I question the PI I hired to find Denzel.

"Salem," my mom cautions. "I'm sure Mr. Chen and his team are working hard."

"Did you run his cards again?"

"Yes, and unfortunately, there still hasn't been any activity," Chen replies.

"So, what now?" Dad's voice cuts into the conference call.

"We aren't giving up. We keep searching. We have a lot of feelers out and favors called in. But this stuff takes time. You need to trust the process."

"What about his old commanding officer?" I ask.

"It wasn't easy to get him to talk to a civilian private detective, but he's fond of your brother. He hasn't seen or heard from him in months."

Goddamn.

"Thank you for all your hard work, Mr. Chen," Mom says. "Please keep us posted."

I grunt and drop my phone on the counter.

I bet if I take a leave of absence and search for him myself, I'd have more leads.

"He has a proven track record longer than you've been alive." I recall Cat's words for me to be patient and let Mr. Chen work.

My doorbell rings. Cillian texted earlier to say he was stopping by.

I head to the door.

"Yo." I pull him into a dap. "What's with the suit?"

"Had a shoot with *GQ*," he tells me.

"And you didn't change?"

"It's part of my new Tom Ford partnership. Need to be seen in it to keep it coming."

"Ah."

He slides his shoes off and follows me to the kitchen. I pull out two beers.

"How'd the call with the PI go?" he asks.

"Shit." I pop the lids and slide him a bottle.

"Damn. What's your gut telling you?"

I shrug. "I'm less concerned about external threats with him." He was trained to protect himself at all costs. "It's the internal stuff that worries me."

"Why would he disappear?"

That's the billion-dollar question.

I raise the beer to my lips and gulp it down.

Every now and then, he gets it into his head that our lives would be better if he disappears. Like he won't be a burden on us or something. He never said it in as many words, but he feels guilty for all the years we spent concerned about him while he was in the service, and more guilt piled on when he got home and wasn't the same man he was when he left. The guilt eats at him, no matter how hard we try to convince him otherwise. "I don't know."

He blows out a breath.

My phone buzzes. I flip it over and tense. "Yeah." I send Blue to voicemail again.

"We gonna talk about the other thing?" he asks.

"What thing?"

He lowers the beer from his lips and side-eyes me.

"Listen, don't come in here busting my balls. Someone had to put their feet on the gas. Plus, Coach commended me on my leadership efforts."

"Leadership efforts." He snorts. "Coach would sell her kidneys if it meant clinching a championship."

I purse my lips, stifling a laugh.

"That doesn't make it right."

"Aight." I take another swig of my beer. "I'll lay off 'em a bit."

"Cool. That's not the thing I was talking about, though."

I shoot him a warning glare.

"That Silencer shit doesn't work on me. Chill. I only want to know our play. What kinda welcome are we giving them?"

My fist grips the bottle. "Whatever happened between me and Blue stays off the court."

He nods and flashes a dark grin.

"I'm serious. It's business as usual."

"Business as usual? So, you didn't tell Coach you plan to rain—what was it?—*hell* down on them?"

I open my mouth, then close it. "Coach snitched?"

"She caught the rest of us in the locker room after you left and practically told us to strap up, quoting you."

I groan. That's definitely not the energy I want to bring tomorrow night. I'm not even sure why I said it. "How many of the guys were left?"

"Damn near everyone except you, Zeke, and Onyx."

"Fu-uck." My head hangs forward.

"Blue?" he asks as my phone lights up again.

"What?"

"That's your nickname for him?"

I shrug the question off and send the call to voicemail.

"'Cause he looks sad sometimes?"

"Nope." I tell him my dad's quote that inspired the nickname.

"Aww." He grins. "You're a romantic little asshole."

I laugh. "Get out."

REAL TALK SPORTS WITH
DARIUS & TODD

"*Before we close out, you'll want to tune in tomorrow. Todd and I will be reporting in after the Lions and Royals face-off. We have front-row seats.*"

"*Figuratively, 'cause have you seen the prices for tomorrow's game?*" *Todd asks.*

Darius laughs. "*Yeah, but we're in there. Is it just me, or was Salem Jones extra emo last game?*"

"*Emo?*" *Todd squints.* "*In the game leading up to his return, you said he was the most ferocious defender in the league.*"

"*It's hard to take him seriously after that cake stunt. What was that for anyway, if the other one's sleeping with his coach?*"

"*The other one?*" *Todd asks.*

"*I don't buy the Royals' statement.*" *Darius shrugs.* "*There's definitely something there.*"

"*To me, his performance last game is the kind of defense that got him coined The Silencer.*"

"*I'm not denying his talent, but I don't know...There's something different about him. Does he still have the grit to lead the defense? This league needs men with backbone.*"

"*Anyway,*" *Todd says.* "*Tune in tomorrow for our post-game coverage.*"

CHAPTER 46
ARNAZ

♫ "Media" ♫
Print lasts forever, they say.
Well, then, so must hate too.
They pick, prod, and flay.
And reveal the wit of fools.

"**B**reathe with me," Sid says while I'm stretching out my neck and bouncing on my heels.

He sucks in air like he's pulling through an imaginary straw, holds, then releases it. He does it again, nodding on the hold for me to join him.

"Wait, I need in," Nick says, tossing his phone onto his shelf and then jogging over.

"Me too," Wes calls out, rolling over in his chair.

For Christ's sake.

I drop my heels and drag in a long breath.

By the fourth round, most of the guys have joined in.

Coach enters, and instead of kicking off his pre-game

speech, he nudges Aiden and the rest of the coaching staff to join in.

"Let's go," he says when we're done.

What?

"No speech?" Johan asks.

"He just got us all locked in." Coach nods to Sid. "When your tank starts emptying, come back to this"—he pulls in a breath and releases it—"and call on your power. Alright?" He reaches his hand in. "Royals on three."

I EXIT the tunnel and spot Salem shooting a corner three with his hoodie up and headphones on.

"Where you going?" Sid asks, stepping in front of me.

"I'll be back." I dart sideways.

"Hold up. Peep where you are."

I look around to find I'm surrounded by light blue and gold Lions jerseys.

We're supposed to warm up on the side of the court that's opposite our bench, and my foot's an inch away from crossing onto the Lions' warm-up side.

Shit. I step back, shaking my head. "My bad."

Salem turns and freezes midcross over, sending the ball bouncing away. Cillian steps in front of him, breaking our stare.

Sid looks over his shoulder, catching his glare. "You good?"

"He keeps his eyes trained that way, and we're straight," Cillian retorts.

"Nah." Sid's gravelly voice hardens. "This our house."

Cillian's lips part in a dark grin. "We'll see."

"It's gonna be *that* kind of night," I murmur.

Sid waves that off. "It's whatever kind of night we say it is. Let's get it."

IT *IS* that kind of night.

The Lions are lighting us up like it's the fourth quarter of game seven of the Finals. We're down eight points with five minutes left in the second quarter.

Sid and Cillian already collected double technical fouls when Cillian tried to shove Sid into the stands after he attempted a reverse layup and got stripped of the ball. Before he could race away, Sid yanked him by his jersey and flung his ass to the floor in front of the photographers.

The crowd loved it, but if the air was thick with tension before, now it's so heavy, we're getting crushed under it.

Nick presses Zyair as he reads the floor for a pass. I close in on Onyx, who's wide open and signaling for the ball.

Zyair lobs it toward him. Reading the arc—it's too short—I kick up my speed. Onyx reads it, too, but by the time his heels lift, I'm already slipping past him, intercepting the ball.

I race toward the rim and lift off for a dunk when a light blue and gold blur hovers in front of the rim and clobbers the ball across the court.

I land, chest heaving, and wipe the sweat from my eyes, bringing the blur into focus. Salem's glare pans the stands, like the whole arena's on his shit list, before striding away like he's on the hunt.

That's the third time he's blocked my shot. No eye contact or shit-talking. It's like I'm invisible.

I shake it off *again* and keep my head in the game.

Sid returns the favor by blocking Zyair's layup.

Salem and Sid square up on our next possession. Sid dribbles slowly as he advances, pausing like he's about to shoot, eyes the rim, then launches left with a swift crossover. Salem buys the fake, shifting right. Sid attacks before Salem recovers and fires a no-look, behind-the-back pass to me.

Double-clutching the ball, I explode toward the rim, veer left, then sidestep right to shake Cillian before launching through the air. One second, there's a clear lane to release an easy floater, then the next, Ezekiel and Zyair swarm in and mob me. Ezekiel denies the shot too hard, forcing Zyair to scramble for the ball before it's knocked out of bounds. He bats it in, and it ricochets off my leg and back out of bounds, securing the Lions the next possession since my leg is the last to touch it.

Nick forces Zeke to turn over the ball. I dive for it at the same time as Cillian. Beating him to it, I roll to my back and wing it to Sid, but Salem intercepts and lobs it to Onyx, who makes a fast break and windmill dunks it in, making our crowd lose their shit.

"Hear that?" Cillian sneers, cranking his head in Sid's direction. "Whose house is it now?"

Sid and I lock eyes.

Yeah, time to light them the fuck up.

Onyx can't get an open look thanks to Nick's tight defense, so he gets off the ball to Cillian, which makes no sense since Sid's locking him out. Salem, who's wide open, gestures for the ball. I transition to defend him. Throwing a side-eye my way, he books it as I draw near. He pings to the opposite wing, but I'm on him before he can turn and get into position to catch and shoot a corner three.

It's the first time we're one-on-one for the night. Not for my lack of trying. Every time I've moved toward him, I'm double-teamed.

Squatting low, I angle to keep my eyes on the ball. When my hand grazes his hip, he stiffens. I push forward, eating up the space he tries to create, and turn to face him. "Can we talk after?"

His jaw tics as he stares straight ahead.

"Just give me five—"

"Don't," he grits out.

The arena quakes as the crowd explodes. I whip around to find Ussef hanging off the rim.

The crowd's so loud it almost drowns out the halftime buzzer.

"Hey, wait." I race to catch up with him.

He ignores me and keeps walking until he disappears into the tunnel.

Damn.

CHAPTER 47
SALEM

I drown out the noise and crash into my locker room chair as the guys pour in, amped up. We listen as Coach schools us on what worked and what to fix for the second half.

"Jones, how's your foot?" a trainer asks as she works on Cillian's shoulders.

"I'm good," I reply, jumping to my feet and peeling out of my wet jersey and shorts for a dry set.

Two more quarters and then I can get the hell outta this town and away from the constant gnawing in my gut to be near him.

He asked for just five minutes.

Like fixing whatever this is can be done in five minutes.

And that fucker...*Aiden.*

I could see him being Blue's type. Why does he look close to our age? He's got to be the youngest assistant coach in the league.

My stomach tightens.

I'M the first on my team to return to the court to warm up, but I'm not alone. *He's* there, getting fed practice shots by none other than his ex-crush or whatever.

I turn and signal for a ball. I dribble and shoot a mid-range three. It misses.

I try again from a different angle. That one circles the rim and rolls out.

I shake my head.

I'm dribbling the ball between my legs when a loud murmur filters from the crowd, catching my attention. I turn to find Blue glaring into the stands, his ball anchored under his arm.

I try to track his gaze, but I can't tell what he's looking at.

He shakes off whatever it is and returns to practicing shots.

I'm running in a layup when the crowd's rumble thunders through the arena.

I spin around as Blue charges for the stands.

The hell?

I take off as Aiden's knocked flat on his ass when he tries to hold Blue back.

Blue barrels through the first row, then the second, before I lose track of him as security swarms in his direction.

I rip past them, hopping over the empty floor seats, when I spot him six rows up, not losing steam.

Where's he going?

My gaze angles above him, scanning the stands, and that's when I see...Darius and Todd.

Todd, with his phone out, pointed at Blue, and Darius, mouth moving, no doubt saying some foul shit.

"Jones," I hear someone yell as I rip through the stands, following the lane that Blue cleared.

I'm gaining on him fast when a hand comes down hard on my shoulder. I whip around and glare at the security guard.

"Get off me!" I growl. My elbow crashes down on his arm, breaking his hold.

Two more close in, but I turn and tear through the lane until I'm an arm's length away and can hear that piece of shit Darius.

"...coming to his boyfriend's rescue."

I lunge forward but am lodged in place as my jersey is tugged hard from behind. My vision whites out as I push forward, but I'm locked in place. I claw at my jersey as Blue scales the final barrier and squares up, two against one. My hands tear through the fabric, and I break free, closing the distance. Blue cocks his fist and hammers it toward Darius, whose knees buckle in anticipation, crashing between the seats.

"I'm here," I say from behind him as he releases a dark laugh, standing over Darius, who's folded in a fetal position. "You good?" I ask.

"Yeah," he replies, a cold chill in his tone. "Never been better."

I glare at Todd, who lowers his phone and backs away.

Blue kneels down, swiping away one of the phones pointed at him. "Look at me." His voice drops just enough for Darius to hear.

"This is your final warning. Remember this moment. You speak my name or his again, and nowhere, not even a game surrounded by ten thousand people, will be safe for you. Get a life, you homophobic dipshit."

There's commotion at my back, most likely security closing in.

Blue rises to his feet, a wall of phones pointed at him. He turns to Todd. "That goes for you too."

"I t-told him to lay off," Todd stutters.

I signal for Blue to go first, but he nods for me to move.

The next thing that happens is a blur.

There's a loud "Watch out" from behind us, and I turn and catch Blue before he falls face-first into the stands.

"That muthafucka," he sneers as he holds the back of his head.

I rip toward Darius, then I'm yanked to the side as a light blue and gold jersey pushes past. Before I can right myself, Easton's there blocking Darius's blow before he hammers a right hook of his own that drops the fucker.

Sid and Cillian close in as Darius sputters, "What was that for?"

"I'm gay, fucker!" Easton fires back, launching another blow, this one against the floor alongside Darius's head. "You talk about them, you're talking about all of us."

Blue and I lock eyes, his murderous glint softened with amusement.

A security guard who has a death wish pushes Cillian hard down the stands.

"What the fuck?" I shout as the guard turns and goes for Sid, who gut checks him as soon as he grabs his jersey.

"Stay down," Sid warns before we're escorted out of the game.

CHAPTER 48
ARNAZ

♫ "Him" ♫

Awake, you reach for me, and I know the beauty of morning.

"That new guard applied excessive force," Sid reprimands the line of security guards outside our locker room door. "We were already walking away. I want to talk to—"

"Consider it handled," Gigi replies, cutting through the line. "There will be an internal investigation into his conduct. If there is a violation of use-of-force protocols, he will be suspended or terminated."

"*If?*" Sid scoffs.

"If." Gigi winks at him.

Yeah, that guy's a goner.

"Gigi." I stop pacing. "I need five minutes in their locker room."

"Not happening, Cade," Jo, my other favorite guard, replies.

"Please." I shift on my feet. "Thought you wanted an invite to the wedding."

Sid smirks. "Come on. Let princess go get his prince."

Jo sighs. "It's your call, boss," he directs to Gigi.

Gigi huffs out a curse. "I swear to god, if you so much as raise your voice in there..."

"You da best." I shoot her a big smile.

"Yeah, yeah. Jo and I get the next two gift baskets."

"Done," I call out as I race down the hall.

Salem

"Nope." Cillian jumps to his feet.

"I just want to talk to him."

My head flies up at Blue's voice.

Arms crossed over his chest, Cillian blocks the entryway.

"Can we talk?" Blue asks, skirting past him and beelining toward me.

"Get out," Cillian orders them.

"Ay," Sid interjects, entering behind Blue. "Know when something's fucked enough."

I shake my head. If it turns to blows, Easton, the brawler in the corner, who's leaned back in his chair and ignoring his fist bleeding all over his shorts, can break them up.

Blue kneels between my legs, and I sit back as I'm hit with the memory from our first time. It rubs me raw.

"You okay?" His voice is soft—cabin-at-night soft.

His hand raises to ghost over the welt where my jersey ripped, and my stomach tenses.

His eyes never leave mine, but his hand trembles against my skin as Cillian and Sid argue.

"Drop it, Cillian," I order.

"Any update on Denzel?" Blue asks.

I shake my head.

His look of real concern kills me. I can't be here. "I need to shower."

"Wait. Can't we talk?" he begs.

"Here?"

"Yeah. Anywhere. Come to my place?"

"I can't. We fly out right after this."

"So that's it?"

I shrug. "I need to focus on my family right now."

"I'm sorry for hurting you."

I can see the sincerity in his gaze, but...

I push my chair back and climb to my feet. "Which time?"

Arnaz

Salem disappears through the side door. My head hangs as I move to stand.

Sid, ignoring Cillian, walks over to Easton and slides into the chair next to him. In less than a minute, he has Easton showing him his bloody fist and suppressing a grin.

"Of course," Cillian sighs. "He hates all of us, but the enemy he likes." He fixes his glare on me.

I wink as I roll out my neck. "You're pecking at bones, sweetheart."

"What?"

"Ain't no more pounds of flesh here." I step closer. "I love him. Get in our way, and I'll go through you."

"Treat him better," Cillian warns.

"I plan to." I turn and walk away. "Sid." I grab a towel. "Watch the door. No one gets in."

The steam from the shower billows from the last stall on the right. I bend down and unlace my shoes, toe them off, then peel off my jersey.

Salem's back is to me as I approach. "Can I come in?" I ask.

He pauses scrubbing himself.

"Please," I add.

His shoulders lift with a small shrug.

Stepping in, I battle a moment of self-doubt before resting my forehead against his back.

He stiffens but doesn't shrug me off.

We trade quiet breaths, soaking in the hot water and thick steam. Wrapping my arms around his waist, I sink into the slow softening of his muscles. The wisp of hope that's starting to grow is snuffed out when he shifts and peels himself away. I'm backing off to give him space when he turns, cups the side of my face, and tilts my head down.

I wince as his fingers graze over the lump where I was punched.

"I'm gonna make him pay," he growls.

He spreads my curls to get a closer look.

"Think Easton did enough damage."

"When you leave here"—he raises my chin—"get this checked."

"It's just a bump," I tell him.

"I want it checked."

I nod against his palm.

The lines on his forehead disappear as beads of water travel down his nose ring and pool at his top lip.

I reach for his waist. "I miss you." My voice cracks under the weight of the ache.

He drops his hands, and the lines reappear, etching his forehead.

"Blue..."

He steps back as I close the distance between us until his back hits the tiles.

Trickles of water sweep across his lashes and cheekbones as he watches me.

The tips of my fingers graze over his stomach, and the skin pebbles under my touch.

"You should leave," he rasps, his Adam's apple rippling from a swallow.

"Okay." I press closer, leaning against his chest, where I can feel his heart beating almost as quickly as mine, and brush a kiss against his lips. "But then I'd still miss you."

I kiss him again, my tongue curling under his top lip.

He shudders against me.

I tilt my pelvis forward, and as soon as our dicks rub together, his hand's around my throat, and my chest hits the shower wall.

I moan as the velvet heat of his erection massages my rim.

"You can't be here," he whispers into my ear.

He parts my lips with two fingers, and I suck, massaging them back and forth on my tongue. He sucks in a breath. "You know how many times"—his fingers drop from my mouth to my dick—"I thought about fucking you in here after our games?"

"How man— Ungh," I rasp into his neck as his other hand strokes my balls in a downward motion.

"Shh," he soothes.

"Fuck me," I beg, already at the edge as his hand fists my cock.

"No," he grunts.

"Please." I widen my legs.

"Mmm." His teeth graze my ear as the metal on his cock grazes my rim, and he rotates my dick with a tight fist. "I said no."

A sharp sting has me biting my fist as a surge of heat, hotter than the water pelting our backs, blazes through me, lighting up every nerve in my body.

Fuuuuck.

His thumb presses into my slit, and sparks flare behind my eyes, and I erupt.

He releases his teeth from my shoulder, then pulls me away from the spray of water and bends me forward.

I glance back as he uses my cum to stroke himself.

His gaze slides between my face and my hole.

He bites his lip as his thumb circles my rim.

I tighten around him as it sinks inside.

"Yo! Gotta dip. Security said our time's up." His eyes widen as Sid's voice rings out.

I take over stroking him. "Come on me," I whisper.

His abs clench as he stares into my eyes.

"I need five minutes," I yell as my hand glides back and

forth over his steely length, relishing its pulse and the strain it's causing my wrist.

He tenses, eyes rolling closed, and I turn, drop to my knees, and catch the first spill of cum on my tongue.

He lets out a low groan as I suck on his head, my fingers digging into his thighs as the metal balls roll against the roof of my mouth.

I pull off him when his toes curl, and he collapses against the wall, chest heaving, face partially concealed by the thick curtain of steam. With a parting kiss to his tip, I start to climb to my feet when I see his fingers still covered with my cum. He shudders as I suck it off.

His cock bobs up like there might be more cum for me, but we're out of time.

"Will you pick up when I call?" I ask, pressing my palm over his chest. "Please."

His chest heaves under my hand as he releases a long breath. "I don't know."

"I get that you're angry."

"I'm not."

I arch an eyebrow.

"I'm not." He pushes off the wall. "Believe me or don't."

"Admit it. You're angry cause I—"

"Look, just go. You got what you came for." His tone sounds defeated.

"What's that supposed to mean?"

"This is all you wanted from the jump, right?" He cuts off the water. "I'm done forcing something that's not there."

"It is there."

"You sure? What's changed besides wanting to bone? What else do you want?"

"Not for it to be like this."

"Then what?"

"For you not to be angry, for starters."

He shrugs. "I'm not interested in casual fucks. I did that. I want more. And I'm not angry—I'm just over it."

"You mean you're over me." My voice cracks.

"No. This!" His finger shoots back and forth between us. "The guessing, the not knowing what anything means. Like now. You're in front of me, and I'm not sure why. I can't figure you out. You do one thing but say another. I think we're on one page, but we're not. Even when you asked me to come to your house a few minutes ago. I did that. I flew across the country to be with you, and where the hell did that leave me? I don't know how to be with you."

"Where are you going?" I ask as he leaves the stall.

He grabs his towel. "I'll finish showering when you're gone."

CHAPTER 49
SALEM

I shift the car into Park and stare up at the four-story white house with a gray roof that looks wider than my brownstone and my neighbor's put together. Climbing out, I open the back door and grab the cake box from the floor. Balancing the box with one hand, I lock the car. Though, looking around at the quiet suburban street, I doubt I have to.

My phone vibrates when I'm a few feet away from the door. I balance the box as I click play on the audio message.

"Good afternoon, Mr. Jones. This is Mr. Chen. We caught a lead in the search for Denzel. You may recall that for the more difficult cases, my team and I outsource a couple of hours to a larger agency with more resources. A junior agent there caught a break. Denzel was seen entering Mexico by car a couple of weeks ago, shortly after you reported talking to him on the phone. His whereabouts in Mexico are unknown, but we're confident we'll have more information soon. I'll be in touch again shortly.

Mexico? I stare at my phone.

With who?

What for?

Placing my phone on top of the box, I wipe my palm against my sweater and then tap the audio record button.

"H-hi, Mr. Chen—" I stop recording and take a deep breath. My parents were also copied on the message. I need to sound calm for them.

I start to hit record again when a car pulls in behind me.

I turn and wave.

"Salem, is that you?" Liz, Blue's mother, asks as she climbs out of the car, grinning widely.

"Hi, Liz. I came to check on Anaïs. How is she?"

"How very sweet of you." She pulls some grocery bags from the trunk. "It was touch and go at first, but I think we figured out the right meds schedule."

I move to help her, but she says, "It's okay. They're light. Come in."

"Is she in a lot of pain?" I ask.

"She's a silent sufferer, like her brother." She reaches into her purse and pulls out her keys. "I only know because I'm keeping track of her meds, and she's needed more painkillers than the schedule allows. The doctor said it's fine, as pain management is important for the first few days, but she had a tough morning."

She opens the door and removes her shoes, and I follow suit. I look down at my socks, not sure what I'm feeling. She catches me and smiles. "Heated marble."

"Oh."

I keep meaning to look into that.

I follow her past a polished brass and glass elevator that has a chandelier with crystal birds sitting atop a brass branch.

She quirks an eyebrow over her shoulder.

"Sorry?" I ask, realizing I missed something.

She nods to the box.

"Oh, I made her favorite."

This time her brows sweep down and bunch together.

"Uh, Fraisier cake," I say.

"Oh." She nods. "She calls you her new bestie."

I smile. "Beautiful home," I observe as we pass a grand room with sculptures and mounted art.

"Thank you," she replies, placing her bags on the kitchen counter and helping me offload the cake.

"May I?" she asks, her hands on the lid.

"Of course." I step back so she can peel it open.

Phew. It didn't shift on the drive.

"Salem...it's stunning." She covers her mouth. "Are those real flowers?"

"Mm." I stare at the flower crown dusted with sugar pearls atop the traditional French cake made from sponge, cream, and fresh strawberries. "They're edible."

She pulls out her phone. "It reminds me of water lilies for some reason." She snaps a picture of the cake. "Have you ever been to Monet's garden in Giverny?"

"Uh, Giverny?"

"In the region of Normandy in France." She snaps another picture. "With your eye for beauty, I think you might enjoy it. One second."

She returns with a glass cake platter. After I lower the sides of the box, she lifts the cake and slides it on.

"Goodness, it really is exquisite."

"You have to taste it first," I tease.

She laughs as she retrieves plates, utensils, and a cake knife.

THE GLASS-PANELED ELEVATOR FACES A WINDOW, and as we rise to the third floor, it feels like we're scaling the row of trees.

"This way," Liz says as I look left and right down the long hallway. "Third door on the right."

Liz gently twists the handle and peeks in. "Good, you're awake," she says, then steps inside. "You have a visitor." Liz nods for me to enter.

Extending the cake first, I announce, "Special delivery."

"Whoa," Anaïs says, her voice a little hoarse. "Is that you, bestie?"

"Guilty." I chuckle.

She's nestled in the middle of a large bed, under the covers and surrounded by pillows, including a wedge pillow that's propping her up. Natural light pours in through the triple-arched windows. Her eyes crinkle at the corners. "I knew you'd come."

"I brought your favorite." I pad over and lower the cake to give her a view.

She grabs her glasses from the nightstand and thumbs them on. "Oh. My. God." Her toothy grin stretches wide.

"Isn't it exceptional?" Liz exclaims.

"Still have to taste it first," I remind her.

She waves her hand over the cake toward her nose. "God, the scent."

"Oh, I used date syrup for the cream, and gluten-free flour for the sponge. I promise it's still delicious. The decorations are sugar-based, unfortunately, but I made it easy to pluck off so you can skip 'em. I read that sugar and gluten can cause inflammation."

Anaïs turns to Liz. "Can we adopt him?"

"Sure." Liz laughs. "Though it might make things awkward for Arnie."

Anaïs looks at me and offers a sympathetic smile. So, she knows.

Of course she knows.

"May I offer you tea or coffee? Mint would probably go well. Or Cinnamon?" Liz asks.

Anaïs and I both answer, "Cinnamon," as Liz makes space for the cake on the coffee table across the room.

"Pull up a chair." Anaïs gestures to one of the two armchairs.

After Liz leaves and I pull up a chair next to the bed, Anaïs removes her glasses and says, "I'm glad I wasn't part of the breakup."

I arch my eyebrows.

"I know you weren't, like, a couple-couple, but it still feels like a breakup to me."

"Yeah, well, my bond with you is tight." I extend my fist to her, and she bumps it.

"He misses you. Like, really misses you. He knows he could have handled things better. He's never been in a relationship. And that's not an excuse; it's just a fact."

"Anaïs—"

"I know. I need to mind my business. Can you blame me, though? I really want you to marry Arnie and join our family."

Time for a change of subject. "How are you feeling?"

"Like I had adhesions cut off my organs," she tells me, then reverts to the previous topic. "So, do you think you'll work it out?"

I shake my head, fighting a grin as she clasps her hands together under her chin and blinks rapidly.

"I don't know," I answer honestly. "The whole situation left me feeling kinda disposable, when I thought I meant more to him."

"You're not disposable to him. Not in the slightest. This is gonna sound like semantics, but it's not that there was another man. It's just that another man triggered feelings from a time when he was at his worst mentally. Did he ever talk to you about that time in his life?"

I shake my head.

She opens her mouth, then closes it. "It's not my story to tell. It's just...he wasn't doing well. And while it hasn't gotten that bad since, it still gets really bad for him in here." She taps the side of her head. "You're dating someone who struggles with his mental health. He retreats when he should reach out.

He doesn't even realize he's doing it. It's like breathing for him. Have you ever dated anyone like that?"

I shake my head. "No. I ha— Ah!" I shriek as a blur of fur jumps into my lap.

Anaïs bursts out laughing. "That's Alfie. He's especially gifted at stealth attacks."

"Christ." My shoulders drop as I pet the furball who decides to couch himself on my lap.

Sighing, I say, "I heard everything you said. I just need time."

"That's good. It's hopeful. I'd be sad if you were adamant that you're through with him."

"He makes me...grrr. He got into it at the game the other day, and I was ready to fight the army of security guards who were closing in on him."

"I caught that game. He filled me in afterward. You looked ready to go to war."

"I'm a chill dude. But come for me or mine, and..." I mutter.

Anaïs beams at me, flashing her teeth.

"What's that smile for?"

"You just called him yours."

I focus on petting Alfie and change the subject again. "They have a lead in the investigation to find Denzel."

"Is he okay?"

"I don't know. He was seen entering Mexico."

"Huh. He has friends there?"

I blow out a breath. "I don't know."

"How are you holding up?"

Liz returns with the tea.

I nod that I'm okay.

She frowns, like she's not sure she believes me.

THE REST of the afternoon breezes by with easy conversation. We finished off three-quarters of the cake, and they made me promise to come back and teach them how to make it.

Heading to my car, I check my phone and see a missed call from Lucien.

"Hey. Isn't it late in Paris?" I ask when he answers my call.

"I flew into New York on a red-eye this morning."

"Ah."

"Are you free to meet me for dinner?" he asks.

"Uh…" I stare down at my sweater and jeans. "Sure. Somewhere casual?"

"How about the Chapel?" he suggests.

"Cool. See you in an hour."

CHAPTER 50
SALEM

"Right this way," the hostess says, leading me to our table.

After years of feeling tens of thousands of eyes on me a few nights a week, you'd think I'd be used to the glances thrown my way, but it never feels natural. Lucien comes into view, impeccably dressed as always, typing on his phone, undoubtedly running his empire with never a minute to spare, not even to remove his coat.

"Here we are. I'll let your server know the full party is here."

At the sound of the hostess's voice, his head pops up.

"Hey!" He eases into a stand, his black tailored coat falling in clean lines.

"What's up?"

"Still single?" he asks.

"Yeah." I breathe around the scrape in my chest. "Why?"

"Good. Now that you're out, we can finally do this..." He leans up and presses a soft kiss to my lips.

My first public kiss that day in the Castro with Blue blinks to life, and I wince from the memory.

Lucien pulls back, peels off his oversized shades, and takes a good look at me. "*Mon dieu. Ce que ça fait du bien.*"

I grin back. "Glad it was worth the wait."

His fingers press into the sides of my waist. "You're actually out."

I huff a laugh. "Wild, right?"

"Come on." He signals for the waiter as he folds into the booth. "We'll celebrate!"

"A bottle of your Bollinger 1996 Vieilles Vignes Françaises, please," he orders when the waiter arrives.

"What are you doing over there?" He shoots me a puzzled glance. "*Viens.*"

Instead of waiting for me to come to him, he shifts to the spot next to me. He leans forward, and I help him out of his coat. Resting it neatly across the bench, he straightens his crisp, waist-length white shirt, patting down the high collar and double chest pockets clasped by small, brown buttons.

He crosses his legs, which are encased in camel-colored wool slacks, then fixes his belt so the braid hangs decoratively to the side.

He winks, his bronze skin flawless, like he keeps to his monthly esthetician visits. "*Oui,* I'm still fabulous."

I smile. "Always."

"Last we spoke, you were baking a cake."

God, that feels like a century ago.

His brown eyes scan my face. "*Merde!*" He frowns.

The champagne arrives.

After we toast, he says, "Tell me."

And I do, starting with the press conference.

He interrupts to ask questions.

Two flutes of champagne later, he's caught up, and with a click of his tongue, he rests his head on my shoulder. "I'm jealous of him. I'd have killed to have put a ring on your finger."

I tilt my head to catch his eyes. "What?"

"I knew you had your eyes set on someone else. But I was happy to have whatever part of you I could."

Wait, seriously? What? He always seemed happy with our arrangement.

"Luci—"

"Relax." He pats my arm. "When you were with me, you were all in. But it sometimes felt like there was a clock ticking, and I wouldn't have you forever."

I lower the flute to the table and wipe my mouth—the bubbly turning noxious in my stomach. "I'm sorry. I never wanted you to feel like there was someone else. I'm sorry if I did."

"Shh. I regret nothing," he reassures.

I don't understand. "Why waste time with me if you didn't think you could have forever? If you wanted marriage?"

He shrugs. "All we really have is right now."

I shake my head. "But it's okay to want tomorrow, to plan for tomorrow, to want to spend the rest of your life with someone."

"Maybe." He flicks his hand side to side. "You're an idealist. It's charming, but it's also intimidating. You see the potential in everything."

"What's wrong with that?"

"You sometimes only see the potential. Which means anything short of it is insufficient. I loved the time we spent together. Why would I have suffered tomorrow's loss when I still had you today?"

"But you wanted marriage?"

"Yes."

"If I want marriage with someone, I could never settle for less than that," I tell him.

"I know." He rests his palm on top of mine. "It's how I knew our time was limited."

"No, that's not what I meant."

"It's okay. Things work out as they should," he says, then adds with a small smile, "I might have met someone."

"Hold on. If I hurt you, Lucien…"

"You didn't. I wouldn't be sitting here if you did."

My back settles against the booth. It's true that he wouldn't stand for being mistreated. Then his words from a moment ago register. "You met someone?"

"His name's Olivier, and he's a physicist specializing in the fundamental physics of quantum mechanics."

"Sounds impressive."

"*Oui.* I try to keep up with his work, but it all goes over my head like my work goes over his. Here he is." He slides his phone over to me.

I whistle. "That's how they make scientists in Paris?" He's built like a club bouncer.

He chuckles. "*C'est trop mignon.*"

Very cute. "He resembles that footballer who plays for PFG," I note.

"*Oui.* He's his older brother."

"Yeah?"

"Mm. Olivier is removed from all of that, though. He didn't know who I was when we met."

"That's perfect for you." He's struggled with guys dating him for money and clout. It's part of the reason we worked. I knew he could be discreet and would never out me, and he knew I didn't want or need his money or influence.

"I don't know about perfect, but I want to see where it goes."

After I fight him to pay the bill, and win, I'm signing the check when I tell him, "Denzel's missing again."

"For how long?" he asks.

"Right after you and I last spoke, I talked to him on the phone."

"Oh, *mon ange, viens là.*" He rests his hand on my thigh. "Can I help?"

"We hired a PI."

"You'll keep me posted?"

I nod. "Ready?"

He reaches for his coat. "I brought you a gift. I'll have it delivered to you next week."

"I told you, no more suits. It's too much."

"I can't imagine anyone else in it," he states.

"Your scientist looks like the perfect muse."

"I prefer him disheveled. What about your guy? Can I make him a suit?"

"He's not my guy." I tilt my chest up, stretching out the tension in my back. "Anyway, he'll probably burn it and send you a death threat scrawled with its ashes."

He laughs. "Possessive?"

A man standing in the corner of the lounge turns slightly, playing it off like his phone wasn't just pointed at us.

"Murderously so," I say, hating the fondness in my voice.

"Hot." He swoons.

CHAPTER 51
ARNAZ

🎵 **"The Lights Will Never Be on When I Come Home"** 🎵
And a dream is buried in a nailed coffin, doused with gasoline,
and set on fire until embers and ashes remain.
A high wind with a sustained speed of 70 miles per hour
transports its silt into my lungs, where it pollutes my brain.

"Another round, please," Sid requests of the bartender.

"How do you know that?" I ask, not believing Sid's reassurance that I have nothing to worry about with Salem and Lucien.

"You know how headlines blow things out of proportion. You said he and Lucien ended things amicably, and now they're just friends."

"They're kissing," I state, shuddering at the image that's been replaying in my mind.

"You saw the videos." He twists in his seat, peering at the crowd sitting before the stage. "It was over as soon as it started. Looked friendly."

I've watched every video and scanned every photo of the two of them on their *date*, feeling both irked that so many people secretly captured the moment and grateful for all the different angles.

"If our *friend* saw you kissing someone on the lips, how would they feel?" I ask.

He purses his lips. "Been there. Katrina. All-Star game when I was playing for Miami. It, uh"—he winces—"didn't go well."

"Exactly."

"Thanks," he says to the bartender, who slides over two Arnold Palmers. Denver's team is hot this season, so we can't afford to drink the night before our game. "He still sending you to voicemail?" he asks me.

I hang my head.

"What's with our boy and the long face?" Ussef's heavy arm lands across my shoulders with a thud before his non-alcoholic beer slams down on the bar.

"He *has* been broody lately, hasn't he?" Sid answers.

"If this is about me being angry that you skipped me again and gave the gift basket to Gigi, I forgive you," Ussef says.

I snort mid-swallow, causing the liquid to go down the wrong pipe.

"I said I forgive you. Don't choke, my man." He pats my back as I gasp for air.

"Th-thanks." I cough through the burn shooting down my chest.

He picks up the fresh bottle that the bartender placed down. "Does it hurt seeing her wear the Cartier cufflinks every day? A hundred percent."

For fuck's sake. "The next two baskets are yours. You can have the next five if it ends this conversation."

"I love you, man." He tightens his hold on my neck, pulling me into a noogie.

My elbow shoots back, but he jumps left, releasing me, before it makes contact.

"Knew that was coming." He swipes up his beer. "Next basket is mine. You heard that?" he says to Sid.

"I thought the next basket was Jo's," Sid replies with a grin.

"Oh shit," I say with a laugh.

"Fuck you!" Ussef spits, storming away.

"I offered you the cake," I call to his retreating back, then say to Sid, "He looks like he's gonna cry."

Sid chuckles. "He'll be aight."

"He'll be aight," I mock, shaking my head. "*You and Salem will work it out. Him and the billionaire designer dude plastered to his lips are just friends.*" I scoff. "You ever feel like you're drowning in all that optimism? What if *you-know-who* stopped talking to you suddenly?" I ask.

His smirk disappears. "They left me once."

My head jerks back. "What?"

He nods. "For a few weeks, the night after my fight with Lucas."

My eyebrows dip. "They left you 'cause you fought with Lucas?"

"Nah. We were rocky before that."

"Why didn't you tell me?"

"You know why."

He wasn't out to me yet.

"How did you fix it?"

His lips spread in a filthy smile. "We talked it out." He downs his drink. "I think I know how to cheer you up," he says before speeding off.

I touch the home screen of my phone and then drop my head to the bar top as I see no new notifications.

What I'd give to see his name on my screen just one more time.

"Good evening. Can y'all hear me?"

I fling a glance over my shoulder at the sound of Sid mic'd up.

"Yeah? Cool," he replies to the din of whistles and shouts. "Good evening, my name is Sid King, and I play basketball for the Los Angeles Royals."

A woman screams, "I love you!" at him, causing more shouts and whistles across the bar.

"Thank you. So, my friend has been down lately."

There's a wave of *awws*.

"And there's only one thing I know that transports him to a place far away from his troubles—music."

No. No way.

Every phone in the spot is pointed at him.

It took less than twenty minutes for the bar to fill up, spilling out to the streets, once word got around that a couple of us were here. Security's doing their best to keep fans at bay so we can enjoy our drinks in peace, but this is testing it.

"Y'all are all in for a treat tonight. We have in the house a man with a voice so beautiful it'll make you feel like your soul's left your body to rest with angels. I could only convince him to do one song, but I promise, all you need is one."

I swipe my hand across my throat, gesturing for him to knock it off, when he glances over at me.

"First, I need y'all to make some noise."

The noise is instantly deafening.

"Nah." He shakes his head. "Y'all can do better than that."

Their roar reaches a fever pitch.

No! I mouth at him.

The fucker nods and winks at me.

He places his hand on his heart. "Knew y'all had it in you, Denver."

Sid signals to Nick, and before I know it, he's stalking over and pushing me toward the stage. "You used to beg us for this and karaoke. You know you want to," Nick taunts.

"You and Sid are on my kill list," I grit out.

He chuckles. "Stop flirting with me."

I'm pushed damn near headfirst onto the stage.

Straightening up, I glare at Sid.

"Just close your eyes and escape," he says, handing me the mic.

"You're on my kill—"

"Yeah, yeah. Love you too."

I stand there for an awkward amount of time before fixing on a band member's Gibson acoustic guitar. Without having to ask, she offers it to me. Another band member offers me his stool.

"Thanks," I say to them both.

I hook the guitar strap around my neck and get situated, adjusting the mic and stool. I massage and stretch my hands quickly to warm them up before I strum a few chords and hum scales away from the mic. There's only one song that comes to mind. It's not mine, but it's the only song that's been on repeat since I lost Salem.

I clear my throat and raise my gaze above the crowd. "If you're out there listening, I miss you. I dream of boring days with you too. This song is for you."

I close my eyes, and with a deep breath, I let go.

CHAPTER 52
ARNAZ

🎵 **"Peace"** 🎵
It wasn't in bed or underneath, the backyard, toilet, patch of
shade, strip of sunlight, couch, kitchen, midnight concrete.
It wasn't inside of me, or the smile of a stranger. I summoned it
by name. I pretended not to need it.
I fucked, I wept, I prayed, I drank, I sweated, I howled, I slept, I
waited.
Never did it come.
Never did I find it.

The sky rumbles as lightning blinks through the dense
gray clouds.

"Is this it?" the driver asks, rolling to a stop.

"I think so." I check the rideshare app for the address.

Carter's Rolls-Royce Black Badge Cullinan comes into view
as we pull into the driveway.

So much for hoping he'd be off traveling.

I'm here for Anaïs.

"Thank you." I climb out and make my way to the door,

tucking my head to shield myself from the rain. Standing under the floral archway, I look out at the street.

With the hectic game schedule, it's taken me longer than I wanted to make it out to check on Anaïs. I'm free for the next three days and plan to spend them making sure she's okay.

There's no way I can be *here* for more than a few hours, so I booked a room at a nearby hotel.

The .25 mg of risperidone my psychiatrist prescribed with a strict warning to take only if I experience a severe panic attack or anxiety sits in the small pocket of the duffel strung over my shoulder. I told her I thought it was unnecessary, but she disagreed after hearing about this trip.

I stretch out my hands and watch raindrops splatter against the cement before lifelessly joining the puddle.

I watch my breath form a cloud in the air.

I'm here for Anaïs.

I ring the doorbell and wait.

I don't need any fingers to count the times I've been here. They moved to New Jersey after I joined the league. And nothing, I promised myself, except for Mom falling sick, would ever make me cross the threshold. I understand Anaïs's choice to recover here, and that she'd only choose it if she had nowhere else to go. I offered to pay for an at-home nurse, but us and strangers—nah.

Plus, Mom, in a head-scratching reversal, decided once we were older and out of the house, that she'd actually give the nurturing mother bit a shot. I've never had use for it personally, but Anaïs allows it for rare times like this when she physically needs the help. I hate thinking about all the ER visits she sat alone in the waiting room.

The door opens. "Arnaz!"

My eyes widen at Mom's outfit.

Chanel makes velour sweatsuits now?

"Come in. How was your flight?"

Is that tomato sauce below the hooded neck?

"G-good," I reply, bending down to unlace my boots.

She looks behind me. "Will Salem be joining us?"

"What? Why would he—"

"Hi, son."

My gaze remains trained on Mom. "Carter."

The air shifts as Mom goes rigid.

I straighten. "Can you take me to Anaïs?" I ask her.

"Maybe we can talk before you leave?" Carter asks.

"Mom?"

"Y-yes." She blinks rapidly. "This way." She shoots him a tense smile, then says to me, "Are you hungry? I made Bolognese."

She cooks now? I'd look around for tells of hired help, but then I'd have to look in the direction of Carter.

"I'm good."

I'm starving, but I'll order something for me and Anaïs.

We enter the elevator in silence, but before it even starts its ascent, she's breaking the quiet. "You know, Arnaz, maybe you can just hear him out before you leave."

"I'm here to see Anaïs, and then I'm gone," I reply tersely.

"God, you're so much alike."

"What?" I glare at her. "I'm nothing like him."

"I just meant—"

"Stop. Please."

"Okay." She raises her hands. "Okay."

When the elevator comes to a stop, she leads the way out. "Your room is here. And Anaïs's is right next door."

"Thanks." I head straight for Anaïs.

I hear the opening tune for *Exosphere* as I push open the door. She has her back to me, and I quietly place my bag down, peel off my coat, and throw it on the chair along with my beanie. I tiptoe over and confirm she's asleep before heading to the bathroom.

I turn on the hot water and push the liquid hand soap spout four times.

One Mississippi, two Mississippi, three Mississippi, four Mississippi, five Mississippi, six Mississippi...twelve Mississippi...

Killing the faucet, I stare at my wet hands.

What did I do wrong?

I leave the bathroom and retrace my steps.

My skin raises like it's separating from my muscles, and my nerve endings send a message to my spine—*be careful, remember the cost of absentmindedness*—as my gaze lands on my coat.

I reach for it and pause with my hand midair.

No, I am not a kid anymore. I'm not afraid of *him*.

I toss the coat back down.

Salem will marry Lucien.

My legs lock in place.

Just fight it.

I ball my fists.

Just this once.

You'll lose him forever.

I snatch up the coat, drag it over to the closet, stab a hanger through the sleeves, and hook it on the rod.

I scrub my hands over my face. *Here five minutes and crushing it.*

I hear a meow at my feet.

I bend down and pick up Alfie, then nestle his head under my chin.

Walking us over to the window, I watch the tree branches thrash back and forth from the force of the wind and rain. When my stomach rumbles, I pull up a food delivery app, copy and paste the address from Anaïs's text, and check out the options. There's a Thai place with decent reviews. I order everything mild in case Anaïs can't have spice.

"Alfie tried to leave through the window too."

My head whips around at the sound of Anaïs's voice.

"I swear he sees ghosts here. Something creeps him out."

That makes two of us.

"How are you feeling?" I ask.

I pad over and get in bed next to her, tucking my knees on top of the comforter.

"I tried to wait up for you. How long have you been here?"

"Only a couple of minutes."

She nods as she covers her mouth and yawns.

"How are you feeling?" I repeat.

"The gas they pumped into my abdomen to be able to see through the cameras has finally worn off. I had a shooting pain in my neck and shoulders for days. And I looked like I was eight months pregnant. Now I just feel achy and tired."

"And your pain on a scale from one to ten?"

"Eh. They gave me the good stuff. Mom and I figured out the right schedule."

"What can I do?"

"Help me outta bed. I gotta pee. It hurts to crunch."

I get to my feet, make my way to her side of the bed, and help her up.

When she hobbles back from the bathroom, she lifts her T-shirt and shows me the stitches.

"Whoa." I count four swollen incision spots. "No wonder it hurts to crunch."

"Yeah. They gave me scans of the organs where they cut out the inflamed tissue. Wanna see?"

"Hard pass."

She laughs as I help her back into bed.

"I ordered us Thai," I tell her.

"Mango sticky rice?"

"Yep."

"Yum."

"Hey, Mom said something weird. She asked if Salem was

with me." I cover her with the comforter and then head back to my side of the bed.

"Yeah...I knew you were coming, so I wanted to wait to tell you in person. He came by and hung out with us."

The hair on the back of my neck stands up. "What do you mean he came by?"

"When we hung out that time after his game, I told him about the surgery. He asked what my favorite cake was and said he would visit me. And he kept his word."

"Was Carter here?"

"No," she says softly. "Don't worry. It was just me and Mom."

He came by?

"Why would he do that if he's done with me?" I wonder aloud.

She reaches for her phone, and a few seconds later, she holds up a photo of the cake.

"Wow."

"Look." She swipes to the next picture, and I smile.

She's making a kissy face with the cake crown on her head. Mom is in the background, laughing.

And when I think I couldn't love him more.

She swipes again. He's bent down next to her, arms slung over her shoulders, and they're making matching silly faces.

He was here in this very room a few days ago.

"Aww, babe," she says, lowering the phone. "You look like you're gonna cry."

"How long did he stay?"

"A couple of hours."

"What day?"

"Uh..." She squints, pursing her lips. "Three, maybe four, days ago."

My head flinches back. "Wait. What day of the week?"

Her eyes roll toward the ceiling. "Friday? No. Thursday?"

I pick up her phone, google Salem and Lucien, ignoring the stab in my gut at the images of them kissing, and scan the date.

I show her the kiss. "So he was here, then went on his date?"

Her mouth dips at the corners. "Yeah...I don't know, Arnie. He is definitely not over you. He said this thing that when you got into it with those jerks at the game, he would have fought all the security in the building to protect you. Something like, if you come for his..."

I slouch and blow out a breath. "I feel like my head is gonna explode." *Or maybe my heart.*

"That's 'cause you love him."

"I keep thinking about how I ran from him. And knowing what I know about him now, he's way bigger of a person than me. I'm not sure I'd have had the confidence to keep pursuing him if the shoe were on the other foot."

She leans her head against my shoulder. "I know. But you aren't him. There are reasons you run. Just like there are reasons Alfie doesn't trust most strangers."

I close my eyes to curb the burn. "Sometimes I think you're the only person who will ever know me. Like *really* know me."

"Hmm." She's quiet for a few breaths. "Maybe I'm the only person you feel safe knowing you. You remember the time we got lost on the way back to that resort in the Dominican Republic?"

"Hmm?"

"When you were young."

Then she was young too. We're only four years apart.

"We got lost on the way back to the resort. And you stopped walking and said, '*Where is everyone?*' And you tightened your hold on my hand. Mom and Carter were supposed to come back for us, but the beach cleared out, the sun set, and they still hadn't returned."

A faint memory surfaces. "The lizard with the aqua and green stripes?"

She huffs out a hoarse laugh. "Yes, you remember. Right before that, though, when I was trying to hide how terrified I was that we were lost, I told you not to worry because Mom and Carter would find us. And you remember what you said?"

I shake my head.

"You said they wouldn't find us because they wouldn't even know we were missing. You were so young to—"

"It's okay," I tell her, even as the memory from that day curls in, tightening my throat.

"I hated crying back then because I needed to be strong for us, but when you ran off to chase the lizard, I broke. I kept thinking you deserved better. You weren't even seven, and you already had a broken heart."

Pressure builds behind my eyes as her voice cracks.

"Anaïs—"

"Just let me finish. I think your heart is still broken. And you hide it in random hookups and ball. I think if it weren't broken, you'd see what I see. That there's no one more deserving of love than you."

My fingers dig into my arm as a bubble grows in my throat.

"I know it hurts, but you need to hear this. I'm honored to be the one who knows you the best, and I will always be that for you, but there's someone else who also wants to know you. Who's also worthy of love. He sat right there the other day with a hurt heart too."

I screw my eyes closed. "I can't—"

The thought of him hurting...

My hand covers my mouth.

"Shhh." She wipes my tears. "It's okay."

I shake my head. "I really didn't want to hurt him."

"You can't always avoid hurting the people you love."

I look toward the window, but all I see is his smile that first time he approached me on the court all those years ago, filled with so much hope.

Hope that terrified me.

How do people do this—live with hurting the people they love?

I never even told him I love him.

Does he know?

"I need his address," I say.

"Why do you think I waited to tell you when you were here?" she says.

I lean down and kiss her forehead. She still wipes my tears before her own. I drag the arm of my hoodie down and clean her up.

"You know you kept me alive," I tell her.

"I didn't—"

"You did. When they ran off Ms. Brown, all I had was you. When I look back, I see how much pain you were in, too, and no one..." My voice catches.

"Arnaz." She shifts to face me. "You gave me purpose. You were the only light in our house." I shake my head, but she holds my chin. "You were the Only. Light. And I saw how that light dimmed every day, and I would have given everything to stop it."

"But it wasn't your job," I insist.

"I don't care. You were more mine than theirs. I was lonely before you came along. Can you imagine if it were just me in their house?"

Oh god.

"Yeah." She breaks into a wet laugh, making me laugh too. "Horrific."

I GET an alert that the food is arriving. I wipe my eyes on my hoodie as she reaches for a tissue and blows her nose.

"I'll be back," I tell her as I rise.

She nods and directs me to the staircase, as if sensing my dread at being cornered in an elevator with *him*.

Food in hand, I'm closing the front door when I hear, "Arnaz, can we please talk?"

"Christ!"

"Sorry. I didn't mean to startle you."

Right.

I make my way toward the staircase.

"I FORGOT TO GRAB PLATES."

"They gave us utensils?" Anaïs asks.

I place the bag down on the coffee table and rummage through it. "Yeah."

"Then we're good."

She's biting into the drunken noodles when I ask, "Did Salem share an update about his brother?"

She swallows. "You heard about Mexico?"

I shake my head as I scoop up the curry.

"He was seen crossing the border into Mexico."

"Mexico?"

"Yeah. Salem found it odd, too, but it's something."

"Hmm."

"Yeah."

"I want to be there for him."

"Then go to him. Show him the Arnie I know. The kid who would stay up all night with me in the ER when I had flare-ups. It's time to go all in. Isn't it?"

Yeah. Past time.

CHAPTER 53
ARNAZ

♫ "Surrender" ♫
The most delicate of delights.

I wait until Anaïs drifts to sleep to head out.

"You're not staying?" Mom asks from the second floor when I reach the ground level.

"I'll be back tomorrow." Anaïs and I have plans to binge our favorite Gothic movies.

Carter appears next to her, changed out of his jeans and hoodie into a T-shirt and sweats. Sweats I recognize from my partnership with Nike.

For fuck's sake.

"What happened to Ms. Brown?" I blurt.

Mom trades a confused glance with Carter. "Your nanny?"

"Yeah." I place my duffel down and cross my arms. "She took us to church every Sunday." I liked being in the choir. It taught me how to sing. "She helped us with homework after school. Then one day, she disappeared."

"Her son was sick, and she had to leave the country and return home," Carter answers.

"Her son was sick?" I shift in place. "I thought it was because you scared her away."

"No, son."

My teeth grind. "You know I hate when you call me that? Like, I want to bash my fist into something hard until I can't feel it anymore."

"Maybe you should go down," Mom encourages him.

"No. Stay there," I demand when he starts to move.

"Okay." He steps back. "I've gotten help. I'm not the same man I was. I've been trying to make amends."

I snort. "When?"

"Pardon me?" he says.

"You heard me. When have you tried to make amends? Was it the time after my back was cut open from trying to save you from falling into the fire? Wait, mmm, no, I don't believe there were any amends then." I start to pace. "Was it when you found out I was gay and tore through the house and broke everything you could in my room? Oh, wait, nope. Don't remember an amends then. Or was it when you left me in the field after dark, covered in animal blo—"

"Stop."

"Oh, I remember," I continue, snapping my fingers. "You mean that time after I totaled Anaïs's car and you couldn't be bothered to show up at the hospital."

"I was there," he says.

"What?" I stop pacing. "Liar!"

"I was there." He grips the banister and sinks onto the step, arms crossing in front of his knees. "Every time you slept, your mother and I would trade places in your room."

I stare at Mom, her face crumpled, eyes wet, and she nods.

"I checked into rehab—again—the day of your release," he tells me.

He was there?

I ball my fists.

So what?

He doesn't get a fucking brownie for doing the bare minimum.

"You made me feel like shit every day for needing anything from you. God forbid I asked for anything that resembled love. Those punishments were the worst. You know how fucking unbearable you made the house for us?"

"I do," he croaks, his face reddening, like he'd rather explode than be here having this conversation.

Hey, he asked to talk.

"I carried shame for years for needing anything from you." I stare at Mom. "And you."

"Arnaz, we were supposed to take care of you," she whispers, tears running down her cheeks.

"Oh, so you did know that?"

"Son—Arnaz—we messed up," Carter says at the same time Anaïs appears over the banister asking, "What's going on?"

"When Mom wasn't working herself ragged to get away from us, she was depressed. I was okay, but Anaïs needed you. She cut herself. Neither of you saw the Band-Aids and lines on her inner thigh."

Mom's head flies up, and she turns to Anaïs. "Is this true?"

Anaïs doesn't respond at first, then she nods, looking away as Mom sobs.

"You know we took turns watering down your alcohol every day after school?" I sneer at Carter.

"N-no." He shakes his head.

"We were scared to death you'd fall and bust your head open like that time you came home covered in blood. 'Cause maybe if you weren't shit-faced, the beast wouldn't wake at the snap of a finger and rage at us. Nothing I did was good enough. Everything I did made the two of you eviscerate each other."

"It wasn't you. Or you." He glances up at Anaïs. "I had all

my worth tied up in football. The alcoholism, the women." He looks at Mom with remorse. If she's surprised to hear about his infidelity, she doesn't show it. "I was broken, and I tried to break everyone in my path."

A dark cackle rises from my stomach. "Not everyone. The perfect Carter Show never missed airtime."

"Everyone I love," he corrects himself. "Imagine if you had everything taken away from you, your NBA contract—"

"What? I'd terrorize my family and cheat on my husband? Negative. I'm not you."

He hangs his head between his arms. "I'm a piece of shit for what I did to you, your sister, and your mom. You have no reason to believe or forgive me."

"You didn't have everything taken away from you," Anaïs breaks in. "*We* were there."

"I know." He raises his head to turn and face her. "I couldn't see that. A man is supposed to provide for his family. And in the blink of an eye, your mom became the only one bringing in money. I had just signed a contract that would have taken us to the next level. And like that" —he swipes his palms together—"it was gone. I worked my whole life to play football. It was all I knew. I didn't know how to be a man, let alone a dad or a husband, without it."

I snatch up my bag.

He turns to me. "I'm sorry for the hell I put you all through."

"I'm sorry too," Mom rushes out. "For abandoning you both when my marriage started to fail."

"Got it." My muscles lock, hardening to contain the surge of rage inside me. "We're done?"

"Listen, I know one talk isn't going to fix us. If you give us a —" he starts.

I raise my hand for him to stop. "This trip is for her." I nod to Anaïs. "I heard you out. Tomorrow and the day after, I'm here for her. Not you or Mom. Respect that."

"I just want to fix this," Carter says.

"Some shit can't be fixed."

"You don't mean that," Mom says. "Please."

"He just needs time," Anaïs says. "We both do. You don't know him. He's been working really hard to heal. He goes to—"

"Anaïs," I interject.

"—therapy, he sees a psychiatrist, he's even figuring out a way to let in someone he loves. And that's a really big deal. It's hard for him to let people in, to trust that they won't turn around and hurt him. I—"

"Anais. Please," I beg.

"—don't know how he's so resilient after everything he went through, but he is. He doesn't give up."

I shake my head, clenching the strap of my bag, as I turn away and stare at the door.

"He's brave. You read the article. To come out that way after being told from the beginning that being gay is wrong. His heart has been broken for a really long time. This was big for him to talk to you tonight. Accept where he is. If you push, you'll push him away."

"We *are* proud of him," Carter says.

My nails dig into my palm as I force my legs to stand strong.

"You can leave now, Arnaz," Anaïs says. "It's okay."

I don't stop moving until the door slams shut behind me. I make it a few steps before my knees buckle, and I crumple to the ground against Carter's car.

Pressure seizes my chest, throat, and back, and my knees sink into the downpour.

Mom's tear-stricken face flashes in my mind.

Get up, I will myself, but I can't move.

I don't know how long I'm stuck there before an arm wraps around my back.

"It's okay."

"No." I push Carter away. "Don't touch me!"

"Okay," his voice cracks.

I stare at his tire as my chest heaves and pain drowns my lungs, ribs, throat...

I fight to choke it down.

"I'm sorry," he croaks.

...but it's scraping, tearing, mangling my sternum.

His arm tightens around me again.

"Get off me." I push away until my back hits the other end of his car. The wet, cold pavement seeps into my bones.

"I don't deserve your forgiveness," he says, collapsing to sit a safe distance away. "I don't deserve this family."

A car pulls out across the street, its headlights lighting up the driveway. I expect him to climb to a stand or shift toward the shadow to avoid a blemish to his perfect image.

He doesn't move.

"For the longest time, when I looked in the mirror, I saw you"—I wipe my eyes and nose on my drenched hoodie—"not as a demon over my shoulder, but your eyes where my eyes should be. And I hate it when people look into my eyes and tell me I look just like you. I can't even leave the house without covering them." I scrub my thumb across the ink on my knuckle. "Every time I looked in the mirror, I felt small. It took me a long time to realize it was you I was seeing, not me. You always tried to prove that I was insignificant. I'm not."

I force myself to stand, legs unconvinced of their strength, breath arrested by the sobs squeezing my chest, and push. Every step feels like it'll be the last before I drop again, but I don't stop until I can no longer feel him watching, until I can no longer see the house.

Pulling out my phone to order a car, I click on Anaïs's text.

Anaïs

I love you

And there's an address.

CHAPTER 54
SALEM

"It's still only thunder, Sim." I reach down and scratch under his chin after he starts trembling again. "I'm sure," I answer as his gaze pings between me and the window.

His head twists toward the fireplace as the wood makes a crackling-pop sound. "It's just fire."

His forelegs start to slide forward on the rug when a rumbling reverberates off the walls, and he shoots up and barks at the window.

"Thunder, Sim." I sigh as I rub my eyes. It's gonna be a long night.

I reach for my phone and connect to my speaker's Bluetooth. I play the video in my browser.

Again.

It came in a few days ago—a text with a link.

> Sid
>
> He's in love with you

My hair stood on end as Blue closed his eyes and sang an acoustic rendition of a song I'd never heard but now can't forget. "Lonely Love Song" by St. Paul & The Broken Bones. His voice, older and deeper sounding than his speaking voice, bled about death and longing. It was haunting.

The opposite of running.

It rooted down and rubbed against a visceral ache inside me.

He was showered with applause as I was swallowed by heartache. The video has over two million views, with people demanding an album. Blue hasn't acknowledged the demand or made any public statement. I get the feeling he never will. This wasn't for the public.

Simba's bark cuts through Blue's voice, startling me.

"What is it?"

He jumps to his feet and takes off toward the door.

There's a growl missing from his bark, which means someone friendly is approaching. It's different from his howl for me and Denzel.

I pause the video, then grab my button-down off the armrest and tug it on.

Standing, I walk over to the security panel to check the camera feed.

Hmm. He's off tonight.

"Good boy." I pet Sim on his head before turning the locks and opening the door.

"Hey, boss," Josiah says, holding up a bag of takeout and a bottle of wine. "Hungry?"

"Uh..." I look down the street. "Were you in the neighborhood?"

He lowers his hands. "N-no. I was sitting at home, bored, and thought I'd check in on you and Simba." Simba pops his head out at the sound of his name.

"Hey, Sim," Josiah says, bending down and showing him some love.

"Honestly, I'd usually welcome the company, but I'm feeling like shit."

"Oh. What's the matter? A cold?"

"Nah. Nothing like that."

He peers up at me, waiting for me to elaborate. "Oh. Is it Arnaz?"

"Yeah." I nod.

He pouts as he stands. "You sure food and wine won't help?"

"Thanks, but I think I'm gonna turn in."

"Okay."

"Hold on one sec?" I step back.

I jog to the kitchen, grab a Tupperware container, and fill it.

"Here." I hand it to him.

"What is it?" He pops back the lid.

"A slice of chocolate cake with coffee and Swiss meringue buttercream and a couple of blood orange cinnamon rolls."

"Mm." He moans. "You made this?"

I nod.

"You stress bake?" His smile darkens. "That's—Listen, if Arnaz doesn't come to his senses, know there'd be a line of men down this block who'd kill for all of this." His hand waves up and down in front of me.

I stuff my hands in my pockets. I know that's supposed to be comforting, but it hurts.

"Here," he says, offering me the food.

"Keep it. I ate earlier."

"Okay, but you have to take this at least." He hands me the wine.

"Okay." I accept it. "Thanks for checking on us."

"See you Tuesday?" he asks Simba.

Sim wags his tail in response.

"Hey, Josiah?"

He looks up.

"I've been meaning to talk to you about something. I really

appreciate your help with Simba, and how you take care of him when I'm not around."

"I love Sim," he says, beaming.

"I appreciate that. It's just…I've noticed lately that you've worn clothes I've left around and sent me pics in them. I'm sure you meant it in a casual way, *but* I need to make sure it's not crossing a professional boundary that I'm uncomfortable with."

"Oh." He winces. "Shoot."

"If you ever need anything while you're here, feel free to ask."

"Oh my god, hearing you say it out loud—I'm so cringe. I'm sorry."

"Thanks for hearing me out."

He nods. "See you Tuesday?"

"Yep. Goodnight."

I lock the door and then crash on the couch. I start the video again as Simba howls and races for the door.

Denzel?

I launch to my feet and bolt for the door, tearing it open, then freeze. Not by choice. My heart and brain are racing too fast to make sense of what I'm seeing.

Blue's standing there, leather jacket drenched, eyes red, jaw scruffy, hand clenching his duffel.

He takes in my open shirt, then looks past me inside the house before searching my eyes.

"It's just me and Sim here." I don't know why I offer that.

Or why I want to fix whatever it is that has him looking so shattered.

"I tried to stay away and give you space…"

I nod for him to continue.

"But…fuck, I miss you so much it hurts. I'm sorry I hurt you by running and keeping things from you. For so long, I felt like, at best, I'm an inconvenience, and at worst, I'm harmful. I didn't believe I deserved you. I'm so sorry I hurt you. I've never been in love before, and maybe everyone is better at it than me, but there'll never be a day that I won't love you, and that I won't try to—"

"You're in love with me?"

He bites the inside of his lip as his head tilts slightly. "Yes." His eyes water. "And I want to fix us. Show you I'm here. I don't expect you to just take my word for it."

I lean against the door. The ache of seeing him cry, of how much I've missed him...I rub my sternum, but it only spreads. "Uh." I force the words out. "I need time."

"Okay." He steps back. "Can I come by tomorrow and we talk?"

"I said I need time, not that I want you to leave."

His lips part slightly. "I don't under—"

"Let's go to bed, Blue. We'll talk in the morning."

"Are you sure?"

"I wouldn't sleep knowing you're in town but not here." I nod toward the steps, holding open the door.

"I would be right back here in the morning," he says, taking a hesitant step forward.

Instead of stepping over Sim, who's lying in the entryway and watching us, he kneels in front of him. "Hi Simba. I'm Blue."

Simba licks his wrist as he pets him.

"He howled when you were at the door. He only howls for me and Denzel."

"You howled for me?" he whispers, leaning down and pressing his forehead to Sim's wet nose. "I have a feeling you and I go way back." He stands. "I heard about the lead in Mexico."

"Yeah. It's something, I guess."

"It's a good lead," he says, leveling a stare at me.

There's something different about him. Like he's cracked open and not trying to hide it.

I wrap my arms around my chest to fight the urge to pull him into my arms.

"You"—I clear my throat—"you, uh, hungry or thirsty?"

"Water?" he asks.

I nod and head to the kitchen and fill a glass. When I return, he's standing and staring into the fire.

My steps falter as I get closer. He's completely still, but tears are trickling from his eyes.

"Hey," I say.

He looks up. "Thanks," he says, reaching for the glass. It's like he doesn't even know he's crying. He downs the water in seconds and doesn't make any attempt to wipe his tears.

"Thirsty. Want another?"

"I can just hold on to the cup and fill it up in the bathroom sink."

"Nah, I can get you another cup. Here"—I reach in to grab his duffel and graze his hand—it's ice cold. The back of my palm reaches up and grazes the side of his face. "Blue, you're freezing. What happened to you tonight?"

He doesn't answer me. His eyes close, and his face leans into my touch. A fresh set of tears spills down his face, all my restraint snaps, and I pull him into my arms. "Hey." I kiss his forehead. "You're safe."

His arms wrap around me, tighter than our last morning at the cabin. He seemed so afraid to let go of me that day. Something he saw in the ruins of the house in the field rattled him. This is different.

"God, I've missed you," I whisper, pressing a kiss to his forehead. I tilt his chin up. My breath hitches when I see more tears pooling in his eyes.

"Don't let go," he pleads.

I'm in love with you. I wouldn't know how to let go. "Your face is ice cold—I want to run a bath for us."

He huffs out a breath. "A bath?"

"Yeah."

He tries to step back, but I hold on to him.

"I didn't come here for you to take care of me. I came here to fix us and—"

"Shh," I reply. "I know. Come on."

I listen to his quiet breaths for a moment as he takes in my bedroom. Something about my bed lightens the heaviness in his eyes. He walks over to my nightstand, and his fingers trail over the open pastry book lying face down on top.

"This way." I guide him to the bathroom.

We silently watch each other as the tub fills, and we undress.

When I go to climb in first, he says, "Please. Can I hold you?"

"Okay," I reply, letting him climb in first.

His hand clutches the side of the tub, and steam blankets his knuckle tattoos. His eyes flutter shut as he lowers into the bathwater. I give him a few moments to himself, slipping out to grab his water refill.

Head leaned back, his stare is distant when I return.

"Here," I murmur, offering him a sip.

He drains the water even faster than the last one.

When I reach for the cup to place it down, he holds on to my hand. "Come," he whispers.

I climb in and lean back against his chest, not sinking against him all the way at first, but when I feel the quickened thump of his heartbeat against my back, I let go and settle all my weight against him. His heartbeat slows.

Arnaz

"Thank you." I break the silence that permeated our bath as I climb into bed next to him. The deep chill in my bones now gone.

"You're welcome. Need anything else?"

He just came back from running downstairs and refilling our waters. "I'm okay."

He nods and kills the lights. "Good night."

"Good night," I reply.

Minutes pass of me battling to stay where I am or shift toward him to close the distance between us.

I want to talk to him.

There's so much I need to tell him.

I listen to the steady rhythm of his breathing for signs that he might still be awake.

"Hey," I whisper, but it comes out too low.

Except he shifts a second later, and I hear, "Yeah?"

"You seemed surprised that I knew which foot your injury was on."

"Huh?"

Not sure why that's what comes out, but I keep going. "During our face-off in Brooklyn, you seemed surprised that I knew. I was on the road—Detroit—and turned on ESPN, and there was a clip of you on the floor in pain." My fingers curl around my pillow as I remember the shock that slammed into me. "I didn't know why then, but I couldn't breathe. I don't remember how, but I ended up on the rooftop of the hotel— just a regular rooftop—to be alone, just to breathe. I was convinced I hated you. Not you, you, but, like, your presence and the way it slammed into me whenever you were near. If I hated you, it's because it seemed like you knew what it did to me."

"If I could have stayed away, I would have," he says, turning to face me.

Thank God he didn't. "I told myself you weren't *that* beautiful or sexy or funny, even if the jokes you threw my way made me grin after I cooled off and was alone. You made me afraid, and when I'm afraid, I fight, which never really worked with you because no matter how hard I tried, I never won any of our fights."

I hear him snicker under his breath. "You got good shots in, though."

"*Tsk.* That was some of my best work."

His gravelly chuckle makes me grin.

"And then you get on TV..." I shake my head. "I never saw it coming. You batting for the same team? Never."

"See, now I'm offended because I spit my best game at you."

"What game? *'I like you watching me. I like what it does to your face,'*" I mock.

He laughs. "Aha. It worked. You remember?"

"Eh. Maybe on some level, I thought about it. But the cake..." I groan and bury my face in my pillow. "It was so good, it made me hard."

He lifts the pillow from my face. "You said it made you hard?"

I try to bury my face under the pillow again, but he pulls it away. I squeeze my eyes shut and blurt it out, "I watched a replay of one of your compilation videos while eating it and jerking off. Then some of the cream got on my hands, so I used it as lube and came so hard as I imagined you bending me over and fucking me deep in this bed."

After a few seconds of silence, my eyes creak open, and I hear, "Wow." There's a shuffle and then he switches on a low reading light, bright enough for me to see the big fucking grin on his face.

His teeth roll over his bottom lip. He opens his mouth, then closes it, then opens it again. "You fucked my cake."

I wince. "I fucked your cake."

He falls onto his back and groans. "Christ, that's so hot. If I ever open a bakery, your testimonial is going on the front page of my site."

"Why do you want to be with me again?"

He snorts. "Because you'd fuck a cake," he quips, and we both burst out laughing.

"What?" he asks when I turn serious.

"I ran at first, after reading your note. I was standing in front of my teammates and coaching staff, who were all drooling in front of the cake, and whatever lies I told myself—that you weren't serious with the press conference—were wiped out by your letter. It was so direct and honest in a way I couldn't deny. So, I ran, and when I got back from the weight room, there were a few slices waiting for me."

"Hmm." He crosses his arms and stares up at the ceiling.

Maybe that was too honest. "What are you thinking?" I ask.

"That you'll want to run—maybe need to at times—but you can't disappear. You have to talk to me. I can't handle anyone else I love disappearing. Especially not you."

"I don't want to run from this. I can't. I tried, and I still ended up back here. I want to be honest with you—that's the only reason I am telling you about the cake."

"Why didn't they film you receiving it for *Royals All-Access*?"

"I asked them not to."

"Why?"

"It was from you. It didn't feel right."

He turns back to his side to face me. "What happened to you tonight before you came here?"

"Wait." I want to take care of him first. "Tell me how you're doing with Denzel?"

He adjusts his pillow, curling it under his head. "I don't

know. It's *something* that he hasn't completely vanished, but he's still not here, nor has he reached out."

"I get that. Did the PI describe how he looked?"

"Crossing the border?" he asks.

I nod.

"Nope."

"Did your dad see the cardiologist?"

"Yeah." His gaze softens. "His heart's okay."

"That's good. How'd he and your mom take the news about Mexico?"

"Confused, but maybe a little more hopeful. They seem to believe the PI is closer to finding him."

"Anything I can do to help?" I ask.

"Keep talking to me. Tell me what happened tonight."

"Okay." My fingers curl around the edge of the pillowcase. "I went to visit Anaïs and had a run-in with Mom and Carter."

He shifts closer. "Run-in how?"

I look down at our hands and cup them together. He releases my hand and strings his arm over the side of my waist, shifting me closer.

I reach up and caress the stubble across his face.

"Tell me," he rasps.

"Carter kept asking to talk. I avoided him at first, but then, after talking to Anaïs about you and me, I realized I'm done running. So, when I was leaving, we talked." *Or whatever the hell that was. For our "family," that's as close to talking as we know how to do.*

"How did it go?"

I shrug. "I didn't hold back. Anaïs was there. Mom was crying. Carter tried to explain his perspective, but everything he said just made me angrier. He followed me outside. I had..." *Collapsed* feels too hard to admit. "I don't know. I was just in rough shape."

"Come here," he says, opening his arms.

I close the rest of the distance between us.

"And you came straight here to me?" he asks.

"Yeah. For a second, I thought about going back to the hotel and coming in the morning when I was in better shape, but—"

"Thank you." He kisses my forehead. "It means a lot that you came to me. That you let me see you hurting."

"I need you to believe me when I say that whatever I felt for Aiden is in the past. Zuri, my therapist, helped me see why his return sent me spiraling, and it's about childhood stuff. I should have told you about it."

He nods. "It's why you froze at Catharine's birthday when I mentioned him?"

"Yes. I tried to forget that chapter of my life. I thought things would fall into place once I was in college, but I was just as fucked up there. I couldn't make friends, I was struggling with being closeted, I hadn't been diagnosed with C-PTSD, or anything else, so I thought the spiral was just me. Aiden was a hands-on coach, and at some point, all his attention started to make me feel like we could be more." I pause. "We don't have to talk about this if you don't want to."

He massages my side. "I want to know. Did it ever become more?"

"No. I made a pass, and he pulled back and cut things off. I got drafted and tried to put all of it behind me. When I spoke to him at Ty's, he explained that he saw me struggling and realized I needed a coach more than a boyfriend."

"And how do you feel about that?"

"I mean, it's hard to fight that argument when everything that happened led me here to you. I think it would have been helpful to know that what I felt from him wasn't all in my head."

"I understand that."

I turn and reach for a sip of water and offer him my glass. After he takes a sip and hands it back, he says, "Your voice—it's incredible. I can't even...ahh. Look"—he guides my fingers across the goosebumps along his arm.

I grin. "I'll sing for you anytime."

"Noo," he groans, rolling to his back and pulling me on top of him. "I can't fall any deeper in love with you. I have a career, responsibilities...I can't be stuck on the couch like I've been, replaying your video over and over for hours."

"Boohoo. Welcome to my world, where every night is dedicated to 'Late Night with Salem.'"

He arches his head to the side. "What's that?"

I bury my face in his neck. "It's when I watch YouTube videos of you until I'm either covered in cum or knocked out."

He huffs out a laugh.

"Shut up."

He kisses the side of my face. "I've been waiting for this— for you to let me in."

I pop my head up and meet his eyes before I kiss him.

I moan at the first taste of his tongue as it pushes past my lips. One second, we're both moaning into each other's mouths, and the next, I'm on my back being spread open.

The entire day rushes out in a hoarse sob when he enters me.

He drinks each sob, latching on to my mouth. "Baby," he rasps, peppering kisses up my face until he's kissing away the tears pooling in the corners of my eyes.

I arch my head and capture his lips. A flash of him and Lucien kissing fills my mind, and I stiffen.

"What's wrong?" he says, slowing on the next thrust.

"Nothing." I close my eyes. "Keep going."

"Hey," he sinks inside of me, forcing out a gasp before he stops moving. "Talk to me."

Why do I feel so raw? I rub the bottom of my palm across the sides of my eyes. The question feels barbed as it's dragged out of my mouth. "Lucien...you kissed."

"Fuck," he murmurs. "Baby—"

"It's okay," I cut him off.

"Hold on. He was congratulating me on coming out and said something about always wanting to do that. It wasn't like how you and I kiss."

I nod even though it hurts. "Did you go home with him?"

"No." He gazes into my eyes, so serious that it snuffs out any doubt. "I can't be in love with you and do that." He presses his forehead against mine.

I stare down at his lips before my tongue traces across the top one and bites into his bottom. "Mine," I grit out.

He slowly rolls his hips, making me bite down harder.

"Yours," he rasps.

I'm NOT ready for morning when it arrives.

I stir awake when he tries to pull his arm out from underneath me and groan, holding on to him.

"Be right back. I'm going to feed and walk Sim real quick," he whispers.

I roll onto my back and scrub my face as he disappears into the bathroom.

Ugh. My bones ache like I went to war and got bludgeoned.

I knew stepping foot in Mom and Carter's house would be hard. I knew there was a high chance Carter would try to corner me again, and I'd have to get big to get him to back off.

I did *not* know that we would talk.

"You need anything?" Salem asks, emerging from the bathroom and grabbing his sweats.

"Can you pass me my pills?" I point to the duffle.

"Yeah." He kneels and rummages through it.

"The small pocket."

"Ah. All three bottles?"

"Not the risperidone."

He reads each of the labels, figures out which is which, and then hands them over. "Is that enough water?"

I nod and shuffle to sit up to sort out the pills.

"How do you feel?" he asks.

Like maybe I need the risperidone.

I shrug. "I don't want to leave this bed today."

"Done. What else?"

I throw the pills back with a swig of water.

"I don't know how to describe it when I'm around them. Mom and Carter. It just leaves me feeling..."

How would Zuri make me describe it?

"...like this feels like it's been poked with a million tiny knives." I point to my stomach. "This feels like it's swollen." I point to my throat. "And this"—I massage my temples—"is all messed up, like someone has one of those air pumps and they're pulsing stale air inside."

"Spacey?" he offers.

"Yeah."

Christ. I probably sound weak as hell. "I'm good, though." I tuck my knees in. "How are you?"

He pauses, rubbing the stubble on his chin. "You're *good*?" He squints. "You just described a stabbing sensation in your gut, constricted air in your throat, maybe your lungs, and pressure in your head. But you're '*good though*?'"

I snicker.

The corner of his lip crooks up, and he mocks, "My whole body feels like it's being turned into minced meat, but, y'know, *I'm good.*"

"Stop." My head falls forward as I shake with laughter.

"Aight, listen. Even though you're *good* and all, we're gonna rest today. I'm gonna hold you, and we're gonna watch TV, eat, and do whatever we want."

God, that sounds amazing.

"I'm supposed to see Anaïs," I tell him.

"I think, after everything that happened, she'll understand if you go tomorrow."

"Yeah, she would." I wish she could come here and be with us.

"I'll be right back," he says, leaning in to give me a kiss.

I try to duck it. He's all minty. "I haven't brushed."

"I don't care," he says, smacking his lips against mine.

Simba jumps up from the floor as he stands. "Get ready to block out the world."

"Like our cabin."

"Yeah." His eyes glaze over. "Like our cabin."

CHAPTER 55
SALEM

I wake and reach for Blue. When my hand pats the cold comforter, I groan and stare down at my morning wood. We spent all of yesterday talking, making love, and never being more than a few feet apart, and still, I miss him.

I drag myself out of bed, throw on my sweats, and follow the sounds to the kitchen.

He looks up as I enter. "Nooo. I wanted to bring you breakfast in bed."

I grunt as I stalk over, pull down his briefs, and hike him up onto the counter.

"I'm making chocolate pan—Fuuuck."

His hands massage my scalp as my lips wrap around his cock.

"Waaaiiit," he slurs. "S-stove."

I grunt as I work him down my throat.

"Baby...wait."

I reach into my briefs to give myself some relief when a stripe of wet sludge slashes against my cheek.

I still and glare up at him.

He snickers, holding a spoonful of batter.

Little shit. When my eyes dart to the bowl of batter, we both freeze and then scramble for it. I'm faster.

I step back and turn off the stove. "You get a three-second head start."

He kicks off his briefs and guns it.

Before I take off after him, I notice the soy sauce sitting on the counter.

I sniff the batter. *The hell?*

Time's up.

I race through the living room, headed for the steps, when I see curls sticking out from behind the couch.

It's literally the worst hiding place in the whole house.

I tiptoe over and flip the bowl over his head.

"Muthafucka," he curses, and before I can jump back, his leg kicks out, and I'm wiped out. He climbs on top of me and rubs his face all over mine, painting it with batter.

"Stahp!" I try to push him off me.

He wraps his hand around my throat. "Fuck me, bitch."

I point to the console table as I drag down my sweats and briefs, the batter making my hand slip on the first attempt. He finds the condoms and lube and wings them at my head. I hold up my batter-covered hands. He snatches up the condom and rolls it on me, then spreads his legs and, squeezing lube on his fingers, starts opening himself up.

God. Damn.

I push him forward onto his knees, line up, and ease inside him. He hisses when I cant my hips. On my next drive, his knees slip in the batter, and he almost takes me down with him.

We both laugh, trying to steady ourselves, only for my knee to give out, and we both land flat, me on top. I wrap my arm under his chest to anchor myself and then thrust into him, hard.

"Ngh," he moans.

Simba barks and then races out of the room.

"Scream my name like you did in the middle of the night," I order. And because I have to earn it, I fuck him hard and without mercy, not stopping even as my name scrapes from his throat, again and again.

Blue's so loud that at first, I think he's the cause of the ringing in my ears. Then he stiffens as we both hear it—the doorbell.

We seem to wordlessly agree to ignore it as my hips pull back and I sink balls deep into him.

What if it's Denzel?

He'd use his key, right?

Fuck.

"Hold on." I kiss his cheek before pulling out and heading over to the security console. He flips onto his back and sits up.

I grin. "It's your sister."

"What?"

Anaïs is waving at the camera like she can see me.

He scrambles to his feet and almost loses his balance, sliding on the batter.

I take us in. "We look wild."

"Wait. It's pouring. She shouldn't be out there." He grabs my sweats and throws them on. "You go upstairs and clean up. I'll let her in."

"Cool." I disarm the security system.

"Hey." He walks over to me, drags off the condom, and strokes my dick. "This load is mine later."

I wink at him. "I love you, but I'm definitely coming in the shower."

He growls and drops to his knees. "You have one minute to come." Grabbing the backs of my thighs, his tongue slides down the underside of my cock before he sucks me down. He presses down on my taint, and my stomach contracts. He tugs on my balls and then inches his fingers back toward my hole. He looks up at me, silently asking permission. I nod, and as soon as his finger rubs against my rim, I groan, the first wave hitting me. When he breaches me, I'm grunting into my fist and shooting down his throat.

He sucks me dry, kisses my dick, jumps to his feet, and smirks as he says, "Like I said, *my* load."

I stand there, panting against a wall with my dick out.

How'd he do that? How does he make me come in, like, thirty seconds?

I scrape up the condom and wrapper—no time to clean up the batter—and drag myself up the stairs on rubbery legs.

Arnaz

I toss the paper towel after washing my hands and race to unlock the door, Simba on my heels.

"What are you doing out of bed?" I ask with concern when I open the door.

She quirks her eyebrow, then swipes a finger against my cheek and tastes it. "Hot!"

I laugh as she wordlessly hands me her bag and pushes past me. "Doctor said I need to walk."

"From New Jersey?"

The sound of a car honking grabs my attention. Mom rolls down her window, waves, then drives off.

"There's no way I'm having a Goth movie marathon without both of my besties," she tells me.

"I wished you were here," I confess. I help her out of her coat and then bend down to unlace her shoes.

When I try to sling my arm over her shoulders, she edges back from my batter-covered chest, and I laugh. "You, I'll hug," she says to Sim. "Except I can't bend down." She squats a bit to scratch his head, then leads the way into the living room. "Are you okay?" she asks me.

"Better than yesterday." I blow out a breath. "My bad for not coming over like I said I would."

"Honestly, it was like a funeral yesterday. Eerily quiet in the house."

"Yeah?" I don't know how to feel about that. "You okay?"

"Mmhm. What about you two?"

"He's stuck with me now," Salem answers from somewhere upstairs.

"Bestie!"

"Hey, you," he says, "Be right down."

"Come on."

She pauses, staring at the mess of batter on the floor that

clearly looks like a torso outline. "I'm so proud of you," she says, making me laugh again.

I'm getting her set up on the couch with her feet up when Salem comes down, looking fresh in gray sweats and a thin black hoodie. He envelops her in a hug. "You hungry?" he asks her.

"For your cooking? Hell yes. I still think about your braised short ribs and mac 'n' cheese," she replies.

"What braised short ribs and mac 'n' cheese?" I ask.

"During bestie date night," she explains.

"Aww, he's pouting," Salem jokes, kneeling in front of the fireplace to get a fire started.

"I don't pout," I grumble.

"Salem, how do you like vampires?" she asks.

"I'm dating one, aren't I?"

"Uh, what?" I snort.

"You hate the sun, you're always biting me, your baseline is melancholy, your handwriting, the tattoos...Come on."

Anaïs and I burst out laughing.

"And you're always watching from the corners like a predator. I saw you at Nick's house."

Ugh. He saw me lurking? Cringe. "Okay, but I'm never truly the predator."

"With us? Yeah, no." He blows me a kiss.

I shake my head as he turns to Anaïs and asks, "Why do you ask?"

"We had plans to have a Gothic movie-thon."

"Bet. I'm down. Let me take Sim on a walk real quick, then get started on breakfast."

"'K. I'm gonna clean up the floor and then shower quick fast. You need anything?" I ask.

Anaïs burrows into the couch. "Throw me the remote?"

I pick it up and pass it to her.

"Hey, Jones," I call out as he grabs his coat and Sim's leash.

"Yeah?" He turns to me.

"I love you."

His dimple appears. "Yeah?"

"Yeah."

"You heard that, Anaïs?" he asks.

She laughs. "Sure did."

"Just making sure I'm not imagining it."

"Fuck you both."

He snickers. "I love you, too, Blue."

CHAPTER 56
SALEM

"Good boy," I tell Sim, scratching behind his ears after he takes care of business, and I clean it up. "What do you think of Blue?" I ask as he stops to smell the base of a tree. "I love him, so you'll see him more. You good with that?" He sniffs the air, then howls.

I grin. "Okay, I guess that's a yes."

He sniffs the air again and yanks at his leash.

"Hold on. No pulling."

He slows down for a bit before yanking again. "Hey, hey. Relax."

When we turn the corner of our block, I check that there are no other dogs around and unhook his leash. He takes off toward home. I watch as he bounds up the steps, and then I freeze.

Seven-foot-four, buzz cut, brown duck jacket, black hoodie, and jeans. I'd recognize my brother anywhere.

"Where the hell have you been?" I fume. He doesn't flinch from where he's bent down, hugging Simba. He probably tracked me from the corner.

"I can explain," he says.

I'm up the steps and in his face in less than two seconds.

"Do you have any idea what we've been through?" I bellow. "We called every fucking hospital across the country! We hired a private investigator! How could you disappear again without calling? Where the hell were you?"

The door rips open. "What's going on?" Blue asks, glaring at my brother.

Denzel flicks a glance my way. "You got him?" His lip quirks up as he nods to Blue. "Hi, I'm Denzel, Salem's brother."

Blue's face doesn't relax despite his mouth forming an *ohhh*. "Arnaz, his boyfriend."

"Boyfriend." Denzel nods. "My parents and I were worried that he'd die with a crush on you."

"Enough," I cut in. "Explain."

"Can we go inside?" Denzel asks. "You woke up half the neighborhood."

I nod for him to move. He lifts his backpack and heads into the house.

After storing his shoes neatly in the shoe bench, he follows me into the living room.

"This is my sister, Anaïs," Blue says. "Anaïs, this is Salem's brother, Denzel."

She sucks in a breath. "Oh my god."

"I didn't mean to interrupt. I can come back," Denzel says.

"Or we can leave?" Blue offers.

"No," I say to him before addressing my brother. "We can do this here or upstairs." I reach for my phone. "I need to call Mom and Dad—they need to know."

"I called them when I landed. Look, you have every right to be angry with me, but just hear me out."

"This better be a hell of a story." I cross my arms.

"It's the truth."

"I'm waiting."

"Uh—after my friend attempted suicide, sitting with him there in the hospital...I don't know. It did something to me. The visions started coming back, like after Iraq. Before I left for the desert, I visited him one more time. He was barely awake, but his nurse sat with me, asked me my story. She mentioned something called the Hearts for Heroes Project and gave me the pamphlet. I stuffed it in my bag and didn't find it again until things got bad."

"Bad how?" I ask.

"I started hallucinating, thinking I was seeing some of my squad mates who had fallen. It was...dark. Darker than it had been for a while," he admits.

"Why not call me, Mom, Dad, your doctors?" I ask.

"I just couldn't. I made the decision that if I couldn't figure it out on my own, I was done."

"Done how?" My voice shakes.

He doesn't answer.

"Done how, Denzel?"

Blue comes over and wraps his arm around my waist.

"The pain was in control," he finally answers. "When it gets like that, it's hard to see a way out."

"I don't understand. You have me, you have people who would have gotten on a plane to be there with you as soon as you called. Why?" I look away as my eyes burn.

Blue leans in, anchoring me with his arm.

"I know. I just couldn't see it," Denzel murmurs. "I'm sorry."

"You need a minute?" Blue asks me quietly.

I shake my head. I need answers. "Go on," I tell Denzel.

"That night, I found the pamphlet the nurse had given me. It had people sitting on the beach in some tropical place, and inside there was a story about a former Marine who has PTSD. She had sold all her stuff and traveled to South America. She talked about taking medicine there that helped her deal with the flashbacks and nightmares from her time overseas. I didn't really believe it, but I was so low, I was willing to try just about anything."

"Medicine? What are you talking about?" I ask.

"Ayahuasca, psilocybin," he answers.

"You're telling me you disappeared for months to get high in Mexico?" I ask incredulously.

"Wait," Blue says, rubbing my chest. "My therapist told me about this. I struggle with C-PTSD," he tells Denzel.

"Me too," Anaïs says.

"Zuri said there are clinical trials that use Indigenous medicine like psilocybin and MDMA to help with what he's describing. It's not about getting high."

"It's true," Denzel says. "It was structured just like a clinical trial. We met one-on-one and in groups with mental health facilitators and Indigenous healers for a few weeks to prepare us. Then we took the medicine, and then there was a period of integration."

"Did it work?" Anaïs asks.

"Not for everyone in my group, but it helped me some. I still need therapy, but—"

"How?" I break in. "How did it work for you?"

"I'd been stuck in a loop of what happened to me overseas —like pieces of memories—the same scenes over and over, but with the sessions, I could zoom out and see the full picture without having to relive it. I've been sleeping better than I can remember in a long time." He blows out a breath. "I also got my appetite back and—"

"Why couldn't you call?" I demand, noticing the tic in his left hand is barely noticeable. "I'm glad you got help, but why couldn't you just pick up the phone and text me or Mom or Dad?"

"I'm sorry. I just couldn't. As soon as I got sleep and started coming back online, I realized how worried you all must've been. I skipped the closing ceremony and got on the first plane back."

I shake my head, staring at the floor. Every day, I'd wished for this moment—him alive and okay, at home with me. And now that he's here, I want to hold him close, but I also want to yell and shake him for all the worry he's caused us.

The terror he experienced serving this country.

I am angry about all of it.

Blue works his thumb inside my closed fist. "It's hard, you know," he says, looking at me but speaking high enough for Denzel and Anaïs to hear. "Whether we mean to or not, we can ask a lot of the people who love us when we aren't well. We can miss how hard it is for them too." He turns to Denzel. "I'm speaking from my own experience. And based on what Salem has told me, he's been worried about you since you enlisted. Now that you're doing better, are you planning to stick around for a while? Be here for him?"

I wipe my face on the neck of my tee.

"Yes. I want to be here in Brooklyn. I'm better around you," Denzel says to me. "I'm thinking of getting my own place nearby and either partnering with the Hearts for Heroes Project or opening my own version here in New York. And I was going to ask for your help. You and I always talked about wanting to do more for vets."

There's a part of me that's wanted Denzel around for years. I still do. But there's another part that's angry we've lost so much time. Then there's the other part of me that feels like I can't care about him this much anymore. It's too hard.

The only problem is that I don't know how not to care about him so much.

I don't know how to make sense of all these parts.

I clear my throat, then say, "I need to take it one step at a time."

"That's fair," Denzel replies as Blue rubs the small of my back.

"It's bullshit that you think you have to disappear to heal.

Please, no more." I raise my gaze to Denzel, then turn it on Blue. "No more."

Blue leans into my shoulder. "I'm not going anywhere."

"Me neither," Denzel adds.

I blow out a breath. "You spoke to both Mom and Dad?"

Denzel nods, and the guilt written on his face tells me he probably got a sense of how worried they've been. "I am going to fly out to see them soon."

I take a second and lean into the support of Blue against my side before blowing out a breath and wiping my face. "Still scrambled eggs with extra cheese and ketchup?" I ask Denzel.

"Yep."

I turn to Anaïs.

"Cheese omelet?" she says.

"Come on," Blue says to me. "I'll help."

"Hey." I turn to Denzel. "We'll talk more later. Your room upstairs hasn't changed."

"I'm sorry," he says, stepping closer to palm my shoulder.

"I'm glad you're safe and here." I pull him into a hug.

"Psst," Anaïs whispers.

I look over, thinking she's talking to me, and catch her mouth to Blue, *Big bro's a ten too.*

"Not the time," Blue whispers back, before mouthing, *Definitely a ten.*

"I saw that," I tell him.

"Sorry." He purses his lips, not an ounce of apology in his voice.

Besides the scar under his jaw and his sharp eyes, Denzel and I do look similar.

Similar enough that I was called Little Denz growing up.

"Denzel, how do you like vampires?" Anaïs asks.

I shake my head as Blue and I head toward the kitchen.

Arnaz

I insist on ordering dinner for us so Salem can continue relaxing.

It was hard to feel him tremble against my side earlier as he tried to hold it together.

He seems like he's the rock for his family. It's a lot for one person to carry.

But he's not alone, and I'll do what I can to help create moments like this.

He's settled into the couch, laughing at Anaïs's secret—and fake—sibling language.

How the hell am I supposed to decipher her sticking a finger in each ear while she's cross-eyed and trying to lick her nose?

We're playing spades—siblings versus siblings.

And they might be tens and all that, but screw them for the silent assassin tricks they've got going on.

The score is 7–2.

"You know there's a room upstairs for you too," Salem says to Anaïs.

She hides her wide grin behind her cards. "You got earplugs, Denzel? Have a feeling we're gonna need 'em, the way these two keep looking at each other."

Denzel nods, eyes bright. "You catching that too?"

"So, doubling back to what you said earlier," I direct at him. "This crush he had…"

"Did you show him the vision board?" he asks Salem, who bursts out laughing.

"Shut your face," Salem replies.

"There's a vision board?" I ask, interest piqued. "I wanna—"

"No." Salem shuts it down.

"Come on," I cajole.

"Hell no." He shakes his head.

"It has 'Marry Arnaz' at the top," Denzel snitches.

My mouth opens wide as Anaïs croons, "Aww."

"Unbelievable." Salem blushes. "You've literally been trained to keep classified intel."

"It's cute," Denzel says. "He's a planner."

That makes us laugh.

When Salem shyly meets my gaze, I wink at him.

Yeah, they'll definitely need earplugs tonight.

CHAPTER 57
ARNAZ
TEN DAYS LATER

♫ "Knives" ♫
"The sharp edges of disquiet return to me like a forlorn lover."

As soon as I wake up, I reach for my phone and start firing off a text.

Me

TODAY'S THE DAY

MY PHONE BUZZES a few seconds later.

Salem

FUCK YEAH BABY!

I HIT play on the video that comes in.

Fuckkkk.

Abs pan down to his cock that's so hard his breath sounds strained as he slowly strokes it...the camera continues downward as he massages and tugs his balls. He flexes the thick bands of muscle carving long ridges into his quads.

Fuck me.

I hit the video-call button.

His deep laughter filters in as the call connects.

"Fuck you."

I'll get him back later. He knows what his thighs do to me.

"I'm sorry." I see a shadowed grin. The hotel curtains are probably still drawn. "That wasn't fair."

"Baby," I groan as I fondle my morning wood. "How could we agree to this?"

"It was your idea."

"Yeah. You keep saying that, though I have no memory of it," I grumble.

"I told you. We had just nutted—"

"After you made me beg for over an hour," I scoff.

He laughs. "You were talking shit earlier that day and needed to be reminded who the fuck I am."

A coil of heat tightens in my lower abdomen and tingles in my groin. I grab my pillow, smother my face, and unleash a growl that burns my chest.

His laughter comes through muffled.

Hold up.

I remove the pillow and glare into the camera. "Why would *you* agree to no orgasms until we raw dog? I say a lot of shit before post-nut clarity kicks in. What's your excuse?"

"Uh, speaking of that." He shuffles to sit up.

"Could you at least put a shirt on?" I groan.

He winks. "You also begged me to piss on you." He rubs his neck, and my mouth waters at the swell of his biceps. "Did you, uh, want that?"

"W-what?"

"Is that something you want—me pissing on you?" He asks.

Do I?

The pressure expands in my balls.

Huh.

Wait, is that a blush spreading over his face?

I wet my lips. "Why?" I drop my voice. "You want to piss on me?"

His gaze darkens. "Baby, is there anything you won't try?"

"With you?"

He nods.

"This!" I point the camera down at my blue balls. "I would never agree to this."

"It hasn't even been a week. We only got our test results back a few days ago."

"Pssh. It feels like a month. How are you so calm? Last night I actually thought about fucking a bowl of spaghetti."

He snorts. "That's like a Tuesday night for you."

"Asshole." I laugh. "Your flight from Phoenix still gets in at 12:30 tonight?"

"Yeah, I confirmed with the jet company last night," he says. "I head straight to the airport after the game. Don't fall asleep."

There shouldn't be traffic at that time. *LA gods come through.*

"You didn't change your mind about me—"

"No. I promised," he replies. "I'll just need a second to, you know, when I get in."

"Cool. Damn...I'm excited."

"Me too. Ready to kick Atlanta's ass and send 'em packing?"

I nod. "You already know."

"Aight. Let's go take care of business."

"Have a safe flight," I say. "Love you."

"Love you."

CHAPTER 58
SALEM

The half-time buzzer rings out, and we pile back to the locker room, up twelve points against Phoenix.

"Good lookin'" I say, catching the towel a locker room attendant throws my way. I crash into the chair, dry off, and down some water.

I'm reaching for my phone when Onyx says, "Hey!" and drops into the seat next to me. "Thanks for having my back with that rebound at the end of the first."

"No doubt."

I unlock my phone and click on Blue's text.

"I thought the spin was good—"

"My bad!" I jump to my feet, cutting Onyx off. "Gotta piss." I grab my headphones and beeline toward the bathroom. I thumb my headphones into my ears and hit play as I pop into an empty stall.

Blue's naked in his bed on his knees with his ass facing the camera. Based on the light, it looks like he recorded it this morning.

His lats are pressed in as he twists his torso to face the camera and flashes me a filthy grin.

Goddamn.

I trail down the muscle of his back to the swell of his sexy ass. I could never work out with him. He'd start a squat and end up on my dick.

I lean in toward the phone as he bends forward, revealing a silver ring pressed against his rim.

Spreading his legs, he rolls his hips forward, separating the globes of his ass to give me a better view.

Fuuuck.

His hand reaches back, and a finger curls around the ring.

A soft grunt spills from his lips as he tugs on it, and a large metal mushroom-shaped bead pops out.

I bite my fist to stifle my groan.

He keeps pulling, his head falling back as he moans, and another bead pops out, this one slightly bigger and shaped like a marble, and another. Imagining him fingering himself open to stuff all of them inside has me reaching into the drawstring of my jersey and compression shorts and pumping myself for some relief.

After the last bead pops out, he bends forward and brings the camera closer to show me his opened hole.

"It can't wait to be bred," he rasps, and the video ends.

Fuuuck.

My strokes reach the edge, and I pull back.

Why the hell *did* I agree to this promise?

I open the camera and snap a picture of my dick.

Me

Cruel. How am I supposed to go back out there with this?

I add the picture of my dick and hit send.

Me

> You're so damn sexy. Sorry in advance for what I'm gonna do to you tonight.

"TIME TO SADDLE UP," someone calls out.

I groan. "Yep!" I call back.

Thank god for compression shorts.

TURNS out being horny as fuck gives you a power boost. We clutched the dub, and I hit a season high of assists, blocks, and rebounds.

After I get through on-court interviews and head back to the locker room, I reach for my phone to check the Royals' final score. Their tipoff was an hour before ours.

I see a text from Blue.

I pop in my headphones even though the cover shot of the video shows him dressed in a beanie and long-sleeved denim button-down shirt.

I hit play. *He flashes me a sweet grin. It looks like he's leaving the Royals' arena.*

Grr. Why couldn't I have a game closer to LA than Phoenix?

"Congrats on the win," someone says.

"Thanks," he replies over his shoulder.

His gaze returns to the camera. "Bring it." His eyes soften. "I love you. Hurry home."

The video ends.

I stow away my phone and race to the shower.

Arnaz

The dinner I ordered for us before I left the arena is waiting in front of my door when I get home. Taking a few bites, I save the rest to eat with Salem late tonight. I head upstairs to shower and prep, then turn on the TV in my bedroom and pull up highlights of Salem's game.

The third highlight shows Phoenix's point guard driving hard toward the basket with a clear path to the rim. In what looks like a split-second decision, Salem steps into the lane, planting his feet. Running full speed with no time to brake, the guard's chest slams into him with a force that makes my neck snap back. Salem's arms spread wide—heels sliding—as he crashes to the floor.

A whistle blows. Offensive foul!

Yeah, boi!

Salem's up on his feet, fisting the air. He grins at the guard, who's whining to the ref about the call before he races away.

I hit rewind.

Brows drawn together, chest erect, fists planted to his sides —he doesn't even blink as the guard barrels toward him.

Fuck, he's fearless.

I pause and swipe up my phone.

Me

This is what you do to me 20 seconds into your highlights

I send him a picture of the bulge in my briefs.

His FaceTime call comes in.

"Why am I seeing sky when you're supposed to be on a jet?" I complain.

"Yeah, there's a delay due to a mechanical issue."

I tense. "What kind of mechanical issue?"

"Not sure. They said it should be fixed soon. The engineer's already working on it."

"Should you be boarding it? Maybe a commercial plane is safer?"

"I don't think it's that serious."

"Salem."

"What?"

I tilt my head and squint at him.

"Alright, alright. I'll go find out. Hold on. I'll call you back."

"What's the name of the charter service? I'll check their reviews." I'm met with silence. "Hello?"

I check the screen. He already hung up.

I hit play on the TV as I wait for him to call back.

Did he mention the name of the charter service this morning? I rack my brain but come up blank.

I'm sure it's fine.

I slide my phone ringer on, so I don't miss his call, and then twist back and forth, stretching out my torso.

There's a chorus of boos from the crowd on screen.

I turn to grab the remote from the bed to rewind when I'm locked in place.

Touch it, and his jet will go down.

I glare at the remote.

It's just anxiety, another voice says.

I lean in, my fingers a few inches away.

Touch it, and he dies.

I step back, my fingers curling into a tight fist. Energy drains from me like I'm hurtling toward a mean post-game adrenaline crash.

I turn and yank the TV out of the wall.

Why hasn't he called back yet? I check my ringer again.

Yeah, I'm definitely crashing. I need to lie down.

I search for something to get the remote off the bed without direct contact. I eye my guitar and wait for the dread that tells me I can't use it to hit. When it doesn't come, I pluck it up and use the body to flick the remote. It crashes to the floor, sending one of the batteries flying across the room.

My phone pings.

> **Salem**
>
> Just boarded. It's all good. See you soon.

> **Me**
>
> What was the mechanical issue?

I call him, and it goes to voicemail.

Hmph.

I kill the lights and grab my headphones. Once my head hits the pillow, I pull up my doomgaze playlist, hit play, and max the volume on my phone.

He's safe.

It's all good.

He's safe.

He's safe.

Salem

The flight is smooth, and despite the delay, we land close to the original arrival time. I text Blue once I'm loaded into the car that the jet charter service arranged to be waiting on the tarmac.

> Me

> Landed

> Driver said traffic will be light once we clear the airport

After twenty minutes, I shoot him another text.

> You still up?

WHEN I REACH THE HOUSE, I pull up the app Blue downloaded onto my phone that controls the lock to the front door. I wait for Bluetooth to connect and then click the button to unlock.

The lights are still on downstairs, but the house is quiet.

"Baby?"

I peel off my shoes and head upstairs.

The bedroom door is open, but it's dark inside.

I tiptoe inside and slide the light dimmer down to the lowest setting before flipping on the light.

He's curled on his side, knocked out.

Heavy bass and hazy guitar strings spill out from his headphones.

How the hell can he sleep with music that loud?

You couldn't tell from how peaceful he looks right now that he has trouble sleeping.

I want to crawl between his legs, but I need to prep first.

CHAPTER 59
ARNAZ

♫ Untitled ♫

A feather caught in the current of sleep and waking pleasure.

A strange quiet stirs me first.

Gone is the noise submerging all other noise.

A warm brush tingles my neck.

I shiver as his voice slinks down my spine.

He made it in safely.

The walls that were pressing in around my throat are pulled back.

Another warm brush passes over my nipples, and then little stings prick down my stomach, making me moan.

"Baby," I rasp, as a barely there lick tickles the tip of my cock.

I roll my hips, but his mouth is gone.

My thighs are parted, then a wet caress over my rim that feels like my toes sinking into warm sand passes over me.

I drag my eyes open, but the weight of sleep and pent-up need presses them back down.

Warm strokes roll across my rim as he licks the skin in long strokes.

I whimper when it suddenly stops. The anticipation steals my breath.

I suck in a breath as cold slick's massaged over my rim and then thumbed inside of me.

"Please," I beg as I'm stretched open, the pace maddeningly slow.

It earns me another finger, but it's not enough.

"Salem," I croak.

There's a husky chuckle as I'm emptied.

I unclasp the sheets, caress the top of his head, and grind my rim across his lips and chin, moaning when his tongue sinks inside me.

I babble guttural pleas as his tongue rotates and reaches deeper. Then his finger's pressing in, his free arm tightening around my waist, holding me down as he reaches so deep that every curl of his finger spreads hot spasms through my body.

I groan as the pace slows, and more slick is fingered inside of me.

My eyes shoot open a few seconds later when a strip of warmth spreads over my inner thighs.

"Fuck," I rasp as his naked, uncut cock glistens with lube, the tip already leaking, the metal heads glistening. He's biting his lower lip as he guides it to my rim. His eyes flicker shut for a few seconds as he spreads his pre-cum over my rim.

"Please," I beg, making the brown of his eyes recede into dark pools.

I fist the sheets as he starts to push in.

I cry out at the same time he utters, "My god."

Air traps in my lungs as my body adjusts to the stretch of him.

My next breath is a hiccup.

He stills inside me as he shifts forward until his lips are on my lips, then thrusts slowly.

When he glides out, leaving just the tip and sinks in hard, shocking my body with pain-pleasure, my vision whites out.

He thrusts again, the pulse of pleasure so intense he wraps an arm under my back as an involuntary shudder shifts me toward the headboard.

"C-can't," I sputter.

"Hmm?" He kisses my lips.

Can't be this good raw.

He quickens the pace of his thrusts.

His piercings and the reach and curve of his dick are so intense against my prostate, my nostrils burn.

"I love you," he rasps, uncurling my fists from the sheets and peppering kisses along my tattoos. "You're so beautiful." He kisses down my arm, and I tremble, contracting around him, eliciting a sharp moan.

He leans in and catches my lips with a soft kiss and then a deeper one.

When I suck on his tongue, his hips snap hard.

"Fuck," I cry out.

"Mhm," he rasps, fucking me fast and deep.

My moans turn hoarse, scraping out one after another.

"Let me hear you," he grunts.

He buries his face in my neck, and a sharp pain has my teeth sinking into his shoulder.

We both groan.

His breath against my ear stutters. "Ready...fuck." He tenses but doesn't stop pounding into me, making me delirious. Rising, he presses our sweaty foreheads together. "Mmh," he pants.

I moan as he catches my bottom lip and bites down.

He rubs his tongue over the bruise. "Can I come in my hole?"

"Ungh, fuck."

"Hmm?"

"Yes," I sputter as I clench around him.

"Fuuccck." He stiffens, his head falling back, as a toe-curling grunt fills my ears.

He trembles like every spill of his release sends electric bolts through his body.

"Don't stop," I beg when his thrusts turn shallow.

His hand reaches down and massages the stretched skin of my rim as his dick tunnels in and out. My fingers dig into his back, the sensation too much.

"Thought you wanted inside me."

I groan. The need to come mixed with the mind-bending dick down keeps me peeled to the bed. "I c-can't," I choke out.

"You want to?" he asks, peppering a kiss on the side of my lips.

"Yes." *So fucking bad.*

"I got you."

My heart races as he pulls out of me and then reaches for the lube.

Pushing my legs together, he straddles me.

Before he can pour the lube into his hands, I stop him. "Come here." I tap behind his thighs, and he shuffles up.

Lowering to my tongue, he hisses as I lick, suck, and tongue inside him to work him open. I suck on his balls as my fingers sink into him.

The push of his walls against my fingers sends a rush of adrenaline through me. I finger him until I can't hold back the need rattling my body.

I groan from soreness as I shift down.

"You okay?" he asks.

"Gonna feel you for a while."

"Mm," he murmurs as though that pleases him.

I get to my knees and line up behind him.

I rub my palm down his spine. "I'll go slow."

I take my time fingering him open some more before I start pushing in.

The tightness sucks me in. Pins and needles spread under my scalp, and white dots stack behind my eyelids.

He releases a throaty moan.

"Fuccccck, baby," I groan. "I'm sorry. This is gonna be quick."

"Quick is good," he rasps. "Damn, you're thick."

I push in further until I'm bottoming out.

I rub his lower back as he winces. "I'm in."

I clamp down harder on my lip as I rock my hips and tunnel inside of the tightest hole I've ever been in.

"You okay?" I ask.

"Yeah," he pants.

On every drive, I feel his deep grunts in the tremble of my thighs.

I push forward, collapsing on top of him and, digging my fists into the bed, I raise my hips and plunge down.

"Blue," he moans.

I bend my elbows to lower and kiss the patch of skin next to his nose ring, then along his cheekbone, and over his stubble. "I love being inside of you."

"Ngh," he rasps.

I sink my weight down until there's no space between us and grind into him.

"Shit," I slur as I look down at my dick sinking inside him, and his tight heat seizes me.

I hear my cry echoing through the room as the first wave hurtles to the surface.

The world reduces to the squeeze of his warm flesh, milking my cum.

Buzzes and shivers roll in, breaking the rhythm of my hips.

Salem

"Okay?" I hear Blue asking, though I can't answer.

I'm floating, can't feel my bones.

Lasting inside him as long as I did used up everything in my chamber.

I was floating, even as he entered me. A wild hum rippled under my skin, melding with the throbbing of being split open by every drag and plunge of his cock.

I grunt as he pulls out of me, then grunt again when he bites my ass.

He tugs on my hips, raising them up, and I look back as his head dips down.

I moan as his tongue pushes inside me, shivering when he suctions my rim, eating out his cum.

The *mmm* sounds he's making, mixed in with the slurps, hit me with the sudden urge to pull him into my arms and sink my cock back inside him for the night.

He pulls back and squeezes my ass. "Goddamn, baby. That ass is perfect."

His leg kicks out as he tries to climb out of bed, but as soon as his foot lands, he wobbles, and I reach out and steady him.

"Where are you going?"

"Was gonna get a cloth, clean you up, and check your hole."

I grin. "Come here." I drag him into my arms. He burrows against my cheek. I push back his curls and kiss his forehead before he catches my lips in an unhurried, sated kiss.

CHAPTER 60
SALEM
THREE WEEKS LATER

H*mm.* I'm standing in the doorway of my bedroom. Well, mine and Blue's. He's here every chance he gets, including last night when I got in from a stretch of road games. I have him for two nights before we both head back out on the road. It's no surprise he prefers being here over Los Angeles, though I fly to him when I have longer breaks.

He's seemed a little off. I didn't think much about it, but that's the fifth time he's picked up the glass and put it back down on the nightstand in the same spot.

I clear my throat.

"Fuck!" He jumps.

"What are you doing?" I ask.

"Nothing." He steps back. "Figured out the Tart-jelly thing?

Pfft. Looks like I'm headed toward my seventh failed attempt. I'm not sure what's clashing the flavors, the gelée or the tartes Tatin, but I need a break. "You just picked up the cup and placed it back down five times."

"N-no I didn't." He rubs his palms on the sides of his briefs. "I'm gonna shower."

"Baby?"

"What?"

"What's got you anxious?"

His brow furrows. "You know what this is?"

I peel off the doorframe and step toward him. "Yeah. Denzel also struggles with OCD when he's anxious. He'll be like, '*Chill, Fred. We're good.*'"

The lines on his face relax. "His OCD is named Fred?"

"Yeah. Sometimes I catch him having full conversations with it. The other day, he said, '*For fuck's sake, Fred. That's dark, even for you.*'"

We both laugh.

"What's wrong?"

"Nothing," he says, frowning at the cup.

"Baby." I pinch his chin and turn his face so I can see his eyes. "You can tell me if something's wrong."

"That's what I'm saying. *Nothing* is wrong. I'm good. Better than I can ever remember."

"So, nothing being wrong is making you anxious?" I question.

He nods. His palm's clammy where it embraces my arm.

I pull him into my chest and kiss the top of his head. "That makes sense."

"How?" he asks, hugging me back tightly.

"New is scary for you. Being in a relationship, one that makes you happy, is new."

"But I want to be with you. I'm not running."

"I know." And I do know that. I can tell sometimes, like today, he struggles with anxiety, but I never doubt that he's committed and wants this as much as I do. "Doesn't mean it isn't scary. What's the thought that made you pick up and put down the cup?"

"Your flight on Wednesday. I had to make sure you'll be safe."

"You're worried about me being safe?"

His forehead drops to my chest. "All the time."

Sounds exhausting. "You've mentioned this to Zuri?"

"Yeah. We're working through it."

"How can I help?"

He shrugs.

"Go shower," I say. "It's my turn for date night, and I'm taking you out."

"WHERE ARE WE?" he asks as we approach a historical factory building in the DUMBO neighborhood of Brooklyn.

"You know how we always talk about missing out on doing stuff because we were in the closet for so long?" I ask as I lead him to the elevator. "I've started making a list for our date nights."

"Really?" He crinkles his nose at me.

When we reach our floor and the doors open, a flash of gold whizzes past us.

The lights are low except in the center of the room, where spotlights of color light up the floor.

"For two?" A white guy with blond hair, rainbow wings, and booty shorts skates up to us.

"What do you say?" I yell to Blue over the music.

His eyes widen, and I follow his gaze to two men slow dancing together on skates.

"First time?" the guy asks, watching Blue's face shift in to a small grin.

"Yup. For us both," I answer.

"Welcome to the only queer roller-skating rink in New York." He refuses the cash I pull out. "First timers skate for free." He reaches into his fanny pack and pulls out two rainbow wristbands. "You can rent skates over there." He gestures with his chin as he snaps our wristbands on. "Makeup counter is that way, but if you just wanna skate, Reese over there"—he points to a guy in a gold bodysuit—"will hook you up. And you can't miss the bar. Our milkshakes are bananas."

"Thanks," we both reply.

"So." I turn to Blue. "Feeling it?"

"Fuck yeah," he says, making me chuckle, as he pulls me toward the skate rental desk.

We're laced up when Blue surprises me and asks the attendant how much for the feathered wings hanging in the shop.

I hand the attendant cash and then grin as Blue loses his leather coat and slides on black wings.

Damn. Between his ripped black jeans, black sweater, tats, and now wings, he's the sexiest dark angel.

"Hello?" He waves his hand in front of my face.

"S-sorry, what?" I stammer.

"Where are your wings?" he asks.

I pull him close and plant a kiss on his lips. "Stop being so damn sexy."

"Put your dimples away," he warns, tugging on my bottom lip.

Whatever my face does next makes him groan and turn to the attendant. "Hey, is there a glory ho—" I laugh as my palm flies over his mouth.

"Ignore him." I shrug off my wool coat and hand it over to the attendant, along with Blue's leather one.

"Where are your wings?" Blue asks again as I start to skate away.

"Uh—" I turn around and pull out my wallet. "The rainbow ones, please."

Blue wobbles on his skates as he tries to turn toward the rink.

"You've skated before?"

He winces, arms flailing. "Once."

"Oh, hell yeah. This is gonna be amazing." I smirk.

"Don't let me fall."

I thread my arms through each wing. "We're definitely falling."

He laughs. "I hate you."

I take his hand. "Come on."

He has a death grip on my arm by the time we get onto the floor.

Staying close to the perimeter, we skate a few laps before he turns to me, panicked, when he has to evade two women taking a time-out against the boards.

"I got you," I tell him, despite being pretty sure I've lost all circulation where he's clutching my arm. "Hey, come here." My thigh slots between his legs as I pull him close. He's not too afraid to let go of the wall and clasp his hands around my neck.

As if sensing my craving for one of his vampire bites, he clenches my lower lip between his teeth as his eyes glaze over.

"Hey, hotties, gold dust or eyeshadow? I have rainbow metallic colors too," someone says.

I pull back from Blue. "Reese, right?"

He spins, lifting his golden wings that shimmer against his brown skin. "The one and only."

I grin. "Hit me with the gold dust." It's hard to resist, given the way it sets his skin aglow.

Blue laughs as Reese pulls out one of those vintage-looking perfume bottles with a pump, rolls back a few feet, then sprays gold dust along my cheekbones.

He appraises his work and winks. "You, honey?" he asks Blue, who surprises me again by asking, "You got black liner?"

Reese pulls out a sheet that has thin black strips that look like stickers, peels two off, and tapes one each along the rim of Blue's eyelids.

I groan. "How am I gonna skate if I can't look anywhere else tonight?"

Reese laughs as Blue blushes while pulling out his wallet and tipping him.

"Come here, vampire angel." I drool as I pull him forward. For a split second, he forgets he's on skates. "It's okay," I encourage him. "Just look at m—"

His body twists, eyes squeezing shut, as a gust of human barrels in from my right. I try to spin as I'm slammed sideways. Clutching the air, I lose Blue as my skates slip out from under me, and I wipe out. Blue lands with a thump next to me, choking with laughter, with a guy sprawled on his stomach, blubbering an apology.

After several failed attempts, we manage to help each other up.

Blue wipes his eyes as the guy skates away. "That was fun." He takes my hand. "Let's do it again."

We do it again. Two more times. Once, when we try to slow dance together, and again when he tries skating backward and freaks out when someone whizzes past him.

But we find our groove.

Stopping for milkshakes, we camp out in front of the tall industrial windows with a view of the lit-up Manhattan Bridge.

Fighting over the final sip, I try to lick it out of his mouth and quickly forget about the milkshake. When we come up for air, he turns toward me with an oat-milk mustache and says, "Last one on the floor can't come until tomorrow night." Then he takes off.

"Cheater!" I call out.

I toss the shake container and race after him.

CHAPTER 61
ARNAZ

"How are you feeling about hugs?" Salem asks.

"Huh?"

"They may ask to hug you. If you're not in the mood, I'll tell them. They won't be offended."

I inhale, the breath feeling snagged in my chest. "And if they don't ask?"

"They will." He caresses my thigh. "Pull in up there." He nods toward a corner spot in the circular driveway. I peer out at the two-story home with green vines framing the windows.

"But if they don't"—I clear my throat—"would it mean they don't like me for you?"

"I don't think that'll be a problem," he says, brushing it off.

I park and kill the ignition. "You don't think?"

"Hey." He shifts toward me. "I love you. They'll love you."

I peer back at the house with its shingled roof and rectangular windows. A sparkle of light to the right of the door has me leaning forward for a closer look. "Are those rainbow wind chimes?"

"Yeah," he says, quirking a smile as he follows my gaze. "They're very proud."

I huff out a laugh as I take in the array of multi-colored glass tubes, star shapes, and feathers.

"Ready?"

"Yeah." I rub my palms on my jeans. "No. Fuck. I'm nervous."

"We can take a walk first?"

I shake my head. "Come on."

He's been excited about this for weeks. Me even more so once the initial terror passed after officially setting a date and time.

I reach for my shades and then pause, dropping them back into the cup holder, before turning and retrieving the bouquet of flowers from the back seat.

Climbing out of the car, I use the driver's door window to straighten out my button-down shirt.

"You're beautiful," he says, holding out his hand.

When we reach the front door, he winks at me before pushing the bell.

I squeeze his hand as my heart starts pounding when a woman's voice calls out, "Be right there."

"I love you too," I blurt out right before the door swings open.

Salem's mom grins at us. "Look at you two! Come in, come in."

Salem chuckles as we step inside. "Hey, Mom." He reaches in and gives her a hug and kiss on the cheek. "I want you to meet my boyfriend, Arnaz. Blue, please meet my mom."

"H-hello, Mrs. Jones," I greet her. "It's a pleasure to meet you."

Her eyes crinkle as her gaze pings between us. A deep brown complexion like my mom, her salt-and-pepper hair is swept back in a thick braid. She's barefoot, wearing an indigo-blue linen shorts set and a black-beaded necklace with a gold accent hanging from her neck.

"The pleasure is mine." She rests a hand on Salem's arm and says, "Oh, isn't he just the cutest?"

Salem chuckles, nodding in agreement.

"May I hug you?" she asks me.

"Sure," I answer. I can't help but smile as she squeezes me tight and Salem mouths, *I told you.*

"None of that Mrs. Jones stuff," she says as she releases me. "Call me Maya." She turns to Salem, and a look passes between them that makes Salem's grin spread.

"Who is it, Maya?" a deep voice calls from somewhere in the house.

"They're here!" she answers over her shoulder as the sound of footsteps draws near.

A tall man with broad shoulders, in a crisp white polo, navy blue shorts, and flip-flops, rounds the corner.

"Hey Dad!" Salem greets him.

"Give him the same adorable intro you gave me," his mom says, making me snicker as Salem shakes his head, laughing.

"Dad," Salem starts, his dimples deepening as his mom squeals. "I want you to meet my boyfriend, Arnaz. Blue, I want you to meet my dad."

His mom and dad trade grins before his dad strings his arm over Salem's shoulder and pats his chest. "Good job. That was a very fine intro."

We all laugh as his dad's eyes cut to me. "Hello, Arnaz."

"Hi, sir, pleasure to meet you."

"Call me Eli. Are those peonies for me?" He asks, a glint of amusement in his eyes.

"Yes, for you both," I say, extending the bouquet to him.

"They're lovely," he says. "Ooh, look at that." He gestures to my knuckle tats. "You know I almost got one of those back in '89?"

"He did," Maya says. "Got as far as the stencil transfer before he high-tailed it outta there."

We all laugh.

"To his credit, when we got our boys' names on us for our 25th anniversary, he was rock solid."

"Let me see yours," Eli says, pulling glasses out of his pocket and thumbing them on.

I hold out my hands, and he reads the letters along my knuckles. "Neat," he says with a hum. "We do hugs yet?"

"I got one," Maya says.

"Guys," Salem says.

"What?" his dad replies. "We've only been waiting five years for this day. You want a hug?" he asks me.

"Sure." I step forward into his embrace.

"Let the man into the house," Denzel says, appearing over his dad's shoulder, leaning against the wall.

Salem grins. "Yeah, let's let Blue in."

"You prefer we call you Blue or Arnaz?" Maya asks as we're peeling off our shoes.

"Blue's fine," I reply.

"You got it."

"Come on in," Eli says. "Maya was just pummeling Denzel in NBA 2K."

We all laugh.

"What's the score?" Salem asks.

Denzel hangs his head as Maya wraps an arm around his waist. "Don't even ask."

"I got next," Salem says. "Winner has to beat Blue. He's a beast."

I wink at him.

"Finally, a real challenger in the family," Maya quips, making us laugh again.

"Ooh. Any chance you're good at Wrath Protocol?" She asks me over her shoulder as we make our way inside. "I keep losing in the Red Zone, and these three can't help me."

"Yeah, you know the backpack you get after you beat Skull

Fall? You have to use the glasses inside to see the hidden room after you scale the beam."

"Oh!" She stops walking. "That's brilliant! I put them on after the Orange Zone and nothing happened."

"Yeah, they only work in the Red Zone."

Salem taps my arm and pulls me to the side. "We'll be right there," he says to his family. "You good?" He palms my waist. "If at any time you wanna leave, just tell me."

I peck him on the lips. "Yeah, I'm good. You think she knows about the watch in the Shadow Round?"

He grins. "I don't know. You should ask he—"

"Hey Maya," I call out, racing away.

CHAPTER 62
SALEM

"Bowling?" I guess.

My back presses against the seat as he steps on the gas and switches lanes. "Nope."

"A Broadway musical?"

"You're never gonna guess."

"Wow." I slow nod. "Someone's smug about planning date night."

He leans forward, his arm slung over the steering wheel as he checks the side window. "How much you wanna bet I'm about to make you lose your shit?"

I snicker. "All this hype for a date that requires"—I stare down at the plastic bag he popped into the supermarket for before we got on the bridge to Manhattan—"a bag of fruit."

"Aight." He turns down Prince Street, and three blocks later, the GPS tells us we've arrived.

"Our date's in SoHo?" I ask as he grabs a rare free spot and parks.

"Yeah." He turns and clasps my cardigan, pulling me closer. "Remember this moment of doubt, fucker."

When I lean in for a kiss, he pulls back.

"Come on," he says, plucking up his coat and the grocery bag from the back before reaching for the car handle.

I look around after we climb out as I button my peacoat. "Besides two town houses, most of the street is filled with industrial lofts."

"Look all you want. You're never gonna guess," he says, locking the car.

Looking both ways, he crosses the street heading toward one of the town houses.

"Blue, hold up," I call out following him.

He keeps walking, throwing a—"Move it, Jones"—over his shoulder.

"Wait, can we just—"

"You get one guess," he says, spinning around, "and two hints. In one minute, I am going to ring that bell." He points to the upscale-looking town house. "That's hint number one. Hint number two is this." He opens the bag and sticks it out for me to see.

"Huh?" I stare at the fruit again and then over at the wide red-brick town house with its high stoop and slender columns framing the door. "I'm so confused."

He grins. "Good."

I glance down at the cobblestone street as he climbs the stairs and rings the bell.

He twists around. "Get up here."

I shake my head but start moving.

The door opens, and I freeze mid-step as I stare up and gasp. Not a quiet, gentle gasp but a full-throated, belly-expanding, audible-from-five-houses-down gasp.

She laughs at my reaction.

Kim Vien, the award-winning pastry chef and owner of one of the most innovative and renowned bakeries in the world, specifically right here in Manhattan.

"Welcome! Please come in."

I don't move. Well, my legs don't, but my eyes widen.

"Hi Kim, thanks for having us," Blue says, offering his hand.

"It's my pleasure," she says, shaking it.

Her eyes are bright, like she's genuinely excited to meet us.

The bun, the freckles, and the thick glasses are all a match to her picture in the back of her famous pastry book that I've been working my way through at home.

"I'm guessing from his reaction that you won date night," she says to him while smiling at me.

Blue holds out his fist, and she bumps it.

"You needed help with the tart thing you've been stuck on," Blue starts explaining, maybe to help me out of my stupor. "So, I grabbed Kim's name from the cookbook and asked Cat to connect us. Her people called Kim's people. Kim called me, and I explained that you've been up late every free night for the last two weeks, muttering around the kitchen, covered in flour and going mad."

"Been there," Kim jokes.

I scoff. "You called an acclaimed winner of not one but two James Beard Awards to help me with my monthly challenge?"

Not to mention the first Vietnamese-American woman ever to win twice.

"Yeah," he says. "You needed help. I know how important it is for you to beat Eli. That's his dad," he says to Kim. "And it was my turn for date night."

"I took you skating," I blurt out.

"It was so fun," he says to Kim. "I fell...well, we fell like, five times."

He's ridiculous!

He's actually standing next to one of the most highly-regarded pastry chefs in the world, telling her about our skating wipeouts. This must be what it's like to be raised around famous people. He's completely unfazed.

"We're letting all of Kim's heat out. Come on."

"Sorry." I jog up the steps.

"Pleasure to meet you, Salem." Kim holds out her hand as I approach. "My husband and I are fans. No offense," she says to Blue. "My husband's from Brooklyn."

"All good," he says as I shake her hand.

"Arnaz told me you've been having trouble with the tarte Tartin and gelée recipe in my book," she says, leading us inside.

"Y-yes," I reply, copying Blue, who peels off his shoes.

"We'll get you sorted. I've prepped some things to help us along. This way."

Blue strings his arms around my waist and tugs me along.

We enter her kitchen, and answers to questions that I've wondered about filter in all at once.

"You have a Miele!" I exclaim, crossing the room to her oven. "I read that the steam injection is excellent for laminated dough."

"That's why it's my favorite," she says. "What do you have?"

"A Wolf. Is that a Brod & Taylor?" I bend down to peer inside.

Blue chuckles, and it hits me that my head is stuffed inside of the proofer. "Sorry," I mutter, backing out.

"Please," she chuckles. "I get to tell all of my friends that *The Silencer* played with my toys."

Blue and I laugh. "Wow," I say, recognizing the ingredients for the recipe on the counter. "You did prep."

"Yep. Before we hop on, please help yourselves to the canapés." She gestures to the tray.

"Thanks," Blue and I reply.

"May I offer you champagne, Chenin, or Lambrusco?"

"Chenin," I answer.

Blue thinks it over.

"I have IPA too," she offers.

"Perfect. *Driving*."

"I can drive us home and skip drinking," I offer.

"All good," he says. "Have fun." He turns to Kim. "Restroom?"

"Sure. There's one in the hall on the left," Kim answers as she retrieves the drinks.

I use the restroom after him. When I return, he's in an apron, sitting on one of the island stools, and eating a mushroom canapé.

"That one's yours." His elbow points to a crisp apron sitting on the chair.

"Thanks," I reply to Kim, who's taking a sip from a champagne flute.

As I raise the neck loop over my head, I feel a tickle in the middle of my chest and take a deep breath.

"He's nervous," Blue whispers, rubbing my back.

"I still get jitters when I attempt a new recipe," Kim shares. "Let's start from the beginning. Which brand of puff pastry did you use?"

"I made it from scratch." I roughly recite the recipe.

"Wonderful. I have one chilling in the fridge that I made a few hours ago. I presume you made adjustments for an in-season fruit?"

"Yes, quinces."

Blue reaches for the grocery bag and brings it over.

Ohh.

He winks at me. "Figured you'd need it to replicate your version."

He unloads the fruit and places it on an empty spot on the counter.

"Excellent choice," Kim murmurs, picking one up. "Why quinces?"

"I considered cranberries and pears at first. Each would work with the Banyuls glaze, but they felt kinda blah."

She nods. "Go on."

"Quinces are sort of old-world romantic. They're older than

apples and peaches by thousands of years. When I thought about adapting the recipe for winter—I wanted to infuse some of the elements of winter so—"

"People could taste winter itself," she finishes.

"Yes! It's inedible raw, but it blooms with heat and time. I like things that demand patience."

I steal a glance at Blue, whose eyes darken just enough for me to notice.

"Like winter," she adds.

I nod. "Like winter. It forces us to slow down."

She stares at the fruit. A soft hush that's easy to let breathe passes between us. "It's an aristocratic fruit," she says before she places it down. "Excellent choice."

"What would you have chosen?" I ask.

"I went with—what was your word choice—*blah*." She uncovers a bowl and shows us cranberries.

Blue snorts, making us laugh.

"I am thrilled to try your adaptation, though," she says. "One more question. Why did you choose this one? I've included winter recipes in the book."

"This is the only one that lets us experience the same fruit in three unique ways that vary in temperature, texture, and flavor. It's the kind of contrast—"

"That achieves perfect balance," she finishes.

"How so?" Blue asks.

She nods for me to answer.

"So, picture three experiences, one dessert," I explain, turning to him. "There's a cold and sweet sorbet, a warm, crispy, buttery tart drizzled with an aromatic Banyuls glaze, and then a chilled, subtly flavored gelée that has a jelly-like texture."

"Sounds like a mouth party," Blue says. "What's a Banyuls?"

"It's a French fortified wine," Kim answers. "They essentially take a high-proof alcohol distilled from grapes until most of its flavor is removed and toss it in with wine grapes during fermentation to stun the yeast and preserve some of the grape's sugars before it turns into alcohol. You end up with a sweeter wine that has a higher alcohol content because of the high-proof alcohol added."

"And you bake with it?" Blue asks.

"Yep," she answers. "The natural grape sugars that are preserved caramelize like a dream once it's reduced."

"I get why you were stuck." He blows out a breath. "Sounds like a lot."

"Nothing the three of us can't handle," Kim says, rolling up her sleeves. "Okay, let's jump in. We'll start the gelée first, since it'll need a few hours to set, then tackle the sorbet, which will also need time in the freezer, and then we'll move on to the tarte Tatin, ending with the glaze. How does that sound?"

"Yes, Coach," Blue says, making us laugh.

Arnaz

We finish six hours later. The last two hours were mostly spent
cleaning up and talking while we waited for things to either
chill, freeze, or bake.

Was it worth the effort?

Hell yeah.

Like all Salem's desserts, it was visually stunning, and the
flavors matched. I could only eat the sorbet and the jelly-thing.
When Kim offered me a tart, Salem damn near smacked his
hand over my mouth because of the butter in the puff pastry. It
was dramatic and hot. I was already making plans for us
tonight after hearing him wax on about wanting to take his
time with quinces and feed me winter.

At least that's how I heard it.

After the non-near-death experience that resulted in me
licking the inside of his palm sealed against my mouth, he
promised he'd make me a vegan tart this weekend.

"That's better than the original," Kim says, polishing off a
second serving. "Quinces...brilliant."

Salem beams.

"Think you might have figured out where you went astray?"
She asks him.

"I think so. It was a couple of small things that added up to
a lot. To start, I didn't get the substitution proportion right for
the fruit, and I needed to pull back on the lemon verbena."

She nods. "Recipes are tricky that way. You sub one thing
for another, and it can change everything."

"I learned a lot tonight," Salem says. "Thank you! You have
to let us treat you and your husband to dinner at my place."

"Really? We'd love that. Maybe I'll take a page from your
book and surprise him for date night," she says to me.

I reach across, and we bump fists.

"May I also ask for you both to sign some things? One for me and one for my husband, who I had to talk down from canceling a business meeting he spent months preparing for because he wanted to come home early and meet you."

Salem laughs and replies, "Of course."

As soon as she's out of sight, he spins me around on the stool, clasps the sides of my face, and kisses me.

I moan too loudly, making him chuckle and pull back.

"You've been edging me all night," I whisper. He knows what it does to me when he's in serious baker mode.

He brushes his lips against my ear. "You're falling asleep on my dick tonight."

I moan again.

When Kim returns, I'm on my feet, selling a drawn-out yawn.

Salem fights a grin, shaking his head.

She extends a Brooklyn Lions fitted hat for us to sign.

I raise my hands. "I feel like it's bad luck for me to sign it."

They both laugh.

"Fair," she says. "How about this?" She holds out a frame with glass but no picture. "Sign the glass? We'll take a selfie, and I'll put our picture inside of it and hang it in my bakery."

"What an honor," Salem says, returning the hat to her.

We huddle together and snap a few selfies, some on Salem's phone.

We're headed to the door when she asks, "You two have plans off-season?"

I look at Salem.

We plan to be together and spend time with our families, travel a bit, but nothing concrete.

"Some plans, why?" he asks.

"A few of my chef and baker friends from around the world meet up every summer for a week. Sometimes all together, other times in different groups. This summer, one group of us plans to meet in Mexico City and the other in Japan. It's real chill. We meet with local chefs and pastry chefs there, try all the foods, check out the local markets, and cook together. Lots of experimentation and ideation. You're both welcome to join us. If you think you learned a lot here, you'll learn tenfold around the larger group. I certainly have. I plan to make both trips."

"Yes!" Salem replies. "Absolutely." He turns to me, and his smile fades. "Wait, sorry, let us discuss it first and get back to you."

"We'll be there," I reply.

"You sure?" he asks.

I nod. "Hell yeah."

"Awesome," Kim says. "I'm sorry in advance for my husband...or really all my friends. We live in kitchens all day and rarely get out."

That makes us laugh.

"Hey," she says to him. "You have that glint and hunger that I see in masters of our craft. Whatever you plan to do with it, I think you'll do well."

I pat his back as he beams and thanks her again.

That's right, so that Beard guy better get ready for the rise of Baker Bae.

"THANK YOU," he says, enveloping me in his arms from behind and squeezing me as we make our way to the car. "I can't believe any of that just happened."

I grin. "I just wanted my boyfriend back."

That's partially the reason. He had been coming to bed late and was back in the kitchen when I woke up. The other reason is that I knew he still doubted whether he had—what everyone who's tried his pastries knows—enough talent and drive to succeed with his own awarded bakery one day.

"She's dope, isn't she?" he asks.

"Yeah. She's a nerd like you."

He grins. "Hey, we really can do our own thing this summer. Sorry if I put you on the spot."

"Baby, it's only two weeks. Not to mention, it's the opportunity of a lifetime. I'm down to chill in Japan and Mexico City. We'll do our own thing after. Maybe Denzel and Anaïs can join us."

"Yeah." He beams. "That would be great."

He unlocks the car, and we climb in.

"What's the verdict?" I ask.

"You definitely plan better dates than I do."

I laugh. "Not that. I meant the bakery with your dad. Is it happening when you retire in a couple of years?"

"I want it, but the hours might be long, and I don't know anything about running a business."

"The second part isn't true. You run your brand, and just like you have Cat to help you, you will learn and can hire help."

"True."

"No bullshit. Sometimes I think you love baking and cooking more than you love ball. I know you love ballin', but it doesn't feel like it hits the same."

"You've noticed that?" he asks quietly.

"Mmhm. And nothing's wrong with that. It's amazing that you have something else, you know? Something that's all yours and can't be taken away by trades, injuries, and contract expirations."

"You're right. What about you and music?"

I reach for my seatbelt. "That's different."

"How?" he asks.

"Music for me is like journaling. It helps me express the things I can't get out any other way. I don't want any part of what comes with making it public. I just want a chill life with you after I retire. No more cameras."

He nods, reaching for my hand and kissing it. "I get that."

I turn on the car and start to pull out when he gushes, "You planned a date with Kim Vien!"

"Told you I'd make you lose your shit."

CHAPTER 63
ARNAZ
TWO WEEKS LATER

🎵 **"By Any Stretch of the Imagination"** 🎵
Of those empty years, those dreams I dared not dream.

"**F**uck," I curse as the knife slices through my finger.

"Ouch," Salem says from the other side of the island. He grabs a paper towel, then reaches over and wraps my finger up. "Add pressure."

"Add pressure," I mock with a sneer. "Where are the bandages again?"

"Ask nicely, and I'll tell you."

"Tell me now, dickhead."

He snickers. "You're still mad?"

"Don't put this on me. You're the one who didn't get enough sleep and woke up grumpy this morning."

"I didn't get enough sleep because someone's flight was delayed, and they got in super late and made mad noise climbing into bed."

I scoff and try to pull my hand back, but he doesn't release it. "Let me go before I bleed on the peppers."

He continues applying pressure.

"And how is it my fault that Simba was excited to see me and almost made me bust my ass trying to get to the bathroom?" I argue.

"Oh, so now it's your fault." He stares down at Simba, who turns his head away from us. "We're making the kid sad." He raises my finger to his lips and kisses it. "The bandages are there in the drawer on the right." He releases his hold.

I yank open the drawer. Two brand-new boxes of bandages sit in the center.

Not just any bandages, though.

"Baby," I breathe out.

"Hmm?" He bends down to peer inside the oven.

I pick up one of the boxes.

"I just called you a dickhead." I groan.

He smirks as I come around the island and back him against the fridge. "That wasn't nice, was it?"

"I love you," I whisper, looking him in the eyes.

Our lips press together, and I kiss him the way I've been fighting the urge to do all day.

"Sweet mercy. Not again," Denzel complains, making us laugh.

"We're clothed, bro," Salem replies.

We didn't realize he was home a few weeks back when I was spread-eagled on the couch, getting pumped deep.

The guy's too quiet. I've never heard him enter a room. I know he's counting the days until his renovated condo in Anaïs's building is ready.

I brush a quick kiss against Salem's lips. "I missed you this morning." He was already out of bed by the time I woke up, in full-on grump mode.

"Yeah?" He grabs my ass. "We'll kick everyone out early."

"Oooh. Tommy, bring the popcorn," Kieran, Sid's cousin, yells.

Denzel groans, covering his eyes and groping the air until he reaches the beer in the cooler, and then he scurries out.

"Last Christmas"—Kieran snickers as I turn and lean against Salem's chest—"Tommy went downstairs to get me a snack and found Ty getting cannonballed."

"In an elf onesie," Tommy adds quietly, handing Kieran the bowl of popcorn.

"It wasn't that bad," Sid calls out from the living room.

"Yeah, it was," Ty yells for us to hear. "He fell into the Christmas tree."

We burst out laughing.

Salem

"Anaïs, come here," Blue calls as we're left alone in the kitchen.

"Wait. Cillian and I are hammering Sid and Ty," she calls back.

"Lies. Ya'll are up one game," Sid replies. "And based on this hand, we're fittin' to run a Boston."

"It'll be quick," Blue says, shivering in my arms as I work his neck with my tongue.

"You either need to stop or finish what you're starting," I warn as he caresses my dick through my jeans.

"We can run downstairs real quick," he breathes against my ear. "The wine cellar, mmm." He grinds against me. "Or theater? No one can hear us down there."

"Wherever." I reach into his waistband. "Right here."

"Okay, no, not right here," Anaïs says, doing an about-face.

I snort and remove my hands as Blue laughs and says, "Wait."

"You summoned me?" She turns around.

He holds up the box of bandages.

"What's that?" She comes closer. "Are those...?"

He nods. "Unicorns."

She covers her mouth. "You told him about the time Carter yelled at you because you..."

He nods.

"Oh, wow," I whisper as her eyes turn watery.

"You made her cry," Blue says to me.

"It's so..." Her head tips back to the ceiling as she fans her eyes.

"I know, right? It's a punch in the heart." His voice cracks. "The best kind."

"Oh, wow, you too," I whisper, kissing the side of his face.

He does that now—cries quiet tears. Sometimes the only proof is his red eyes, but he always seems better after.

"Here," she says, opening the lid of the box and pulling out a medium-sized bandage. She peels back the paper. "Christ, I can't see." She pauses and fans her eyes again. "Salem here, you do it."

I take the bandage and raise his injured finger. Kissing his palm before removing the bloodied paper towel, I say, "Hold on." I reach under the sink for the antiseptic. "What do you think for the next family bake-off we make a unicorn cake?"

The monthly challenge has expanded to include guest appearances from Denzel, Blue, and Anaïs. Blue tries to help, coining himself "assistant pastry chef," and for the most part he is helpful—only one-third of the eggs he cracks requires us to pick out the shells. Denzel cleans up as we work, making sure to make appearances for Mom and Dad on camera. Anaïs licks all the bowls clean and teams up with Mom to supply endless dad jokes.

"Okay, but we all need to wear matching unicorn onesies!" Anaïs exclaims.

"I'm down." I laugh.

We turn to Blue. He watches as I wrap the bandage snugly around his finger.

A fresh set of tears pools at his lids. "Fuck yeah. I'm in."

When we're alone again, I tell him, "Thank you for organizing tonight."

He nods. "I know how much you love to host and have friends and family around."

Arnaz

"Oof," I grunt as the side of my face hits the wine cellar's brick wall.

"What do you think of when you watch me?" Salem rasps, reaching around for my belt buckle.

I *was* watching as he laughed with Ty and sat with Denzel, who isn't big on social gatherings, and made sure Anaïs ate enough, and asked questions about Sid, Tommy, and Kieran's childhood.

I kick my pants and briefs away, then flip us so he's against the wall. "I like watching you be in the world."

"Hmm?" he hums.

It's the only explanation I have for the months of hiding away at night to watch him as I fell asleep.

I kiss his neck and start working on his belt. "I can't stand the distance."

Once I get him naked from the waist down, he pulls me closer, until we're slotted against each other, and takes us both in hand. "Where do you want to be?" he asks as he drizzles lube over our cocks.

"Closer," I pant as he presses the head of his cock against mine. Rolling his foreskin over my dick, he grips our two heads together, then begins slowly stroking.

"Where do you want to be?" he asks again.

"Inside of you. Fuccck." My head falls back as I tunnel into the velvet walls of his skin, his metal points pressing into my sensitive head.

"You about to nut?"

"Yeah," I rasp. Shit is instant when he does this.

He works me until my toes dig into the floor, and my breath starts to choke up.

I gasp when he releases me, and my head falls forward. He holds me as I catch my breath and nibble on his collarbone.

He shudders as I tug on his piercing and drop my mouth to his shoulder and suck on it.

"Mm, stop if you want me," he warns.

"I need to be inside you." I turn him around, and he spreads his hands on the wine barrel as I step behind him.

Nibbling on his ear, I rub my erection through his crease.

His head dips between his shoulders as my tongue trails down the ridge of bone, over his spine, until I'm kneeling behind him.

Licking up the back of his thick thighs, I suck on the globes of his ass, making him tense, as I sink my teeth into the flesh, then relax, as I trail soothing circles over it with my tongue.

"Baby," he moans as I lick across his rim, head tilting sideways, fanning my tongue back and forth.

His thighs tremble as I suck on the walls of his crease and reach between his legs to massage his balls.

Picking up the lube, I squeeze some on my fingers, then lower myself more so I can roll one of his balls into my mouth as I sink a finger inside him.

He groans as I breach the tight ring of muscle and alternate tongue kissing his heavy balls. I add a second finger, eating up his sweet grunts as I stretch him open.

"Fuck me," he pleads as I curve my finger and light up his prostate.

I keep massaging that magic spot, feeling the heat of his thighs on my face as he trembles and sweats.

When the pressure between my legs becomes damn near blinding, I push off the floor and slather lube on my shaft.

Kissing between his shoulder blades, I rub the head of my cock over his rim.

"Ready?"

"Yeah," he says.

The raw sounds of our gasped moans echo through the cellar as I push into him.

My head drops to his back as I'm enveloped in soft, tight heat. I slide out to the tip and thrust back in.

The sound of him saying "baby," dripping with desire and affection, coated in his impossibly deep voice...*fuck*.

I raise his arm and lower my tongue to his pit as I bottom out inside him.

"Blue," he moans.

"Hmm." I thrust harder, wanting him louder. I move to his other pit.

"God," he grunts as I hit his prostate. "How's it this good?"

"I love you," I rasp as I snap my hips, watching my abs clench as my dick disappears inside of him.

He looks at me over his shoulder, submerging me in the depths of his soulful eyes. "I love you too."

"Mm...I'm close," I pant, wrapping my arms around his waist and slamming into him.

He grunts as I slap his hand away from his dick and take over stroking him.

When I corkscrew my hand and flick the side of his piercing, he tenses. Gripping the sides of the barrel, he clenches around me and erupts. His husky moans echo through me, and my abs contract, my eyes slam closed, and I let go, releasing inside him.

He curses as I grind into him, staying buried deep, filling him with shallow thrusts.

He bears my weight as my heart hammers against his back, and I catch my breath.

When I pull out, I drop to my knees and spread his cheeks.

"Fu-uck," he groans as I eat my cum out of him.

I tap his legs. "Sit on my face."

"God, I love you," he mutters as I lie on my back, and he lowers down to my tongue.

CHAPTER 64
SALEM

"Coach, put him back in," I beg.

Coach Derek groans. "Not this again."

"Why's he benched?"

"For Christ's sake, he's been out two minutes for rest," he snaps.

"Oh." My head darts to the side. "Grandpa's tired?"

Blue fires a middle finger at me while popping his gum.

"I get it. Not everyone can handle the heat of the playoffs."

"Fuck you going on about?" He glares, nostrils flaring.

"Nope." Coach Derek reaches his arm out to move me along. "Don't poke the bear."

"He the bear?" I grin. "That pretty thing?"

"Fuck you call me?" Blue asks, lip curling.

"Alright." I shoot him a smirk. "I guess I eat bears."

He nods slowly, staring straight ahead, his gum chewing picking up pace.

"There's no fun beating y'all if he isn't in, Coach."

"Y'all down thirteen points," Blue grits, knee springing up and down.

"How much you wanna bet if you put him in, we'll go on a fifteen to nothing run?" I ask.

Blue snorts.

"Cool, stay there, sweetcakes. Play or not, you'll still lose," I taunt.

"For fuck's sake." He jumps to his feet. "Let me shut this fucker up real fast."

"Nah, stay there." I wave him off. "But bundle up. It's about to get brr, bitch."

Coach sighs and shakes his head. "I warned you." He waves toward the court. "Cade, warm up."

I grin, racing backward.

"Fuck you grinning for," Blue sneers, tearing away the snaps on his pants. "You 'bout to lose."

"Yeah, yeah." I blow him a kiss. "Love you too, little bear."

EPILOGUE- SALEM
WEEKS LATER

I pop the cake onto a rack to cool.

I know this moment where everything in my life is good, perfect even, won't always stay.

My brother is upstairs sleeping, Blue and Sim are over there on the couch, and my parents are good.

Blue sometimes needs to go away, even when we're in the same room, but he always comes back.

All I can do is love him and give him the space that he needs.

I'm learning to trust.

Trust that I can let go.

Trust that, even if it isn't within my control, it just might turn out all right.

After all, life has taught me that with an ounce of courage and a sprinkle of fate, you just might end up scoring the man of your dreams.

EPILOGUE- ARNAZ

Z*uri told me that my homework is to try to talk to you. We've been sitting with you more. She asked if I felt ready to talk. I told her I'm not sure there's a point.*

Plus, you probably won't hear me because you're hiding in the corner of the room.

You can come out whenever you want, you know.

Zuri says you may need some convincing.

I asked her how I'd do that, and she said to sit with you. She said that if I can't speak to you, maybe I could write to you.

We were always too nervous to sit still long enough to read back then.

I guess that's not my problem. All I can do is try.

I won't bullshit you. The next twenty or so years are shit for you.

Externally, it looks like you're winning at life, but inside, you're as lost as you are now...angrier too.

But you survive.

Anaïs survives too.

She even figures out what's causing her pain every month, and she gets surgery. It's not a cure, but it helps. You can stop crying over that now.

Them? They're still around.

I know that matters to you because no matter how shitty they were to you, you were always so terrified of them leaving.

They don't leave. But they're also never there. Not for the years that mattered anyway.

But they live.

And you...

My pen pauses.

I just went to flex my feet, but there's a seventy-pound dog stretched across my legs. He loses his shit whenever he sees you.

He howls for you.

My stomach is rumbling again because in the oven there's a dairy-free cake (oh yeah, the rashes and stomach aches—cow's milk. Anaïs finally figures it out in a couple of years).

The cake's there because you asked for it. Seriously, if you said right now that you wanted a chocolate cake shaped like a Transformer, the guy over there in the kitchen would make it for you.

Speaking of him...

My hand stills.

You know how right now you're terrified everyone's gonna leave? Well, that fear never fully goes away, though you'll tell yourself you don't care if they do.

'Cause, like, people are trash.

Not him, though.

He's part of the reason I can sit here and do this.

You love him with every inch of your being. You love him so much it aches. You try really hard not to. And every time you run, you end up back with him. You'll still feel like the floor is gonna cave in and you'll lose him, but I can't help you with that. I haven't figured it out.

But you don't run anymore.

You still retreat into the quiet corners of yourself.

He knows you need it.

But he's there whenever you come out.

With cake.

Oh, and you figured out that your favorite dessert is any one he makes (you'll be asked that one day).

Guess what?

He loves you back.

Hard.

Oh, and come closer for this. Guess what I have wrapped around my ring finger?

A unicorn bandage.

It's my thing now.

The man in the kitchen says he's gonna replace it with a gold band one day.

He didn't argue with me when I said that if it isn't big enough to fit over the bandage, then it has to go around my neck.

He just said, "Okay, Blue."

And I finally learned why he calls me that. Blue.

And it's not why I thought. It's because I give him hope. That whenever he's near me, he believes in tomorrow.

Can you imagine?

Us giving someone hope.

He's...God, he's different.

He isn't the type of man who sees the good and beauty in everything, but he'll observe a life-worn thing and sense its goodness and beauty. There is a difference.

That's him now, telling me the cake will be ready soon, so I gotta go.

I'm not here to convince you to come out of the room.

But you should know that you eventually figure out there's more to life than survival.

That in the end, we're safe.

You'll wake up one day and look around and finally realize you're home.

The End

Craving more time with Salem and Blue? You're in luck. Sign up at https://kitgrey.myflodesk.com/bonus-content-access or **scan the QR code below** to unlock an exclusive bonus scene!

East & Ray's childhood best-friends-to-lovers story is next. Coming soon!

THANK YOU!

Thank you for reading Salem & Blue's story.

At the heart of this story is a simple but powerful question:

What would it take for these two human beings to reach their happily ever after?

Given their backgrounds, perspectives, and goals—what kind of healing, understanding, and journeys are needed to get them there?

Sometimes, the answers aren't pretty. Sometimes they're really hard. Choices are made out of fear. Courage shows up later, once it feels safe enough to lower the walls. There can be so much yearning—and still, we run.

This book explores the reality that sometimes **falling in love and being happy is the scariest feeling of all.**

For *some* of us, it's not as simple as grand gestures or off-the-charts chemistry.

We have to dig deep.

We need to process our past and continue healing so we can show up for our own happily ever after—especially if we're survivors of trauma or painful experiences.

Every story demands its own unique process.

For Salem and Blue, that meant plotting—and a ton of research.

I needed to know everything about them: their backstories, Enneagram types, quirks, desires, deepest fears, astrological signs. I delved into clinical psychology research on chronic trauma, shame, dissociation, and the complex, shame-based internalization of unrequited love. I also consulted with a psychodynamic and relational therapist. I had to close my eyes, slip into their minds, and see the world through their eyes.

And wow, are they different. Beautifully, uniquely, messily different. The kind of difference that makes the journey to their HEA so fulfilling and healing to write.

Because the truth is: No two people ever start at the same place in a relationship.

I hope you enjoyed spending time in their world. Thank you for joining them on their journey to a happily ever after.

ACKNOWLEDGMENTS

To N, my best friend and partner—thank you for your steadfast support. You are my rock. I'm so grateful for your fierce protection and unwavering encouragement.

To my editors—Jo, Shauna, and Jenn—thank you for your sharp eyes and hard work helping to polish this manuscript. Your contributions made all the difference.

To Jo—thank you for the care you give my manuscripts. It goes above and beyond anything I could ever ask for. I squealed when I finally met you in person—but somehow managed to resist hugging that brilliant brain of yours.

To my beta team—Lys, Sharanya, Dee, Tanya, and Taylor—thank you for taking the time to read an early version of this story. Your honesty, encouragement, and thoughtful feedback helped guide and shape the revisions. I'm deeply grateful for each of you.

To Taylor, thank you for lending your basketball expertise and for reviewing those scenes with such care.

To Pauline, thank you for creating beautiful promo graphics and for helping fine-tune Lucien's French dialogue. Your creativity and support mean so much.

To Shawna (#hero), thank you for sweeping in and taking charge of the ARC process. I appreciate your quick support and behind-the-scenes magic.

To my hype team—you are, without a doubt, the greatest hype team in the universe. Period. Your energy and excitement light up every single post. I see you, and I appreciate you.

To my ARC team—thank you for volunteering your time to read Arnaz and Salem's story, writing reviews, and helping get the word out. Your enthusiasm makes such a difference.

To my friend C.P. Harris—Thank you for being my writing buddy over the last few months. Your morale support and cheerleading helped carry me across the finish line.

And last but not least—thank you, dear reader. I'm so grateful you picked up Blue & Salem's story. I truly hope you enjoyed it.

ABOUT THE AUTHOR

Kit Grey lives for love stories—both the ones she devours and the ones she creates. When she's not lost in the pages of a book, she's busy crafting angsty, emotional, high-heat romances of her own.

Though she's a private soul who treasures the quiet moments where her imagination can roam free, **connecting with readers** makes the journey so much more meaningful. For early access to sneak peeks, book updates, and exclusive content, be sure to sign up for her newsletter at **KitGrey.com**. You can also hang out with her on **Instagram and Facebook**.

Scan the QR code below to stay in touch.

ALSO BY KIT GREY

Loving the Legend is available on Amazon, Audible, and KitGrey.com/shop. Scan the QR code below to learn more.

For art, signed and unsigned paperbacks, and swag, visit KitGrey.com/shop or scan the QR code below.

9 798989 766581